Hannah Elliott's mind shuts down.

The station is being torn apart in front of them, silent bursts of fire shredding the modules, the command center ripping in half. Cargo cruisers are coming about, trying to flee, chased down by the metal spheres. One particularly large ship splits down the belly, its cargo spinning out into the void, tiny silver particles glinting. Food containers, probably destined for the station restaurants.

She's still in the sim. She has to be. She's fallen asleep, and her jump-lagged brain is in the middle of a horrible lucid dream. She's definitely not here, on a tourist vessel shaped like an upside-down turd, watching an entire station get blown to pieces.

Atsuke's still on there. So's Donnie. The tattooed guy in the VR room. And the little girl on the bench in the dock. Everybody.

The people on the tour ship's main deck are screaming.

By Rob Boffard

ADRIFT

ROB BOFFARD

www.orbitbooks.net

Copyright © 2018 by Rob Boffard
Excerpt from *A Big Ship at the Edge of the Universe* copyright © 2018 by Alex White
Excerpt from *The Corporation Wars: Dissidence* copyright © 2016 by Ken MacLeod

Cover design by Charlotte Stroomer—LBBG
Cover images by iStock
Cover copyright © 2018 by Hachette Book Group, Inc.

Orbit
Hachette Book Group
1290 Avenue of the Americas
New York, NY 10104
orbitbooks.net

Simultaneously published in Great Britain and in the U.S. by Orbit in 2018
First U.S. Edition: June 2018

Orbit is an imprint of Hachette Book Group.
The Orbit name and logo are trademarks of Little, Brown Book Group Limited.

The publisher is not responsible for websites (or their content) that are not owned by the publisher.

The Hachette Speakers Bureau provides a wide range of authors for speaking events. To find out more, go to www.hachettespeakersbureau.com or call (866) 376-6591.

Library of Congress Control Number: 2018933281

ISBNs: 978-0-316-51911-3 (trade paperback), 978-0-316-51912-0 (ebook)

Printed in the United States of America

LSC-C

10 9 8 7 6 5 4 3 2 1

For Cat

Chapter 1

Rainmaker's heads-up display is a nightmare.

The alerts are coming faster than she can dismiss them. Lock indicators. Proximity warnings. Fuel signals. Created by her neuro-chip, appearing directly in front of her.

The world outside her fighter's cockpit is alive, torn with streaking missiles and twisting ships. In the distance, a nuke detonates against a frigate, a baby sun tearing its way into life. The Horsehead Nebula glitters behind it.

Rainmaker twists her ship away from the heatwave, making it dance with precise, controlled thoughts. As she does so, she gets a full view of the battle: a thousand Frontier Scorpion fighters, flipping and turning and destroying each other in an arena bordered by the hulking frigates.

The Colony forces thought they could hold the area around Sigma Orionis—they thought they could take control of the jump gate and shut down all movement into this sector. They didn't bank on an early victory at Proxima freeing up a third of the Frontier Navy, and now they're backed into a corner, fighting like hell to stay alive.

Maybe this'll be the battle that does it. Maybe this is the one that finally stops the Colonies for good.

Rainmaker's path has taken her away from the main thrust of the battle, out towards the edge of the sector. Her targeting systems find a lone enemy: a black Colony fighter, streaking towards her. She's about to fire when she stops, cutting off the thought.

Something's not right.

"Control, this is Rainmaker." Despite the chaos, her voice is calm. "I have locked on incoming. Why's he alone? Over."

The reply is clipped and urgent. "Rainmaker, this is Frontier Control: evade, evade, evade. *Do not engage.* You have multiple bogies closing in on your six. They're trying to lock the door on you, over."

Rainmaker doesn't bother to respond. Her radar systems were damaged earlier in the fight, and she has to rely on Control for the bandits she can't see. She breaks her lock, twisting her craft away as more warnings bloom on her console. "Twin, Blackbird, anybody. I've got multiples inbound, need a pickup, over."

The sarcastic voice of one of her wingmen comes over the comms. "Can't handle 'em yourself? I'm disappointed."

"Not a good time, Omen," she replies, burning her thrusters. "Can you help me or not? Over."

"Negative. Got three customers to deal with over here. Get in line."

A second, older voice comes over her comms. "Rainmaker, this is Blackbird. What's your twenty? Over."

Her neurochip recognises the words, both flashing up the info on her display and automatically sending it to Blackbird's. "Quadrant thirty-one," she says anyway, speaking through gritted teeth.

"Roger," says Blackbird. "I got 'em. Just sit tight. I'll handle it for y—. Shit, I'm hit! I—"

"Eric!" Rainmaker shouts Blackbird's real name, her voice so loud it distorts the channel. But he's already gone. An impactor streaks past her, close enough for her to see the launch burns on its surface.

"Control, Rainmaker," she says. "Confirm Blackbird's position, I've lost contact!"

Control doesn't reply. Why would they? They're fighting a thousand fires at once, advising hundreds of Scorpion fighters. Forget the callsigns that command makes them use: Blackbird is a number to them, and so is she, and unless she does something right now, she's going to join him.

She twists her ship, forcing the two chasing Colony fighters to face her head-on. They're a bigger threat than the lone one ahead. Now, they're coming in from her eleven and one o'clock, curving towards her, already opening fire. She guns the ship, aiming for the tiny space in the middle, racing to make the gap before their impactors close her out.

"Thread the needle," she whispers. "Come on, thread the needle, thr—"

Everything freezes.

The battle falls silent.

And a blinking-red error box appears above one of the missiles.

"Oh. Um." Hannah Elliott's voice cuts through the silence. "Sorry, ladies and gentlemen. One second."

The box goes away—only to reappear a split second later, like a fly buzzing back to the place it was swatted. This time, the simulation gives a muted *ding*, as if annoyed that Hannah can't grasp the point.

She rips the slim goggles from her head. She's not used to them—she forgot to put her lens in after she woke up, which meant she had to rely on the VR room's antiquated backup system. A strand of her long red hair catches on the strap, and she has to yank it loose, looking down at the ancient console in front of her.

"Sorry, ladies and gentlemen," she says again. "Won't be a minute."

Her worried face is reflected on the dark screen, her freckles making her look even younger than she is. She uses her finger this time, stabbing at the box's confirm button on the small access terminal on the desk. It comes back with a friend, a second, identical error box superimposed over the first. Beyond it, an impactor sits frozen in Rainmaker's viewport.

"Sorry." *Stop saying sorry.* She tries again, still failing to bring up the main menu. "It's my first day."

Stony silence. The twenty tourists in the darkened room before her are strapped into reclining motion seats with frayed belts. Most have their eyes closed, their personal lenses still displaying the frozen sim. A few are blinking, looking faintly annoyed. One of them, an older man with a salt-and-pepper beard, catches Hannah's eye with a scowl.

She looks down, back at the error boxes. She can barely make out the writing on them—the VR's depth of field has made the letters as tiny as the ones on the bottom line of an eye chart.

She should reset the sim. But how? Does that mean it will start from scratch? Can she fast-forward? The supervisor who showed it to her that morning was trying to wrangle about fifteen new tour guides, and the instructions she gave amounted to watching the volume levels and making sure none of the tourists threw up when Rainmaker turned too hard.

Hannah gives the screen an experimental tap, and breathes a sigh of relief when a menu pops up: a list of files. There. Now she just has to—

But which one is it? The supervisor turned the sim on, and Hannah doesn't know which file she used. Their names are meaningless.

She taps the first one. Bouncy music explodes from the room's speakers, loud enough to make a couple of the tourists jump. She pulls the goggles back on, to be greeted by an animated, space-suited lizard firing lasers at a huge, tentacled alien. A booming voice echoes across the music. "Adventurers! Enter the world of Reptar as he saves the galaxy from—"

Hannah stops Reptar saving the galaxy. In the silence that follows, she can feel her cheeks turning red.

She gives the screen a final, helpless look, and leaps to her feet. She'll figure this out. Somehow. They wouldn't have given her this job if they didn't think she could deal with the unexpected.

"OK!" She claps her hands together. "Sorry for the mix-up. I think there's a bit of a glitch in the old sim there."

Her laugh gets precisely zero reaction. Swallowing, she soldiers on.

"So, as you saw, that was the Battle of Sigma Orionis, which took place fifteen years ago, which would be ..." She thinks hard. "2157, in the space around the hotel we're now in. Hopefully our historical sim gave you a good idea of the conditions our pilots faced—it was taken directly from one of their neurochip feeds.

"Coincidentally, the battle took place almost exactly a hundred years after we first managed to send a probe through a wormhole, which, as you ... which fuelled the Great Expansion, and led to the permanent, long-range gates, like the one you came in on."

"We know," says the man with the salt-and-pepper beard. He reminds Hannah of a particularly grumpy high school teacher she once had. "It was in the intro you played us."

"Right." Hannah nods, like he's made an excellent point. She'd forgotten about the damn intro video, her jump-lag from the day before fuzzing her memory. All she can remember is a voiceover that was way, way too perky for someone discussing a battle as brutal as Sigma Orionis.

She decides to keep going. "So, the … the Colonies lost that particular fight, but the war actually kept going for five years after the Frontier captured the space around Sigma."

They know this already, too. Why is she telling them? Heat creeps up her cheeks, a sensation she does her best to ignore.

"Anyway, if you've got any questions about the early days of the Expansion, while we were still constructing the jump gates, then I'm your girl. I actually did my dissertation on—"

Movement, behind her. She turns to see one of the other tour guides, a big dude with a tribal tattoo poking out of the collar of his red company shirt.

"Oh, thank God," Hannah hisses at him. "Do you know how to fix the sim?"

He ignores her. "OK, folks," he says to the room, smooth and loud. "That concludes our VR demonstration. Hope you enjoyed it, and if you have any questions, I'll be happy to answer them while our next group of guests are getting set up."

Before Hannah can say anything, he turns to her, his smile melting away. "Your sim slot was over five minutes ago. Get out of here."

He bends down, and with an effortless series of commands, resets the simulator. As the tourists file out, the bearded man glances at her, shaking his head.

Hannah digs in her back pocket, her face still hot and prickly. "Sorry. The sim's really good, and I got kind of wrapped up in it, so …" She says the words with a smile, which fades as the other guide continues to ignore her.

She doesn't even know what she's doing—the sim wasn't good. It was creepy. Learning about a battle was one thing—actually being there, watching people get blown to pieces …

Sighing, she pulls her crumpled tab out of her pocket and unfolds it. Her schedule is faithfully written out on it, copied off her lens—a habit she picked up when she was a kid, after her mom's lens glitched and they missed a swimming trial. "Can you tell me how to get to the dock?"

The other guide glances at the outdated tab, his mouth forming a moue of distaste. "There should be a map on your lens."

"Haven't synced it to the station yet." She's a little too embarrassed to tell him that it's still in its solution above the tiny sink in her quarters, and she forgot to go back for it before her shift started.

She would give a kidney to go back now, and not just for the lens. Her staff cabin might be small enough for her to touch all four walls at once without stretching, but it has a bed in it. With *sheets*. They might be scratchy and thin and smell of bleach, but the thought of pulling them over her head and drifting off is intoxicating.

The next group is pushing inside the VR room, clustered in twos and threes, eyeing the somewhat threadbare motion seats. The guide has already forgotten Hannah, striding towards the incoming tourists, booming a welcome.

"Thanks for your help," Hannah mutters, as she slips out of the room.

The dock. She was there yesterday, wasn't she? Coming off the intake shuttle. How hard could it be to find a second time? She turns right out of the VR room, heading for where she thinks the main station atrium is. According to her tab, she isn't late, but she picks up her pace all the same.

The wide, gently curved walkway is bordered by a floor-to-ceiling window taller than the house Hannah grew up in. The space is packed with more tourists. Most of them are clustered at the apex, admiring the view dominated by the Horsehead Nebula.

Hannah barely caught a glimpse when they arrived last night, which was filled with safety briefings and room assignments and roster changes and staff canteen conversations that were way too loud. She had sat at a table to one side, both hoping that someone would come and talk to her, and hoping they wouldn't.

In the end, with something like relief, she'd managed to slink off for a few hours of disturbed sleep.

The station she's on used to be plain old Sigma XV—a big, boring, industrial mining outpost that the Colony and the Frontier fought over during the war. They still did mining here—helium-3, mostly, for fusion reactors—but it was now also known as the Sigma Hotel and Luxury Resort.

It always amazed Hannah just how quickly it had all happened. It felt like the second the war ended, the tour operators were lobbying the Frontier Senate for franchise rights. Now, Sigma held ten thousand tourists, who streamed in through the big jump gate from a dozen different worlds and moons, excited to finally be able to travel, hoping for a glimpse of the Neb.

Like the war never happened. Like there weren't a hundred different small conflicts and breakaway factions still dotted across both Frontier *and* Colonies. The aftershocks of war, making themselves known.

Not that Sigma Station was the only one in on the action. It was happening everywhere—apparently there was even a tour company out Phobos way that took people inside a wrecked Colony frigate which hadn't been hauled back for salvage yet.

As much as Hannah feels uncomfortable with the idea of setting up a hotel here, so soon after the fighting, she needs this job. It's the only one her useless history degree would get her, and at least it means that she doesn't have to sit at the table at her parents' house on Titan, listening to her sister talk about how fast her company is growing.

The walkway she's on takes a sharp right, away from the windows, opening up into an airy plaza. The space is enormous, climbing up ten whole levels. A glittering light fixture the size of a truck hangs from the ceiling, and in the centre of the floor there's a large fountain, fake marble cherubs and dragons spouting water streams that criss-cross in midair.

The plaza is packed with more tourists, milling around the

fountain or chatting on benches or meandering in and out of the shops and restaurants that line the edges. Hannah has to slow down, sorry-ing and excuse-me-ing her way through.

The wash of sensations almost overwhelms her, and she can't help thinking about the sheets again. White. Cool. Light enough to slide under and—

No. Come on. Be professional.

Does she go left from here, or is it on the other side of the fountain? Recalling the station map she looked at while they were jumping is like trying to decipher something in Sanskrit. Then she sees a sign above one of the paths leading off the plaza. *Ship Dock B*. That's the one.

Three minutes later, she's there. The dock is small, a spartan mustering area with four gangways leading out from the station to the airlock berths. There aren't many people around, although there are still a few sitting on benches. One of them, a little girl, is asleep: curled up with her hands tucked between shoulder and cheek, legs pulled up to her chest. Her mom—or the person Hannah thinks is her mom—sits next to her, blinking at something on her lens.

There are four tour ships visible through the glass, brightly lit against the inky black. Hannah's been on plenty of tours, and she still can't help thinking that every ship she's ever been on is ugly as hell. She's seen these ones before: they look like flattened, upside-down elephant droppings, a bulbous protrusion sticking out over each of the cockpits.

Hannah jams her hand in her jeans pocket for the tab. She wrote the ship's name for the shift in tiny capitals next to the start time: RED PANDA. Her gaze flicks between the four ships, but it takes her a second to find the right one. The name is printed on the side in big, stencilled letters, with a numbered designation in smaller script underneath.

She looks from the *Panda* to its gangway. Another guide is making his way onto it. He's wearing the same red shirt as her, and he has the most fantastic hair: a spiked purple mohawk at least a foot high.

Her tab still in hand, she springs onto the gangway. "Hey!" she says, forcing a confidence she doesn't feel into her voice. "I'm on for this one. Anything I need to know?"

Mohawk guy glances over his shoulder, an expression of bored contempt on his face. He keeps walking, his thick black boots booming on the metal plating.

"Um. Hi?" Hannah catches up to him. "I think this one's mine?"

She tries to slip past him, but he puts up a meaty hand, blocking her path. "Nice try, rook," he says, that bored look still on his face. "You're late. Shift's mine."

"What are you talking about?" She swipes a finger across her tab, hunting for the little clock.

"Don't you have a lens?"

This time it takes Hannah a lot more effort to stay calm. "There," she says, pointing at her schedule. "I'm not late. I'm supposed to be on at eleven, and it's …" she finds the clock in the corner of her tab. "Eleven-o-two."

"My *lens* says eleven-o-six. Anyway, you're still late. I get the shift."

"What? No. Are you serious?"

He ignores her, resuming his walk towards the airlock. As he does, Hannah remembers the words from the handbook the company sent her before she left Titan: *Guides who are late for their shift will lose it. Please try not to be late!!!*

He can't do this. He can't. But who are the crew chiefs going to believe? The new girl? She'll lose a shift on her first day, which means she's already in the red, which means that maybe they don't keep her past her probation. A free shuttle ride back to Titan, and we wish you all the best in your future endeavours.

Anger replaces panic. This might not be her dream job, but it's work, and at the very least it means she's going *somewhere* with her life. She can already see the faces of her parents when she tells them she lost her job, and that is not going to happen. Not ever.

"Is that hair growing out of your ears, too?" she says, more furious than she's been in a long time. "I said I'm *here*. It's *my shift*."

He turns to look at her, dumbfounded. "What did you just say?"

Hannah opens her mouth to return fire, but nothing comes out.

Her mom and dad would know. Callista definitely would. Her older sister would understand exactly how to smooth things over, make this asshole see things her way. Then again, there's no way either her parents or Callie would ever have taken a job like this, so they wouldn't be in this situation. They're not here now, and they can't help her.

"It's all right, Donnie," says a voice.

Hannah and Mohawk guy—Donnie—turn to see the supervisor walking up. She's a young woman, barely older than Hannah, with a neat bob of black hair and a pristine red shirt. Hannah remembers meeting her last night, for about two seconds, but she's totally blanking on her name. Her gaze automatically goes to the woman's breast pocket, and she's relieved to see a badge: *Atsuke*.

"Come on, boss," Donnie says. "She was late." He glances at Hannah, and the expression on his face clearly says that he's just getting started.

"I seem to remember you being late on *your* first day." Atsuke's voice is pleasant and even, like a newsreader's.

"*And*," Donnie says, as if Atsuke hadn't spoken. "She was talking bakwas about my hawk. Mad disrespectful. I've been here a lot longer than she has, and I don't see why—"

"Well, to be fair, Donnie, your hair *is* pretty stupid. Not to mention against regs. I've told you that, like, ten times."

Donnie stares at her, shoulders tight. In response, Atsuke raises a perfectly shaped eyebrow.

He lets out a disgusted sigh, then shoves past them. "You got lucky, rook," he mutters, as he passes Hannah.

Her chest is tight, like she's just run a marathon, and she exhales hard. "Thank you *so* much," she says to Atsuke. "I'm really sorry I was late—I thought I had enough time to—"

"Hey." Atsuke puts a hand on her shoulder. "Take a breath. It's fine."

Hannah manages a weak smile. Later, she is going to buy Atsuke a drink. Multiple drinks.

"It's an easy one today," Atsuke says. "Eight passengers. Barely a third of capacity. Little bit about the station, talk about the war, the treaty, what we got, what the Colonies got, the role Sigma played in everything, get them gawking at the Neb ... twenty minutes, in and out. Square?"

She looks down at Hannah's tab, then glances up with a raised eyebrow.

"My lens is glitching," Hannah says.

"Right." This time, Atsuke looks a little less sure. She reaches in her shirt pocket, and hands Hannah a tiny clip-on mic. "Here. Links to the ship automatically. You can pretty much just start talking. And listen: just be cool. Go do this one, and then there'll be a coffee waiting for you when you get back."

Forget the drink. She should take out another loan, buy Atsuke shares in the touring company. "I will. I mean, yeah. You got it."

Atsuke gestures to the airlock at the far end of the gangway. "Get going. And if Volkova gives you any shit, just ignore her. Have fun."

Hannah wants to ask who Volkova is, but Atsuke is already heading back, and Hannah doesn't dare follow. She turns, and marches as fast she can towards the *Red Panda*'s airlock.

Chapter 2

"Mom, check out that star!"

Corey Livingstone leans way back, pointing straight up through the tour ship's viewing dome. The star is the lone red one in a black void filled with thousands of dim, white pinpricks. It's just beyond the other ships cruising above their docking station. He can see himself there, too, reflected in the glass, the *Apex Space* logo on his white T-shirt just visible. And he can see the top of his mom's head, which means she either didn't hear him, or is pretending not to.

"It's not a star." Malik sounds bored, his eyes fixed on his hologram in front of him. "Just a mining ship."

"How do you know? You didn't even look."

Malik shrugs. Like always, he has the movie editor open on the holo—Corey can see footage of their dad on the diving board of the hotel pool, running on a silent, three-second loop. No sooner do his feet leave the board than he's back on the edge, right foot forward, making the jump, over and over again.

Corey wrinkles his nose. Malik is fifteen, only five years older than him, but sometimes he acts like he's thirty. And, of course, he thinks he's so bàng because he uses outdated tech like the hand-held holocam, a stick of black plastic with a big hologram display floating above it. He claims it's because it has better image quality than his lens, which isn't true. Malik is only doing it because Shanti Evans at school did it first.

He looks back up through the dome. "Mom, you see it?"

"In a second, honey," Anita Livingstone says, not looking at him. She and his dad, Everett, are arguing about the return tickets. Again. They're doing that weird thing where they both speak quietly without looking at each other. Their index fingers are touching, linking their lenses, which they wouldn't even have to do if they'd just let them all get neurochips like everyone else. His mom had the thirty-day trial shot last year, which she claimed gave her a headache, and that was the end of *that* discussion.

"No, seriously, check it out," Corey says. "Is that Phobos-B? I think it might be, but I don't know if—"

"Dad." Malik doesn't look up. "Could you tell him to go bother someone else please?"

"But, Dad, look, it's—"

"Very nice, Corey," his dad says, glancing up towards the dome for perhaps a third of a second. As always, he's wearing an old denim shirt and faded jeans, although at least he didn't bring his nasty work shoes on this trip, with their spatters of reactor sealant. He squints, frowning at something on his lens. "They're supposed to be here," he says. "The station cloud should have them."

"Well, it obviously doesn't." His mom drops her finger from

his. She's wearing a green shirt, unbuttoned, over a tank top and slim pants.

"But they were there when we checked in. I even said …"

Corey's finger wavers, then drops. He slouches in the bucket seat, one of about two dozen on the tour ship's main deck.

His gaze drifts to the ships crossing above them. *Antares D6 cruiser, cold fusion drive, three hundred crew capacity. AI-controlled, minimal range.* A big cargo carrier slides into view, and Corey blanks for a second before the answer comes—of course it does, it's on the big poster on his wall at home showing all the main Frontier ships, upper left corner. *Vector Leviathan. Got a hold big enough to take an entire squadron of Scorpion fighters.*

His imagination lights up with scenes of a quiet cargo hold, the fighters stacked like toys, flight-suit-clad pilots waiting silently for their go signal. Fat chance. These days, it's probably just hauling asteroid slag or something. That's what a lot of the old combat carriers are doing—getting rented out to the big companies as freighters. It's kind of sad, even though it's still pretty crash seeing one up close.

At the edge of the dome, he can just see the tip of the Horsehead Nebula, a tight cluster of stars that glow like a fistful of diamonds. Corey lingers on them for a second, then looks back at the cargo carrier.

The Neb is amazing, but once you'd been looking at it for a week solid, you kind of got over it. And it was just getting to that point of the trip where they'd run out of stuff to do, which was why they were on this lame tour in the first place.

Man, he's looking forward to going back to Earth.

Sigma was pretty cool—at first, anyway. It was the only place in the whole Frontier that you could actually get a good look at the Neb, and getting here had felt like an actual adventure. There's only one jump gate—the other one got blown up in the war—and it cost a lot to get this far out. It's weird how people can invent something as amazing as a jump gate network, and then spend almost thirty years fighting over it and blowing it up, but whatever.

They'd gone swimming, and eaten in some OK restaurants,

and—of course—spent hours looking at the Neb from every angle they could. The only time he'd been really bored was when Mom and Dad had sent them to some dumb kids evening, where a bunch of the staff did this really embarrassing play with audience participation.

They'd almost called on Corey, but if there was one advantage of the growth spurt that had propelled Malik to nearly six feet, it was that Corey could hide behind him when he had to. He still couldn't wait until he got his own spurt—he hated his body, hated his pudgy five-foot frame and his stupid hair that his mom wouldn't let him get cornrows in, like Malik had.

He hadn't wanted to go to the kids' thing—he doesn't even like *thinking* of himself as a kid—but Mom and Dad said they wanted some alone time. That meant s-e-x, but when they got back to the room it didn't smell like s-e-x. It didn't smell like anything.

What if the Vector *did* have a fighter or two in the hold? One they hadn't decommissioned yet? Maybe if he was nice to Mom and Dad, they'd let him go ask. Maybe whoever owned the Vector would let him sit in a Scorpion fighter cockpit—he'd done that once, in the Frontier War Museum on Europa, and it was awesome. Totally zhen.

Besides, what if aliens attacked the station or something? They'd need somebody to fight them off, and he could definitely fly one of the Scorpions, if he had to. Well, they wouldn't let him, not at first, but if all the other pilots got blown up, and there was one ship left … He smirks as he imagines his brother filming him doing it, swooping back and forth. Much better than their dad on a stupid diving board.

He'll have to time it right. No point asking while Mom and Dad are like this. Maybe later, when they're back in the room …

The ship rumbles, jerking him out of his thoughts. He shifts on the uncomfortable seat, folding his arms, his gaze tracking back to the red star. Malik was right (not that he'd ever admit it—he'd rather get called on at the kids' evening). It *is* a ship, the shape starting to form as it closes on the station. Probably just another Antares.

Adrift

The tour ship they're on is old. *Really* old. They came in through the airlock in the bar on the lower level, and most of the lights were off, which meant his mom nearly lost her balance on the stairs. Corey doesn't know why. They've been on a bunch of these ships before, and they're all identical. Same bar, same stairs leading to a big main deck on the upper level, same grimy walls. Same rows of scratched and dented plastic bucket seats, bolted to the floor. Each of the rows has seats back-to-back, which is annoying, because you're always bumping someone's head when you tilt yours up. There aren't any safety straps on the seats, although Corey can see the brackets for them. Either they took them out, or never bothered to put them in in the first place.

Without even trying, Corey can picture the layout of the rest of the ship in his head. Cockpit in front of the main deck, with a small passage leading to it. Bathroom under the stairs in the bar. The rest of the lower level taken up by astronautics and the fusion engine—you can't get there through the bar, but there's a trapdoor on the floor of the main deck, just off to his right.

There's an escape pod at the back of the main deck, the door covered with red warning signs. A super-dense, curved gravity well covers the entire bottom of the ship, cradling it like a hand. It's your standard Maverick tour vessel: twenty-four-passenger capacity, plus a three-person crew.

There's hardly anyone around, though. A young couple at the front. Both of them are wearing leather jackets, and the woman's long brown hair hangs down her back in a swooping ponytail. The man is enormous—six-six, easy, with shoulders like steel beams, tight against the leather. His left hand and arm are metal, which is kind of strange, because most people with switched-out limbs get them covered in skin-type material so they look real. Not this guy.

Does it make a noise when he turns over in bed? Or during s-e-x? Either way, Corey's a little bit jealous. Only a little bit—losing an arm just to find out the answers wouldn't be fun—but he's seen that series about people with prosthetics going one-on-one against droids in the ring, which wasn't bad, even though the droids usually won.

Maybe *that's* why the guy got his arm switched out. Even droid fighters need vacations now and then.

There's an old woman to their left in a thick grey tracksuit, with a giant, unclipped fanny pack on her lap. She sees Corey looking, and smiles, the dark skin around her eyes wrinkling. Corey flashes her a smile back.

The last person is a man in a green polo shirt and suit jacket. He looks a little like Terio Smith, the point guard for the Austin Djinns back home in Texas—same shaped face, same big shoulders. He's staring at nothing, absently twisting the hem of his shirt in his fingers.

How awesome would it be if the man actually *was* Terio Smith?

The man glances at Corey, then away, his mouth turned down. Corey looks at his shoes, annoyed with himself. The man's a lot older than Terio, late thirties. Plus, he's going bald on top, his hairline crawling back. And if Terio Smith *was* here, there's no way he'd be on a crappy tour like this one.

Maybe the man is *related* to Terio Smith—they do kind of look alike, after all. He could tell everybody he met Terio's cousin, get a photo or …

He sighs. Kicks his feet against the chair supports.

One more day. Then they'd head to the gate, and jump back home through the wormhole. He'd have a whole week to mess around with Jamie and Allie before school started. Maybe Jamie'd finally managed to finish that new engine model—it'd be useful when they finally started building their own ships.

Jamie would design them, Allie would do all the business stuff and Corey would fly them, all the way out of Sigma Station and beyond, further than anyone had ever gone. They'd already picked out a name for their company: 866 Industries, after the first three digits of the Universal Location Coordinates for Austin.

Of course, he'd have to join the Navy first. He wasn't wild on the whole boot camp thing, but being Frontier Navy meant that he'd *really* get to learn to fly, even if they weren't doing too much fighting any more. But who knows what kind of secret tech they had? Stuff they only showed the top pilots?

There's a soft click, and a man's voice issues from a nearby speaker: a recording, loud and perky. "Thank you for choosing Sigma Destination Tours. We value your business. This comfortable, spacious vessel will provide all the amenities you need on your adventure. We hope that—"

The recording is cut off abruptly by another voice, this one not pre-recorded. It's a woman this time, deeply bored, with one of the thickest Russian accents Corey has ever heard.

"Ladies and gentlemen, welcome aboard the *Red Panda*. I am Captain Jana Volkova and I will be your pilot today on our tour of Sigma Station. The tour guide is running very late but will be here soon so in the meantime I will tell you about this ship. Restrooms can be found at—"

There's a long pause, as if the mic has cut out, before the captain's voice comes back, "—under the stairs near the bar. After your tour starts, our staff member Barrington will be happy to serve you a range of bev ... oh, sorry, I just looked at the staff roster and he didn't come in for work today, and we are short-staffed, so no bar service, sorry again. Safety reminders, should the gravity well fail, you will find handholds located along the struts across the main viewing area ..."

Corey's mom is staring into the middle distance, which means she's working on her briefings. Again.

His dad notices, too. "We're supposed to be on vacation, 'Nita. We talked about this."

"What difference does it make?" she says, blinking. "You heard the captain. We're waiting."

"All the same. We're here to relax."

"I'm just catching up on my reading," she says, not noticing as Corey mouths the words along with her.

He doesn't blame his dad for being annoyed. It's not like Mom is going to be able to beam back her notes to the office—even if she could, it'd take years and years and *years* for anybody to get them.

Usually, her lens is direct-connect to the Frontier government servers. Won't work all the way out here, though, so she had to download everything before she came. Like always, she has her handbag with her: a giant tote made of shiny green fabric that she takes pretty much everywhere. Corey snuck a look in there once; all it has are weird creams and bottles of painkillers and four or five pairs of sunglasses, plus a few boring political books that she could easily get on her lens but which she claims to prefer reading in her hands.

He can't remember a trip they'd been on where she *wasn't* reading, or writing memos, or drafting policy. The only time she's even looked remotely guilty about it was when Corey saw her doing it in a restaurant on Titan, eyes flicking left and right while Mal and his dad talked basketball. Or movies. He can't remember.

Anita Livingstone works for a Frontier senator. She's a deputy legislator, which Corey knows is pretty high up. He sometimes wonders how she got together with his dad, whose office is in an industrial area in Austin and who spends most of his time driving from place to place, installing home fusion reactors. He'd asked them once, and they given each other the strangest look, as if both remembering something slightly different. "Just in college," his dad had said, which was kind of a boring answer.

He kicks his legs, drumming them against the chair support as the captain drones on, glancing at the holo display floating above his brother's hand cam. Malik tweaks the tracker with his thumb, adding in some special effects: a cartoon explosion from Everett's feet as he leaves the diving board.

There's a clunk from the airlock below them, then the sound of running feet. Seconds later, a woman pops out of the stairwell like a cork from a bottle.

She's young, early twenties, with arms and legs that remind Corey of the thin arms on space construction bots, and she looks harassed. She's wearing a red T-shirt that's too big for her, the tour company's bright white logo across the back—a weirdly shaped silhouette of a ship, zooming across the words SIGMA DESTINATION TOURS. In one hand she clutches a crumpled tab. Corey blinks. Mal's holo might be old, but actual tabs are prehistoric.

Captain Volkova's voice booms through the main deck. "OK, I see the guide has arrived, so we can begin the tour."

With a clunking shudder, the ship disengages from its dock.

Adrift

The view outside the dome begins to change, sliding to the right. The tour guide drops her tab. She bends down, flustered, trying to scoop it up, and has to dodge back as she almost bumps heads with the male half of the couple at the front. Malik already has his holo up, filming the encounter.

Corey looks back up at the dome. The red ship is gone.

"All right," says the tour guide. A tiny mic clipped to her T-shirt collar broadcasts her voice through the ship's speakers, the sound crackly and distorted. "Sorry I was a little late, ladies and gentlemen, but we can get started now. My name is Hannah, and I'll be your guide for this tour around Sigma Station. As you probably know already, the station is not only a luxury hotel, but an active mining centre, processing at least twenty mil—"

She stops, looking down at her tab, tapping at it experimentally. Idly, Corey wonders why she doesn't just use her lens. "Yes. Twenty million tons of helium-3 a year, although it is also a popular tourist destination which ... I guess you also know already, and you've probably had a good look at the Horsehead Nebula, which around here we call the 'Neb.'"

She gives an awkward laugh. Every sentence she speaks rises in pitch until, in the middle, it drops again, coming to rest on a low note. It makes Corey want to put his hands over his ears.

"And if you take a look through the dome now," Hannah says, "the station itself should just be coming into view."

Corey glances up and his mouth falls open.

They'd seen the station from the outside once before, when they were coming in on their transport ship (*Diablo F400, needle nose, twin fusion engines*). But that was a fleeting glimpse, and the station was just a dark shape, shadowy and indistinct. From here, it's silhouetted against the glowing expanse of the Horsehead Nebula, and Corey can't believe how big it is. Dozens of cylindrical modules, each the size of a city block, with what must be a million twinkling lights. The giant command sector hovers above the station like an umbrella. A dozen ships are in view, slowly coasting through space, moving in and out of the cavernous station dock.

Corey isn't the only one staring. Every other passenger, even not-Terio-Smith, is craning their necks to look.

At that moment, Corey spots the red ship again. Only, it's not red. The light from the Neb made it look that way from a distance, but it's actually painted a dull orange. He doesn't recognise the silhouette—it's sharper and more streamlined than the Vectors or the Antares, and it's still not close enough for him to pick out the details.

Whatever it is, it's moving crazy fast. It must have been a hundred miles away when he first saw it, and now it's almost on them.

"So when the war ended ten years ago," Hannah is saying, reading from her notes, "the Belarus Treaty allowed the Colonies to keep ten planets around the Talos core, with the remaining ninety-six occupied planets and outposts being ceded to the Frontier—including this station."

She taps at something on her tab. "The station holds around ten thousand people full-time, plus there are usually anywhere between fifty and a hundred mining ships docked or in orbit. They arrive using the Sigma jump gate, which is too far away for us to see from here but which you've probably … Yes?"

The old woman with the grey hair is holding up a shaky hand. "I read the Frontier got a raw deal out of the treaty?" she asks.

"Oh no, ma'am," Hannah says, smiling. This time, she doesn't have to refer to her notes. "That's a common misconception. It's true that the Colonies got to keep some valuable mining outposts, but the Frontier got a much larger chunk of territory, plus control of the jump gate network. And when you consider that the war only started because the Colonies decided to keep the resources they were sent out for instead of firing them back through the gates like they were supposed to, I'd say it's a good compromise. Everybody got what they wanted. Mostly. Does that sort of answer your question, ma'am?"

"Oh, please don't call me ma'am," the old woman says, returning Hannah's smile. "And yes, thank you."

Corey glances at his mom—Anita Livingstone is staring daggers at Hannah, and he can understand why. She's spent the past two years trying to get the treaty changed, arguing that the Frontier *did* get a raw deal out of it. *Please don't let her start arguing with the tour guide …*

Adrift

The *Red Panda* starts to turn, and the orange ship slips out of sight. They're heading further out from the station, coming past the loading docks, giving the incoming ships a wide berth. D6 cruisers shine in the light from the Neb.

"So here's a little factoid about the station you might not have heard," the guide says, leaning on the word *factoid*. "When we first set out to build permanent gates—ones we could actually send humans through—this was one of the first completed. It meant we had a lot more volunteers prepared to leave Earth, which, as you know, was a pretty crucial issue after the sea levels rose. So when you jumped through the gate on your journey to Sigma, you were jumping through history!"

She beams at her audience, and gets precisely zero reaction back.

"OK, ladies and gentlemen," says the pilot. "There will be a slight acceleration now, so please hold onto your seats and do not walk around, thank you."

There's a rumble as the *Red Panda*'s engines take the strain. As it does, the orange ship comes into view again.

It's much closer now—close enough for Corey to finally pick out the details. The ship is huge, easily as big as an Antares, with an aggressive, pointed nose and thin, almost needle-like fins. It's slowing down, its thrusters pointed forward, ejecting white puffs of gas as it comes to a slow cruise above the station.

A shiver sneaks up Corey's spine. He thought he knew just about every type of ship there was, but this one? He's never seen it before.

The other passengers have seen it, too. His dad catches the old woman's eye and shrugs, smiling. The couple near the front are asking Hannah about the ship. "I'm not sure," the guide says. "It's probably just another mining vessel."

A tiny opening appears on the side of the orange ship. Small metal spheres begin to pop out, dispersing into the vacuum. Each looks to be about the size of a small hovercar.

Two spheres become three, then a dozen, then two dozen, drifting like a cloud of flies. Thrusters on the spheres activate, one after the other, sending them on a curving trajectory towards the station.

"What are those?" his dad says, pointing up at the spheres. The rest of the passengers are just as confused, craning their necks to look up through the dome.

Corey can't move. He can't tear his eyes away from the cloud of spheres. One changes course, zipping away from the pack, colliding with one of the cruisers near the station dock.

A ball of silent, swirling flame erupts, the cruiser's body cracking in two. Corey's eyes go wide, and the old woman sucks in a horrified breath.

"Um ..." Hannah says.

Then the rest of the spheres reach their targets, and, without a sound, Sigma Station explodes.

Chapter 3

Hannah Elliott's mind shuts down.

The station is being torn apart in front of them, silent bursts of fire shredding the modules, the command centre ripping in half. Cargo cruisers are coming about, trying to flee, chased down by the metal spheres. One particularly large ship splits down the belly, its cargo spinning out into the void, tiny silver particles glinting. Food containers, probably destined for the station restaurants.

She's still in the sim. She has to be. She's fallen asleep, and her jump-lagged brain is in the middle of a horrible lucid dream. She's definitely not here, on a tourist vessel shaped like an upside-down turd, watching an entire station get blown to pieces.

Atsuke's still on there. So's Donnie. The tattooed guy in the VR room. And the little girl on the bench in the dock. Everybody.

The people on the tour ship's main deck are screaming.

The family at the back are going nuts, the two parents pulling their boys in, trying to shield them as if one of those spheres is about to come hurtling through the viewing dome. The old woman is still seated—she's pulled herself into a tight ball, like a centipede curling in on itself, fingers clutching her fanny pack. Her mouth is moving, whispering something rapid and panicked—a prayer, maybe. The man in the suit jacket and polo shirt is on his feet. He's shouting, and every word is a horrible wail: "*Hooohmygod! Hoooh! Hoooooohno!*" To Hannah, it sounds like he's gasping for air, barely pausing for breath between each one. His eyes are enormous, locked on the chaos outside the ship.

"Jesus fucking Christ," says a stunned voice to Hannah's right. It's the man in the leather jacket. He's got an Irish accent, and he too is on his feet. The woman with him has her hand over her mouth, staring in horror.

Hannah can't move. Can't think. The orange ship is still just visible, the hole in its belly is still shooting out those spheres. Hundreds of them, whirling away, heading for different parts of the station.

"We gotta get out of here," says the man in the suit jacket. When Hannah doesn't respond, he bellows at her. "You hear me? We gotta go now!"

Hannah opens her mouth, but can't get the words out. She swallows, tries again. "If everybody could just stay calm—"

The captain's voice booms over the speakers, clear and urgent. "OK, everybody on the main deck stay sitting, and hold on!"

Hannah nearly loses her footing as the *Red Panda* turns, the inertial dampeners straining. The thrum of the engines increases, the dampeners fighting to keep them stable as the pilot banks hard. Hannah grabs one of the plastic chairs for support, but her fingers are slimy with sweat. She can't get a grip. Her right knee bangs against the deck, hands splayed out in front of her. There's a curious metallic taste in her mouth.

A shadow crosses the viewing dome. Hannah looks up, and there's a ship heading right towards them.

It's a tugboat, its cabin destroyed, its back half shorn almost clean off. Someone—the father of the two boys, she thinks—gives an angry roar, as if to scare the thing off. As it gets closer, Hannah sees a burned, human-looking shape in one of the pilot seats.

The *Red Panda* banks again, sending the destroyed tugboat sliding to the left, only just missing them. Hannah's shoulders are trembling under her oversized T-shirt. A sphere rockets past the dome as she gets to her feet, making her flinch. Her own words echo back at her in her mind: *The station holds around ten thousand people full time.*

"What do we do?" It's the boys' mother. Her face is white, and her voice almost a shriek. The old woman's prayer is audible now, her voice hitching, reeling off something in Spanish. All the passengers, even the old woman, are looking at Hannah. She can feel the stunned terror radiating off them—it reminds her of the waft of dry heat you get when you open an oven that's been on for a long time.

They're staring at her because she's the one in charge. She's the one standing at the front, the one with the notes and the official T-shirt, and they want her to tell them what they have to do.

"Um," Hannah says, barely aware that she's speaking. "Just ..." Then she turns and runs.

In seconds, she's in the tiny corridor leading to the cockpit, pushing through the grimy door. The passengers are screaming in startled fury behind her. Somewhere, deep in her chest, there's a tiny beat of horrified shame. She doesn't care. She can no more face the passengers right now than she can breathe in space.

The first thing she sees through the cockpit glass is another station module erupting in a massive gout of flame. It's close, less than a mile away, and it's happening in absolute, perfect, horrid silence. Hannah flinches, banging her head on a ceiling strut, sending darts of light shooting through her vision. *This isn't happening.*

The cockpit is small, with a horseshoe-shaped control deck surrounding a single battered chair. Hannah can just see the back of the occupant's head, greying hair pulled into a severe bun.

"Captain, we have a proximity alert," says the cheerful voice of the *Red Panda*.

"*I know!*" The pilot changes from English to Russian, spitting a torrent of abuse as she reaches out, hammering on the control panel.

Adrift

She's an older woman—fifty, at least—with a heavily lined face and a receding hairline. She wears a short-sleeved white pilot's shirt with epaulettes, and her wrists are heavy with gold bangles. A cigarette—a homemade one, not a NicoStick—hangs from one corner of her mouth. Hannah can't remember the last time she even smelled tobacco.

The pilot turns, twisting in her seat, bloodshot eyes landing on Hannah. "Guide? What are you doing here? Get back! Get to the cabin! Deal with the passen—"

She cuts off mid-sentence to yank the control stick to the right, twisting the *Panda* around to avoid a chunk of debris the size of Hannah's parents' house. Hannah screams, and ducks. A dim, unfocused thought crosses her mind: why is there an actual control stick in the cockpit, when the pilot could easily control the ship with her lens?

Volkova flips a switch and starts speaking again. "Mayday, mayday, station control, this is the *Red Panda*, XT560 dash T1, requesting instructions, do you—*pizdets!*"

Hannah is almost knocked off her feet as the *Red Panda* shudders from an impact. She's almost certain one of the spheres has found its mark, that she's about to be sucked right through the wall as the ship undergoes explosive decompression. Then a car-shaped chunk of metal appears in the viewport, spinning away from them, torn wires sprouting from its edge. The *Red Panda* smacked right into it, hard enough to shake the ship.

They're above the station's command module now. Hannah can see right through it, right down to the main station modules below. The wreckage is spitting gouts of purple-blue flame, twisting and coiling like snakes.

We should be shooting back. Hannah might not know Sigma Station well, but she knows that it has some defences—long-range torpedo batteries, designed to intercept threats before they get close. That kind of thing. And yet the attacking ship is still there, hanging above the chaos like a malevolent god, untouched. It doesn't make sense.

"What's going on in here?" It's the man in the suit jacket, slamming through the cockpit door, bracing himself on the wall as Volkova pulls out of the roll. The drumbeat of shame in Hannah's chest gets louder, thumping in time with her heart.

With a grunt, the man thrusts himself into the cockpit, propelling himself along. Something inside Hannah, some nugget she retained from the guide orientation sessions, reasserts itself. She steps in front of him, hands raised. "Sir, if you could just return to the main cabin ..."

"*Are you out of your mind?*" the man screams at her. He tries to push past her, reaching out and putting a hand on the captain's shoulder. "We have a right to know what's—"

Volkova twists around in her seat. For a half-second, Hannah is sure she's going to lunge forward and take a bite out of the man, like a rabid dog.

"Get out!" Volkova bellows into his face. Another ship drifts past, spinning wildly, broken and torn.

"The hell with this," the man says, tearing himself away. "I'm getting on the escape pod."

"No!" Volkova roars the word over her shoulder, but the man is gone, pushing past Hannah before she can even blink, ripping the cockpit door open and vanishing through it.

Escape pod. Of course.

She's taken two steps when Volkova grabs her, iron fingers knotting the fabric of her T-shirt, pulling her back. Hannah only just manages to stay on her feet.

"Stop him," Volkova says. The sharp whiff of booze on her breath is unmistakable. "They launch the pod, they die."

"But—" Of course they need to launch the pod. What is the captain talking about?

Volkova pulls her close. Despite the booze on her breath, her eyes are clear.

"This is a crap ship," Volkova says, jerking her head at the control panel. "Short-range, no weapons, moves like a pig in mud. You cannot even control it with a lens—you must use a stick. But the escape pod is even worse. No control—drift and drift until *boom*. Plus, it sends out an automatic locator beacon. Easy to find, easy to kill."

"I can't," Hannah says, barely able to get the words out. The shame has reached a thundering crescendo, and the thought of going back out there to face the passengers is almost too much to take. She swallows, forces herself to speak. "Why can't you do it?"

Volkova shoves her away. "Didn't you hear me? This crap ship's crap autopilot is going to get us killed. I have to fly it, so you need to control the passengers. *Go!*"

Chapter 4

As he sprints back onto the *Panda*'s main deck, all Jack Tennant can think about is the minibar in his room.

There'd been a whole row of tiny Nova whisky bottles, lined up like soldiers on one side of the fridge. When he'd left his room this morning, for the first time since he arrived on the goddamn station, all but one had been drained. Did he bring it with him? He can't remember.

He wasn't even supposed to be on Sigma. He'd wanted to go to Kepler-186, check out the new boutique resort there—the kind of thing the Europa Central Feed had sold him on when they hired him as their hotel critic in the first place. But the economy was in the toilet and readers wanted family package experiences and yadda yadda yadda, and so they'd sent him to fucking Sigma.

Jack had retired to his room (small, dilapidated) more or less immediately. He'd spent three days lying in bed, ordering up room service (tiny portions, steak overcooked) when he got hungry, watching movies he'd seen before and pillaging the minibar for everything it had. This morning, he'd finally emerged, bleary and unshaven, wearing his last clean shirt and jacket. He'd been tempted to wing it, make the whole thing up. His editor wouldn't even notice, mostly because—as he tried to remind himself as often as possible—he was a hell of a writer.

In the end, he'd decided not to. He might hate this job, but he'd be damned if he'd compromise his ethics.

His early horror gives way to a furious, panicky purpose. He bursts onto the main deck, arms pumping, eyes hunting for the escape pod. Someone on his right, he doesn't see who, is yelling, asking what's going on. The irony is, he can hear them perfectly— the ship's engines might be firing hard, but the destruction around them is completely silent. Whoever it is grabs his shoulder, and he twists away, almost toppling over one of the plastic bucket seats.

It's the man with the robot arm—he and his wife are standing side by side, eyes huge. "What did they say?" the woman says, in a thick English accent. "Where's the guide?"

"Forget her. We're getting out of here."

And *there's* the escape pod, a door in the back wall, big and square, festooned with warnings. They should be able to get everyone in there—even the pilot and the tour guide, if they've actually got the balls to leave the cockpit. Once they're out, they can—

A sun-bright bloom of fire fills the dome above them. Jack looks on reflex, and the after-image sears itself onto his retinas, the old woman's startled scream slamming his eardrums shut.

He blinks hard, squeezing stinging tears out. The family—Mom, Dad, the two boys—are huddled in a tight ball at the far end of the line of seats. The dad's face is just visible over his wife's back. He's shaking his head, from side to side, as if what he's seeing is a hallucination he can dislodge if he just shakes hard enough.

The old woman is still in her seat. Jack grabs her by the arm— more on instinct than anything else—pulling her upright, ignoring her squawk of protest. He drags her down the aisle between the seats, shouting at the others to follow him, nearly falling as another vibration shudders into the cabin.

"This vessel is experiencing unsafe conditions," says the *Red Panda*'s cheerful voice. "Please remain in your seat."

Jack reaches the escape pod door, still dragging the old woman. There's a big green button in the middle of it, protected by a transparent plastic cover. He scrabbles at it, fingers trying to pry it off, but it won't move. The thick plastic clip on the bottom of the cover is stuck.

"You're hurting me," the old woman says, with something like wonder.

Jack ignores her. "Help me with this," he says over his shoulder, speaking to anyone in range. When no one responds, he twists around, his gaze landing on the father of the two boys. "Hey, I need help here, come on!"

"I don't—"

"*Just pull!*" Jack turns back to the door, beyond caring if the man understands him or not. He braces his feet, puts every bit of force he has into pushing the clip back. How could they possibly make it this hard to open an escape pod? His mind is blaring nonsense words, terror and anger stirring them up like a swarm of hornets. He still hasn't let go of the old woman.

Hands on his, pushing down, someone forcing themselves in between him and the door. He tries to resist, but whoever it is has him off balance, and he stumbles back. It's the goddamn tour guide. She's shouting at him, waving her hands, her voice lost in the mad buzzing sound in his ears.

Jack lunges forward, hunting for the button cover. He'll smash it if he has to—there's got to be something here that can dent the plastic, a fire axe, something ...

"Wait a second, just *listen* to me," the guide is saying. When Jack ignores her, she leans into him, grunting as she tries to shove him back. She's tall, gangly, but she's planted her feet. He can't get past.

Fine. He'll shove her sideways if he has to. He's on the verge of doing it when the cabin lights blink twice, then die completely, leaving them in flickering shadow. Bursts of light from outside the window turn the cabin into a nightmare.

The guide raises her voice, piercing the darkness. "If you go in the pod, you die."

The lights come back on, dimly at first, then glaring bright. "I said, you're *hurting* me," the old woman says, finally yanking her arm from Jack's grip. It pulls him slightly off balance, and gives the guide a chance to get in front of him, blocking the button with her body.

"Why can't we use it?" says the mother of the two boys. It comes out as a hysterical yell.

"Right," says a voice over Jack's shoulder. Robot arm guy. His lilting Irish accent is at odds with his size and with the panic in his voice. "You do know you can't keep us here, yes?"

The guide's eyes are huge. She has the same look she had on her face just before she ran, before she went and hid in the cockpit. A burst of indignant fury surges through Jack, but before he can act on it, she says, "The pod's got no control. You'll just drift until one of those things find you. At least here, the ship has—"

"But it's an *escape pod*," the woman in the leather jacket says.

Jack blinks. This is insane. Everybody on this ship has gone insane. They're standing here, arguing, in the middle of a firefight. Well, they might be happy to get blown to bits here, but not him. He steps forward, mouth set in a thin line, ready to grab the tour guide's shoulders and physically move her out of the way.

One of the boys screams.

It's the younger one, the one with the fuzzy mop of hair, and it's the kind of scream that nobody can ignore. Everyone turns to look at him, and then they look at where he's pointing, up through the viewing dome.

They're not just close to the hotel. They're heading right for it, moving at full speed towards one of the ruined modules. It has huge chunks torn out of its side, the outer surface pitted with dark holes. The sight makes Jack's tongue go curiously dry. In that instant, he is desperate for a drink, the need overpowering, the phantom taste of Nova curling up the back of his throat.

The *Red Panda* is heading right towards one of the holes in the module wall. A hole that is way, way too small for them to make it through.

Chapter 5

Corey can't remember when he first read about Maverick-class touring vessels—it was probably something he skimmed over on the way to the really cool part of the book, with its Vector carriers and Antares cruisers and Frontier Scorpion fighters. But he can see it clearly in his mind now, an exploded diagram with measurements in tiny writing.

Maverick. Fifty metres long, thirty metres from gravity well to upper viewing dome, twenty-five metres wide. Safe operating distance of ten metres outside the docking arm.

There is no way—no *way*—that the hole is bigger than their ship. They're coming in from below, the *Panda* yawing, the hotel approaching fast. Through the gap, Corey can see what looks like a chandelier. It's surrounded by a cloud of glittering particles, and as Corey stares at them he realises they're shards of glass.

The man in the polo shirt, the one who looks like Terio Smith, goes back to yanking at the escape pod door, shoving the guide away, swearing to himself in quick, shocked bursts. A second later, Corey's view is blocked by his dad's body, climbing on top of him again, shielding him. Corey can smell his dad's aftershave, thick and pungent. His mom is holding Malik. Distantly, Corey wonders how they decided who should shield who.

"Just hold on, Corey," Everett Livingstone says. It's impossible to miss the terror in his voice. "Just hold onto me."

Up until now, none of this felt real. He was either dreaming, or it was some kind of educational thing, a historical sim, something arranged by his parents to keep them busy. But as he stares at the module, the truth finally hits home. The pilot's crazy. They're never going to fit through. It's going to be like trying to shove a basketball into a coffee cup.

Corey shuts his eyes tight, and buries his face in his dad's shoulder.

And as he does so, he feels the ship *turn*.

There's a huge thud, and the squealing of metal on metal echoes through the cabin. The lights flicker, and the world outside the viewing dome goes black.

Corey can still smell his dad's aftershave.

Very slowly, he opens his eyes. They're still in the *Red Panda*, still moving. It shouldn't be possible. But unless the afterlife is exactly like real life in every way, that's what just happened.

"Dad?"

"Corey, just hang on."

"No, Dad, look!"

Everett blinks at him, then looks over his shoulder. Corey takes the gap, sliding across the bucket seat, the edge digging into his backside. His mom is refusing to release Malik, who is trying to squirm out from underneath her, one hand clutching his tablet tight.

For the first time since the spheres appeared, the *Red Panda*'s main deck has gone quiet. Everyone, even Not-Terio-Smith, is looking up through the viewing dome. The guide's mouth falls open. Under her freckles her skin is drained of blood.

They're inside Sigma Station, coming slowly to a halt. The ship is in the only area big enough to take it: the atrium, the giant space inside the hotel module, the one with the chandelier and that corny fountain with the angels. The captain must have known where she was aiming, brought them right in.

But why? To protect them? How is being inside going to help?

The atrium's undergone decompression, and there's debris everywhere. Smashed marble. Broken plates. A jacket, still on its hanger, the sleeves floating freely. And bodies. Corey's eyes land on a man floating halfway in and out of a doorway, dressed in a black porter's tunic. In the light from the *Panda*, his skin is puffy, his eyes almost swollen shut. Frost has started to form on his skin.

Corey's mom moans, turning away. He just stares in astonishment. He can't even begin to think how they got through the gap. There's a long scratch on the surface of the viewing dome, but that's all. However they did it, Volkova has positioned them just right, bringing the *Panda* to a stop, filling the atrium. The jacket bumps against the viewport, caught for a second before sliding away.

"Christ," says Not-Terio-Smith. The collar of his green polo shirt is skew, the button line pulled sideways on his chest. His fingers knot the hem, back and forth.

"Look," says the tour guide—*Hannah*. That's her name. "As long as we're in here, we're safe, so—"

"You call this *safe*?" says the man with the robot arm.

There are gaps in the atrium walls, the viewing windows shattered. At that second, a metal sphere rockets past, thrusters puffing white gas, less than fifty metres away. Corey's mom screams, pulling him to her again.

The sphere vanishes. Through the gaps, they can make out more ships coming apart, flaming briefly against the blackness before dwindling to nothing.

"I'm—" Hannah swallows. "I'm sure there's someone coming. We just have to sit tight."

"What if they don't?" Malik says. Corey glances at him, and sees his brother hit the holocam's record button, doing it almost absent-mindedly. His finger jitters so much that he touches it twice, and he has to reactivate it.

"Of course someone's going to come, honey," says his mom, automatically. Something bangs off the dome. In the instant before it spins away, Corey sees that it's a frying pan, liberated from one of the kitchens, still covered in grease.

The old woman is still praying loudly, eyes shut tight, the fanny pack clasped to her chest like a rosary. Suddenly, Corey feels a burning need to explore the ship. Right now. There might be something they can use, down in astronautics or the engines. Maybe he could go and talk to the pilot—the one who, somehow, got them inside the hotel. But, really, it's because he just wants to get away. The main deck, with its hysterical adults and the big window above their heads, is just too much right now.

He slowly lifts himself off his seat, but doesn't get more than three steps before his mom reaches out and clamps a hand around his wrist. She pulls him in, holding him to her chest like he's five. He can hear her heart through her shirt, pounding hard, and that's when he starts to get *really* scared.

"Don't cry, honey," his mom whispers into his head, her own tears soaking his hair. "Just stay with me."

Corey tries to tell her that he's not crying—he's way, way too scared to cry. Another object collides with the *Red Panda*—something much bigger than a frying pan. There's a scraping, grinding sound as whatever it is drags along the hull underneath them. Corey feels like if his mom holds him any tighter, he's going to pass out.

"Guide!" The captain's voice bursts out of the speaker in the wall, loud enough to make Corey's ears ring. "Guide, come to the cockpit. Now!"

Chapter 6

Volkova is still hunched over the controls, playing the stick, keeping the *Panda* away from the walls of the atrium. Sweat drains down the lines on her face—the top half of her shirt is transparent with it, her white undershirt showing. As Hannah pushes inside, a chunk of wall or floor—she can't tell which—bumps off the cockpit glass. Volkova doesn't flinch. The cigarette is still jammed in the corner of her mouth, burned down to the filter. Hannah isn't sure she's even noticed.

The ship's computer speaks, sounding like someone walking through a park on a warm spring day. "Captain, you have strayed from your recognised flight path. Do you wish me to inform Sigma Station Traffic Control?"

Volkova ignores the voice. "In two minutes, I'm going to shut down everything," she says, before Hannah is even through the door. "You go and tell the passengers they must be quiet, OK?"

Hannah blinks. "What?"

"Captain, it is my duty to inform you that shutting down any function of this vessel without authorisation violates—"

"*Da zayebis!*" she spits back, speaking over the ship's voice. "Guide—go, now."

Adrift

"Shut down everything? What does that even—"

"*Everything!* Light, air, gravity, toilets, engines, heat, everything. The passengers must be very, very quiet. No moving, OK? Make sure they hold tight to the hull, and stay still. Maybe the balls don't look inside the hotel, maybe they do, so I will lower the temperature to disguise our heat signature."

"Captain, Sigma Station Traffic Control is not responding. Would you like me to play some music while I try again?"

Hannah fights through the tangle of Volkova's words, hands braced against the cockpit walls. "Why?"

"Because I am the captain, and this is an emergency, and you do what I say. OK?"

Hannah gapes at her. As she does so, she finds she's angry.

She's not trained for this. She's a history major. The safety course they did the night before might have covered things like fire, or what to do if a guest had a heart attack, but it definitely didn't cover what to do in the event the entire station got blown to pieces. She's angry at herself, for having run from the passengers when this all kicked off, but now some of that anger is being directed at the *Red Panda*'s captain.

And why not? It's all very well for her, sitting in this cockpit and issuing orders, but Hannah's the one who'll have to carry them out. She's the one who's going to have to face the passengers again. How can Volkova expect her to do that? Expect her to know what to do?

Callie would know. Callie would do it before the captain even asked. She'd have everything under control, and isn't that the real reason you're angry, Hannah Banana? Because someone expects you to be like her?

"Tell them yourself," she says, through gritted teeth.

"What you say?"

"You've got a mic. *You* tell them what's going on."

Volkova swivels in her seat, eyes bugging out. The cigarette butt waggles furiously. Hannah expects her to shout, maybe even to finally snap, but she doesn't. She gets control of herself, exhaling hard through her nose as she looks back out through the cockpit viewport, satisfying herself that there's nothing coming at them. For the first time, she doesn't look like she wants to kill someone.

"If *I* tell them," she says, looking back at Hannah, "I will have every passenger in the cockpit yelling a million questions at me. I must stay at the controls. Focus, you understand?"

"But why? Why turn off the power?"

"You're not seeing what I see," Volkova says, pointing to a gap in the hotel's outer wall. Hannah can just see another metal sphere cruising past. "They're not stupid. They hunt light and thruster signature. Sound and heat. So we have to be dead, like a destroyed ship."

"Will that even work?"

Volkova exhales, shrugs. "If humans control the balls, then maybe they think it's impossible for a ship to be inside the hotel. Maybe they don't even look for us. But if an AI controls them, they'll look everywhere. So we must be like … what is word, *oblomki sudna*. Wreckage. Dead. We do that, maybe they …" Volkova waves her hand in the direction of the sphere, giving an up-down whistle.

"But without air—"

"Our CO_2 filters can last one hour. We will be cold, but OK. Now, *please*, go and tell the passengers. Understand?"

There's a blush rising in Hannah's cheeks, and for the second time in ten minutes she wants to sink into a hole and blink out of existence. She takes a breath, then nods, heading back towards the cockpit door.

As she pulls it open, she stops. "How'd you even get us in here? How'd we fit through that gap?"

For a second, she's not even sure Volkova heard her. Then the captain half turns, a strange smile on her face. Several of her teeth are gold, glinting in the light from the cockpit controls.

"The gravity well on the bottom of this ship is super-dense reinforced alloy," she says. "Foot thick. Has to be, so we don't float around. I went as fast as I can, pulled up, used the alloy to smash through the hole. I made it bigger."

Hannah gives a dazed nod. Just before she pulls the door closed, Volkova calls out. "Remember: after the lights go off, no movement, no sound. The ship must be dead!"

Chapter 7

"Can anyone see ..." says the woman with the ponytail, squinting up at the viewing dome.

Jack wishes people would finish their sentences. It seems like no matter what anyone says, they lose track of their thoughts halfway through. It's unbelievable just how annoying it is. Even as the thought occurs, the boys' mother says. "We should maybe ..." and then trails off.

Nobody's screaming any more. Nobody seems to know what to do. The shock has collapsed over them like a wave.

The explosions outside the station are fewer now, but there's no way to really tell how bad it is out there. In a way, that's the worst part. One of those metal spheres could be heading right for them, and they wouldn't know about it until they were blown out into space.

Jack is twisting the hem of his shirt in his hands, doing it automatically, hard enough to leave the fabric stretched and kinked. That stupid trick the shrink on Europa taught him, the little trigger mechanism to get his mind off things. He yanks his hands away like they've been burned. What a crock of shit. It's never worked. Not once.

A surprisingly lucid thought burns through his mind. No leadership. That's the problem here. No one to take charge. No one to take *responsibility*. Got the tour guide running off every five seconds, insane pilot putting them into all kinds of dangerous situations, and no one's held accountable. When he tries to suggest something sensible, like getting the hell out of here, he gets shut down.

Another unseen vibration rumbles through the ship, making the lights flicker. The old woman has started to sob, the sound coming in huge, hitching gasps. Jack grips his shirt again, tighter this time, the action automatic.

The parents of those two boys are arguing, hissing at each other in sharp whispers that needle the edge of Jack's hearing. He wants to tell them to shut up. Instead, he just twists his shirt tighter, gritting his teeth. His hands are shaking. A drink would fix that—and why the fuck shouldn't he go down to the bar? If they aren't going to let them onto the escape pod, why should he—

The guide comes hurtling out of the cockpit passageway, red hair flying out behind her. She slows to a jog, then to a fast-paced walk, arms pumping. "OK, everyone, listen up!"

The man in the leather jacket gives Jack a knowing look. The old woman sits up straight, and the boys' father gets to his feet, fingers gripping the back of a chair. His wife sits stock still, her mouth a thin line.

"We're going to shut down the main systems," the guide says. "The whole ship. So if you could find a handhold and—"

"*What?*" says the woman with the ponytail.

It opens the floodgates. The parents are on their feet, the man with the metal arm, everyone talking at once. Jack's voice is the loudest. "How are we supposed to breathe?" he says.

The guide is still trying to speak, her hands raised, desperately trying to get everyone to calm down. She doesn't look at him, and that pisses him off even more. "Hey. Miss. Talking to you," he says. "What are we supposed to do about air? And heat?"

"We'll be OK. Now would everyone please *just listen!*"

"How do you know they haven't gone already?" says the boys' father. "It looked like it was—"

"Of course we don't know, Ev," his wife says, her voice shaking. "Just listen to her."

"We can't take the risk," the guide says, shaking her head. Her voice is strong, but she looks like she's about to pass out.

"Who *are* these people?" the old woman manages to say. "Why are they doing this?"

"I don't know," says the guide. "But we can either stay online, and hope they don't find us, or we go dark and wait it out."

"But for *how long*?" Mom has her arms around her boys, holding them close. They look extremely uncomfortable, although Jack can't tell if it's from her tight grip, or from what the guide is proposing.

The guide licks her lips. "An hour, no more."

Adrift

In a voice that she almost manages to keep from shaking, she tells them what the captain wants to do. When she finishes, nobody moves. They all just look at each other, frozen in shock.

Jack's thoughts tangle together. There's got to be something else they could do. Some other way. But in the end, he moves when the rest of them do, making their way to the edges of the deck. The old woman has gone white, and the guide has to help her, leading her to a nearby hold.

Jack sticks an arm through one, pulling the inside of his elbow into it, cursing himself for going along with this stupidity. The handhold is as thick as a man's wrist, made of metal that's been painted over one too many times. When he puts his other hand on it to brace himself, the sweat on his skin nearly makes him slip.

The couple in the leather jackets are one handhold down. Jack catches the man's eye again, shaking his head in bewilderment.

"We're ready, Captain," the guide shouts, as she grabs a handhold of her own. She's on one a few steps from the family, all of whom are clustered around a single strut, holding tight to one another.

The captain's voice comes through the speakers, so loud it nearly blows Jack's head off. "OK, shutting down the gravity well. Hold on."

Briefly, Jack wonders what the hell *she's* holding onto. Probably strapped herself into that nice, comfy seat. Then there's a rolling *whump*, the floor shifts beneath his feet, and he's floating.

It's not a pleasant sensation. His natural instinct is to keep his feet planted, but they're being teased upwards, pulled off the ground by a gentle, implacable force. He extends his legs, but that just makes it worse, and in seconds he's parallel with the floor, his arm aching from holding tight to the metal bracket.

His stomach is expanding and contracting: a slow, sluggish motion that makes him feel like he wants to throw up. There's a gentle tightness in his sinuses, an insidious pressure inside his skull. How long has it been since a ship went zero-G? It's certainly never happened to him. Gravity wells existed long before he was born, and he's never heard of them failing, not once. The idea of dealing with no gravity is absurd, something from the very earliest days of deep space travel, when people didn't know what the fuck they were doing.

He's going to die here. They'll write a little obituary for him on the feed, and then they'll hire another hotel critic, and that'll be it.

"Please stay calm," says the *Red Panda*. "There has been a disruption in localised gravitational forces. Be sure to secure yourself before assisting other—"

The voice cuts off with a squawk. The lights go next, clicking off in sequence across the cabin. A second later, the engine shudders to a halt, and all Jack can hear is deafening tinnitus. He floats in silence, trying to ignore the nausea and the ache in his arm and the squeeze in his sinuses, wishing he was anywhere else in the universe. Anywhere else at all.

"Can we—" someone says.

"*Shhhh*," says the guide.

Jack has a sudden urge to laugh. There's no way this is going to work. No way. He looks over his shoulder. Like him, the *Red Panda*'s passengers are all trying to stay in one spot, arms and hands clutched tight to their holds. And outside …

The hairs on his scalp prickle. It doesn't look real. When the *Red Panda*'s interior was lit, the outside was a world of shadows. Now, he can see just how bad the damage to the hotel is. It's like a giant monster slashed at the wall, rending and tearing, speckling the wounds with cold stars. There are things floating out there—bodies, some of them, their shapes unmistakable. From somewhere beneath them, there's a burst of fiery light, hot and silent.

White vapour puffs in front of Jack's face as he breathes. With the engine shut off, the ship is bleeding heat fast. The metal against the crook of his elbow is already growing cold, biting through his jacket fabric.

They're not going to last an hour. They might not even last ten minutes. They'll freeze to death long before they get out of here.

But ten minutes go by. Then twenty. Jack's stomach is a bubbling cauldron, and his lips are going numb with the chill. He squeezes his eyes shut for a few seconds, and, when he opens them, one of the metal spheres is right outside the ship.

It's tracking past them, *inside the hotel*, moving on puffs of vapour that make Jack think of his breath condensing in front of his face. Up close, the multiple sensors on its body stick out like pimples. They turn towards the *Panda*, dark eyes flicking left and right. Thrusters on the sphere's body activate, slowing its course, bringing it to a stop in the middle of the viewing dome. Jack doesn't know if the sensor is a heat scanner, a camera, or something else entirely. He just stays as still as he can.

For three whole minutes the sphere hovers in front of them. Jack is starting to shiver—the cabin's temperature is below freezing now. How long will it be before someone does something stupid? Makes a noise, or sneezes, or triggers that sensor in some way that none of them will see coming?

The war between the Colony and the Frontier might have taken place in distant systems, away from the Core worlds, but plenty of Jack's colleagues reported on it, and there was no lack of feed footage. The battles were fought with missiles and plasma and kinetic impactors. These? He's never seen anything like them, not even that one time someone in Frontier Defence leaked a bunch of weapons schematics to Ajit on the news crew.

The spheres aren't like missiles. They don't have a single method of propulsion—there are multiple thrusters, all across the body—and they move like they're sentient, tracking targets relentlessly, changing direction in a split second, defying the physics of space travel. It makes his skin crawl.

The word *alien* creeps into his mind, settles there, refusing to budge.

The sphere's thrusters come to life, slowly moving it away from them, heading towards one of the holes in the module's outer wall.

That's it. Keep moving, you son of a—

There's another bang as something collides with *Panda*—a chunk of hotel floor, just visible through the viewport. It hits so hard that it starts them moving again, drifting sideways, the world outside the dome spinning on its axis. The muscles in Jack's arm spasm as he fights to hold onto the bracket.

From the other side of the ship, there's a panicked gasp. Jack looks up to see that one of the kids is floating loose, the younger one, arms moving in frantic windmills, trying to grab hold of anything he can. His mom is reaching for him—their fingertips brush, but he slips away, moving towards the centre of the main deck.

Jack looks over at the receding metal sphere. It's not receding any more. It's starting to turn, coming back towards them, the sensors on its body swivelling like eyes.

Chapter 8

Corey Livingstone isn't really a big reader.

He's got a few books on his lens—the *Quasar Lizard* trilogy, which is pretty crash, and a couple on the history of the Great Expansion, which are *really* crash. But, mostly, he digs comics and series and messing around with Jamie and Allie. Books always have these weird expressions in them. Like: *his heart was in his mouth.*

He's never understood that one. How'd they even come up with that? Why would being scared mean your heart climbed all the way up into your mouth? It seemed kind of icky, more than anything else—he'd mentioned it to Jamie one time, and they'd spent more than a few minutes wondering what it would be like.

Jamie had remembered an old expression about eating your heart out, and *that* had sent them on a tangent that left the series they were watching forgotten in the background. Eating your own heart, they concluded, was both really hardcore and really, really gak.

But as Corey drifts into the open space above the main deck, as he watches the sphere approach, it really *does* feel like there's something in his mouth. His tongue feels like it's grown to five times its normal size, clogged with gummy, sour saliva. He can't stop himself spinning, no matter how hard he tries—every movement he makes is exaggerated, sending him in unexpected directions.

He's upside down now, head pointing towards the floor. His mom and dad are reaching out for him, silent terror on their faces. His mom tries to spring after him—she's pulled back by his dad, who is looking desperately for another way to help him. And Malik—*Malik is filming him*. Holo up, eyes glued to the screen, tracking his movements. Corey stares at him, stunned, wanting to rip the holo out of his brother's hands and smash it against the wall.

Everyone else? Everyone else looks like they want to throw up, pass out, or just die right there. They can't get to him—and they don't dare try. He's too far above the chairs to grab hold of one of them, and he's not close enough to the dome to use that, either. He'll reach the other side of the cabin soon, but it's not going to happen before the sphere gets there—it's closing fast, only thirty yards away now, navigating smoothly past a floating chunk of debris, coming right at them. And Corey isn't sure he'll be able to land quietly.

Maybe if he stops moving ... but it doesn't matter, he just keeps right on going, the laws of physics not giving a shit whether he stays still or not. He jerks back into life, clawing at the air, his brain telling him he can swim through it even when his frantic movements get him nowhere, doing nothing but sending him into a wobbly, uncontrolled spin.

He can't stop shivering—he's so cold that he's not even sure he still has all his fingers. And in the middle of his terror, there's a bright core of shame. How can he be a pilot if he can't even control himself in zero-G? You can't fly a Scorpion fighter into deep space if you can't even figure out how to move your arms without gravity.

Twenty yards away. Corey can see the sphere's sensors scanning left and right. Any second now, he's going to collide with the wall, and collide hard. He could try to spin himself around, but the movement might alert the thing's sensors. For a second, his toes are pointing at the wall, and he thinks he'll be able to cushion the landing. But he can't hold the position, turning head over heels in midair, the wall getting closer. Corey braces himself, closes his eyes, his heart climbing back into his mouth, squatting there …

But when he hits the wall, there's no sound—and it doesn't feel like a hard surface. Corey looks down, confused, only to see something between his feet and the wall. An arm. The old woman's arm, covered in soft, grey tracksuit fabric. He hadn't even realised she was there. Her right hand is holding tight to the wall bracket, but she let her other arm drift into Corey's path, her armpit at his left toe, her wrist at his right knee, muffling the impact.

In a smooth, effortless movement—one that looks like it should come from someone much, much younger—she pulls Corey in, wrapping the arm tight around his legs, holding him in place. She's looking up at him, and it's pretty easy to figure out what she's trying to say.

He stays as still as he can, only breathing when it feels like his lungs are about to explode. Relief floods through him. And not just him: he can feel it coming from everyone on the main deck. He glances across, to Hannah, and sees her close her eyes, exhale a long puff of white vapour. He tilts his head back: his mom looks like she's doing everything she can not to shout his name. His dad, too. Malik, of course, is still filming him, and Corey feels another burst of stupid, pointless anger.

From where he is, he can only see a fraction of the viewing dome, and the sphere isn't in sight. It could be right above him, that sensor thing looking right at him. His hair tickles his forehead, the strands drifting in weird directions, and an itch starts to creep along the bridge of his nose.

He has never been this cold. The vacuum of space hovers at almost absolute zero—minus 273 degrees Celsius—and there isn't a ship in the universe that can hold onto heat for long with its engines shut off. Definitely not a little Maverick vessel like the *Red Panda*. Corey's fingertips are so numb they're starting to burn, and his lips and nose throb with gentle, insistent pain. His breath is starting to freeze on the wall in front of him, the condensation turning to ice crystals.

And is it his imagination, or is it getting hard to breathe in here? The air is ice-cold, but stale somehow. Corey's eyes go wide as he realises what's happening. Without any new oxygen being pumped in by the ship's air recyclers, it's up to the passive CO_2 filters to keep the air breathable. But they're not meant to work alone for this long; they're being overloaded, clogged with excess particles.

He really, really doesn't want to die. Not by freezing, not by suffocating, not by anything, not ever. If he dies now, he'll never fly a ship, never go to flight school. He'll never see Austin again, or Jamie, or Allie. He'll never be able to help Mom and Dad stay together, and he'll never get to tell Mal that he's a giant dick for filming him while he was in trouble.

The sphere hovers for a few moments more. Then, as if satisfied, it spins in place and moves away, its thrusters firing.

His thoughts are slow, and dull, like glass that's been covered in dust and left to hang out for a thousand years. He has to keep breathing, no matter what, that his breaths need to be deep. But all he wants to do is close his eyes for bit. Just for a few seconds ...

A voice. Crackly, like someone speaking with a mic too close to their mouth. "I see the attack ship moving away," the voice is saying. "We are OK now, I think."

The *Red Panda*'s engines rumble to life, and the lights in the main deck flicker on, one after the other. It takes Corey a few seconds to understand what's happening, and, when he does, he can feel hot, embarrassed tears pooling in the corners of his eyes. They made it.

The ship's voice comes on, picking up exactly where it left off. "—assisting other passengers. If you require medical attention, please stay where you are, and the crew will be with you shortly. Thank you for travelling with Sigma Destination Tours."

Corey breathes a shaky sigh. Engine's up, which means heat, plus the lights, which means that gravity'll—

Gravity. Corey's eyes go wide as he realises that he's not hanging onto anything, that the old woman is never going to be able to hold him up when the gravity well kicks back into gear.

Then he's falling backwards, arms flailing, legs bending in a weird direction as the old woman tries to hold onto him. He hears his mom shout his name, and then he hits the floor so hard that his teeth clack together.

Chapter 9

Hannah has to keep telling herself not to look out of the viewing dome.

The *Red Panda* is drifting a short distance from what used to be Sigma Station—now nothing more than a galaxy of shredded metal and spinning debris. The Horsehead Nebula glimmers behind it in perfect, colourful splendour, edged with deep space, inky-black.

When Hannah got a good look at the Neb, on the way to the dock, it didn't feel like this. It felt vast, but manageable: a backdrop, something that could be ignored if she wanted. Not any more. The debris gives everything scale, perspective. The pieces will keep moving forever, shooting out from the ruined station, getting further and further apart.

If the *Panda* waits long enough—and why wouldn't it, because where the hell are they going to go?—the debris field will disperse. It'll be like it never existed.

Hannah's legs feel heavy, as if her feet are encased in concrete, and there's a ringing in her ears that she can't get rid of. And no matter how hard she looks, she can't see any other intact ships out there. Not even any escape pods. There might still be people in the hotel, alive, trapped—but there's just no way to tell for sure. And she can't stop dwelling on just how remote this place really is. Sigma is way, way outside the Core systems, accessible only by the single jump gate.

No. No way. They can't be the only ones. There's got to be another ship out there. Surely they can't be the only ones left?

The *Panda* started to move a few minutes after the attacking ship departed, taking its spheres with it. Hannah didn't understand why they didn't leave a few behind, drifting like traps for whoever came upon the station next. And she's still not entirely sure how Volkova managed to get them out of the hotel. There was plenty of grinding against the hull as she manoeuvred them through, along with distant swearing from the cockpit. When Volkova next came over the speakers, she said she needed to fly them out to a safe distance, where the debris was more scattered.

There must be something we could have done—some weapons system we could have used. Nothing. Total blank. And compared to the attacking ship—hell, compared to everything—they're tiny. The *Panda*'s main deck is maybe a touch bigger than her apartment in college, and even when you add on the rest of the ship, it isn't very much at all.

There's a noise to her right. The man in the suit jacket—the one who wanted to get on the escape pod—is retching up chunks of thin gruel. He's bent over, hands on his knees, back and shoulders shuddering as the liquid spatters on the deck's surface. Hannah's first instinct is disgust, but she can't even blame him. Not really.

Her head feels too light on her shoulders, like it's going to float away. She sits down, and the motion turns into a controlled fall, her backside thumping heavily onto the seat.

The man with the metal arm is shaking his head, his real hand over his mouth, alternating between staring up through the dome and down at his feet. He's saying something, over and over again, very quietly. Hannah has to concentrate, realises it's the words "Fucking hell." His Irish accent was softer before, almost unnoticeable. Now, it almost sounds like he's deliberately leaning on it. The words sound strange, elongated.

His wife, or girlfriend—Hannah can't remember if she wore a ring or not, and can't see the woman's left hand from here—

is sitting stock still, shoulders hunched, eyes on nothing at all.

"Is anybody still out there?"

It's the old woman. Despite dropping the boy she grabbed earlier, she made it down OK. She addresses the question to Hannah, her voice shaking, but immediately looks up through the dome, as if knowing she won't get an answer.

The mother of the two boys is sobbing quietly, her arms wrapped around her sons. The younger one is still shivering.

"Hey, does anyone have a signal on their lens?" the boys' father asks, voice trembling.

Metal arm man wipes his mouth. "Nothing here, mate."

Shock, Hannah thinks. Isn't that what's supposed to happen after something like this? They need to keep warm and hydrated. There are bottles of water in the bar, she's sure of it, and isn't that where they keep the first aid stuff, too? A first aid kit would have blankets, wouldn't it? That'd help with the keep warm part at least. And it would give her something to do.

"Stay put, everybody," she says, sounding a lot more decisive than she feels. "I'm just going to—"

"OK," says polo shirt. He's stopped throwing up, and, despite a face the colour of sour milk, he looks livid. He points a finger at Hannah, the tip trembling slightly. "What's your name?"

His tone—angry, accusing—loosens her fragile grip on the plan. "Sorry?"

"I want your name, and the name of your tour company and its parent company. Pilot, too." He raises his voice, as if the main deck is crowded with people, and he has to make himself heard. As he speaks, Hannah thinks of a flag in a high wind, snapping and fluttering, threatening to tear loose from its moorings. "Everybody here is a witness. They put us all in danger."

"Sir, if you could just lower your voice ..."

"I'm gonna sue," he says, wheeling on her. "My *feed*'s gonna sue. I'm here on business, and your company just ignored all safety precautions."

"Hey," Hannah says, hurt.

"You better get yourself a good lawyer," the man says. "Because if you think—"

"Don't talk to her like that," says the mother of the two boys, her voice cracking. "It's not her fault."

"Well, then, whose fault is it, exactly?" says robot arm. He points at Jack. "Because he's got the measure of it. They must have known that ship was coming. They wouldn't've just let it waltz right in. So that means they sent us out there when they knew it was on the way." He speaks calmly, reasonably, but there's an odd look in his eyes, haunted and suspicious.

The boys' mother folds her arms. "But you can't just accuse—"

"Why should we listen to you?" says polo shirt. "Your kid almost got us all killed."

The woman looks like she's had a bucket of cold water thrown in her face. "Excuse me?"

"He's right." The ponytailed woman says. Next to him, she looks almost child-size. "If that lady hadn't been there ..."

"Let's just all calm down," the boys' father says.

Their mother shoots her husband an angry look. "I'm not just gonna *calm down*. They don't get to talk about Corey that way." Her younger son cringes.

Polo shirt laughs. The sound is sharp and coarse, stripped of any humour. "Maybe I should sue you, too. You put us in danger just as much as—"

And then they're all shouting, in each other's faces, the shock and dismay boiling over and filling the air with angry noise. The mother is tapping polo shirt man's chest with her finger, her husband trying to get between them. The guy in the polo shirt smacks the finger away. Robot arm squares his shoulders, and now ponytail is involved, arms folded, sneering into the other woman's face.

And Hannah doesn't have the faintest clue what to do about it. Any of it.

A piercing whistle blocks out the noise. It goes on for a few seconds before trailing away, and, when it does, everyone has turned to stare at the old woman. She still has her index fingers in her mouth, and pulls them loose with an audible pop.

"Didn't know I could still do that," she says.

"We're not done," Jack says. "It's—"

"No. That's still the pilot, and the young miss over there is still the guide. They're in charge here, and we're going to do what they say. So," she looks up at Hannah, "what do you want us to do?"

Everyone turns to look at her, and for half a second her mind is a total blank.

Inspiration hits. It doesn't look like anyone's injured—in shock, maybe, but not badly. What she needs to do is get these people acquainted. At least if they know each other's names, they might find it a little harder to yell at each other.

She clears her throat. "Why don't we all just sit down for a sec?" she says, lowering herself into one of the plastic chairs.

One by one, they all follow. The parents sit on either side of their children, while the other three—polo shirt, robot arm and ponytail—sit opposite them. An empty chair separates them from the old woman.

"OK," Hannah says, putting her hands on her knees. "Maybe we should all introduce ourselves. Since we're all here, I mean."

Polo shirt looks away from her, mouth turned down in contempt.

"I'll go first," she says. "I'm Hannah Elliott, which I ... I guess you know already, since I stood up in front earlier."

She waits for somebody to go next. Nobody does.

"Uh, how about you?" she says, turning to the mother of the boys.

The woman blinks at her. "Anita," she says. "Anita Livingstone."

She introduces her sons, neither of whom look up from the floor—the younger one, Corey, looks like he wants to vanish into it. Malik, the one with the cornrows, is still clutching his ancient holo camera.

Their dad gives the group a small wave. "Everett," he says. "Ev."

The old woman is next. "Lorinda Anna Maria Esteban," she says. "I'm from out in the Kuiper Belt. My husband and I did mining there."

"And where is your husband?" Hannah says. Dull horror floods through her as the realisation hits: *He's not with her. He was back on the station.*

Adrift

Lorinda Anna Maria Esteban looks confused, and then her eyes go wide. "Oh! No no no. No, he passed a few years ago. It's just me."

"Thank you," Hannah says, more relieved than she wants to admit. After a moment's awkward silence, she turns to the man in the green polo shirt, trying to push what he said to her before to the back of her mind. "What about you?"

He stares at her. His eyes are bloodshot at the edges. When he blinks, it's twice in quick succession, each time. There's a very tiny dot of vomit at the corner of his mouth. Hannah can't stop looking at it.

After a few seconds, he says, "Jack."

"Name's Brendan O'Hara," says the other man, raising his metal arm in a greeting. "And this is my—"

The ponytailed woman puts a hand on Brendan's leg, as if to remind him that she can speak for herself. "Seema."

"Are you married?" says Lorinda.

Seema raises her left hand, waggling her fingers. An elegant diamond ring sparkles. "Newlyweds," she says. "We're on honeymoon."

There's an appreciative *aaah* from the group, the kind of automatic reaction made when someone says the words *newlywed* or *engagement* or *honeymoon*. Even Hannah finds herself doing it.

"Great. Are we done?" says Jack, pushing himself to his feet. "Wonderful. How the hell are we going to get out of here?"

Everyone looks at Hannah again. She pauses for a moment, then takes a deep breath, not sure what she's going to say but knowing she has to say something. "Let's think about this. My guess is whoever did this thinks the whole station is—"

"It was a Colony ship," says Anita Livingstone.

"Bullshit," Jack says.

Anita gives him a withering look. "Like you would know the difference."

Her husband sighs, as if he knows what's coming.

"How can you be so sure?" Seema says.

Anita straightens. "I'm a political consultant. I work on the lobbying team for Senator Daniels."

Hannah feels a slight hitch in her stomach. *Daniels*. She marched against his policies in college, more than once. This woman works for him?

Anita pauses, as if choosing her words carefully. "We're re-negotiating the Belarus Treaty. The Frontier wants a little more territory in the Colonies. There was … well, a lot of sabre-rattling behind the scenes. We knew the Colonies put what's left of their military on alert, even though there was no chance they were going to do anything—nobody there really wants to go to war again, not when the last one hit them so hard."

"I didn't hear about this at my feed," Jack says. Anita rounds on him, angry, but he talks over her. "Anyway, if you were working on the treaty, why are you on vacation?"

Lorinda tries to jump in. "Let her—"

"And you can't tell me it was a Colony ship just because of your *sabre-rattling*. There's no way the Colonies would have that kind of tech. No way."

"Who else would attack us, then?"

"She's right," Corey says, raising his head. "It was definitely Colony."

"And you know that how, young man?" says Brendan.

Corey shrugs. "I just do, OK?"

"Oh, we're listening to the kids now." Jack shakes his head. "Great. Fantastic."

"Let's say it *was* a Colony ship," Seema says. "How did they even get here?"

"Jump gate," says Lorinda, decisively.

"Nope," Jack says. "There's no way a ship full of Col scum gets into a wormhole. Frontier controls the whole network."

"Maybe they had a visa."

Jack rolls his eyes. "A visa. Sure, OK. Big ship with never-before-seen weapons tech, we'll just grant you a Frontier travel visa, enjoy your trip. Do you know how tightly controlled those things are? The second a ship popped out of a jump gate it's not supposed to pop out of, it'd get blown to pieces by the auto-turrets. Couple of impactors, and boom."

"Could have bribed their way in," Everett says. "You hear stories.

People smuggling, stuff like that. I was reading on a feed, the Roses Cartel apparently compromised a couple of officials, and—"

"*It's not the fucking Roses,*" Jack says, sounding as if he's trying hard not to explode.

"How do you know?"

"He's right," says Brendan. "It's not their style. Roses'd never put themselves on the radar like this. It's not worth it. The only reason the Frontier lets 'em operate in the first place is 'cos they keep their shenanigans quiet."

"Has anybody ..." Lorinda thinks for a moment. "I mean, have we considered the possibility that they might not be human?"

"You can't be serious," Seema says.

"Why not? We've spread out into the Galaxy, but we've still only mapped a tiny fraction of it. Who's to say they aren't out there? Maybe we just hadn't found them yet, and this was first contact."

"Blowing up a way-out station is *first contact*?" Jack's voice drips with scorn.

"We might not be the only ones who got attacked," Lorinda says.

In the silence that follows, Hannah's imagination goes to work. It's easy to picture more ships out there: a coordinated attack on multiple targets from a hostile force—one with tech no one had ever seen before. She looks up through the dome again, at the endless, expanding debris field. At the cold stars beyond them.

"Hold on," Everett says. "We're not ruling this out, but I think it's unlikely it was alien. The ship was ... different, but it wasn't *that* different."

"Seems a little thin," Lorinda says.

"I'm just saying. If it really was aliens, then why would they build a ship like that? It was too ... human, I mean. Too *us*. And it had a gravity well." He sees their blank expressions. "Alien life probably wouldn't need the same gravity conditions we do. And even if they did, are you seriously suggesting they invented the same tech as us?"

"Exactly." Jack finally wipes his mouth. "Thank you."

Everett continues. "But more importantly, how'd they get

here *without* using a gate? Could they have made their own wormhole?"

"No way," Corey says. "We can't do it."

"Corey—"

"No, you don't get it. We can't make a wormhole ourselves, just use the ones that're already there."

"Everyone knows that already," Malik says, sounding as if he wants to hurl Corey out of the airlock himself.

The pieces line up in Hannah's head. Humans had first discovered a network of tiny wormholes dotted across their solar system a century before. It was the biggest discovery in history—even if it took a while to figure out how to make use of it.

Wormholes—Einstein-Rosen Bridges, to give them their scientific name—collapsed in on any matter that entered them, shredding it down to its component molecules. To send anything and actually have it survive the trip, you had to inject the wormhole full of exotic matter: special particles with negative mass.

It took huge energy to create the particles, using special colliders—and the larger the thing you wanted to send through, the more particles you needed. At first, anything bigger than a basketball-sized probe was a no-go—it just took too much energy to produce the amount of particles needed to send bigger objects. In one of her more diligent moods, Hannah had tried to read up on the physics of it, and had given up after five pages.

Then a researcher in Moscow—Hannah always forgets her name—had figured out that you could widen the throat of the wormhole at the entry and exit points, meaning you could use the same amount of exotic matter to send much larger objects through. All you had to do was build a permanent, fixed gate at each end, stretching the wormhole throats open.

Now the probes being sent through the wormholes had a mission beyond just a look-see: construct the exit gates, using whatever resources happened to be in the area. With the gates in place, holding the wormholes open, actual ships with actual humans inside them could make the jumps, which in turn led to the Great Expansion.

Humans had spread not just to other planets in their solar

system, but far beyond to it, to a hundred different worlds. They couldn't choose where the wormholes led to, but they could choose which ones they built gates on, expanding to the most resource-rich sectors of space.

That, Hannah knew, was why the war had started in the first place, when the people who'd spent a large chunk of their lives making this all happen—the Colonies—decided they'd rather keep the resources they found for themselves than feed a solar system most of them had long forgotten. A lot of them had never even been to Earth. It might have still been the headquarters of the Frontier Senate, but they just saw it as a creaky old planet with a fucked climate, filled with old men and women trying to give them orders.

"So they came here through the Sigma gate." Brendan sees Jack about to protest, and cuts him off. "They must have done. And my guess is they did to the defences what they did to us. So right now, they're going *back* through the gate to escape. It's logical."

"Unless they're hanging around and shooting every ship that comes through," says Lorinda.

"Or they used one of those metal balls to blow the gate up after they jumped," Malik mutters.

Everybody looks at him, and he drops his head. A chill settles over Hannah. Because Malik is right—they might have done just that, and there's no way to know for sure.

"What if it came back?" Corey's eyes are huge. He hops off his seat, spreads his hands. "Ships sometimes go missing when they jump through a wormhole. What if, like, a ship went missing, only when it came back, it thought no time had passed? And we were still at war? It'd see the station, and just … boom."

A few seconds silence. Then Malik says, "That's dumb."

Corey rounds on him, but their dad gets there first. "It's not dumb. It's an interesting idea. But Corey, I don't think that's what happened. Ships have gone missing, all right, but it hasn't happened in decades. And it doesn't mean they got … trapped in time, I guess you'd call it."

"But, Dad—what if it's happened before, and we just don't know about it?"

An idea pops into Hannah's mind, bright and sharp. Surely they could send a distress call? What if ...

Her shoulders sag. They're in deep space, and even a message sent by a powerful transmitter would take at least a month to reach the nearest outpost. Maybe longer. The quickest way to deliver messages was still by using jump gates, travelling across the galaxy faster than any beamed message could ever go.

Could they send a signal to the gate? See if it was still there? Maybe ... but she didn't think the *Red Panda*'s transmitter was strong enough. Not on a ship designed to go no further than a few miles from the station.

"Hang on," Jack is saying. "Frontier's got trading ships coming into Sigma all the time, right? Right? So it won't be long before someone realises something happened."

"Assuming there's still a gate for them to come through," Anita says.

Jack ignores her. "Point is, we gotta stay here. If rescue *does* come, and we're somewhere else—"

Everett clears his throat. "Actually, that might not be such a good idea."

"Why not?" Seema says, folding her arms and looking Everett up and down. It's such a theatrical, offended gesture that Hannah almost laughs.

"Well," Everett runs a hand through his thinning hair. "According to military strategy ..."

Seema frowns. "You're a military strategist?"

Everett blinks, knocked off his stride. "No. I run my own business. I install home reactors. But I *read* military strategy sometimes—" a brief glance at his wife "—and this is a classic manoeuvre. They'll destroy a forward-operating base, then wait for the rescue teams to arrive. Additional casualties, mass panic ..."

"OK," Hannah says, not sure where he's going.

"What I mean is, they might still be nearby. If we hang around too long, we could get caught in another firefight. I'm not sure we can handle a second one." He reaches out and ruffles Corey's hair, awkward and hesitant.

Adrift

"But that's crazy," says Seema. "Jump gate ain't more than a few hours away. How long could it possibly take them? And who's to say that if we make a run for it, that ship won't take us out?"

"I'm just—"

"Yeah, OK, Evan," Jack says. "We'll pass on the analysis."

"Everett."

"Huh?"

"It's Everett. Not Evan."

"Whatever. Look, you're not the one in charge here."

"And you are?" says Anita, bristling.

"Let's vote." Hannah's voice is louder than she intended. "There's enough of us. We can decide together. How about it?"

Silence. Neither Jack nor Anita will meet her eyes.

"Fine," Seema says, turning her headlight gaze on Hannah. "Let's get it over with."

"Alrighty," Hannah says, folding her hands in her lap. "All those in favour of staying here?"

"Maybe it should be a secret vote?" Lorinda says. "We could write on slips of paper or something."

Brendan puffs out his cheeks, and Jack mutters something that sounds to Hannah like *For fuck's sake*. They're saved from having to debate this new wrinkle when Anita raises her hand. "I vote we stay here."

Everett frowns. "'Nita, I'm not sure that's such a good—"

"Seconded." Jack flicks up his hand, the other one still twisting his shirt. Anita's hand hovers in the air, an expression of confusion crossing her face—she clearly hadn't intended to side with Jack on this one. Hannah half expects the vote to be retracted, but Anita says nothing, just lowers her hand to her lap, mouth set.

Brendan and Seema raise their hands, too. No one else does.

"Great," Hannah's hair is stuck to her forehead again, and she has to forcefully peel off a couple of strands. "And those in favour of heading out?"

She lifts her hand. So do Corey, Everett and Lorinda.

"Four on four," Brendan says. "Now what?"

"Hang on." Jack points at Malik. "He hasn't voted."

Everyone turns to the teen, who looks like he would do anything to be able to hide behind his holocam.

Anita nudges him. "Come on, hon. Your vote counts, too."

Speaking very quickly, Malik says, "I vote we stay here. I vote we wait."

"*What?*" Corey swings around in his chair. "Come on, Mal, you *know* that's a dumb idea."

"Well, Mom voted for it!"

"Maybe if you weren't stuck with that stupid holo up your ass all—"

"Do *not* speak to your brother that way," Anita says, rounding on her son. "Ev, tell him."

Everett doesn't tell him. For a moment, the two sides of the family just look at each other, as if waiting for someone else to make the first move.

Jack cuts in. "Doesn't matter. We voted, all right, and it's five-four to stay here. So could we—"

"What about the pilot?"

Jack turns to Lorinda. "Huh?"

"The pilot. She gets a vote, too, doesn't she?"

"And if she votes to leave, it'll be a stalemate again," Seema says.

Lorinda refuses to look away. "Maybe. But we still need to do this right."

"We could always flip a coin, if it comes to that," Hannah says.

"Flip a ..." Jack closes his eyes. "All right, you know what? I'm going to get a drink. Do whatever you want."

He heads towards the stairs leading to the darkened bar. Corey and Malik are still hissing at each other. Anita and Everett have gone quiet, and Lorinda flashes Hannah a weak smile.

"Well," Hannah says, with a conviction she doesn't even remotely feel. "I guess I'll go talk to the captain."

Chapter 10

Hannah is about to open the door to the cockpit when she blacks out.

One second she has her hand on the door handle, cold metal under her fingertips, and the next she's slumped against the passage wall. There's a headache blossoming at the base of her skull, her tongue thick in her mouth.

"I'm OK," she says, and then a wave of nausea stronger than any she's felt before hits her. It feels as if someone has grabbed her stomach on either side, then twisted in opposite directions, like a person wringing out a wet towel.

She breathes through her nose, inhaling and exhaling, concentrating hard on each one. Slowly—very slowly—the nausea falls under control.

Suddenly, Hannah is mortified at the idea that anyone might see her. She looks up, but nobody has. Lorinda is deep in conversation with Malik, Everett and Corey. Anita is off to one side, arms folded. Brendan and Seema are muttering to each other, heads bent, and Jack is already in the bar, out of sight.

"I'm OK," Hannah says again. She takes another harsh, sour breath, and steps into the cockpit.

The smell has become worse, cigarette smoke blending with the harsh tang of sweat. The one in Volkova's mouth is fresh, only just lit. A cardboard coffee cup, balanced on the control panel, is half full of butts, swimming in a cold, black stew. For the second time, Hannah wonders why she doesn't just smoke NicoSticks. Maybe she's got used to the smell.

There's something else, too: a bottle of clear liquid, propped up against a screen. Its label side is turned away, but Hannah can read the word водка through it. There's a small trapdoor in the floor, the lid thrown back, exposing wires and blinking lights. Volkova must stash the booze down there.

The ship's computer is speaking as Hannah enters—the same jovial male voice. It's not an actual AI; more like a simple computer system, modded to make it sound human. Then again, it's not like you'd expect a decent AI on a ship like this.

"Captain, the station command mailbox appears to be full," the computer is saying. "Please communicate with other Sigma Destination Tours vessels to locate a clear quadrant, and await further instructions."

"Is that you, Guide?" Volkova's voice sounds as if she's suffering a mountainous hangover. She doesn't turn to look at Hannah, doesn't lift her hands from the controls. The *Red Panda* is hovering a short distance from the ruined station, away from the larger chunks of debris.

Hannah licks her lips. Her mouth is still cottony. "Any sign of the other ship?"

"*Nyet*. Nothing."

"That's good, right?"

Volkova just shrugs.

"Captain," says the *Panda*. "Contacting Sigma station control for further instructions. Station command mailbox appears to be full. Repeating attempt."

Volkova ignores the voice. "What about the passengers? Are they good?"

Hannah leans against the control panel, perching on the edge. She almost slips, putting her hand out for balance. "Um, we ... there's been a vote."

"A vote?"

As Hannah explains what happened, Volkova's eyebrows beetle towards her hairline. "You're crazy," she says, when Hannah is finished. "Of course we're staying here."

"But—"

"But nothing. The *Red Panda* may not have radar equipment, but the enemy ship definitely has. No, we stay here, we wait. If rescue comes, we're in right place."

It unsettles Hannah to hear the captain echoing Jack's thoughts. She pushes it away. "What if they don't come? What if the gate ..."

"Then we make another plan. But for now, we stay here." Volkova turns back to the viewport. "Go tell the passengers. I'll keep us from crashing into ... what are you doing?"

Adrift

The nausea is back, foaming, filling up Hannah's stomach. This time, she isn't sure she's going to be able to keep it down. Thick, sour saliva coats her mouth.

"*Yob tvoyu mat,*" Volkova says to herself. Hannah hears her scramble up from her seat. There's a thump, and then something appears in front of her face, a receptacle of some kind. "Here. You throw up, at least you're not throwing up on the floor."

Hannah raises her head, just a little. The receptacle is a slim cardboard box with thick sides—one that used to hold the *Red Panda's* log book, an old-fashioned ledger with dog-eared pages. The book is on the floor now, spread open spine-down.

A few seconds pass. Hannah's stomach subsides, but panic replaces the nausea, as raw as a piece of abraded skin. She closes her eyes, tries to get it under control. "I can't," she says. "Please, you've gotta talk to them. They won't listen to me."

"Let me tell you a story," Volkova says.

The words are so out of place that Hannah almost forgets her panic. "Story?"

"*Da.*" Volkova keeps talking. "I was in the Frontier navy. Flew Scorpion fighters, during the war. We were in the Bellatrix system—you know where that is?"

"Uh ..." It was one of the battles in the war—a distant one, over jump gates in a far-flung system. Hannah's tutor had mentioned it once in a college seminar.

"Colony and Frontier forces converged for control of the jump gate," Volkova says. "I was second-in-command of my squadron, and our mission was to defend the Frontier capital cruiser. OK?"

"OK ..."

The captain takes another puff of her home-made cigarette, tilting her head back to exhale the smoke. "The battle went on for hours. Kinetic impactors everywhere. The Colonies had a big, big upper hand—they had ship-killer nuclear bombs, you know the kind? And very fast Crisis fighters. My commanding officer, he was on the other flank of our capital cruiser. I saw I had a clear path to the Colony frigate—one with their bombs. The *Xi Jinping.*"

Hannah nods. The details are coming back to her now.

"So." Volkova points, as if sighting the frigate in the distance.

"I asked our officer for permission to engage. She was much too busy—fighting off the advance by the Colony ships. I knew our window was going to close. We wouldn't be able to take out the frigate at all if I didn't do something. So I took two other members of my squadron, and made a run for the *Jinping*."

She leans forward, locking eyes with Hannah. "They spotted us from ten kays out. Lit us up—*pa, pa, pa*." She clicks her fingers rapidly. "But we were good pilots. Best in the Frontier. We dodged the ordnance, made it through the enemy lines, and we targeted the frigate engines."

Volkova claps her hands together, making Hannah jump. "*Jinping* was destroyed. The Colony forces had no idea what to do. They just scattered." She grins. "My commanding officer got very angry with me, but by then the battle was done." She taps her chest. "President-elect Greenwald pinned my Victory Star, right here. Wingmen, too."

Hannah's eyes are wide, her panic forgotten. This explains how Volkova saved them—how she managed to pilot the *Panda* into the station, pull off those moves.

But then she frowns. "What does any of this have to do with—"

"Because," Volkova pauses, lighting another cig with a metal lighter that looks like it, too, might have been at the Battle of Bellatrix. "You needed something to distract you. You're acting like a crazy person, and this is not a time for acting crazy."

Hannah is about to interject when she stops. She's not nauseous any more, and the panic feels like a distant memory—like the cockpit is on a different ship to the rest of the *Panda*.

"Also, sometimes, to make a point, you *need* a story," Volkova says. "It's like putting a foundation under a building. If the foundation is not there, the building falls over. Bang."

She leans back in her chair. "Your story ... it is not good. It's boring, like mine before I joined the navy. I grew up in an apartment block in Nova Petersburg, and my father planned for me to study accounting. I told him no. I wanted to fly. To make my own story. You're very young, maybe you haven't had a chance yet. *This is your chance.* Build a foundation. Make it strong."

"But—"

Adrift

"And this is the point, Guide: sometimes you don't *have* a choice. You be the commander, or all the soldiers die. You take the line, you make the decision."

"But *you're* the captain," Hannah says.

She gets an eyeful of smoke as Volkova exhales. "You're not listening. OK, so I be the commander. I tell the passengers what to do. Then in an emergency situation, when I have to pilot the ship, they still expect me to give orders. Not good. But if *you* are the commander ..."

She leans in closer, jamming the cigarette back in the corner of her mouth and putting her hands on Hannah's shoulders.

"You will be fine, *da*? You can do this. You take care of everything inside the ship, and I—" she gestures out of the viewport. "I will take care of everything outside. We must work together. As long as I am here, we will be safe, and you can do your job. You can command the passengers. Besides," she says, leaning back and pointing at Hannah's chest, a sardonic smile on her face. "You're wearing a red shirt. Commander colours."

Hannah half smiles, then stops. Something pulls her memory, something she's sure they talked about in one of her college seminars a couple of years ago. Something about the Battle of Bellatrix.

She almost has it when a sound pierces the cockpit. It's a warning noise—a muted, high-pitched beeping, something that couldn't be considered good news in any circumstances. Hannah's mind immediately leaps to the Colony ship, its orange slashes filling her mind. She scans the window, sure that it's come back for them, that she's about to see one of those metal spheres coming right towards them. There's nothing but the darkened remains of the station, silhouetted by the Neb.

"Captain," says the AI. "I'm detecting an anomaly in our automatic suppression systems."

Volkova leans around the pilot's seat, silencing the alarm, scrolling through screens so fast that Hannah can't keep track. What she stops at is a ship schematic, a segment flashing bright red.

"Huh," Volkova mutters.

"What's happening?" says Hannah.

Volkova tries to smile, can't quite manage it. "Remember I said you must be the commander?"

Chapter 11

"How the fuck …"

Jack pulls open another cardboard box, not bothering to finish the sentence, staring in glum fury at the plastic-wrapped serviettes inside. He's on his knees, head bent below the counter. The boxes are stacked under the bar, a dozen of them tightly wedged beneath the countertop, and he's had to work hard to winkle them out. The two mini-fridges behind him sit empty, the bare shelving visible through the glass doors.

The first box held cans of JamFizz, presumably to fill the fridges behind Jack. Every one after that contained bar supplies: serviettes, extra glasses, those stupid little plastic cocktail olive skewers shaped like miniature rapiers. Jack pulls open another box, pulling at the tape with his bare hands. It bunches and twists, and he has to resist the urge to go in with his teeth.

He gives a final yank and the tape comes free. He flips the box open to find that it contains tiers of napkin rings, each one with the Sigma Destination Tours logo printed on it.

"How the fuck," he says again, completing the sentence in his head: *How the fuck does this place not have anything to drink?*

The *Red Panda*'s bar is below the cockpit, down a set of stairs from the main deck. It's a narrow room, with a long, scratchy counter running along one side, set a few feet from the wall. There's a metal basin and a rack of glasses above the two fridges. An icemaker sits alongside the rack, dry and empty.

The stairs are on his left, with a unisex bathroom underneath them. The airlock is opposite the stairs. Although there are a few chairs and tables in the bar, they're bolted to the floor on the far side, creating a clear path between the stairs and the airlock.

Like the main deck, the bar is lit by grimy fluorescent lights that make Jack think of hospital corridors. He looks around, hoping to spot another stack of boxes he might have missed, knowing he won't. The whole thing is absurd. Cruel, even. This isn't a bar. It isn't worthy of the name. It's completely unfit for purpose.

Rage overtakes him. Hot, blinding, pointless anger. He upends the box, shaking it, sending napkin rings clattering to the floor. Then he kicks out at them, crushing and snapping them against the surface of the nearest fridge, sweeping others aside with a swing of his arm. The way they scatter, rolling and bouncing across the floor, makes him think of the debris field outside. The thought short-circuits; for a moment, his mind is a complete blank.

When he comes back, he's astounded to find his face wet. He plucks a tear from below his eye, stares at it like he's never seen one before. Why the fuck is he crying? For the people on the station? He didn't know any of them, can't even remember the name of the PR flunkie who welcomed him off the shuttle.

He puts the heels of his hands over his eyes, makes a helpless groaning sound. As if in response, the hull of *Panda* creaks, the metal responding to the vacuum. He stares at the bar fridge by its feet, barely noticing the smashed plastic napkin rings.

How thick is the hull on this thing, anyway? A foot? Less? And zero shielding, outside of the thickened gravity well. One little hit, one tiny bit of spinning metal angled just the right way, and the whole damn thing'll turn itself inside out. *Pop.*

He needs a drink. There must be something he missed. He starts to rise, then slumps back. *Stop torturing yourself.* There's nothing there. A second helpless groan sneaks from his mouth, like steam escaping a pipe.

On some level, he knows the drinking is messing him up. There have been more than a few hangovers where he just wanted to die then and there, where he finally thought the booze would kill him. Weirdly, it wasn't as horrifying as it should have been—and definitely not when his head felt three times its size and even the dimmest light through the window of his tiny-ass apartment on Europa made a giant bell start ringing inside his skull.

Being dead meant he wouldn't have to think about what happened in São Paulo, and that was just fine by him. Besides, if you were gonna go, there were worse ways to do it than out of your mind on good whisky. It was the kind of death people remembered.

Oh, it's a problem. It's *definitely* a problem. It's just that it never really felt like one worth solving. Especially not now, when he's about to become a casualty in a war that ended *ten goddamn years ago*. Another chunk of bad luck, to go with the ten thousand or so other chunks that have been piled on him since he left São Paulo. And Hector.

"Can we help you out there, mate?"

Jack looks up to see Brendan O'Hara leaning over the bar. The man's thick, blocky face is set in a sympathetic frown. His prosthetic hand grips the edge of the bar, and there's a slight tenting in the sleeve of his jacket from the bulky metal arm. He looks exhausted. Like he hasn't slept for ten goddamn years.

"Nah," Jack says, letting out a disgusted breath. "Not unless you know where they stash the single malt."

"Course. Got it right here, along with celery and hot sauce for a couple of Bloody Marys."

Jack blinks at him. The guy's making jokes? Now? Then again, why the hell not?

Brendan reaches out his real hand—it's the size of a catcher's mitt, big as the rest of him, the skin ever so slightly rough—and pulls Jack to his feet. "Bartender's lucky he wasn't working today," Jack says, dusting himself off. "I'd have something to say about the no-booze policy, believe me."

"Not sure I'd use the word *lucky*," Seema mutters. She's behind Brendan, staring at the airlock with a blank expression. She's undone her ponytail, the hair tie wrapped around one of her fingers, jacket off.

Jack winces. "Oh yeah. Shit. Fair point."

He leans on the bar, arms akimbo, his fingers fanned across the grimy plastic surface. He still isn't entirely sure why Brendan agreed with him so quickly upstairs—he's not used to having people agree with him, something which he's perversely proud of.

Still, if they want to hang out down here, in this shitty little bar, fine by him. Better them than the damn tour guide, or that other woman. The political consultant with the useless husband and the two rugrats. Better here than up there, with a big, wide window onto the shit-show outside. Without wanting to, he pictures the station's PR person, a perky woman with green bangs and an expensive smile.

"S'alright." Seema takes a shaky breath. She looks pale, and frightened. "What *is* there to drink?"

"JamFizz. Think I saw some fruit juice, too."

Seema walks over. Up close, Jack can see that she's strong—not built like Brendan, but the arms under her tight green T-shirt are thick and muscular. She's got a tattoo on her left bicep: a band of thorny branches, circling it. It's one of those tats with LED ink, making the green branches glow ever so slightly against her dark skin. "I'll take a JamFizz, please," she says.

There's a moment where Jack thinks about rationing, about saving what they have. Then he decides: *fuck it.*

"No ice," he says, reaching behind him. "Got some soychips if you want."

Seema grimaces. "Any nuts?"

"Sure. I keep 'em right by the prime rib."

A tired smirk makes its way across Brendan's face. "JamFizz for me, too, cheers."

Jack digs out three cans, then manages to find three clean glasses. The nuclear-orange JamFizz hisses as he pours it, white foam whooshing up the sides of the glass. Vaguely, he remembers that they don't sell it on Earth any more. Something about sugar. Not that it matters now.

The three of them clink glasses and drink deep. The drink barely satisfies Jack at all—like flicking water at a four-alarm fire. When they finish, none of them say anything. Jack meets Brendan's eyes for a moment, can't hold them. Maybe they should have made a real toast, said something to commemorate the … the people who …

That blankness threatens his mind again. He pushes it away, although he can't help but look down at the napkin rings, smashed and broken by his feet.

The silence is way too awkward. "So how'd you two end up here?" he says.

Seema waggles her left hand, flashing her wedding ring, and Jack shakes his head. "Sorry. Honeymoon, right?"

"Family clubbed together and bought us this trip," says Brendan. "We didn't want to leave the little one behind, but you know how it is with newborns. They thought we could use the R&R."

Jack looks between them. "Little one?"

"Marcus." Seema looks down, and it takes her a little too long to form her next words. "He's four months."

"You know, you can plan as much as you want," Brendan says, sounding as if he's forcing the cheer into his voice at gunpoint. "But life gets in the way. Not sure what went wrong. Or right, I suppose."

"We were engaged anyway," says Seema. "So after Marcus was born we thought ... well, why not? And then my parents offered to look after him for a while so we could see the Neb."

"Seems is an artist," Brendan says, glancing at his wife. "She wanted to take some photos."

Jack grunts, and takes a swig of JamFizz. "You guys from Earth?"

"Yeah. London."

"Huh. Really." Distantly, he wonders what the hell he's doing. Making small talk, when the entire universe just exploded. "Thought it was pretty tough to live there after the sea levels ... you know."

"Nah. London's been through plenty worse. Thames is just a bit bigger now, is all."

The Thames. Jack never did get to London before he moved out to Europa—North and South America, that was it, with a couple of weekends in the Mexican Archipelago that he can't really remember. Not that it matters now. Even before this whole thing went down, he was never going back to Earth. Fuck it. Useless planet, anyway. When you think about it, not hard to see why the Colonies didn't exactly feel keen to send back their resources.

Adrift

"Planning to move out to Titan after we get back, though," Brendan says. "Already put a down payment on a nice little place."

"What about you?" Jack asks him. "What do you do?"

"Her assistant, believe it or not." Brendan nods at Seema, who gives a wan smile. "She's a terrific artist, but she just hasn't got a head for business. That's what I did, back in the land of the living—data research. When her stuff started taking off, we decided that I should step in to run things."

"Is that why we haven't been paid from the last commission yet, Pooka?" Seema says, taking a sip of her JamFizz. Her tone is light, but her hand is shaking, just a little.

He raises an eyebrow. "Pooka?"

"Silly nickname." Brendan wraps his fingers around his wife's. "On the contrary, my cushla, they made payment just before we left."

Jack has to stop himself from rolling his eyes. He's always hated cute couple names. He takes another sip of his drink, then puts it down, disgusted. He can still taste stomach acid in the back of his throat from when he threw up.

His gaze lands on Brendan's arm, the metal hand flat against Seema's back. The fingers are unusually long—a good inch beyond those on the man's other hand. His wedding ring, a thin gold band, is much larger than a regular one. Thicker, too, and—

"Seen something interesting?" Seema says. When Jack looks up, he sees a dark, almost hostile look on her face.

"Oh, come off it, Seems," says Brendan. "He's just looking."

Seema's expression immediately dissolves. She composes herself. "Sorry. People stare sometimes. It's rude."

"I really don't mind that much." Brendan squeezes her shoulder. Then he lifts the arm, turning the palm face up. In the quiet bar, the servos sound a little too loud.

"Motorbike accident," he tells Jack, looking a little less haunted than before. "Was doing a race on a trip to Mars when I came off on a hairpin. Nasty business. I was in hospital for …"

He stops when he realises that Seema is crying.

She lowers the glass to the bar, setting it down gently. Then she buries her face in her hands, shoulders heaving silently. For a second, Brendan looks utterly defeated—like he's shrunk a whole foot in size. He reaches out for his wife, pulling her into an awkward hug. She still hasn't made a sound.

Jack hates it when this happens. Everything he wants to say always feels like the wrong thing. All the same, he can't even imagine what it must be like. At least the family upstairs is together. Seema and Brendan's kid—Martin? No, *Marcus*—won't even know what happened to his mom and dad.

After a few moments, Seema pulls away from Brendan. Her skin is puffy from crying, her eyes red.

"Ignore me," she tells Jack. "I'm just ... struggling a little."

"Don't worry about it."

But looking at her makes him think of London. Hadn't he watched something about it a little while back? How the floodwaters had got everywhere, dissolving the foundations. All those monuments and old buildings looked strong on top, but underneath they were crumbling.

"Anyway, how about you?" Brendan asks, as if nothing had happened. "How'd you land up on this pleasure cruise?"

"Nothing as interesting as your story. I'm a hotel reviewer. For the Europa Central feed."

"A hotel re—" Brendan's eyebrows shoot up. "Wow."

"Yeah." Jack forces himself to drain his JamFizz, idly spins the can on the bar. Weirdly, he feels a little better. And Brendan and Seema aren't bad—or at least, they're not nearly as annoying as the other people on this particular pleasure cruise.

"How long do you think it'll take?" Seema says, wiping her nose as she glances at the airlock.

"Not long, I reckon," Brendan replies. "Not once they figure out no ships are coming back through the jump gate. I say a day. Maybe less. We stay here, we'll be fine." He grips his wife's hand even tighter. "We're the lucky ones, right? We survived."

"Yeah," Jack says bitterly. "It's a miracle."

Silence. He realises Seema is looking at him.

"What do you mean?" she says.

Jack frowns. "What do you mean, what do I mean?"

Adrift

"You just called it a miracle."

"Yeah, it's a figure of speech. So what?"

"What are you on about, Seems?" says Brendan.

But Seema's shakiness is vanishing now. She leans on the bar, arms folded. She looks, to Jack, like someone who's just been told that there really is a way to break out of the jail that everyone said was impossible to escape from. It's the same determination Jack saw when she gave him shit about staring at Brendan's arm—steely, on edge, hostile.

Seema, he's starting to realise, is strung up tighter than a model on one of the live bondage channels he sometimes signs on to. Not that he's surprised. She's a mom, and she's a long, long way from her kid. They both are. It's kind of surprising that Brendan still has enough energy left to crack jokes.

"Don't you think it's a little weird that we're the only ship that survived?" Seema says. "Like, from the whole station, only one ship makes it out?"

"Come off it," Brendan says again. "We might not be the only ones. There might be others."

"We'd have heard from them by now. Or seen them."

"No." Jack shakes his head. "I mean, the odds … it was a big station. Someone had to survive. Why not us?"

"Right. Exactly." Brendan puts his hand over Seema's. "Babe, just think for a second."

She rips her hand away. "Don't you tell me that. I *am* thinking, all right, and none of this is square." She looks at Jack, her eyes a little wild. He has to force himself not to flinch. "You know what I mean? Like … it doesn't add up. Us being the only ones."

Jack takes a deep breath, righting himself. *This is absurd.*

"Sorry. I'm with Brendan on this one," he says. "I think it's just shitty luck. Most things are."

And yet, even as he speaks he's turning the idea over in his mind. No, they have to be rational about this, and, right now, Seema is several miles from rational. But …

But.

It's been a while since he was an actual reporter, since he actually had to ask questions of people who didn't want to give him the answers. But you never lose the instinct. You might not have got on a bike in years, might have even sold it, but that doesn't mean you forgot how to ride. Your feet would automatically find the pedals, even when there was nowhere to go.

At that moment there are shouts from the main deck. Shouts, and running feet. The three of them exchange a look, then abandon their drinks, heading for the stairs. Brendan gets there first, followed by Seema, but Jack has long legs and he and Brendan reach the top at the same time.

The first thing he sees is Hannah's head. She's been swallowed by the floor at the back of the main deck, a trapdoor sprung open next to her. Everett, Anita and their boys are on their feet, and Lorinda Esteban is staring at the tour guide in shock. Hannah is barking instructions, yelling at Everett to follow her as she vanishes into the floor. He complies, a stunned look on his face, closely followed by his wife.

"What's going on?" Jack yells across the deck. He has to do it again before Lorinda turns to look at him, her eyes huge.

"Fire."

Chapter 12

Corey is almost at the hatch when his mom grabs his arm. "Stay here," she says.

"But—"

"No. *Stay*."

Like he's a dog being told not to crap on the carpet. *Thanks, Mom.* But his mom looks pale, and it's that, more than her words, that makes him do what she says.

"I'll look after them," says Lorinda. "Go."

Anita flashes her a smile of thanks, hustling to the hatch. Corey's dad is just disappearing out of sight, and she climbs in after him.

Adrift

The other three adults—the ones who were in the bar—all head down after her.

"Bakwas," Corey mutters.

"All right, boys," Lorinda says, not appearing to have heard him. "Let's just hang out here. They'll be back soon."

"I don't get it," Malik asks her. "Where's the fire?"

"Engine," Corey says, frowning at the hatch. "Like she said."

"So why isn't there an alarm?"

Corey shakes his head. Sometimes his brother can be a real chutiya. "Because people would get scared. The whole point is to get them to stay where they are. There's probably an alert or something in the cockpit, and then the automatic systems deal with it."

"OK, *genius*. If there's automatic systems, then why's everybody heading down there?"

Corey looks at the trapdoor. The automatic systems *should* have kicked in, shutting down the fire the second it started, drenching it with suppressant foam. Every ship had to have that, no matter how small—it was the law. That meant the *Red Panda*, too.

The engine is right at the back of the ship, on the lower level. When they were flying into the hotel, there was the ear-splitting scrape of something against the hull. Could that have started the fire in the engine? Maybe damaged the suppressant systems? It's easy to see a couple of torn wires sparking, their insulation slowly burning, getting hotter and hotter …

"I'm going down," says Malik, getting to his feet.

"Don't be an asshole, Mal," Corey says, forgetting for a second that there's an adult in the room. A grandma, actually.

"Don't swear, *Cor*." His brother goes down on one knee by the hatch, transferring his holo controller to his other hand. Is he seriously going to film *everything*?

Of course he is. That's Mal. The same Mal who'd made him jump into the warm and sticky pool at Southeast Towers in Austin, making him do it over and over for two whole hours because the shot wasn't quite right. The Mal who spent most of last year bugging their parents for an expensive editing program, never shutting up about it, until Corey wanted to kill him. Who would never let Corey sit in the window seat on a shuttle, in case he got in the way of a shot. He won't show Corey any of the movies he's working on, won't even let him in his room at home. He used to play soccer with Corey all the time, but they haven't done that in forever.

Mal didn't know anything. Worse: he didn't *want* to know anything. If it wasn't seen through a camera, he just didn't care. Technically, Corey is sort of the same, with spaceships and stuff, but that's different. He does other things, too. He hoverboards and plays basketball at school and hangs out with Jamie and Allie. And he doesn't treat his brother like a movie prop.

"Stop right there, mister," the old woman says, getting to her feet with a grimace. "I told your mother I'd look after you, so you're gonna stay right where you are. Besides—" she digs in her fanny pack. "I've even got something to keep you both occupied."

It's a toy—a tiny action figure, a little dinosaur in red plastic armour, its teeth bared. A tiny, badly painted purple tongue pokes between them. It's still in its plastic packaging.

Corey blinks in astonishment. "Is that ... is that a *Reptar*?"

"I have no idea," the old woman says, sounding a little desperate. She starts to tug at the packaging, grunting as she tears open the back panel. "I bought it for my sister's grandson. Saw it in the gift shop this morning, on the way over here. Apparently, you can link it up with a lens and make it walk around and jump up on tables. I haven't really looked at that yet. We could try if you—"

Malik tilts his head, looking at them like they've gone insane. Then, in one movement, he turns and vanishes into the trapdoor. With surprising speed, Lorinda goes after him, but stops when she reaches the edge, her face flushed red as she stares at the ladder. Corey thinks he hears her mutter under her breath, something that sounds like *shit*.

She's still clutching the Reptar toy in one hand. Corey isn't sure what she was thinking—even *he's* getting a little old for shows like *Quasar Lizards*, never mind Malik.

He can't help but look up through the viewport at the debris field. If the station was still around, there'd be a big, fat rescue ship rushing out to them, even if the suppression systems were working right. It'd scoop the *Panda* up in its belly, get it into a pressurised environment, get the passengers out. Not going to happen now. There's nobody coming for them—nobody who even knows they're here.

A cold line of ice water runs down Corey's spine. He shivers, has to make himself stop.

"I'll go get him." Corey crouches down, lowering his legs over the edge—only to be brought up short when Lorinda grabs his arm, in almost the exact same place his mom had her fingers around before. He can smell something nasty: Jack's puke, still puddled by the wall to his left. It's just starting to crust over.

The old lady's grip is a lot softer, but it stops him cold. "Uh-uh," she says. "You're not going anywhere."

Corey smiles at Lorinda. "I never said. Thanks for catching me before. That was really nice of you."

She blinks, then smiles back, opening her mouth to reply. But as she does so, her grip on his arm loosens just a little.

Corey slips out of it. He hears Lorinda cry out, her hand brushing the back of his T-shirt. She's not nearly fast enough—in less than two seconds he's through the trapdoor, dropping right down. The ladder whooshes past him, and he lands hard, almost falling. He never worried about making the drop—it was only ten feet, barely enough to need a ladder for—but the landing is awkward and he only just manages to stay up.

"I'm really sorry!" he shouts up at Lorinda, a hot flush of shame already creeping onto his cheeks. He *is* sorry, and he's probably going to get in bad trouble later, but he meant what he said about her catching him. He can tell her that, and it'll all be OK. And, anyway, all he wants is a look.

He takes a breath, and gets a mouthful of hot, acrid smoke. It's not the smoke of a campfire, or even like the kind when his dad burned something in the kitchen. It's got a taste to it, a nasty one. He coughs, bending over, feeling like the smoke is coating the inside of his throat.

Bending over brings him closer to the ground, where the air is a little clearer, so he drops to one knee. The *Red Panda*'s astronautics section is a tiny room, dimly lit, the walls lined with boxy modules festooned with wires and blinking lights. This is the ship's brain: its navigation, its proximity sensors, its voice, its heating and air.

On a more expensive ship, they wouldn't have this room—everything would be on a single quantum chip, in its own cryo-pod. But quantum chips are expensive to maintain, and rooms like this one aren't. Something goes wrong, you can just pull out a module and replace it, which is a million times cheaper than sending a quantum chip into a lab.

Corey blinks against the smoke, trying to pull in enough fresh air to hold in his lungs. He can just see beyond astronautics to the engine compartment; the door is open, and Seema is hanging on the frame, staring at something just out of his line of sight.

His dad's voice cuts through the noise. "Aim it round the corner—"

"It's not long enough," Hannah says.

And then his mom, furious. "Malik, get back upstairs! *Now!*"

Corey hesitates. If his mom sees him down here, she might do something a little worse than ground him for a few days. And, besides, he doesn't want to get the old lady in trouble. Maybe he should …

But the old lady is already in trouble, no matter what happens, and so is he. Corey runs in a crouch, trying as hard as he can not to suck more smoke into his lungs.

He doesn't bother to sneak past Seema. She makes a grab for him, misses completely, and then he's inside.

The engine room is even more cramped than astronautics. Most of its floor space is taken up by a huge, shielded cylinder, covered with a hundred different warning labels. The miniature fusion core. The walls are a mishmash of touch screens and digital read-outs, their glow shading the smoke strange colours. It's much thicker in here, so thick that Corey has to go down on all fours just to get another breath.

A metal panel has been torn loose from the wall, lying off to one side, exposing a space less than two feet across. Hannah and Corey's dad are crouched over by the wall, the red tube of a fire extinguisher between them. There's an oxygen tank, too, with a thick plastic mask attached to it—his dad is holding it to his mouth whenever he leans into the vent, squeezing his eyes shut as he lets off another burst of spray. Jack and Brendan are behind them, shouting instructions. Off to one side, Mom and Malik are screaming at each other.

The smoke. It's not just coming from the hole in the wall. It's coming from everywhere, seeping out through gaps in the panels, harsh and hot. Whatever's going on in there, the automatic systems either aren't working or can't handle it, which is probably why the grown-ups are trying to use the fire extinguisher.

An uncontrolled engine fire is about one of the worst things to happen to a ship. If they don't kill it soon, they're just ... *screwed*. It won't damage the fusion reactor—nothing short of a direct hit on the engine compartment would get through the shielding—but it'll stop the thrusters working. They won't be able to move, and if that Colony ship comes back, or a big chunk of debris crosses their path ...

That's if they don't die from smoke inhalation first.

Corey's dad is half in, half out of the vent, trying to squeeze the extinguisher cylinder between his body and the vent wall. His shoulder won't fit—he tucks it in, pulling it close to his body, but there's just not enough room. The vents are there so technicians can send in special drones, ones small enough to navigate the ship's internal systems and conduct repairs. Corey's seen video of them before. Almost guaranteed there won't be any on the *Panda*. And the vents can't take an adult, but—

The idea arrives fully-formed, bright and blazing as the midday sun. The entire sequence of events unfolds in an eye-blink, all the way to the rescue ships arriving, to the *Red Panda*'s captain explaining to a Fleet Commander how he, Corey, averted disaster ...

And it's gotta be him. No one else can do it. The grown-ups won't fit, and neither will Malik, who's probably just going to stand around and film the whole thing anyway.

OK, bro. Film this.

He sprints across the room, staying low, skidding to his knees in between Hannah and his dad, ignoring the startled shouts from Jack and Brendan. His dad is trying to tuck the extinguisher cylinder under his arm, winkling it in close so he can squeeze into the vent. His eyes are streaming, turned red by the smoke, the oxygen mask wrapped around his face. Corey fights to keep his eyes open against the sting as he reaches for the cylinder. He'll grab it, then dive into the passage before anyone—

He's brought up short by a vice-grip hand on his shoulder. His mom, eyes huge and wild, screaming at him to get back. Corey stares at her, one hand on the cylinder. Doesn't she get it? Doesn't she understand what's happening?

Then it feels like every adult in the engine room is there, too, pulling him away, their angry voices blending into a single confused, buzzing roar. Not quite fast enough. Not even his mom can hold onto him. He surges out of their grasp, half falling towards the vent, hands questing for the extinguisher. His dad has it resting on the floor now, and Corey grabs it, pulling the short hose with him. There are hands on his back, fingers plucking at his shirt, but he barely notices. He feels like he weighs nothing, as if his body is made of air.

Corey sucks in a huge breath, then hurls himself forwards into the vent.

Chapter 13

He lands with a bang, the extinguisher wedged underneath him and his lower legs sticking out of the pipe. The heat wallops him in the face. It's so dry that it sucks the moisture right off his lips, off the surface of his eyeballs. He doesn't dare open his eyes, or take another breath—if he does, he's sure his body will just burn right up.

He's aware of bundles of wires, of more metal plates under his fingers. The vent is covered in slick, bubbling foam, slimy against his skin.

A hand wraps around his ankle, pulls him backwards. Then it's gone, whoever it is letting go like he's on fire—for all he knows, he might be. Angry voices pierce the smoke. Hannah, his mom, that guy Jack. All of them shouting. Corey pushes himself forwards again, trying to avoid the hot spots, but the tunnel is narrower than he thought it was. He's not wedged tight, but the ceiling presses on the back of his head, the walls uncomfortably close to his shoulders. The cylinder underneath him pushes his body upwards, squashing him …

He has to take a breath. His lungs feel like they're going to tear through his ribcage. But if he does, all he'll get back is smoke. No, this wasn't a good idea. This wasn't a good idea at all.

Something bumps his shoulder. At first he thinks it's someone trying to pull him out of there, but then he sees it. It's not a hand. It's the oxygen mask, the one that was around his dad's neck. They've thrown it to him. *They think he can do this.*

He gropes for the mask, fighting the burn in his lungs and throat, telling himself to hold on for a few more seconds. There's no way he's getting the string on the mask around his head, so he settles for using his free hand to jam it in place.

Oxygen, cold and sharp, floods his lungs. It smells like disinfectant, but it's still the best breath he's ever taken.

He wants to look back over his shoulder, see who passed him the mask. He can't do it. Now that he's in, there isn't enough room to turn around. He forces his eyes open, doing his best to ignore the stinging smoke.

A suppressant nozzle juts from the top of the vent, dribbling bubbles of useless foam. There's a second one further along, utterly dead, right where the vent turns ninety degrees to the right. Beyond the turn, glinting off the metal, there's the orange glimmer of flames.

Another breath, then he squeezes himself further down the passage, using his right knee to push the cylinder along underneath him. He barely moves three inches. He tries again, carefully placing his free elbow, holding the mask tight to his face. No good. He needs to get free of this cylinder, or he'll cook long before he reaches the fire.

The foam doesn't come directly out of the cylinder—it comes from a thin hose, made of flame-resistant nylon, with a metal nozzle at the end. Corey grabs the hose, pushing his body sideways to take pressure off the cylinder. If he can get ahead of it, pull it along behind him, then he can get around the corner. As long as the hose doesn't do something horrible, like coming loose from the extinguisher …

Six inches. A foot. Corey's wrist and elbow are screaming at him as he worms forward. The extinguisher is heavy, and it's almost more than he can handle to pull it along. He doesn't know how far he is from the vent entrance; they might not be able to pull him back out. Terror swells through him, a freak wave a hundred times higher than the others. His eyes feel three times their size, gritty and dry in their sockets.

His head comes around the corner. Then his shoulders. The fire consumes the passage, the heat nearly knocking him out. It's not crackling, like a regular fire—it's *spitting*, the flames hissing like a wounded animal.

The hose. It's still behind him, level with his chest, curling over his hip to the cylinder behind him. He teases it forward, inch by inch, trying to ignore the fact that the heat on his face is going from painful to excruciating. It's like he's opened the oven in their kitchen at home, and someone is holding his face to it, not letting him pull back from the surge of dry heat.

He keeps pulling until the nozzle is level with his chest, until he's got it pointed right at the base of the fire. But he can't make it stay put—the tip of the nozzle keeps arcing up towards his chin, the stiffness of the hose pulling it straight. He'll have to use his free hand to hold it in place, which means he's going to have to drop the mask so he can activate the cylinder.

There's no time to think it over. No time to figure out if it's even possible. Corey takes one last breath of oxygen, then drops the mask and reaches back.

His hand lands on the scorching floor of the vent, making him yelp. Where's the cylinder? Surely the hose can't have—

Adrift

He finds it. Then he finds the top, and the trigger, and then he's pushing down as hard as he can and the vent fills with bubbling, expanding foam.

The nozzle slips out of his fingers, flicking back towards his face and sending gobbets of foam thudding against his chin. Corey splutters, sucking in a mouthful of smoke that twists his throat into knots. The whole vent is vibrating around him, as if he's in the intestine of an angry monster. As he fights to get control of the flailing nozzle, he tells himself to keep his finger on the trigger, to keep squeezing as hard as he can.

Somehow, he does. Somehow, he holds the nozzle in one place, smothering the fire and turning the smoke so thick that for a few seconds he can't tell the difference between it and the foam. Everything is scorching, slimy, stinging, his lungs about to tear out of his chest.

Then the fire is gone. He blinks, eyes leaking stinging tears, sure he's imagining it. But it's been blanketed in lumps of foam, and he can't hear the spitting sound any more.

He tries to shove himself backwards on his elbows, but stops when his feet jam into the wall at the point where the pipe doglegs. He has to get around it ... but how? He can't link the thoughts in his head. His legs are at a strange angle, his knees facing the wrong way in the pipe. He's still holding the extinguisher nozzle—his fingers welded to it, the cylinder squeezed tight to his body.

Fingers brush his ankle, someone reaching as far as they can down the pipe. Doesn't matter. They're not going to get him out unless he turns, and he doesn't have the first clue how to do that. He takes a breath, and inhales a blob of foam. His throat clogs instantly. Hacking coughs burst out of him, bracketed by panicky inhales.

It's as if his body takes over. He twists, shoving himself around the dogleg, worming backwards, moving on instinct. The fingers at his ankle move up his calf, grip tight. He raises his head, still coughing, and gets a look at Hannah's panicked face.

Then his mom and dad are there, and then everyone is hauling him out, into the light.

Chapter 14

Hannah always wanted to be a mom. It was something she was quite comfortable daydreaming about—something that would happen far in the future, when she'd paid off her student loans and had a job curating a big museum or overseeing a research programme at a university.

Her parents had exchanged a fleeting, slightly worried look when she'd mentioned it the first time, before plastering wide smiles on their faces and saying how nice it'd be to have a grandchild. She still thinks about that look at odd moments. Every time, she tells herself that it doesn't matter *what* they thought. It's her life, not theirs.

She didn't know who the dad would be—her fantasies bounced between Sandro Sawyer from the *Uncommon Valor* movies, and a cute guy she'd known in her sociology seminar—but the picture of the daughter was completely clear. She would be a punky, independent little monster who Hannah could take to the park, and build blanket forts with.

But now, looking at Anita and Everett Livingstone as they hold a coughing, blinking, foam-flecked Corey tight, she's not sure she could do it. If she was in Anita's position, she'd just start screaming.

They're all back on the main deck. Some of the smoke made it up here, and the air is ever so slightly hazy. Nobody's saying anything—everyone's staring into space, or occasionally shaking their heads in disbelief. There are no arguments this time. No yelling. Just a kind of stunned lethargy—as if the adrenaline everyone was running on has drained away. Everywhere Hannah looks, she sees haggard faces and exhausted eyes.

It's not hard to see why. There's only so much anyone can take before they stop being able to respond—it was why people switched off during the war, reports of battles from places like Sigma barely peaking their emotional radar. It's the same even when it's up close, when it's happening right in your face. Eventually, your body shuts itself down. It dulls the world, files off the rough edges as a survival mechanism.

Everything that's happened on the *Panda*—all the arguments, the fire, nearly losing Corey—and it hasn't changed a thing. Hannah can't help looking up through the viewport, and as she does so, it's like the black is pulling at her. Like it's about to lift her right out of the *Panda*. Turn her into another piece of debris, drifting until the end of time. The only thing stopping it from happening is that very thin, very clear piece of glass above her head.

"All passengers, please st-st-stay calm," says the ship's voice. "There is a situation in the engine room. The main deck has been sealed for your prrrrrrr-protection, and the authorities have been notified. Please stay seated, and only move to the escape pod if you are instructed to by a Sigma Destination Tours sta-sta-sta-sta-staff member."

The main deck isn't sealed. Hannah's not even sure it can be. She's long since tuned out the message, which has been repeating every couple of minutes ever since they came up here.

Volkova has already confirmed that one of their thrusters is non-functional, but the other three are still working. They're still mobile, for now. And yet, Hannah can't help feeling like she screwed up. She had a plan: a calm, controlled, clear response to an emergency. If the suppression systems really had failed, they were going to find the extinguisher, pull away the panel, deal with the problem.

But that plan went out of the window the moment they realised the fire was too far back, and it grew wings and vanished over the horizon when Corey Livingstone appeared. If the vent had been just a little bit narrower, if Corey had got stuck or they hadn't been able to get him the oxygen mask ...

You got lucky, rook.

Someone sits down next to her, and she looks up to see Lorinda. The old woman is pale, like she's aged another decade in the past half-hour.

She looks over at Anita, who is arguing with her husband again. "What am I going to say to her?"

"What do you mean?"

"I was supposed to watch her boys, and they both … they were *so fast*. And I'm not very good with ladders …"

Hannah licks her lips. "I'm sure you did everything you could." It sounds lame, even as she says it.

Licking her lips makes her more aware of how thirsty she is. Thirsty, and hungry. She does a quick calculation in her head— they've been on the ship for three hours, and the last thing she had to eat was the night before, a stale cheese sandwich that she'd stuffed in her mouth in the staff canteen. No, wait, there was the apple and a bowl of cereal this morning. Anyway, even if the passengers ate before they got on board, they're still going to need food before long.

It would be so, so good to stay here, on this chair, to close her eyes and go to sleep and pretend none of this is happening. Instead, Hannah gets to her feet, moving like she's Lorinda's age. Her hands are coated with black particles, and they leave dark smears on her jeans. As she looks back up, she sees a brightly coloured object on the seat next to Lorinda: a little action figure, a dinosaur in a red spacesuit. Its packaging sits next to it, the back torn open.

"What is … what's that?" she says.

Lorinda picks it up. "I thought they might want to play with this. I guess not. Do you have kids at all?"

Hannah shakes her head.

"Me neither." She cradles the toy in her hands. "We tried, but we never quite managed. My sister does, though—I bought this thing for her grandson. My grandnephew. Or nephew twice removed—I never remember which it is. Although I suppose they're a little younger than—"

"*Reptile formation!*" the toy barks.

Its voice is loud and crunchy, and it's followed by a series of ear-piercing bleeps. Hannah jumps, and Lorinda yelps, almost dropping the toy. "Sorry! Sorry everyone. It linked with my lens automatically."

Jack sighs, long and loud. Lorinda flashes the rest of them an apologetic smile, then looks back down at the toy, turning it over in her hands.

"You know who I keep thinking of?" she says. "The woman

who cleaned my room, in the hotel. She was about the same age as his mother—my nephew, I mean. We talked once or twice, and she said she was from the Colonies—got a special visa for what she was doing. Apparently the hotel brought in a whole bunch of them, and she was telling me about how she had some leave coming up, and how excited she was to go back home ..."

Hannah can't do this. Even thinking about the people on the station is too much. It fills the *Panda* with ghosts, drains her energy.

She straightens up, raising her voice to the others. "I think it'd be a good idea if we figured out how much food we have on board," she tells everyone, "and where it all is."

"What for?" says Anita. "We know there's some in the bar, and the Frontier'll be here before long, won't they?"

"Right," Brendan says. "You get hungry, just eat a pack of soychips. Why're we even bothering?"

Because I need this. Because I've got to be able to do something right, or I'm going to collapse.

"Because we have to plan for every eventuality," she says, hating how formal the words sound.

"Yeah, because the Frontier's just going to ignore one of their outposts going offline all of a sudden," Jack says.

"Unless there was more than one attack," Lorinda says, not looking at him.

"Jesus Christ." Jack's hands are hanging down between his knees, as if he's preparing to break his fall when he hits the floor. "It's not aliens. OK? Fucking ... *aliens* didn't attack us."

"I didn't say that."

"It's the goddamn Colony pissed off with *her* damn treaty." He points at Anita, who bristles. "Anyway," Jack goes on. "It doesn't matter. You watch, pretty soon there'll be a bunch of Frontier response ships inbound, and then we can all go home and let them figure it out."

"And what if they *don't* come?" says Seema, giving Jack a look that Hannah can't quite figure out.

He raises his eyes to meet hers. "They will."

"We still need to eat," Hannah says.

"Yeah, so? We just go down to the bar and help ourselves."

"Stop acting like this is normal."

Seema's words are almost a snarl, and they bring everything on the main deck to a grinding halt. For a few seconds, nobody moves.

Brendan takes two steps towards his wife, puts an arm around her shoulders. It's his metal one, but she doesn't appear to notice.

"My cushla," Brendan says, emphasising each syllable. "Calm. Down."

She rips away from him, red eyes flashing. "No. Don't you do that. Don't you ever do that to me. Our boy is not going to … to …"

Seema falters, her face collapsing. Brendan stands, awkward, as if he doesn't know whether to touch her or not. He glances at the rest of them, as if embarrassed to have an audience.

"You have a son?" Lorinda says.

"Yep," Brendan says, distracted. "Four months. Back on Earth."

He takes a hesitant step towards his wife—but it's Anita Livingstone who gets there first. She pulls the shaking Seema into her arms, hugs her tight. Hannah can see her whispering in Seema's ear—she can't hear what's being said, but, then again, she doesn't need to. Anita's a mom, too. And she nearly just lost one of her own sons.

After a long moment, Anita reaches out for Brendan, pulling him in, almost forcing him into the hug. The three of them stand there for a few seconds before pulling apart. Nobody else has said anything.

Seema wipes her eyes. "I'm sorry," she says, looking Jack in the eye. "Didn't mean to …"

"S'alright." Jack looks too exhausted to complain. "Don't worry about it. You'll be back with your boy soon."

"For sure," Anita says.

Brendan flashes her a weak smile. He's not as emotional as Seema, but there are dark circles under his eyes, and there's a definite slump to his shoulders.

Hannah clears her throat. "The Frontier's probably on the way right now," she says, less sure than she sounds. "But all the same, we need to know what we're working with."

Adrift

"Waste of time, you ask me," says Jack.

"No," Hannah says. "We ..."

And suddenly she doesn't know what to say. There are good reasons to inventory their food, but they've popped out of her head, like they were never there.

Lorinda puts a hand on her arm. "I've got some energy bars in my bag. And I think there's a juice box as well."

"And there might be some in the escape pod." Everett Livingstone pulls himself to his feet. "Emergency rations, something like that."

"No," Anita says. "We need to watch the boys."

Everett gives her an exasperated look. "'Nita, would you just—"

"You know what?" she says, turning away from him. "It's fine. Just go."

He stares at her back for a long moment, then starts trudging towards the escape pod.

"I can do the bar." Hannah gives Jack a pointed look. "Can you help me?"

He holds her gaze for a moment, then shrugs and nods.

"If you can bring what you find downstairs," Hannah says to the others. "That's where most of the food is anyway, I think, so ..."

"Wait. Hold on." Corey has managed to winkle out from his mom's arms, standing on unsteady feet. His voice sounds like he has Volkova's smoking habit. "Someone should tell the pilot before we open the pod. Otherwise she'll freak out."

"I'll go," Malik says. Corey gives him a disbelieving look, but Malik just shrugs, heading to the cockpit. Anita pulls Corey in again—he resists at first, then sinks into her arms. Hannah realises she's shaking.

"All passengers, please st-st-stay calm. There is a situation in the engine room ..."

Hannah heads downstairs, Jack following a few steps behind her. The bar has got colder since she was down there last, and the air prickles against her bare arms.

There are three glasses on the counter, one still half full of JamFizz. She's about to say something about needing to conserve supplies when her thirst ratchets up another notch, her throat going from uncomfortable to excruciating in less than a second.

She snags a glass from the rack, shoves it under the tap. The water is ice-cold, so cold it hurts to drink. It's the sweetest, most delicious glass of water she's ever had in her life.

"Pour me one while you're at it," Jack says.

Hannah jumps—she'd almost forgotten he was there. He's leaning on the bar, arms folded, looking expectantly at her.

She raises an eyebrow. He stares at her for a long moment, then rolls his eyes. "*Please* pour me some water. Christ."

"Here," she says, filling up a glass. As he drinks, she says, "Sure you're not going to sue if you spill some down your shirt?"

He drains the glass, wipes his mouth. "Let's just get this over with."

In the end, there isn't much to do. There's a box full of warm JamFizz, minus the three Jack, Brendan and Seema already drank. There are maybe two dozen packets of no-brand soychips, most of them garam masala flavour. *At least it's one I like*, Hannah thinks, as she and Jack stack them on the bar. They work in silence, not looking at each other.

Malik brings Lorinda's energy bars down, adding them to the pile. He's followed by a grim-faced Everett. "Nothing in the pod," he says.

"You sure?" Hannah asks, dismayed.

He shakes his head. "Not a damn thing. And there's *supposed* to be. Emergency rations, MREs, stuff like that. It isn't there."

"Did you check the—"

"Storage lockers, yeah, I did. Three of 'em. Refrigeration's on but there's nothing inside."

"Shit." Jack drums his fingers on the bar, eyes passing over the suddenly very small pile of chips and chocolate bars. "What kind of tour company skips out on its pod food?"

One I should never have signed on for. Hannah digs the heel of her hand into her forehead. It's easy to figure out what happened. Either Sigma Destination Tours forgot to restock their pod, or they never bothered in the first place. After all, the *Red Panda* and its sister ships would never be more than a short distance from the station—and what inspector was going to bother coming all the way out here?

Another burst of guilt, one she can't explain. After all, *she* wasn't responsible for stocking the tour ship's escape pod. The guilt is replaced by anger. With the station intact, launching the escape pod without any food would be a minor annoyance, something a Sigma functionary might get a disciplinary hearing for. Now? It might kill everyone on board.

No. It won't come to that. The snacks will keep them going until the Frontier forces arrive, which shouldn't be more than a few hours. She does a quick count in her head, then starts pulling out chips, making a pile for each passenger, adding a JamFizz to each.

They've got enough for about two days here—three if they ration. And it's not like they're going to die of thirst, which is far more worrying than dying of hunger—there should still be plenty of water in the bathroom tanks.

Do you know that for sure? Who's to say the same person responsible for stocking the bar wasn't responsible for filling up the water supply …

Everett scratches his stubble. "Would there be any food in the cockpit, or—"

"Don't think so." Hannah pushes a pile of food and drink towards him. "Can you help take these upstairs? You and Malik?"

"Sure. Right." He and his son gather the food, making their way up the steps.

"Now what?" Jack says.

Hannah bites down on her irritation at him. It's easier now—for the first time since this whole thing started, they've got some control. Not a lot, but enough. She might not be able to stop a whole station being destroyed, but she can handle doling out soychips.

"OK," she says, putting her hands on her hips. "We could probably use some sleep. I think … yeah, there should be some blankets somewhere."

But there aren't. A search of the bar reveals a single, rigid foil blanket, sealed in plastic and stashed in the first aid kit—useful for someone with hypothermia, but not exactly helpful when you've got ten people who need beds. Hannah digs through the rest of the kit, hoping to find a second blanket, pulling out bandages and boxes of nanoplasters and a couple of packs of nanomed capsules, but there's nothing.

Hannah sighs. They'll just have to deal with it. She can ask Volkova to turn up the ship's temperature a little—the bar is freezing cold now, and she can't imagine the main deck being much better.

"Could you just do one last check upstairs?" she asks Jack.

"For blankets?"

"Maybe we'll get lucky."

"How do you not *know* where they are?"

"What do you mean?"

"You're an employee of the tour company, yes? You should know the facilities on company ships, and you should know what to do in an emergency. So do we have blankets here, or not?"

"I don't know."

"Why—"

"Because today was my first day."

He says nothing. Just stares back at her.

The hell with this. She needs to eat, and so does the captain. She's pretty sure Sigma Destination Tours doesn't exist any more, which means she's officially unemployed, and therefore not contractually obliged to be polite to passengers who aren't polite to her.

God knows what she'll tell her parents if they ever see each other again. *Yeah, sorry. I lost the job. Tour company got blown up.*

She pushes past the startled Jack, heading up the stairs. Halfway up, she turns back to him. "By the way, you might wanna clean up your puke on the main deck. It's starting to stink."

The look of disgust on his face is totally worth it. She takes the last few steps at a skip, bounding onto the upper level.

The cockpit stinks, too. It's a cramped space to begin with, and cigarette smoke has mixed with Volkova's sweat to turn the air into a swamp. The captain is bent over a control panel, peering at it, navigating through a set of menus at lightning speed. On another screen, there's a command terminal, a set of instructions written into it. The computer is repeating its message again, but, as Hannah ducks inside, it cuts off mid-sentence.

Adrift

"Ha!" Volkova slaps the panel. She spots Hannah, and flashes her a mouth of yellow teeth. "Not easy to turn off the voice, but I worked for Sigma for twelve years. I know all the tricks."

"Is that a good idea?" Hannah says. "I mean … don't we need it?"

"For what? It's a dumb computer. It's not helping."

Hannah's too exhausted to protest. And, besides, Volkova's right. The ship itself might have a voice, but it isn't a true AI. People who don't bother to stock an escape pod with emergency rations aren't going to shell out for a decent artificial intelligence.

Not that it would help them if they did. AIs had been restricted ever since the Dallas Incident—that little clusterfuck happened long before Hannah was born, but she's seen the video, and it was nasty. Even if the *Panda* had an actual AI, it would be hard-coded with heavy-duty failsafes, and wouldn't do anything without being ordered to.

Anyway, the ship's voice and personality had obviously been chosen by someone who knew they'd never have to listen to it on a daily basis. Volkova could shut it up? That was A-OK by Hannah.

The cardboard coffee cup is now almost completely full of wet cigarette butts, so she's surprised to see that there isn't one in Volkova's mouth. "I ran out," the pilot says, when she sees Hannah looking. "You have any? I'll even take a NicoStick, if you got one."

"Sorry. Don't smoke."

Volkova mutters something under her breath, but smiles when Hannah passes her the bag of chips and a JamFizz. She looks spent, like she's been wide awake for three days.

A thought occurs to Hannah—one that she should have had hours ago. "Why can't we see the gate from here?"

"What you mean?"

"The gate." Hannah points out of the cockpit viewport. "Shouldn't we be able to see if it's still there? It's not that far."

Volkova takes a slug of the soft drink. "The albedo's not good."

"Al … what?"

"Albedo. You work in space, you don't know this? It means reflectivity. The gate is two miles wide—not very big, so it doesn't give off much light. Hard to see until we're maybe a hundred miles out."

"So how do ships find it?" Another thought flickers in her mind, and her face lights up. "They must use a signal, right? Could we find it? See if the gate is still—"

"Oh, there's a signal. Or there was. I already tried to pick it up. Nothing."

"What does that mean?"

"Could mean anything. Ship transponder is crap, too. I never used it to pick up the gate signal before—no point. Or I might not have the correct frequency. Or perhaps it just fried itself. Who can say?"

Hannah sighs, defeated. *Shit.*

"You should get some sleep," she says. "I can stay up and watch for the rescue."

"*Nyet.* I am fine."

"But—"

"*Fine.* And I will sleep. Right here, and I'll turn comms up very, very loud so it will wake me if someone calls."

"Should we have ... I don't know, heard something by now?"

"Too soon," Volkova says. But there's a shadow on her face that Hannah doesn't like.

As she steps away, the ceiling speakers give a haughty bleep, followed by the *Panda*'s voice once again urging them to try all the facilities on their comfortable and spacious touring vessel. Volkova's swearing sweeps Hannah out of the cockpit.

Chapter 15

The soychips have almost zero taste, although the JamFizz is OK, colder than Hannah thought it would be. She eats sitting in the passage leading to the cabin, back against the wall.

Adrift

The other passengers are clustered in small groups around the main deck, and Hannah sees more than a few yawns. Corey and Malik are having an argument of some kind, something about the escape pod, which is wide open at the back of the deck. It's a cramped, windowless module, with a triple-decker rows of jump seats stacked on top of each other. Unlike the seats on the main deck, there are uncomfortable looking straps hanging down from the headrests. A place for emergencies, for serious short-term use only.

Hannah carefully folds up the chip packet, slotting it into the JamFizz can. Then she rests her head against the wall, and closes her eyes. Just for a second.

She knows it's a dream, but it doesn't feel like one. It's more like a memory. She's back on Titan, at her parents' house, sitting at the kitchen island. She's eating toast—made from real bread, which is one of the luxuries her mom refuses to skimp on. It's spread thick with honey, the good stuff, from the Acedalia plantations on Mars. Not too sweet, and thick as caramel.

Are you sure you've got everything you need? her mom says. She's fussing over Hannah's backpack, trying to slide a sealed box of sandwiches into a side pocket already jammed to bursting.

I'm fine, Hannah tries to say. Either she has a mouthful of toast or it's a dream where she can't speak, but no sound comes out. She doesn't much care. There's artificial sunlight from the light banks at the top of the dome, shining through the windows, dappling the counter, and Hannah can hear birds chirping somewhere. Those, at least, are real. Perfect Titan morning.

Her dad smiles. *For the last time, she's OK. They'll feed her on the shuttle. You don't need to—*

I know, her mom says, giving up on the side pocket and opening the main compartment, looking for room. On the other side of the island, Callista—ten years older than Hannah, with the very first lines of grey starting to appear in her jet-black hair—is blinking rapidly, looking at reports on her lens. Despite the fact that it's the weekend, she's dressed well, her tailored suit jacket a contrast to Hannah's grey hoodie.

Her dad is looking at her, a slight frown flicking across his face, like a cloud passing before the sun. This time, she hears herself speak. *You OK?*

Hmm? Oh, fine sweetie.

She sighs. *What is it?* She'd forgotten this part—pushed it out of her mind, more like. Why is she reliving it now? If this is a dream, can't she just skip forward or something?

He looks at her for a moment, then folds his hands on the table in front of him. Inwardly, Hannah sighs. It's the thing he does when he wants to Talk Serious. He's done it since Hannah was a kid—lately, she's even seen Callie doing it once or twice. Can't they just leave it today? Of all days?

You know we want you to be happy, he says.

Oh, come on, Dad. Not now, please.

We're just not sure you're making the right decision here.

Hannah reaches down for her duffel bag, not meeting his eyes. *We've been through this. It's the only job I could get.*

And I keep telling you that you just have to think outside the box. I know your degree wasn't in business like your sister's, but—

And you could always go work with Callie, her mom says. *You guys are hiring right now, aren't you?*

Callista's gaze switches from middle distance to close up. *What? I mean, yeah, we've got some junior positions open, if you wanted to apply or whatever.* Her eyes meet Hannah's, a sympathetic smile spreading across her face. *Not sure I could be involved though—I could make a recommendation, but it'd be nepotism if hired you, so—*

Oh, please, says Hannah's dad. *You run the place! It's your company. What you say goes.*

Callie takes a sip of her coffee. *You and Mom hire her, then.*

Um, hello? Hannah says. *Right here.*

Ah, it'd be too many politics at my place, her dad says. *Too many people.* He points at Callie. *You're still small, though. Agile. She'd slot right in. And you could teach her about marketing, right? She can learn from the best!*

Callista's smile brightens for a second, then fades. She goes back to her reports, and Hannah stares at her, wondering what happened. Where's the Callie who stayed up with her for hours flicking through boys on Red Heart? The one who had shitty taste in music and loved reading ridiculous slash fiction aloud when she was drunk? When was the last time she'd even *been* drunk?

It'd just make us a lot happier if you were doing something you could advance in. Her mom wraps her arms around her dad. *This tour guide job ... I just don't see where you'd go from there. It doesn't pay very well.*

This again. She knew it was coming—knew it from the minute her dad folded his arms. What gets her is that they think they're sugar-coating it, and it just makes it worse. She knows what they're really trying to say. *Take responsibility. Do something important.* Isn't that what she's doing? Didn't she hustle to get this gig? Admittedly, she has no idea to transition to an actual museum job, but she sure as hell isn't going to do it working for Callie's marketing startup, or in her dad's logistics company.

She bites back on the familiar anger, taking another delicate mouthful of toast, barely tasting the honey. A shrug worms its way across her shoulders.

Her dad gives her another sad smile. *We're just gonna miss you, rook*, he says.

She knows something is wrong, that he *said* something wrong, something different from the memory, but she can't figure out what. She tries to tell him that she's going to miss them, too, but suddenly she's outside the house, clambering into a cab. She's at the rear, dropping her bag into the trunk. The blowback from the hover generators is hot and dry against her bare ankles. The street is quiet, empty.

We love you! her mom shouts. Her parents are on the front porch of their gabled house, arms around each other, Callie alongside them. Her dad pushes his glasses back up his nose again. Hannah's already said her goodbyes, hugging them all tight, and she waves as she climbs into the cab. She's going to miss them, even Callie.

Please speak your destination, says the cab's automated system.

Hannah opens her mouth to tell it to take her to the shuttleport, and that's when she sees the metal sphere. It's diving out of the blue sky, heading right for the house, coming in so fast that it's nothing more than a silver blur.

She opens her mouth to shout a warning, but no sound comes out. Then the sphere hits the house and the world vanishes in a searing ball of light and Hannah is pounding the cab's windows and everything is shaking—

"Guide," says Volkova. Her voice rips Hannah from the dream. She blinks up at the pilot, and for a second she can't remember where she is, or what she's supposed to be doing. She was dreaming, she knows that, but the dream is already fading.

"Whrshm," she says. It feels like most of a tube of glue was used to stick her eyes shut, and the rest was squirted into her mouth. Has she been drinking? Then she smells smoke, and puke, and remembers.

Volkova glances towards the cockpit. "We must head to the gate. I'm taking the ship out."

"Whuh—" Hannah licks her lips, tries again. "Are the other ships here? Frontier?"

"No. So we must go to—"

"I thought the plan was to wait until they got here." She lifts her head, winces at her stiff neck.

"Too long," Volkova mutters. "And still no signal."

It takes Hannah a few seconds to work out what Volkova is saying. Her eyes fly open. "How long was I sleeping?"

"Eight hours? Nine?"

"Jesus." She pulls herself to her feet, using the wall to keep her steady. Her head is packed with lumpy cotton wool.

"No comms," Volkova says. "No signal, like I say. By now, the other ships would have come. There's nothing out there, and I don't like it. Not one tiny bit."

Hannah glances at the main deck. The Livingstones are sleeping sitting up, Corey cradled in his mom's arms, Malik resting his head on his dad's shoulder, his holocam tucked into his armpit. Brendan and Seema are lying on the floor, spooning, using their leather jackets as pillows. Lorinda is up, her back to Hannah, eating something, and Jack is sitting up with his arms folded, head tilted back. His mouth is open, his tongue just visible.

Adrift

"If there aren't any ships ..." Hannah says.

"*Da*. Maybe the gate is gone. Defences, too. If the Frontier was coming, they would be here by now. I can find the gate without signal—I know where the quadrant and sector is, and I get close enough so we can see the exact location."

"Really?"

Volkova scratches the side of her neck. "Increasing acceleration on three thrusters, with gravitational forces ... I think, maybe ... It will take maybe two hours, two and a half."

Hannah rolls her neck. Getting her thoughts in order is like trying to grab slivers of soap in a hot shower. The gate might have been destroyed after the ship travelled through it, one of the metal spheres set to detonate post-jump. On the other hand, the ship might be hanging around the gate, destroying any Frontier vessels that came through.

Could it really do that? No, it'd be too risky, surely, even for something that well-equipped. Sooner or later, the Frontier would figure out what's happening, and they'd send something too fast or too well-armoured for the other ship to handle.

Still ...

As if drawn by a strong magnet, she looks up through the viewport again. A large chunk of debris is just drifting past the *Panda*—a ripped, shredded metal plate the size of a big car, scorch marks crossing it like tiger stripes. There's still enough surface undamaged for the metal to be slightly reflective. The reflection is soft and distorted, but the *Panda* itself is visible on the plate's surface, suspended in an ocean of black. The metal drifts a little further, and the reflection vanishes.

Hannah feels the familiar dread lighting up in the pit of her stomach. The problem is, they just don't know what's out there. After the attack, they could afford to wait for rescue. But Volkova's right—it's been far too long. They're already digging into their food supplies.

"Let me talk to the passengers," she says.

Chapter 16

Corey's mom is strangling him.

She's not doing it on purpose. He fell asleep nuzzled into her, and, as she drifted off, her arm tightened around his neck. He wakes up with his throat buried in the crook of her elbow, her head pressing into the back of his.

He really doesn't want Malik to see, which is stupid, because he was snuggling up to his mom before when his brother was awake. Doesn't matter; he needs to squeeze out, or his mom is going to do to him what the smoke didn't.

He tries to slip through, but his chin catches on her arm. He twists his head sideways, doing it gently so he doesn't wake her, but she responds by pulling tighter. And now his mouth is smushed into her arm. Great.

Anita Livingstone sighs with sleepy pleasure.

"Mom, get off me," he says, only it comes out as "Mmgeroffee," the words muffled by the fabric. She doesn't move, so he tries to winkle one of his hands into the space between his throat and her arm. That just makes it worse. Not only does it not help, but now his hand is trapped as well.

OK, now he *really* needs to breathe. He taps his mom on the leg. When nothing happens, he grabs hold and shakes her. Still nothing. Is she unconscious? How can she not—

"What's that you're eating?" someone says.

Anita Livingstone jerks awake, and Corey wrenches himself free, sucking in a huge gulp of air. His dad and brother are coming awake, too, blinking in the low light.

The question came from Seema O'Hara. She's up on one elbow, looking at Lorinda, who is slowly turning around to face her.

The *Red Panda*'s main deck is a mess. There was a half-hearted attempt to keep the floor clear of chip packets, but over the past few hours they've drifted all over the place. The packaging from Lorinda's Reptar figure lies dead centre, the plastic ripped open. The deck still stinks, with a thin curl of body odour sneaking into the mix, and the viewing dome is dirtier than it was before, the glass smudged.

"I didn't know anyone else was awake," Lorinda says to Seema.

Seema points. "You can't just take when you're hungry, yeah?"

Corey looks down at Lorinda's hands, where there's a chocolate bar still half in its wrapper. His own stomach wakes up, growling in protest.

"This?" Lorinda waggles the bar. "It's for my teeth."

"Doesn't matter. Should've gone with the rest of the food. You can't just keep stuff for yourself."

Lorinda's eyes narrow. "Like I said, it's for my teeth. It's a dental health bar." She looks down at it, frowning. "Tastes pretty crappy, to be honest. I only eat it because my dentist says—"

"So?" says Brendan. He's awake, too, sitting up, his eyes slightly bleary with sleep. Jack snaps awake, blinking hard and looking around him.

"Oh, for God's sake." Lorinda holds out the bar. "You want it? Take it."

"That's not what I—"

"No, go on. I insist. I only had about two bites. Still plenty for you."

The body heat from Corey's mom kept him warm, holding off the chill air in the main deck. Now that he's away from her, he's freezing. Should it be this cold? What if the primary heat exchangers—

"Hey, team." His dad appears in front of them, squatting on his haunches. He nearly squashes Anita's tote bag as he does so, has to manoeuvre it out of the way. "How're we all doing?"

"I'm OK," Corey says. It's a lie. He'd do anything right now for a shower, and his mouth feels like a cat took a shit in it. But he's learned that whenever his dad asks how *we* are doing, it's best just to say that he's totally fine.

He's also *really* hungry. He'll have to grab another pack of soychips, even though he doesn't really feel like soychips. What he feels like is a big, juicy hamburger, with lots of gooey cheese and a slice of pickle. And real meat. Definitely real meat this time.

"You sure?" says his dad.

"I don't want your chocolate," Seema is saying. "I just mean you should have told us about it."

"He's right," says Jack.

Corey licks his lips. "I'm gonna get some water, actually."

"Good idea," says his dad. "I'll come with you."

"Hold on," Anita says. "We need to talk about what just happened."

"Aw, *come on*, Mom."

"No," she says, spreading her fingers across her knees. "We're going to talk about it, and we're going to do it as a family."

"'Nita, can't this wait?" Everett puts a hand on his wife's, but she pulls away, index finger raised.

"Corey, honey, you could have got hurt. Or stuck in there."

"If I hadn't been there, the engines woulda burned up!"

Behind him, Jack is on his feet, staring down at Lorinda with his hands on his hips. She returns the look, holding the chocolate bar like a weapon.

Anita continues as if Corey hadn't spoken. "I told you to stay up here. I'm just ... I'm disappointed you didn't listen to me."

"What about Malik?" Corey says. "He went down there before I did. Why don't you wake *him* up and shout at him?"

"Hey," says his dad. "You don't talk to your mother like that, you hear?"

Anita gives him a surprised look, followed by a terse nod. "Exactly. Thank you. I'll be speaking to your brother when he wakes up, and he's in *just* as much trouble as you are. You need to think about others, not just yourself. We've talked about this before."

Corey stares at his mom and dad. They've both gone crazy. They're acting like he flunked a test at school, or stayed out at Jamie's place for too long, or finished the last bag of pretzels in the snack cupboard. Don't they get it? Don't they understand the situation they're all in?

His mom's job is all about talking to people—Corey remembers listening once, fascinated, as she told him what she did at work during a long shuttle ride up to Washington (Mal, of course, hadn't been listening—he'd been filming the cabin, occasionally pointing his camera out of the window to capture the curve of the Earth).

She'd told him about the Senate, and about meetings with the President-elect, and about getting people "on-side." She kept using a word: compromise. He had to ask her what it meant, and was secretly proud when he realised his mom made people agree with her for a living. It felt like a superpower.

But, of course, every superpower had its downside. Whenever Corey does something wrong, his mom always wants to talk it out, sit down and very calmly explain why he messed up and what he should do about it. His dad doesn't even try to stop her. How could he? Fusion reactors don't talk back, so he usually lets Corey's mom take the lead, fading into the background. Which she's probably OK with.

In a way, it would be better if they yelled and screamed at him. It wouldn't last as long, and at least they'd be doing it together. And don't they get it? He's fine. Yeah, the fire thing was scary, but he got out. Just like they'll get out of this, when the Frontier's Scorpion fighters arrive.

Anita pushes a stray hair out of her face. "Corey, you have to understand ... that was scary for both of us." A quick look at her husband. "We didn't want you anywhere near that fire."

"What your mom is saying—" his dad begins, and then the chocolate bar smacks him in the back of the head.

Lorinda has her hands to her mouth, staring at him in horror. "*Dios mio*, I'm so sorry."

Everett rubs his head, more surprised than angry. Anita reaches out for the chocolate bar, but Corey gets there first, scooping it off the floor, desperate to get away from this conversation. He walks over to Lorinda, handing her the bar. Behind him, he hears Malik awake with a start.

"Thank you, dear," Lorinda says. "At least someone on this ship has some manners."

Jack steps forward, hand out. "Give me the damn bar."

This time Lorinda's aim is true, and the chocolate smacks off Jack's chest. "Take it," she says. "Hope you break a tooth."

Seema's eyes flash. "You need to just—"

"OK, everyone?" says Hannah. Corey jumps, as do most of the

others—they didn't see her come up. She looks tired, but focused, her arms folded over her red T-shirt, hands cupping her elbows.

No one says anything. They don't even look at each other. To Corey, it feels like they've all been caught by a teacher doing something bad. Which is weird, because the last thing he can see Hannah doing is standing in front of a class of kids. She'd get eaten alive.

His throat is screaming for water. He tries to slip around the back of the plastic seats, thinking he can head down to the bathroom, but his dad stops him with an outstretched arm. "How're we looking up there?" he asks Hannah.

She doesn't respond immediately. Instead, she perches on the edge of one of the chairs, pushing aside an empty soychip packet, then rubbing her exposed arms.

"We think …" She stops, tries again. "At least, the captain thinks we need to head to the gate."

Brendan frowns. "I'm sorry?"

"I thought the whole point was that we were waiting for help," says Seema.

"We're not so sure help is coming any more," Hannah says. Talking quickly, she lays out the conversation she had with the captain.

"That's ridiculous," says Jack. "Just because we haven't heard from them doesn't mean they aren't there. Maybe we just need to boost our receiver range."

"Won't work," Corey says. They all turn to look at him, and he shrugs. "Maverick ships have a pretty basic comms system. You can't really make it stronger."

"How do you even *know* that?" Jack says.

"What about plugging it directly into a power source?" Seema asks. "The comms system, I mean. Would it boost the range if we gave it more juice?"

Corey scrunches up his face. "It'll fry it."

"Maybe they just don't know we're here," Anita says. "Shouldn't we be sending a distress call of our own? Even if it's a weak one?"

"Good idea," Brendan says. "Let's just let that nice Colony ship know we survived the hotel blowing up."

"I'm just saying we should keep our options open."

Adrift

"We're going to vote," Hannah says. "Same deal. All those in favour of heading to the gate, raise your hand."

"Again?" Jack says. "Great. Why not just redecide everything after a few hours? Why stop here?"

Hannah glares at him. "The situation's changed."

"No, it hasn't," Seema says. "We're still in exactly the same place we were in ten hours ago."

"There's new information. So we—"

"Wait a minute," Everett says. "We head on out, make our way to the gate, assuming it's still there. Then what? We try to jump through? Will this ship even make it?"

"And what if the other guys find us?" Malik says.

Hannah takes a breath, tries to speak slowly and calmly. "We've got enough for a couple days, but probably no more than that, even if we ration it. We could stay here, for sure, but if nobody comes we might be in trouble. We take a risk now, maybe we never *have* to run out of food. And at least this way we'd know for sure about the gate."

"Well," says Brendan, clapping his hands together. "Sounds like you and the captain have decided. Why even bother voting?"

Hannah meets his eyes. "Because this affects everyone. We're going to do it right." She lifts her hand. "I vote we make a move, and so does the captain. Anyone else?"

Nobody moves. Then, slowly, Lorinda puts her hand up. Corey follows.

The rest of the Livingstones look at each other. Everett raises his hand. Anita and Malik don't.

Come on. Please. Corey tries to catch their eyes, willing them to actually do the smart thing for once. At least when they were mad at him, they were agreeing on something. Now it's like that never happened.

Hannah looks around, dismayed. She clears her throat. "And … and all in favour of staying?"

"'Nita?" Everett looks at his wife expectantly, his hand hovering.

Slowly, Anita Livingstone raises her hand. Malik, too, after a sideways glance at Jack. Corey closes his eyes, his hands balled into fists.

"Well, that's that," says Jack, raising his hand and immediately letting it drop. Then he notices that Brendan and Seema haven't raised their hands. In fact, they're not even looking at him. They're arguing, heads bent together, whispering to each other. Corey can't hear what they're saying.

"Hello?" Jack says.

Seema holds up a finger—*not now*—and hisses something at Brendan.

He stares for a second, mouth open as if to respond, then his mouth snaps shut. He gives her a terse nod.

"I vote we leave," says Seema, giving her hand a little flick upwards.

"Really?" says Jack.

Brendan lifts a metal finger. "Sorry, chap. We're a package deal."

"They're not coming," says Seema. "We need to go to them."

"So it's settled," Hannah says, getting to her feet. "I'll tell the captain we can head out."

"How long before we get to the gate?" Everett asks.

Hannah flashes her smile. "Your travel time today will be approximately four hours," she says, putting on a ditzy Southern accent. "Just sit back, relax, and *enjoy* the flight."

Dead silence greets her words. Lorinda manages a weak smile. Hannah turns, red flush spreading across her cheeks, and vanishes into the cockpit passage.

"So what now?" Seema says.

"What do you mean, *what now*?" Jack says. "You just voted. That's what now."

Seema tilts her head, an amused smile flashing across her face. Jack meets her gaze for a moment, then shakes his head. "Whatever. I'm gonna see if there's any coffee we missed in the bar."

Seema's eyes brighten. "God, yes. I could murder a coffee."

"Don't get your hopes up. Worth looking, though."

She, Jack and Brendan head back downstairs, talking in low voices.

Corey's family are doing what they usually do. His brother is back on his holocam, head down, and his parents are having another argument. *Can't they just be nice to each other? Just for a little bit?*

The dental health bar is still lying on the floor. He picks it up and hands it to Lorinda.

"Thank you, dear," the old woman says. "Think I've lost my appetite, though. Do you want it? Or your mom maybe?" She grins. "Keeps your gnashers nice and healthy."

"I'm good," Corey says. "Hey, ma'am, about earlier, I'm really, *really* sorry. I didn't mean ..."

He trails off. Lorinda looks away for a moment then back at him. "It's all right. Just promise me you won't do something like that again. Not sure you'll be that lucky twice in a row. And don't call me ma'am, please, dear. Makes me feel ancient."

"You got it. Sure thing."

"And listen ..." she beckons him closer, then points to his mom and dad. "You watch out for them, OK? Even if they don't get along. They're going to need you and your brother both before this is all over."

Corey nods. Below them, the *Red Panda*'s remaining thrusters fire up, and outside the viewing dome the remains of the Sigma Station begin to move further away.

Chapter 17

There's no coffee in the bar. Of course there isn't. Jack doesn't bother to spend more than a few seconds looking. He pours himself another JamFizz instead, takes a sip, grimaces. The bottom level of the *Panda* has got cold, cold enough that he can just see his breath, but, unbelievably, the sugary soda is still warm.

Oh, who gives a shit? Jack drains it as fast as possible, then makes his way over to the table where Brendan and Seema are sitting. He feels stoned—as if the events of the past day were a weird hallucination, but at least he feels better than he did when he woke up. Jerking out of sleep to find he was still on this goddamn ship, the dull, leaden feeling in his stomach as he realised where he was, felt like God herself was shitting on him.

He's hungry again, the damn soychips long since digested. Water isn't going to be a problem, even if they run out of JamFizz, but the Frontier better hurry the hell up all the same. What he wouldn't give for a steak sandwich—real Europan steak, not the stringy excuse for one he was served on the station—and a cold beer, so cold that the glass almost hurt to wrap your fingers around.

As he steps out from behind the bar, he sees Malik Livingstone coming down the stairs, gripping that old hand-held camera. Why does the kid even have one? The parents didn't seem like the type of people who ban their children from using lenses.

Malik starts when he notices them, as if he genuinely wasn't expecting them to be there. "Hey, I, um ... can I get something to drink?"

"Sure," says Jack, at the same time as Brendan says, "Yeah, of course."

Malik steps past Jack. He carefully puts the holocam down on the bar, face up, then vanishes behind the counter. A moment later, they hear the click of a JamFizz can being opened.

"Would you guys mind if I shot some footage of the bar?" he says, still out of sight. "Just like a five-second sweep?"

"Uh ... OK," Jack says.

Malik pops up, smiles. "Awesome. Thanks. Just stay where you are and act natural. Do what you were doing before."

They sit and stand in awkward silence as he raises his camera, sweeping it horizontally across the room. Jack shifts, realising that he needs to piss. It seems strange, having such a basic urge at a time like this.

The sweep takes about fifteen seconds, not five, and Malik seems to realise it. When he reaches the end, he quickly lowers the camera. "Done," he says, a little too loudly.

"You get anything good?" Brendan says. It's a throwaway question, asked automatically, so Jack is a little surprised when Malik gives a very serious nod.

"Yeah, absolutely," he says. "I've pretty much been filming since we got here. I think I got most of the … what happened to the station, too."

Above them, the *Panda* speaks. "Passenger! Thank you for documenting your adventure. Did you know you can upload your own images and video to the Frontier Public History Archives? Share your trip with other travellers, and become part of history as you—"

"Jesus," Jack mutters.

"—navigate the galaxy. Please enjoy the rest of your journey on this Sigma Destination Tours vessel."

None of them say anything, and the ship's voice falls silent.

Seema makes a small, guttural sound, like she's swallowed a tiny bone. "I am so sick of that thing."

Malik doesn't appear to hear her, and doesn't seem bothered by the AI's interruption. He flashes them another quick smile, then heads for the stairs. Halfway there, he stops, turns back. "Can I ask you guys something?"

Brendan shrugs.

"Well, it's just that …" He lifts the camera, as if about to start shooting again, then lets it drop. "How do we know the ship that attacked us isn't still out there?"

"We don't." Jack looks pointedly at Brendan and Seema. "Which is why it would have been smarter to stay."

"That's kind of what I thought, too." Malik toes the raised edge of a floor panel. "I know we have to vote on stuff, but if we get blown up, nobody'll ever know what happened to us. I mean, they'll probably figure out about the station and everything, but they won't know about what happened *after*. With hiding in the hotel and the fire and everything. They'll just never know."

"What's her name?" Brendan says.

Malik looks up. "Huh?"

"Your girlfriend. Or is he a boy?" He sees the expressions on Jack and Seema's faces, and actually laughs. "Come on, now. You can't seriously tell me that was difficult to work out." He turns back to Malik, eyebrows raised expectantly.

After a moment where Malik looks like he wants a black hole to appear and swallow him whole, he says, "Shanti."

"Shanti." Brendan says the name as if tasting it. "Lovely. This a girl at school?"

"Yeah." They can barely hear him. "Grade below me."

"How long have you been together?"

"She's not my girlfriend," Malik says quickly. "Well, she might be. We kissed once. I don't know, I just ... I don't want her to not know what happened."

To Jack's surprise, Brendan stands, the servos in his arm whirring as he walks over and puts a hand on Malik's shoulder.

"Everybody's going to know what happened," Brendan tells him. "Want to know what I think? We keep saying it's rotten luck, and from a certain view, yeah, it is. But we made it out of there. I'd say that makes us more lucky than not. I think our luck's going to hold, and then the cavalry's gonna get here, and that'll be that. You'll be back home with your Shanti before you know it."

He says the words to Malik, but it's impossible for Jack to miss who he's really talking to. Seema is sitting very still, hands folded in her lap, face expressionless.

Brendan grips both Malik's shoulders. "And do yourself a favour, son. Just ask her. That was the mistake I made with Seema—took a bloody age before I worked up the courage to ask her to marry me. And she has the world's scariest mother—thought about defecting to the Colonies a couple of times, just so I wouldn't have to have her at the wedding."

"Oh, please," Seema says.

Malik is nodding, a smile sneaking onto his face, despite his exhaustion. Watching him, Jack feels oddly useless. Then again, he's never been good with kids—something Brendan and Seema obviously don't have a problem with.

"So that's who you've been filming for?" Brendan says. "This Shanti person?"

Malik shakes his head. "Nah. She's not really into that too much. It's all going in my show reel. I need a good one if I want to get into TFA. That's the Titan Film Academy. It's the best in all the Frontier systems."

"Is that right?" Brendan says. Malik nods again, and Jack gets the oddest thought: they're all talking like their lives are just going to pick up where they left off. The kid's still putting together his show reel for college. The old woman's chewing on that bar for her teeth.

Well, why shouldn't they? After all, there's no way the Frontier hasn't noticed the sudden lack of activity from Sigma. They'll be here soon. It's only been ten hours. Everyone's overreacting.

"Keep shooting," he says to Malik. "We might need it before this is all over."

The boy's expression suddenly changes to one of horror. "Please don't tell my mom and dad about Shanti. Or Corey. Mom would freak if she knew. She thinks I'm too young for—"

"Not a word," says Brendan, smiling. "On our honour."

Malik looks relieved. "Corey especially. He sort of does things without thinking. I remember this one time? One of my friends was sick in hospital with grey lung—I don't know if you know it, but—"

"We know." Seema's smile is tight.

"All from Earth here," Jack gestures to the three of them.

"Right, right. I mean, they can cure it now, so he got better. But, like, when he was coming home from the hospital, a bunch of us wanted to throw this surprise welcome back party at his place. Corey somehow got involved, and he got so excited he ended up telling people at school, so by the time Ajay came home it was like, oh, yeah, thanks, guys."

"I get it," Brendan says. "We won't tell about your girl."

Malik flashes them a hesitant thumbs up, and jogs up the stairs.

Jack waits a moment, then crosses to the bar. He tries to pull a chair closer with his foot, forgetting for a moment that they're bolted to the floor, and nearly topples over. Brendan snorts.

"Glad I amuse you," Jack says, as he sits down.

"Well, someone has to." Brendan shivers, sending a short *brr* through his lips. "Poor bloody kid."

Seema gives him a baleful look. She has her hands between her legs, her jacket collar pulled up. Jack still hasn't fully forgiven her for voting against him, but it's hard to muster any enthusiasm for the feeling.

"So, no coffee," Brendan says. "Let's go up. It's freezing down here."

"Hang on." Seema leans forward, steepling her fingers, resting her elbows on the table. "We never got to finish talking before. About what's happening."

They both give her blank looks.

"About us being the only surviving ship."

"This again." Brendan sounds defeated, and he gives Jack a knowing look.

"Don't do that." Seema's voice is very quiet.

"Do what?"

"Treat me like that. Like I'm crazy. You always do."

"Babe, I'm not saying that."

"Then what are you saying?"

"Enough." Jack rubs his face, digging his fingers into the bony ridge above his eyes. "All right?"

"And you." Seema's voice is still very low, but there's no mistaking the wounded look on her face. She leans forward, tapping the table, very gently. As if this was a committee meeting, with minutes and an agenda. "You're just going to accept what's happening here. Is that it?"

"I'm not accep—" He realises he's almost shouting, and has to pull himself back. "What do you want me to do here?"

"I want you to pull your head out your arse. This whole situation stinks, and you just want to sit there and pretend you don't smell it. Well, not me. I'm getting back to my boy, and if you aren't going to help me, you can fuck off. Yeah?"

Her husband speaks gently. "We're not leaving Marcus. You're his mum, and I'm his dad, and that's that. But, Seems, I don't see a conspiracy here. I really don't, and keeping on at this isn't helping."

But there's something in his eyes. Not disbelief exactly, more like eagerness. It reminds Jack of how Seema looked before, when he used the word *miracle*.

Seema takes a deep breath. "OK," she says, giving Brendan a slow nod. "OK. But I still don't think we're being told the full story."

Jack's stomach growls again. "How do you mean?"

"We've spent this whole time reacting. The attack, the fire, everything. We need to take the initiative."

"Seems ..."

"No. Listen. Have either of you actually spoken to the pilot? Or seen her?"

"Yeah," Jack says. "During the attack, I went to the cockpit. She was there."

"For what, like five seconds? None of us have seen her since, or been in there. We've just trusted that she knows what she's doing, and that we'll just follow behind like good little soldiers."

"What about the votes?" Brendan says. But he sounds less sure, glancing at Jack as if looking for support.

Seema gives him a tired smile. "You really think the pilot cares? She thought we were wrong, she'd just do what she wanted anyway, and none of us could stop her. And I'm tired of the middleman shit, with the guide going back and forth. We need to be in that cockpit. We need to know what the pilot knows. Use your brain, babe."

"I *am*." There's no mistaking the annoyance in Brendan's voice.

"Your gut then. Or if you can't do that, then trust mine. Pooka, remember that commission we got offered on Mars?" She glances at Jack. "Business guy in Acedalia wanted a triptych—that's three pieces of related—"

"I know what a triptych is. What's your point?"

"It didn't feel right. I walked into his office, and I just ... *knew*."

"Cushla, that was different, though," says Brendan.

"Yeah? How? If I'd taken that job, it'd be months of work down the drain, and we'd have ended up with nothing. Why do you think they shut him down like two months later?"

As Jack looks between them, a memory of Hector surfaces. They'd been on the rooftop of Hec's place in São Paulo, shirts off, backs sticky with sweat in the late afternoon sun. A bucket of Antarctica Cerveja, the ice long melted. Hec was showing off, demonstrating something they taught him in police training.

Jack had protested that he didn't need to know it; plenty of criminals hung out at luxury hotels and resort spas, but they weren't the kind that usually needed to be aggressively disarmed. "Don't matter," Hector had told him in that gorgeous accent of his. "You gonna come to São Paulo, you gotta be prepared."

That was the thing with Hector. Sometimes, he just got an idea into his head that he couldn't let go of. This was one of them. So he'd insisted on showing Jack how to disarm someone holding a gun: walk slowly towards the attacker, hands raised. Then, when you were close enough, bring your hands inward, like you were going to clap them together. Strike the inside of the wrist, and the back of the hand, moving your head quickly to the side. "It'll go off, probably," Hector had said. "But it'll go flying, too."

Jack doesn't really remember the technique. He'd been concentrating on Hec's body. Afterwards, with the sun still baking down, he'd given it even more of his attention. The memory is so vivid, so bright, that he can almost feel the sun on his back as Hector's fingernails dug channels in his skin.

He shakes himself off. He might miss Hec, but he doesn't miss that annoying, irrational, single-minded focus. He doesn't miss Hec's obsessions—which you couldn't even really call obsessions, because they kept changing. Things that *had* to be done, *had* to be taken care of, right that instant. It was what made him a good cop.

Seema reminds him a little bit of Hector. And not in a good way. She isn't acting rationally. She's momma bear separated from her cub, and she's lashing out, desperate to remove the threat. He doesn't need that right now. Hec can't help them. Seema and Brendan might be the only people on this ship he could conceivably talk to without wanting to pour bleach into his ears, but that'll change if she doesn't can her bullshit.

He rises off his chair. "I gotta use the head."

"The head?" Seema says.

"Yeah. The washroom." He gives her a very pointed look. "Assuming that's all right with you?"

She rolls her eyes, but says nothing.

There's a unisex symbol on the door of the bathroom, which is squeezed under the stairs. It's such a narrow space that Jack has to turn sideways to make his way in. There's a toilet, a tiny basin, a miniature bottle of dry foam sanitiser. An opening next to the sink has a little scruff of paper towel protruding from it. There's no mirror, but the wall above the toilet is covered in yellow warning labels, informing the user that anyone who smokes in the bathroom will be subject to a fine of twenty thousand universal dollars or a prison sentence of five years—or both. *Good to know.*

The bar is cold, but this little room is absolutely freezing. His breath forms white clouds, and when he unzips himself the feel of the cold air on bare skin nearly makes him gasp.

The sound of his piss hitting the toilet's plastic surface is dull, muted. In the quiet, he can hear the hull of the ship creaking and groaning, just audible over the hum of the engines.

You're just going to accept what's happening here. Is that it?

It's a miracle.

He looks down, dismayed to find that his free hand has twisted the hem of his shirt into a tight knot. He lets go like it's burned him, slaps the sink. Again. The cheap metal surface flexes, threatens to dent.

What a useless piece of shit this ship is. Useless, cheap, lowest-common-denominator junk. If they get out of this—no, *when*, not *if*—he's going to have a word with one of the business reporters at the feed. There's no way a company with standards this low is fully legal. It's a shady outfit, run by cost-cutting shitheads, and he'll be very happy to bring it down. Starting with the two idiots in charge of this ship.

And then, he's going to have a beer. Ice-cold, in a very large glass. For a second, he can actually taste it, feel the froth crisping against his lips.

He looks at the wall with the warning labels, which is just reflective enough to show a distorted version of himself. "Stop it," he says, his voice no more than a growl.

He takes what must be the quickest piss in his life, zipping up so fast that he nearly catches his dick in the ice-cold metal. The toilet is chemical, the thick pink liquid draining quickly, with hardly a murmur.

When he turns the tap above the basin, there's a long, agonised metal groan from the ceiling above him, and a distinct lack of water. He frowns, turning the tap as far as it'll go. A single drop of water sneaks out of the opening, clinging to the edge of the tap. Nothing else.

"Guys?" Jack says.

Chapter 18

Hannah is no stranger to space travel. She's done short-range hops plenty of times: with her parents, class field trips, even a weekend on Io's artificial beaches during spring break. She knows that stars don't appear to move when you do. It doesn't stop her staring at the white pinpricks outside the *Red Panda*'s cockpit viewport, sick with worry.

They've moved away from the debris field now—there are only a few pieces around them, winking against the black. Hannah had been looking forward to this, hoping that it would calm her nerves. It hasn't. If anything, the empty blackness outside has made things worse. The Nebula is behind them now, with only a faint wisp visible on one edge of the cockpit glass.

A light year is a distance of around six trillion miles. It's a meaningless number, utterly incomprehensible. The stars outside the viewport might already be dead—turned into huge supernovae, extinguishing themselves, a fact which nobody would even realise until they'd already been gone for thousands of years. The idea of those stars being gone—of there being nothing but blackness ahead of them—is horrifying.

Against distances like those, they may as well be standing still.

"Few hours," Volkova says, muttering to herself. "Then we'll see. Guide, pass the bottle, please."

"Huh?"

"The bottle. By the aux thruster control there."

The vodka bottle is two-thirds empty, nestling up against the control panel. Hannah looks at Volkova, taking in her dishevelled hair and bleary eyes. "Is that a good idea?"

"What do you mean? Vodka is always a good idea. Come, give."

"What if the other ship comes back?"

"If the other ship comes back, we're all dead. And in my old squadron, I took an oath never to die sober."

Hannah half laughs. "Right. Your old squadron. They win Victory Stars, too?"

"Exactly. Yes. Now, *please*."

She holds her hand out for the bottle. Hannah wavers for a second, and then she puts the bottle to her own lips, tilting her head back to take a slug of booze.

She's never been a big drinker—beer mostly, with the odd badly mixed cocktail. She's had vodka once or twice, but it wasn't nearly as good as this stuff. The first taste is like hot cinnamon, and it's so good that all she wants to do is go on drinking. Then she's hit by an alcohol burn so intense that it makes her cough, spraying droplets of vodka across the control panel.

She expects Volkova to shout at her, but, instead, the pilot laughs. "Good, yes. Now please, for the love of God, *give*."

Volkova drinks deep, swallowing the vodka with no more difficulty than if it were a glass of water. Hannah can feel a buzz building behind her eyeballs, and it makes it a little easier for her to deal with the idea that the Colony ship could appear at any second.

Up until now, the thought has been like a splinter on the ball of her thumb, one she can't dislodge. It's why she's hanging out in this cockpit, with its stench of cigarette smoke and sweat. It's easier to ignore the thoughts here, where Volkova is in charge, and it's *definitely* easier to ignore them after a shot of vodka.

Volkova passes the bottle back. Hannah almost says no, then changes her mind. The second hit goes down a lot easier, and tastes just as good. No more, though—this stuff is lethal. She can take almost throwing up in the cockpit once—doing it twice might be a little rude.

"What do you think we'll find?" she says. "When we get to the gate?"

"Depends. Maybe the defence system is still active, in which case it can protect us. Even if it is destroyed, maybe the gate is still there, and our Colony ship is just shooting anyone who comes through. If that happens, we go far away as possible, wait for someone to send a ship too big to destroy. If not ..."

Volkova shrugs, then notices the expression on Hannah's face. "Sorry. I know it's a bad situation."

"It's OK. I just ... I keep thinking about what I was going to do. You know, when I got another job."

"You don't want to be a tour guide?"

"Yes. I mean ... I did, but it was just a first job. It wasn't the only thing I wanted to do. I thought I could find another gig when I was out here, if I didn't like being a guide."

"*Da?*" Volkova says, in the tone of someone who isn't really interested. "Then what?"

"I figured I'd get a job at a museum. You can't really get one without experience, but I thought, you know, if I came out here first ..."

She trails off. Suddenly, she's sick of that lie, a story she told her parents and her friends when they asked what her plans were. In reality, this was the only job she could get, and she had absolutely no idea how human resources at the Martian Museum of Natural History would view a stint as a guide for the world's cheapest tour company.

"What about you?" she says. "If this hadn't happened, what would you be doing?"

The captain doesn't answer. Not surprising—it's a ridiculous question. *What would she be doing? What do you think she'd be doing? She's been flying for Sigma Tours for twelve years. She'd be right here, in this seat, taking passengers around the station like always.*

After a few moments, Volkova says, "Passengers OK?"

"What? Oh, yeah, fine."

"Maybe you should go check. See if they need any help. Anyway, I have work to do. Can't just talk all day."

"Uh ... OK?" Hannah puts the bottle down. What is Volkova talking about? The passengers don't need her help—and it's not like there's anything to do right—

Adrift

But Volkova's shoulders are way too tight, and she's gripping the controls like they're about to escape. Of course. When your working life is spent entirely by yourself in a cockpit, it must be pretty jarring for someone to suddenly be in there with you all the time—especially when it's not built for two people to begin with, and there's no emergency to deal with. This is Volkova's space, and Hannah's set up camp in it. Set up camp and started drinking the supplies.

She smiles—something made easier by the vodka, which has set the inside of her cheeks alight. "You got it. See you in a bit."

"*Da*. Thank you."

Anita and Lorinda are the only people on the main deck. The old woman has her eyes closed, head resting on a jacket, while Anita is doing something on her lens. Hannah stops at the top of the stairs. "Where are the boys?" she says, hoping that the cheerful note in her voice doesn't sound too forced.

"What?" Anita looks over to her, blinking. "Oh. They went downstairs."

"OK. Thanks." Hannah tries to think of something else to say, but can't. She turns to go; she should probably make sure Jack isn't trying to chisel his way through the airlock door or something. Then, she stops.

"Um, can I just ..." she closes her eyes briefly, wondering how to phrase it.

Anita glances up. "Yes?"

Screw it. Hannah pushes herself off the railing, folding her arms. "You said you worked for a senator?"

"Tom Daniels, that's right."

"OK. Yeah. That's what I thought. Because I just ... I mean I wanted to ask ... do you really think negotiating the Belarus Treaty was the right idea?"

Anita sighs, very quietly. "As a matter of fact, I do."

"I don't get why you'd want that? Haven't we taken enough from the Colonies? They already pretty much lost the war."

"Well, it might stop their ships attacking us, for one thing." There's an edge to Anita's voice now, one that wasn't there before. Behind her, a puzzled Lorinda looks back and forth between them.

"But that's all the Frontier Senate does. Take and take and take. I just … I'm trying to understand, like, how could you be comfortable with that happening. How can you rationalise—"

"Rationalise?" Anita folds her hands in her lap. "I don't have to rationalise anything. We thought the treaty swung a little too far in favour of the Colonies the first time round, so we went back to the negotiating table. That's how it works."

"You can't just change things when you get bored with them."

"You make it sound like we snapped our fingers and rewrote the whole thing. It's taken *two years* of back and forth. Committees. Subcommittees. Diplomatic back-channels." To Hannah, her laugh sounds cold. "And in the end? Everybody got what they wanted. They got increased aid packages and lifted sanctions, and we got them to give us a few outlying worlds, and agree to a reduction in their military spending. Seems to me—" she fixes Hannah with a pointed look "—that might be a pretty good idea."

"Yeah—those outlying worlds?" Hannah leans on the words. "You're just going to mine them for helium-3. What about the people living there? Do they get a say?"

"We've got a full relocation package ready for them. We're even offering them Frontier citizenship, if they want it." She sighs. "I know there are parts of the treaty that might be … controversial, but it's about keeping the Frontier safe."

"Oh, *come on.*"

Anita's smile is as chilly as the main deck itself. "You don't have kids, do you?"

Hannah is about to respond when there's a noise behind her. She turns to see Everett coming up the stairs. "Hey. Do you know what's up with the water?" he says.

Her retort to Anita is still on the tip of her tongue, and she has to force herself to focus. "What do you mean?"

"We're only getting a little bit out of the tap."

Anita has returned to her lens, blinking her way through documents, and it makes her feel a little silly. Hannah blinks. What is she doing, arguing about politics? Now? How much vodka did she *have*?

She follows Everett down into the bar. Brendan, Seema and

Jack are huddled together at the far side, arguing about something. Hannah doesn't bother to ask what their problem is, heading straight for the bathroom. It's only when she's halfway there that she realises the temperature in the bar has dropped even further. It's *freezing* in here.

There's a panel above the flimsy bathroom door, perhaps two feet square, with a recessed handle. Hannah stands on tiptoes, gritting her teeth as she touches it, the icy metal biting into her skin. It takes a few seconds of futile pulling before she realises she has to lift the handle up and out. When she does so, the panel swings to the side so suddenly that she almost topples back. The slight buzz she got from the vodka ramps up, threatening to make her lose her balance entirely.

The water tank itself is the size of a large upended bathtub, multiple pipes leading off it. She can just see its bottom half through the open panel. She grasps the edge of the opening, and uses it to pull herself up so she can put a hand on the plastic surface. It's ice-cold, too, and when she raps on it with her knuckles, the noise sounds wrong. Like there's not enough air inside.

There's a valve on one of the lower pipes. She tries it without much hope—even if she gets it off, she won't be able to see inside the tank itself. Nothing. It's stuck fast.

"See anything?"

The voice makes Hannah jump. It's Everett, standing behind her, and she can hear more footsteps coming down the stairs above them.

"I got it," she says, flustered. Last thing she needs is a bunch of people standing around dishing out instructions.

"You sure?"

"... Yeah, I'm good. Some ice in the pipes, that's all."

"Ice?" Everett peers over the top of her head.

"Is that a *valve*?" Jack says. "What is this, the 1800s?"

"This whole ship is from the 1800s," Seema mutters.

"We really run out of water?" Malik says from behind them.

Everett slides in next to Hannah. As he does so, she spots a small access hatch on the tank itself—one the company probably uses to clean it, assuming they ever get around to that kind of thing.

The panel is secured with a twisting handle. Everett is about to turn it when Hannah stops him. "Wait. What if we're wrong?"

"What do you mean?"

"I know I said it was ice in the pipes but ..." She can see the panel flying open, a thousand gallons of precious water cascading down on them.

"Maybe there's a sensor?" Anita says. "Or a camera?"

"I'll go and ask." Corey dashes off before his mom can say anything. He's back in less than a minute, looking confused. "The captain says no. Also, she said the ship was crap, and that it was a stupid question, and that I should stop bothering her."

"Yeah, the captain's smart like that," says Mal, smirking. Corey nails him in the shoulder, which only makes the smirk bigger.

Everett thinks for a moment, then taps the panel. "Put your hand here," he tells Hannah. He looks around, settling on Jack, and calls him over, too. "We'll all hold it shut so I can open the safety lock. Then we're going to *slowly* let it open. You feel any pressure from behind, even a little bit, you hold it shut so I can lock it again."

"Is that actually going to work?" Jack says.

"Well, we're not holding back the sea or anything," says Everett. His voice is calm, but it's impossible to miss the nervous edge to it. "Three people should be enough. We might lose a little bit if it's still liquid, but that's all. And I'm open to other ideas, if anyone's got 'em."

No one says anything. Carefully, Hannah, Jack and Everett position themselves, hands pressed against the hatch. "Remember," Everett says. "You feel even a little pressure—"

"Yeah, just do it already," says Jack.

"Be careful," says Anita from behind them.

Everett turns the catch. Slowly, the three of them lean into the panel, Hannah having to stand on tiptoe to apply enough pressure. Why didn't they just get Brendan over here? With his arm, he could probably have held the hatch in place by himself.

"Feel anything?" Everett says.

Hannah shakes her head. Slowly, very slowly, they let the pressure off the panel. Hannah is expecting—hoping, actually—that she'll feel a sudden push against her hands, and that she, Jack and Everett will get a wave of icy water in their faces before they slam the panel closed. That would mean they've still got—

"Shit," says Jack.

The water behind the panel is frozen solid: a thick wall of ice, wedged in place.

Chapter 19

Hannah's heart sinks. This is not good. And who knows what condition the pipes are in? The ice might have burst them completely, somewhere they can't see.

"OK," says Anita, scratching her chin. "So we heat it up again. There's got to be a way to do that, right?"

Hannah exhales, long and hard. "I hope so."

"Any other water tanks on board?" Everett is frowning at the ice, like it personally offended him.

"Bigger problem," says Brendan. "What if the whole ship gets like this? I mean, this cold?"

Hannah closes her eyes, trying to think. "We know the main deck's heating circuits still work. Even if the bar's down, we should be able to hold it off."

"Maybe we can fix it ourselves," says Anita. "Where would we find the broken part?"

For some reason, everyone turns to Corey.

"What you all looking at me for?" he says, giving a helpless shrug. "I don't know."

Hannah has a sudden urge to send Corey into the space above them, have him crawl through just like he did in the engine room. But he's not *that* small, and, anyway, the last thing she needs is to have a pissed-off Anita on her hands.

"Maybe they were damaged in the attack," Everett says. He

has his hands on his hips, staring up at the ceiling, brow furrowed. "Or when we busted into the hotel?"

"Maybe we could melt some of it," says Brendan.

"Captain's got a lighter," Hannah replies.

"Actually …" Everett turns to look at the bar. He taps a finger against his lips, thinking hard.

"Actually … what?" says Seema.

"I was thinking of something a little more permanent." Everett strides past them, dropping to his knees by one of the bar fridges, yanking the door open and sticking his head inside. "Do these have condensate pan heaters? Or a defrost cycle?"

When nobody answers him, he lifts his head back over the bar. "Never mind. I'll figure it out."

"Is that even going to work?" Jack asks.

"Don't see why not. Be a lot easier if I had the right tools, though. And it's more of a long-term solution—it'll take me a while to put together. I need to insulate the coil so it doesn't short."

Long-term solution. Hannah shivers, making herself focus on the tank.

They can't just not have water—even short term, even with the stockpile of JamFizz, that's not good. It wouldn't be good under normal circumstances, let alone when they're all stressed and exhausted. And, more than that: maybe this is a way to finally stop these people from wanting to tear each other's throats out. A way to take their minds off the fact that their only way out of here might already be destroyed.

And isn't that what Mom and Dad always wanted her to do? Take responsibility? This might not be exactly what they had in mind—but, then again, they aren't here, and she is, and this is something she can finally, finally, handle.

"All right." She turns to the others. "I want everybody to get something they can use as a chisel. A screwdriver, a … a pair of scissors. Anything."

"I don't get it," Jack says. "You want us to tunnel into the ice? Why?"

"Yep. Make a space for Ev's … whatever he's building."

Adrift

"Why bother? We could just hold it to the ice after he builds it, melt it that way. That'll work, right?"

"Sure. But if he can't make it work ..."

"Oh, I'll get it working." For the first time since he came on board, Everett actually sounds happy.

"Even so." Hannah meets Jack's eyes. "This is a backup plan. We knock some of the ice out, put it in the glasses so it can melt."

She wants to tell him that she knows it isn't strictly necessary, that whatever Everett is doing will probably be enough. But she doesn't know how to phrase it. Jack isn't the kind of person who would buy the idea of them needing to band together as a group, and Hannah isn't sure she has the energy to try and convince him. If a little lie gets him focused on the task at hand, she's happy to tell it.

She's saved by Seema, who pulls something out of her pocket and passes it over. It's an old-fashioned penknife, a little rust on the red handle. "Will this do?"

Hannah feels a burst of triumph, taking the knife and flipping the blade open. "Yes. Exactly." She waves it, a little wildly. "Anything like what Seema has."

Gently, Seema takes the knife from her, pulling the blade back in and flipping out the bottle opener, with its thick, flattened end. "Let's not mess up the blade, yeah?"

Hannah nods, blushing a little. "Right. Sorry."

While Everett works on the fridge, yanking out power cables and pulling off panels and dispatching his wife to retrieve a roll of tape from the ship's first aid kit, the others get to chiselling. There isn't much to work with: Seema's knife and an old pair of nail scissors from Anita's cavernous bag are the only things they can find that would make a dent in the hard ice. They'd hoped to find some cutlery behind the bar, but, of course, there's nothing back there. You don't need a knife and fork to eat soychips.

Hannah is lost for a few seconds, realising how long it'll take them to chip away with just the penknife and the scissors, but Brendan gets an idea. With Everett's agreement, he smashes the glass on the second fridge, driving a metal fist through the pane. Malik pulls off his shirt, wrapping it tight around his hand and snagging one of the bigger chunks. "So I don't cut myself," he tells a horrified Anita.

Taking it in turns, Hannah, Jack, Brendan and Malik hack away at the ice, while Lorinda and Corey hold glasses up to catch the falling chips. The outside is grimy, crusty with frost. But, before long, bigger chunks start to come loose. A line of glasses grows on the bar, slowly melting chunks of ice dripping into them. Soon, everyone around the bathroom is soaked and shivering, piles of slush growing on the floor around them.

Despite the fact that she can no longer feel her hands, Hannah can't help smiling. For the first time since the attack, they've stopped thinking about what's going to happen to them. *It's working*. It's not going to work forever—she can already picture a bigger section of the ice coming loose, crushing someone's arm underneath it—but it's a good start.

After they've chiselled a foot-deep hole in the ice, Hannah calls time. She's exhausted, her shoulders trembling, but her smile grows bigger as she walks over to the bar. She even high-fives Malik, barely feeling the impact on her frozen palm. Everyone else is the same—even Jack and Seema look happy, for once. Hannah passes the woman her knife back, then lifts one of the glasses that has more liquid in it than the others, and raises it to them in a toast.

"Shouldn't we save it?" Everett says from the other side of the bar. He's still not finished with his makeshift ice melter, and is adrift in a sea of wires and metal plating and shreds of tape. A heating coil lies on his lap like a pet snake.

"Think we've earned this one," Hannah replies. She takes a small sip before passing it to Brendan, who winks at her.

"Agreed." Jack has a glass of his own. "Oh hey, Captain, come on down. You want a drink?"

Hannah turns to see Volkova on the stairs, and the smile drops off his face.

"Captain?" Anita says.

"Come upstairs," says Volkova. "Everyone needs to see this."

Chapter 20

The jump gate is gone. Destroyed.

The ring, usually two miles wide, has been blasted to pieces. Big chunks of the structure still remain: huge, curved sections of polished metal with jagged, torn edges. The chunks are surrounded by hundreds of shards of loose debris, including what remains of the gate's auto-turrets.

Jack wants to look away. He's *desperate* to look away. But neither he, nor any of the other passengers, can tear their eyes from the viewing dome.

There's one particular piece: the jump gate's giant, cylindrical reactor. Half of it, at least. No way the Colony ship did this from up close—the energy released when the reactor was destroyed would have torn it to shreds. It's all too easy to see what happened. They jumped, and left a few spheres behind to close the door.

Jack looks beyond the gate; maybe he'll be able see the wormhole. But there's nothing there. Without the gate forcing the wormhole throat open, it will have shrunk back to its original size: a tiny dimple, all but invisible unless you know what to look for. An untrained observer, trying to find one against the blackness of space? No chance.

It wouldn't help them anyway. Even if they could somehow enter a wormhole that hadn't been forced open by a gate, there's no exotic matter around to shield them. They'd be torn into sub-atomic confetti.

Years to build this gate. Less than a day to destroy it. Less than a day to close off this section of the Galaxy for good. With them as the only humans for light years in every direction.

The main deck is silent. Even the *Panda*'s engines seem muted. Jack looks down at his hand: he's still holding a pint glass, half full of icy water. He stares at it, and then the anger is there, boiling up from inside him.

He hurls the glass across the deck. It smashes against the

wall, and he hears someone gasp. He doesn't know who, doesn't care.

"*Fuck,*" he shouts. How could this have happened to him? He's not even supposed to *be* here.

Even in his fury, he can see the irony. They're not trapped—they can go wherever they want. It's just that it'll be hundreds of years before they reach anywhere. As if to remind him of just how much time they have left, his stomach chooses that moment to wake up, growling in annoyance, sending a shivering ache through him.

He doesn't have another glass to throw, so he slams his foot into the nearest plastic chair. The material's too tough for him to make a dent in, but he doesn't care. He kicks the chair again, suddenly more angry at himself for wasting the water in the glass than anything else. Then he slumps onto the seat, chest heaving. The rage ebbs, drawing back like the tide, replaced by a terrifying apathy. He doesn't want to do anything. He just wants to sit here, and not talk to anybody, for a very long time.

The thirst, held at bay by the first few sips of water, begins to creep back up his throat.

"All right," Seema says, far too quietly. "So what do we do now?"

Nobody says anything. Anita's pulled Corey in close, her hands on his shoulders as they stare upwards. Hannah has gone very pale.

Seema licks her lips. "I said—"

"Nothing we can do." Volkova is sitting on one of the plastic seats, arms folded, head down.

"There has to be something." Seema spreads her fingers, patting the air as if telling everybody to calm down. "Because we're not dying out here. Is there a message we could send? A distress signal, or—"

"It won't work," Hannah says.

Seema swings around. In the space of half a second her expression goes from one of forced calm to full-on, twisted fury. "Don't say that. *Don't you say that.*"

Hannah isn't crying, not yet, but it's impossible to miss the redness in her face, the hitching tone in her voice. "I'm sorry. I don't know what—"

"Figure something out. That's your job, innit?"

"Nobody's going to die," Anita says. She's got both her sons now, holding them close.

Jack tries to tune them out, not wanting to think, not wanting to do anything. He turns his head to see Volkova looking at him.

She blinks slowly, as if she isn't really seeing him. In that moment, she looks twenty years older. She gets to her feet, moving with agonising slowness, and starts walking towards the cockpit.

He almost stops her. Demands she do something. Only: what's the point? All the flying in the world isn't going to get them out of this. He even knows what she'll probably suggest: heading for Bishop's Station, even though there's no hope in hell of ever reaching it alive. There's nothing else they *can* do.

At least we've got some ice, he thinks bitterly. His gaze tracks back to the viewing dome, to the slowly spinning debris. It's not just the gate. There are pieces of ship floating there as well—at least two or three, judging by the shape of the wreckage. They must have been here when the Colony ship arrived—maybe they'd only just come through. They wouldn't've known what hit them.

Were they trading vessels? Fighters? Maybe he should ask the kid, the one who knows so much about ships. He'll do it later. Right now, he just wants to sit where he is and wipe his brain clean.

But how? How is he supposed to do it when he can't even have a drink? The thought of another JamFizz makes him want to scream. He closes his eyes, the anger building again, his mind *refusing to turn off*.

It had been that way ever since Hec had told him to leave. He could even pinpoint the exact moment when it had first started: in the hospital waiting area, sunlight streaming through the windows and painting the sterile tiles with gold.

He remembers the nurse's face: her stupid, bovine face, telling him that no, *Senhor Alarcón não quer visitantes*. Smiling thinly at his useless, scattershot Portuguese, refusing to let him past. There was no way that Hector would have told her that. No way. But he had, and there wasn't a damn thing Jack could do about it. Not then, and sure as hell not now.

He should have stuck it out. He should have pushed the goddamn nurse aside, marched into Hec's room, told him—

His thoughts move in familiar directions, the paths so automatic that he doesn't even realise it's happening. Usually, he manages to fight them off. This time, he doesn't bother. Who gives a shit? He rolls in them, lets them wash over him.

After a while—he isn't sure how long—Jack looks up. Volkova is gone. Malik Livingstone is buried in his holocam again, but Corey and his parents are still staring out of the dome, shocked expressions on their faces. So is Brendan, although his wife has her head bowed, hands in her lap, shoulders moving in silent, hitching sobs. Lorinda—God, he'd almost forgotten about her—is sitting opposite him, rooting through her bag. Hannah is off to one side, her back to him, head bowed.

This is worse than after the attack—worse than when he'd thrown up, which he can still smell. At least he felt something back then. Now? The emotion's been sucked right out of the room.

Nobody's looking at anyone else. Nobody's asking: *what's next? What are the options? What pointless vote should we have now?* Even Seema appears to have given up. At least, he thinks, she was wrong. No one's messing with them. There's nothing going on behind the scenes. They were attacked, they survived, and now they're stranded. End of.

He runs through their options—it's pointless, but it feels like something he should do. There aren't any other jump gates in this part of space. The nearest settlement is light years away. They could go back to the station, try to ... what? Find supplies? They'd have better luck holding hands in a prayer circle. Could they take the escape pod? No—as much as he hates to admit it, Hannah was right about that. All that would happen then is that they'd be adrift in an even smaller vessel, with next to no power.

"Would anyone mind if I went outside for a bit?" Lorinda says.

Jack blinks. Nobody else reacts to her words, so maybe he imagined it, or didn't hear her right.

Lorinda clears her throat. "I said—"

Adrift

"What do you mean, go outside?" Everett says. Jack gets a bizarre image of Lorinda putting her coat on, stepping out for a breath of fresh air.

"I mean, to take a closer look at the gate."

They all turn to look at her. Everett and Corey exchange a confused glance.

Lorinda gestures to the open pod. "There's a suit back there—two, actually. If one of you can help me into it, I think I might—"

"Why?" Hannah says.

"There may be something out there we can use. A comms module, a distress beacon. Maybe even some food—the freeze-dried stuff is still good, even if it spends time in a vacuum. Happened to us once, back at our mine."

Jack lowers his head, slowly scratching the nape of his neck. "You wanna go. Out there."

"No, I said it purely for your entertainment." Lorinda gets to her feet, carefully placing her bag on the seat behind her.

"But you can't even climb down a ladder," says Corey in amazement.

Lorinda sighs. "True. But I'm not bad in zero-G—or don't you remember how I caught you before?"

She winks at him, and starts walking towards the escape pod, using the backs of the plastic chairs for balance. Jack stares at her back. *She's crazy. Cooked. All of this has snapped her mind.*

"Ma'am," Hannah says. "I really don't think—"

"First off," says Lorinda, not breaking stride, "I've asked you repeatedly not to call me ma'am. Second, I don't believe it makes one damn bit of difference to our situation if I go outside or not. Third, as I keep saying, we might find something of value out there, and four, I'm quite comfortable in low-gravity environments."

"Yeah, but ..."

"But nothing. I spent my whole life mining asteroids, so how about we stop with the pointless objections, and let me do as I please?"

"But you'll *die*." Corey Livingstone is looking at her like she's not only being stupid, but like she's told him she's grown an extra head.

She grins at him. "Nonsense. I, young man, am going to live forever."

"You can't just take a suit," Jack says.

"Why not?"

He opens his mouth to tell her exactly why they might need it later, but he doesn't have a single thing to say.

"Glad that's settled," Lorinda says. "Now then: are you going to stand around, or are you going to help an old lady into her spacesuit?"

Chapter 21

Corey's friend Allie is pretty good with numbers. If—*when*—they actually start their ship company, she's going to handle the business side. It's always seemed kind of strange that she wanted to do that, instead of being a pilot—when it comes to 866 Industries, *she* was the fearless one.

As he watches Lorinda struggle into her suit, helped by Hannah and his dad, Corey can't help but think of the one time Allie went a little too far.

They were out by the dried creek bed, round the back of her house: a deep, meandering depression baking in the hot afternoon sun. Allie lives near the edge of the Austin suburbs, her house in the shadow of the mine, the hundred-foot-tall mountains of earth dumped on the surface from the tunnelling operations below it. The dump stretched for ten square miles: quarries and dirt roads and acres of barren, orange earth, broken by the shadows of the vast cloud seeders that dominated the Austin sky.

Corey, Jamie and Allie weren't supposed to go into the dumps, but they'd done it anyway, more than once, sneaking through a tunnel some kid had once made under the rusted fence.

The site was supposed to be able to detect anybody with a lens or a neurochip trying to gain access, but they'd heard from Mohammed Al-Mukhtar at school that his uncle worked on the scanners, and they'd all been shut down for maintenance since forever. The earth on the huge mounds of dirt was soft and grainy, but once you'd slid down it a couple of times, you kind of got over it. The creek bed was far more promising.

On this particular day, they had their hoverboards with them, and one of them—Corey can never remember who—suggested they build a kicker off the edge of the creek. There'd been some argument about whether this was a dumb idea or not, but they were bored, itchy with heat, and they'd got tired of racing through the creek itself. A ramp to jump off, Allie told them, would be bàng. And they'd be able to make it to the other side of the creek, easy. It wasn't *that* wide.

It took most of the afternoon to build. The dirt at the edge of the creek was hard-packed, and Allie had to go and fetch a couple of shovels from her mom's garage. But in the end, they had a steep ramp, rising to a lip like a sideways apostrophe. The top of the ramp was two feet above the ground, eight feet above the dried creek bed, and that was when Corey and Jamie started thinking that maybe this wasn't such a good idea after all.

Not Allie, though. Allie hadn't said anything, just given them this look, like she couldn't believe she had to put up with such losers. Then she'd activated the board, hopping onto it, knees bending to take the impact. "One of you make sure you get this," she said, pointing towards the creek, as she shot off in the opposite direction. "It's gonna be *good*."

He and Jamie had done a quick round of rock-paper-scissors-fire-water, and he had ended up on the other side of the creek, in the full glare of the sun. The sweat baked on his forehead as he looked up towards the ramp, activating the camera on his lens.

Jamie waved at him, letting him know that Allie was coming. He narrowed his left eye, zooming in on the ramp, which suddenly seemed as high as a ten-storey building.

He heard the rumble of the board before he saw it, a low hum with a clattering undertone from the dirt and pebbles it was displacing. Allie came hurtling over the top of the ramp, ass out like she was doing a squat, one hand gripping the edge of the board. In the second she cleared it Corey thought she really *was* going to make it to the other side of the creek.

Then he saw the look of panic on her face, and her back foot sliding off the board, and he realised she wasn't. He saw it all through the camera, saw her topple over backwards as her board shot forwards. She slammed into the ground so hard that Corey felt the impact rumble through his shoes. A second later, the front edge of the board cracked against the other side of the creek, its generator shattering like a light bulb. Then he and Jamie were sprinting towards their friend, a curiously dry taste in Corey's mouth.

Allie sat up before they got there. There was huge cut on her forehead, oozing blood. Below her skate shorts, her knees were raw meat. She blinked at them, her eyes huge.

"Ow," she said, as if she'd just skinned her knuckles.

Then she kind of slumped over, and Jamie had to run and get his dad. Allie ended up spending the night in hospital, the cut on her forehead eventually turning into a wicked scar. It was a couple of weeks before they all went hoverboarding again, even though it was the perfect summer for it, and they never did build another kicker.

Corey didn't mind too much. He didn't think about what he liked to call Allie's Leap too often, but, deep down, he knew how lucky she'd been. If she'd come off her board a second later or earlier, or if she'd hung on, she'd have been eating through a tube for a few months while the nanobots fixed her, instead of sitting in the dirt saying "Ow."

If Lorinda goes too far out there, she can say *Ow* as much as she wants. They won't be able to hear her. And they won't be able to do anything to help. Corey turns away, jamming his hands into his pockets.

The Reptar figure Lorinda brought on board has made it down to the bar, perched next to a couple of glasses, arms raised to attack. Corey has no idea how it got down there—last he saw it, it was on the main deck. Seeing the toy makes him think of Jamie, and he looks back at Lorinda, feeling more helpless than he has on this entire trip, even when they went zero-G.

The spacesuit isn't exactly top-level Frontier tech. It's clumsy and bulky, with white fabric and neon-yellow markings. There are thrusters at the shoulders and waist. They're fed from a backpack, moulded to the suit, that holds both the oxygen and the propellant. Lorinda has to stand with her arms out, like those scarecrows Corey's seen in old pictures, while Hannah clips her gloves on.

His dad is fiddling with her oxygen, muttering to himself, his brow furrowed in concentration. Corey doesn't know why he's bothering. The suit might look old, but if it's in the escape pod it's designed to be used by people who have probably never been in space before. You shouldn't have to mess with it to get it to work.

They're in the bar, a few steps from the *Red Panda*'s airlock. Despite the freezing temperatures, the rest of the passengers have clustered on the stairs, watching the proceedings. Corey wishes they wouldn't. It reminds him that there's nothing else upstairs, and nothing outside, either. It reminds them of just how screwed they are, a million times more screwed than they were with the fire, or with the frozen water supply. And what does Lorinda even think she's going to find out there? Another gate?

"So," his dad says. "You've got about two hours' worth of oxygen in here. At least, that's what I can tell from the—"

"Yes, yes, yes," Lorinda says, tapping at something on the suit's oversized wrist control. She sounds relaxed—excited, even. "Next thing you'll be telling me that I don't have to spend an hour in the airlock to depressurise. I know how a spacesuit works, Everett. Besides, I won't be out there nearly that long. I'm just going for a little look."

"I'd still be more comfortable if you let someone else do it," Hannah says. She looks as if she's about to throw up.

"I'll be fine, dear. I've spent more time in space than you have."

"I just don't see what you're going to find out there," Hannah tells her.

Lorinda shrugs. Corey doesn't think he's seen anyone in a space-suit manage it before. "Freeze-dried rations, if I can find some. They're nasty, but I'm a little bored of soychips. Now; perhaps you can help me with my helmet?"

"What? Oh. Sure."

But you'll die, Corey's original idea comes back to him: the one about the Colony ship disappearing during a jump, reappearing, thinking that the war was still on. His lips are suddenly dry. They don't have the faintest idea what's out there, and now Lorinda wants to go right into the middle of it.

"Watch out for the reactors," he says, pushing himself off the bar.

Lorinda looks up. "I beg your pardon?"

"The reactors on the destroyed ships. They're fusion, probably, so they might still be hot, even though they're in the vacuum. You'll burn yourself if you get too close."

She's not gonna burn herself, it's almost absolute zero out there, stop being a dumbass.

"Got it," Lorinda says. "Anything else?"

"What?"

"Anything else I might need to watch out for?"

"Just ... come back safe, OK?"

She smiles. "I will, kiddo. Thanks."

Hannah slots the helmet over her head, sliding it one click to the left to lock it in place. Corey hears the tiny hiss as the seals kick in, even over the rumble of the engine.

Chapter 22

Lorinda Anna Maria Esteban floats towards the ruined gate.

She pivots gently, using the hand controller to spin herself around a piece of debris, with only a light burst on the thrusters to help her. It's amazing how quickly the old moves come back. She hasn't done a walk in a long while, but it's like she never left.

The suit's thrusters are powered by a highly compressed propellant in her pack. Her movements are controlled by a joystick, connected to a module on her left wrist, that slots right into her hand. She tweaks the stick, gently squeezing to adjust the thrusters, her motions helped along by servos in the suit gloves. Her lens, automatically synced to the suit's processor, displays her data. Her old layout presets still work just fine.

She hasn't felt this alive in ages.

Lorinda is sixty-five years old, and feels like it. Oh, there are plenty of anti-ageing solutions people use, or nanobots that can repair tired bones, but no insurance company is going to cover them—and she and her husband definitely didn't have the funds to. It doesn't bother her too much, even if she has to wake up three times every night to use the bathroom.

She doesn't handle stairs well, and ladders are out of the question. But space? Space is easy on her bones. Space makes her feel like she did when she was thirty, when she spent more time outside their habitat than inside it. Space she can *do*.

It's not that she minds regular gravity. It's much easier to concentrate on the day-to-day running of a mining company when your coffee mug isn't floating away every five seconds, and you can actually sit down at a desk instead of having to tether yourself to it. So the company office on Asteroid ZX5-B73K, Kuiper Quadrant 25, had its own gravity well. She and Craig could do their jobs and eat their meals and sleep in relative comfort. Make love, too— contrary to what they taught in high-school biology, you *could* have sex in zero-G. It was just so much better to do it the other way round.

Sex aside, she was always more comfortable bouncing around in zero-G than she was riding a desk. Craig was more than happy to stay in Central, manning the comms, handling the day-to-day stuff and the buyers' calls while she oversaw the equipment and directed operations outside. Even after decades on the Belt, her eyesight was still OK—she'd had a scary incident with a cataract a few years back, but their insurance (the one that wouldn't cover anti-ageing meds) was paid up, and cataracts *were* in their coverage. No wriggling out of that one.

The Hale Mining Company—named for Craig's grandmother, after she helped them out with some startup capital—might not have been the largest operation in the Kuiper Belt, but it had got pretty big by the end. Seven employees, a dozen asteroid rigs and a couple of six-figure contracts that meant they were able to pay their rig-hounds a decent bonus every year.

"You're too friendly with the clients," she'd told Craig once. "We could be getting double-annual from Calomar, but you let him buy you a beer once in a while and you think he's your pal."

Craig had shrugged. "So you go talk to him next time he's out here."

"Maybe I will."

He'd smiled, and gone back to his dinner. They both knew she wouldn't—she'd rather get her hand caught in a rock vacuum than handle a contract negotiation. And truth was, she didn't mind too much. As long as they could pay their rig-hounds, and she could snuggle into bed with Craig after dinner, safe in the knowledge that the Europa Bank wasn't going to jump through the local gate with a repo vessel, she was happy.

And then, one day, Craig was gone. He'd been sitting in Central, like always, talking to her on the comms—something about the risotto he was planning on making for dinner—and then the line had gone silent. She'd assumed a malfunction, a pain in the ass but not critical. After all, she didn't need him to repair a faulty back-line fuse.

She'd gone in, de-suited, and found him at his desk. Blood clot, the doc had told her later. Nothing anyone could have done. Quick and painless.

For Craig, maybe. For her, not so much.

Not so much at all.

They'd never had any kids. That was the thing about living in space. She had no doubt that the radiation shielding at Central and on their suits worked just fine, but forty years of life in the Belt had a price. One not even Craig's grandmother could have helped them pay.

Selling up had been startlingly easy—not just the decision, but the whole process. What else was she going to do? Sit in the office while Mitchell Cheng handled the rig-hounds? She could have done—their claim was square, as was the paperwork proving it, so no one was going to take it from her. Other companies had tried, bigger ones than Hale, and a quick visit to the Frontier Mining Ops offices put paid to them. But after one week as the new Central command, Lorinda knew she was done.

Calomar, who by then was one of their biggest clients, came out for the memorial service—and this time Lorinda was the one buying *him* a beer. The payment—cash only, thank you very much—had been enough to set her rig-hounds up with two years' salary each, while they looked for more work. Cheng'd probably blown most of it at the first bar he could find, but that was his problem, not hers. And the money had been enough to finance the travel she and Craig had always talked about. First stop: the famed Sigma Station, home to the best views of the Horsehead Nebula in the entire Frontier territory.

She could almost hear Craig's sardonic tone, the drawl from his Texas upbringing. *Look how well that turned out.*

"Quiet, bucko," she says to herself, as she tacks around another spinning hunk of debris. "Mama's working."

"Say again?" Volkova's voice sounds tinny over the helmet comms.

Shoot. She'd forgotten she was on an open comms line. "Nothing. Sorry."

"You doing OK out there?" Hannah's voice this time.

The *Red Panda* is a tiny dot behind Lorinda. She's facing away from it, but there's a helpful display in her helmet, linked to a camera on her oxygen tank. She pulls the control stick down, tilting herself towards the centre of what used to be the gate. "Just fine. I'm going in for a closer look."

Most of the wreckage has been blown into the distance; Lorinda can see the pieces spinning away, where they'll drift until the end of time. But a large portion of the debris is still there, turning in place, the pieces brushing by each other in a silent dance that sends smaller splinters of them flying. The debris field stretches for miles, just like it did at the station.

Lorinda angles herself towards one of the larger clusters. The Neb is behind them, throwing soft light across the remains of the gate, highlighting it against the black. There are fragments of what look like a robot probe—more than one, judging by the number.

Makes sense. The first thing the Frontier would have done, when they realised the Sigma gate was down, would be to send probes to figure out what happened. No problem for the Colony ship, which could have sat here picking them off at its leisure.

The Colony ship. It *had* to have gone through the gate—it was the only way out. Could there be another gate nearby? One they didn't know about? That didn't make sense either. Gates took a long, long time to build—it's not like the Colonies could just knock one up without anyone noticing.

But if the Colony ship *did* go through the existing Sigma gate, then how did it get away from the Frontier at the other end? What the hell is going on here?

The Frontier must have sent probes when the gate went down, but Lorinda can't see any active ones flying around. Then again, by now they're probably aware something is badly wrong, which means they'll be putting together something a little more substantial than a basic repair probe. That'll take them a good long while, if she knows the Frontier. Not that it matters. Unless they figure out a way to rebuild the gate in the next few days, it's not going to help anyone on the *Red Panda* get home.

Still, maybe she can find something out here …

She might be comfortable in space, but there's no denying that it's harder than it was when she was young. There's an ache in her knees, a gentle, throbbing pain that she knows she'll have to deal with later. Fingers, too. At least her feet don't hurt. They do when the gravity's Earth-normal—she's spent far less time in that environment than outside, and the soles of her feet are smooth and sensitive as baby skin. She's used to it by now, but when it comes to her poor paws, she'll take zero-G any time.

She glances at the heads-up display on her lens, noting her oxygen supply. It's lower than it should be. She's breathing too fast, working her muscles harder than they've been worked since she left the Belt. Something smears across the helmet glass: a tiny drop of sweat, stretched out by zero gravity. The systems in modern suits usually do a pretty good job of keeping skin dry, which means she must be sweating buckets.

"See anything?" Volkova says. Her voice is fainter now.

"Nothing yet."

Not that she knows what she's looking for. That's really the rub, isn't it? With the gate destroyed, there isn't even a way to send a message to anyone. All she can do is get in close, and have a look-see. You never know.

Bullshit. There's almost certainly no freeze-dried food floating around, and the electronics in any comms module are likely to have been killed by the vacuum. Being out here is better than the endless bickering inside that damn ship.

Maybe she just won't go back. It'd be a good way to go—turn off the oxygen and just drift away.

"I don't like this," says Volkova.

"I'm OK." Lorinda tweaks her shoulder thrusters, sending herself into a very gentle somersault.

"*Da*, you OK now. But when we are rescued, maybe I have to tell my bosses why I let a passenger go for a walk in space. Not a good conversation."

Despite herself, Lorinda smiles. She hasn't said too much to the captain before this, but it's hard not to like her. All at once, she feels guilty for wanting to stay out here.

Volkova continues. "Besides, if you die, I'll only have the guide for company. The guide, and a bunch of passengers who act like little babies. You are the only person who doesn't. Should never have let you go for—"

Silence.

"Captain, come in?" Lorinda can't see the *Red Panda* any more—it isn't on her tank cam, or anywhere in her field of view. There's nothing but the silent, twisting debris. Her heart begins to beat a little faster. The dropped comms remind her of the day she lost Craig, cutting a little too close to the bone.

She tries again, keeping the nervousness out of her voice. "*Panda*, can you hear me?"

A tiny *ding-dong* sound answers her, followed by a cheerful male voice. "Hello, and thank you for attempting to contact the *Red Panda*, registration number XT560 dash T1, a Sigma Destination Tours vessel. We are having trouble connecting your transmission, but we aim to do so shortly. Thank you for your patience."

Terrible, tinny jazz music fills her helmet. Lorinda breathes a sigh of relief. The voice means that at least the *Red Panda* is still there—although, why wouldn't it be? It's probably just a problem with the signal.

"Disable music," she says.

A saxophone solo kicks in, screeching in her ear.

She winces. "*Red Panda*: disable—"

Something collides with her right leg.

It's a piece of debris. A big one. She doesn't know how she missed it, but it sends her into a wild spin. There's a second of sickening *hiss*, and she's sure she's got a leak, sure that any second her suit is going to decompress. Then the hiss cuts off, replaced by a muted beeping. She can't find the source of it; nausea is rolling up from her stomach, twisting her intestines. She's breathing even faster now, drops of sweat hovering in front of her eye.

She blinks, and her eyelash catches one, splitting it into smaller globules which sting her retina. The debris field whirls around her. She doesn't know where the Red Panda is, and she certainly can't find the spot she was aiming for.

She works the thrusters, very gently, switching between spurts from her waist and shoulders, slowly bringing herself to a halt. The damn sax is still playing, but, right then, she has a burst of inspiration. "Close connection," she says, and the music cuts off.

She breathes a shaky sigh. That was not good. She has to be more careful.

There's a piece of debris a few hundred yards away, something that looks like the front section of a trading vessel. Maybe she can get into the control room, get some of the data off the computer. God knows what use it'll be, but it's better than nothing. She tries to raise the *Red Panda* again, and cuts the connection when she hears the same message as before. She's worried, but only a little. Communication will only become a problem when she tries to get back inside, and she can burn that bridge when she comes to it.

Lorinda smiles, marvelling at how one of Craig's favourite sayings came so readily to the front of her mind.

She's pointed directly at the wrecked ship now. She gives all the thrusters a full burst, her shoulders aching as she shoots forward. The O_2 meter on her lens reads just under 75 per cent—more than enough for what she has in mind.

She's almost at the ship when she realises she's overcompensated slightly. The last thrust has caused her to tilt forward, as if she's leaning over a precipice. She's about to correct it when she looks down, and forgets about everything else. Her mouth falls open, and she exhales a hot, horrified breath.

The *Red Panda* is maybe half a mile below her, side-on, its viewing dome pointed in the direction of her three o'clock. And coming up beneath it, like a shark in murky water, is the giant bulk of the Colony ship.

Chapter 23

"Can we try her again?" Hannah says.

"We tried her three times already." Volkova is frowning at the screens, as if they've personally offended her. "Nothing. Comms are down, like the heating system for the water."

"Then can we get in closer?"

Volkova sighs. "There's too much debris this time. I don't want to risk a ship rupture. Just because we're all dead anyway doesn't mean I want it to happen sooner."

Hannah doesn't quite know what to say to that. She's a little surprised at how calm she is. She hasn't had a blackout, or a panic attack. Volkova hasn't had to tell her another story to lift her spirits. Instead, she just feels numb. The idea that this ship is the last place she'll ever see is an abstract concept, one she can't get her head around. It feels like a movie. Like the credits will roll at any second, and she can disconnect her lens and be somewhere else. Somewhere safe.

Somewhere with *food*. She's been trying to ration her second bag of soychips, taking one at a time, and it's getting harder to resist. She can't stop herself thinking about it. More importantly, she can't stop thinking about lasagne—the one her dad used to make, maybe once or twice a year, with meat that had to be imported from Earth. It's like a cut on the roof of her mouth that she keeps wanting to touch.

And she's thirsty again, which worries her. They've got more than enough water to drink, for now—just chisel some off and wait for it to melt—but it's like her body needs double its usual amount, just to function. Hardly surprising, given what they've been through.

The cockpit speakers leap to life, issuing a series of loud clicks. Volkova groans, and, a second later, the *Panda*'s computer begins to speak. "C-c-captain. We are out of range of Sigma Station comm—"

The voice cuts off abruptly. Two seconds later, it comes back— only this time the voice has changed, going from a cheerful male voice to a sultry female one with an Australian accent. "Setting two. We are out of range of Sig—Sig-Sig-Sigma Station communications array. Do you wish to issue a distress beacon?"

"Stupid voice is glitching," Volkova mutters, tapping at the controls. "Thought I shut it up the first time."

The cockpit door clicks open, and Jack steps in, ducking his head under the door frame. Hannah winces. She's just *not* in the mood right now.

"She find anything?" Jack says, leaning on the back of the captain's chair. The space is almost too small for the three of them.

Volkova glances at Hannah, with a look that says, *You deal with him.*

"We can't reach her," Hannah says. "She's out of range, or something." She's not, but it seems easier than telling him the comms might be dead.

"Out of range?" He peers out through the glass. "That's crazy. She can't have gone that far."

"Captain," says the *Panda*, sounding as if it's about to suggest they all slip into something more comfortable. "I am d-d-d-detecting multiple passengers in the cockpit area. I am detecting removal of a passenger vaaaaaacuum safety suit from the escape module. These are not—" the voice glitches again, this time coming back male, with a light Scottish brogue "—optimum conditions for piloting this vessel safely. Do you wish to issue a distress beacon?"

"Like a fucking cockroach," Volkova says to herself, stabbing at one of the on-screen options.

An alarm goes off. Three quick, urgent beeps, repeated, hollow and terrifying. Hannah's head snaps around, flicking between the screens, trying to find the source. There's something very different about this alert noise, something guttural and insistent, something very, very bad. A moment later, the ship says. "Projectile lock. Projectile lock."

"*Blyad!*" Volkova grabs the stick and the debris field starts to slide away.

"What the hell?" Jack says, his voice almost drowned by the beeping.

Then they see it.

The Colony ship drops into view like a spider moving smoothly down a thread of silk. It's closing fast, its angled cockpit pointed right at them. Against the Neb, its fins look like long needles. It's perhaps two miles away, maybe less, and, as Hannah looks at it, the air catches in her throat, becoming a solid blockage.

It doesn't make sense. How can it still be here? With the gate destroyed, it's stuck, just like they are.

Hannah can't speak. Can't even move. The metal spheres begin to appear: tiny white dots exiting the bigger ship. Jack has gone paper-white.

"Can we talk to them?" Hannah says, her voice kicking back in. "Surrender? Something?"

"No surrender," Volkova says. "*Never surrender.*"

Then she swings the *Panda* around so that the Colony ship vanishes. She slams the stick forward, the engines roaring to life. On the main deck, Malik Livingstone is shouting. Any second now, they'll hear the *thud-bang* of a sphere impact, followed by the freezing, boiling darkness of decompression.

"Projectile lock," says the Scottish voice. "Projectile lllll—" The voice cuts off with a squashed, distorted yelp.

They're heading right for the debris field, banking in a slow arc towards it. Hannah finds her voice again. "What are you doing?"

"What do you think?" says Volkova.

"I thought you said we couldn't get too close!"

The captain spits another barrage of angry Russian, one hand locked on the stick, the other dancing between the control panels. They're *very* near the debris now—the nearest piece, what looks like a chunk of gate, looms in the viewport.

"Do something!" Jack roars.

"*Shut up!*" Volkova yells back. "Just shut up!"

The debris is almost on them. Any second now, it's going to smash through the cockpit glass. Hannah squeezes her eyes shut, turning her face away.

The impact doesn't come. She opens her eyes, then wishes she hadn't. More debris looms, appearing from all directions.

"What's happening?" Brendan is in the doorway, holding on with both hands. Everett and Seema are behind him, their eyes wide.

Volkova does something with the controls, something hard and wrenching which makes the ship drop, like it's falling down an elevator shaft. The inertial dampeners whir into life, fighting against the movement, not quite managing to beat it. Hannah's feet rise off the floor, and her stomach threatens to climb into her throat. Suddenly, she's back on Sigma, watching that historical sim play out on the VR, watching Omen and Blackbird and Rainmaker curve and twist across the battlefield. *Thread the needle.*

It looked almost impossible when Rainmaker did it, and she was in a Scorpion fighter, built to dance through the vacuum. How the hell are they going to do it in a tour ship?

The ship's voice returns. Now its voice is male Indian, the accent gentle and lilting. "Deploying countermeasures. Deploying countermeasures. Sorry, countermeasures are not installed on this ship class. Do you wish to contact customer service to order this feature?"

"Jesus—" Seema gets out. But her words are cut off by a loud rumble, rattling through the ship, fading away to be replaced by even more alarms and Volkova's furious swearing. One of the displays near Hannah's head is flashing, showing a schematic of the ship with its back end blinking in an ugly red. The sight freezes the blood in her veins.

"Did we get hit?" she shouts.

"It hit the debris behind us," Volkova says, spitting the words over her shoulder. She's still fighting with the controls, slicing the ship through the closely packed debris. She's trying to out-manoeuvre the spheres, getting the wreckage from the gate in between them and the *Panda*. Hannah stares at Volkova in stunned amazement—*Jesus*, this woman can fly.

But it might not be enough. Another chunk of debris fills the cockpit glass. It's not a big one, but they're coming at it fast. Volkova snarls, twisting the stick, trying to bank the *Red Panda* away from it.

Chapter 24

Lorinda hangs in the debris field, watching with mute horror as the spheres close in on the *Red Panda*. There are two of them still chasing—there were three, but Volkova managed to fake one out, smashing it into a piece of debris. It's one of the best pieces of flying Lorinda has ever seen, something she didn't even think was possible in a ship like the *Panda*.

"*Red Panda*, come in," she says, forcing the words out. Her only reply is the same oblivious voice, thanking her for her attempt at contact. She cuts the connection, swearing. She hasn't sworn in years, and it sounds far too loud in the cramped helmet.

The air around her face is heavy with floating blobs of sweat—the suit's cooling system has overloaded, refusing to suck in more moisture. The glass is a smeared nightmare, one she can only see through in patches. As she watches, the *Panda* passes below her, moving out of sight, the spheres trailing, closing fast.

The worst part is the silence. It's like the station all over again; all that destruction, and not a single sound.

She can't move fast enough to intercept the spheres—and, even if she could, what the hell would she do when she got there? She squeezes the thruster control anyway. She doesn't have a plan, doesn't have anything *close* to a plan, but it's better than doing nothing.

Even then, there's no telling how long she'll be able to keep going. Spacewalking might be like riding a bike, but she's never felt this tired. The aching numbness has spread from her fingertips to her forearms, leeching into her elbow joints, curling up to nestle in her knees.

She spots the *Panda* below her, at her seven o'clock. The spheres are even closer now, but the ship is still winding its way through the debris, getting in so close that it's a wonder it's not being smashed to pieces. Not that it matters. Sooner or later, Volkova will make a mistake. The spheres won't.

Lorinda looks back at the Colony ship. It's hanging off to one side, not moving, drifting in the blackness. An unexpected wave of anger rolls through her, fresh and sharp. Who the hell *are* these people? Why are they doing this?

She turns her head, intending to find the *Panda* again, when she stops.

They haven't sent any spheres in her direction. They're ignoring her completely: either they don't know she's there, or they don't care. And why would they? Once the *Red Panda* is destroyed, they can just turn and leave.

She's never felt terror like this. It's one thing to face death inside the *Panda*, but it's something else entirely to face it out here, where a single wrong move could end her. It's enough to freeze her in place for a few moments, the blood rushing in her ears. She makes herself think of the *Red Panda*, of Corey Livingstone and his family.

She thinks of her sister's grandson, her grandnephew or nephew twice removed or whatever the hell he is, the one she was going to give that lizard toy to. She'll never be able to see his reaction, never be able to find out if he loves it, or reacts like Corey and Malik did. It's that—that tiny little fact—that finally pushes past the fear. She can't do anything about the spheres …

But maybe she can do something about that damn ship.

Adrift

She bites her lip, focusing on the bright pain, using it to eclipse the ache in her arms and legs. Could she smash the ship's cockpit? Decompress it? No chance. Even the glass on their Central mining module back in the Belt was reinforced: primary and secondary layers, pressure panes, scratch coating. The Colony ship probably has double that—she'll just bounce right off.

What about disabling the engines somehow? If she could get to one of their thrusters ...

... but that won't stop the guidance systems or AI from working, and that means the spheres will keep on coming.

Could use the ship's spheres against it? She won't be able to control them, or get them to turn on their controller. But perhaps she doesn't need to.

She interrogates the idea, trying to find problems with it. There are many, but not as many as the others, which means it's the best idea she's got.

"All right, bucko," she murmurs. "Here we go."

Lorinda Anna Maria Esteban summons every bit of energy she has left, and squeezes the control stick, propelling herself towards the ship. It's upside down in relation to her, which makes it harder. Lorinda swallows, letting muscle memory take over as she flies above the debris, looking for the openings releasing the spheres. It feels like an age before she finds them, two black holes on either side of the ship's bulbous belly.

She's lost sight of the *Panda* entirely—for all she knows, it could be destroyed already. She doesn't dare look. And she has no idea if this is even going to work. If they target her before she gets there ...

"*Dios mio*," Lorinda says. She's barely aware of the whispered prayer. "Don't let them spot me. Let me be small. Lord, let me be a speck of dust out here. Just a little speck of dust."

She pushes the thrusters harder, burning her propellant, ignoring the warnings flashing up in her helmet. The ship is less than a mile away now. She can make out more detail in the bays the spheres are launching from. The spheres are arranged in a long line, locked to a railing running back down into the ship. From a distance, it makes the bay she's approaching look like an eye, with the sphere as the pupil surrounded by a dark iris. She's going to have to do this carefully, and she's going to have to do it fast.

The terror comes back. She makes herself think of Craig, imagines his voice in her ears, his soothing drawl crackly and amused. *Got yourself into a bit of a pickle, darling. Don't you fret, though. Nothing you can't handle.*

A hundred yards now. She can just make out the details inside the launch bay, see more spheres lined up. Right now, her back is to the ship. She needs to come in feet first, bending her knees to absorb the impact. It'll hurt like hell—it's hard not to think of bones and joints shattering, like a dropped champagne flute—but it's the only way.

Carefully, oh so carefully, she works the thrusters, sending tiny jets out to the side. She tilts backwards in relation to the Colony ship. It's then that Lorinda realises that if this works, everybody in that ship is going to die. There's no way they'll be able to seal themselves off in time. The thought almost stops her cold.

Too late now. It's them, or the *Panda*.

Lorinda makes contact with the side of the Colony ship, her knees screaming, a stabbing pain shooting through the joints. But she's still OK. For now. Her suit isn't damaged, and her legs didn't splinter into a thousand pieces. She works her thrusters, moving slowly towards the line of spheres.

The bay they're protruding from is larger than she first thought, a circular hole at least fifteen feet across, like the barrel of a gigantic gun, the muzzle flush against the ship's hull. Inside the barrel, the spheres are attached to a thick rail in a long line, held in place by stout brackets. As she watches, the outermost bracket disengages, the sphere's thrusters activating, sending it exploding away.

The rail moves the line of spheres forward, another taking the first one's place. At full clip, like back at Sigma, this thing must be able to launch spheres at an insane rate. No sooner has the thought occurred than two more fire, moving almost too fast for her to track.

Do they know she's here? Would they have cameras near the sphere bays? She pushes the thought aside—if she doesn't work fast, it's not going to matter one bit whether or not they catch her.

Chapter 25

There's no room left in the *Red Panda*'s cockpit. Everyone on the ship has crowded in, the Livingstones pressed up against Brendan and Seema, Jack having to bend his head as he's squashed into the cockpit wall next to a white-faced Hannah. Every second brings another glimpse of one of the spheres, another piece of debris coming right at them, another sickening lurch from the ship as Volkova yanks the stick back and forth.

Everett is muttering. "Watch the left, watch the left."

"What if we—" says Brendan. He's cut off by a yelp from Anita as a chunk of the gate nearly explodes through the viewport. Volkova turns aside at the last second, her knuckles bloodless against the control stick.

The whole thing reminds Jack of the last football game he watched, a party at the house of someone he can't remember, the kind of party where everyone's drinking out of plastic cups and eating from bowls of sweaty chips. Everyone clustered around an old-school wall holo, yelling and thumping their armrests. He remembers thinking how stupid it was, how nothing they said or did would have any impact on the game.

"Projectile lock," says the *Panda*. "Projectile lll—" It switches back to its original male voice. "Activating playlist: Urban and R&B."

"No!" Volkova shouts. The muscles in her neck stand out, hard as iron. "Cancel command."

This time, the ship responds. "Playlist cancelled, Captain."

"What if we shoot back?" Corey Livingstone shouts.

"*With what?*" yells his brother.

"We could put something in the airlock and depressurise and—"

"Don't be an idiot." Malik looks like he's about to throw up.

"Well, it's better than just standing here!"

"Both of you." Jack can't tell if the expression on Anita Livingstone's face is one of terror or anger. "Get to the escape pod."

"No, Mom! We're not leaving!"

The ship shudders, then lurches sideways. Ordinarily, the gravity well would keep them upright, but its inertial sinks are starting to struggle. They're not meant to deal with the strain Volkova is putting them through. Jack finds himself hurled on top of Brendan and Anita, collapsing in a tangle of limbs. Someone's fingers are in his mouth, one eye squashed against a shoulder. He struggles to his feet, pushing away, just in time to see a bloom of fire from somewhere above them.

"Ha!" Volkova shouts. "Two down! *Eto tebya tochno nauchit!*"

"What's she saying?" Seema yells.

Jack ignores her, reaching out a hand to help Brendan to his feet. Hannah is clinging onto the wall, like she's standing on a ledge with the wind tugging at her. As Jack looks past her, he sees something that almost makes his heart stop.

A third sphere is coming for them. It's shot ahead, fully in view now, cruising around the debris field, avoiding the bigger chunks. It's just starting to turn towards them, and there are very few pieces of debris in the space ahead. It occurs to Jack that the spheres might have some kind of machine learning—if one fails, the others may analyse the data, work out why so they can avoid doing the same. Either that, or they're human-controlled, and the people on the Colony ship have got tired of this game.

"OK, *gondoni*, I see you," Volkova mutters. Her hands dart out, flicking switches faster than Jack can register. He can't be sure, but it feels like the *Red Panda* shudders to a halt, the sphere coming right towards them now, a mile away, closing fast.

"Captain, reverse thrust detected," says the *Panda*. "Should *error error command not understood.*"

"What are you doing?" Jack says. He has a sudden urge to

reach over, push Volkova out of her chair, take over, get them *out of here*.

"Full thrust. Put us back into the debris."

For a second, there's nothing to prove they're moving. Then pieces of debris begin to appear, slipping into view. The sphere is dead centre in the cockpit viewport.

"Can anyone see Lorinda?" Hannah says.

"Forget Lorinda," says Seema. "Why haven't we turned around?"

"Wreckage is too close." Volkova leans to the side, fingers darting across switches. "We turn now, we crash. We have to go straight backwards."

"How are you even steering?"

Volkova taps the side of her head, not looking away from the approaching sphere.

"Are you serious?" Jack says. "You're doing this from *memory*?"

"Isn't there a camera?" says Anita. "A rear-view mirror? Something?"

"No reverse camera," Volkova says, hissing the words through gritted teeth. "Cameras side and bottom, but not on the back."

"Then how are we—"

"*I know where the wreckage is*. I can steer us."

For the first time in forever, nobody says anything. Nobody can look away from the approaching sphere. It's less than half a mile now, a white dot against the blackness, getting bigger every second. Volkova is muttering to herself, and with a dull thud of horror, Jack realises she has her eyes closed. She's tweaking the stick, gently moving them from side to side.

Hannah's face is drained of blood. "Captain, it's getting closer."

"We gotta turn," says Brendan. "Can you go any faster?"

"Not yet," Volkova says.

"But—"

"*Not. Yet.*"

Chapter 26

Lorinda is a few feet away from the line of spheres when whoever is controlling them realises she's there.

Ahead of her, the bay doors begin to slide shut, the protruding rail with its cargo of spheres starting to retract. She doesn't waste time looking for something on the outside to keep them open—there won't be anything. With an economy of movement born from thousands of hours in space, she launches herself forward, firing the thrusters at just the right second to give her enough of a boost. She executes a long, languorous forward flip, grabbing the edge of one of the closing doors, using her momentum to spin herself inside the bay.

A second later, she slams against the interior wall, her breath harsh and ragged, her aged body screaming at her. The doors aren't closing at speed, but she's got perhaps fifteen seconds before they lock her in here.

Lorinda is still in zero-G, outside the reach of the ship's gravity well. Now that she's inside, she can see that what she thought was a simple launch bay is more like a long tube, stretching deep into the interior of the Colony ship, with the sphere rail vanishing into darkness.

There's got to be something she can use. She looks around, wincing at how much effort it takes to turn her head, and spots a recessed panel in the wall. She has no idea if it's connected to the closing door, or if the electronics behind it are thermally shielded, and she doesn't bother second-guessing herself. She grabs the grips on the panel—like all access ports on ship exteriors, they're designed to accommodate suit gloves. Then she braces her feet against the wall, and *pulls*.

The panel snaps right off. Steadying herself with a quick thruster burst, Lorinda goes to work, plunging her hands into the opening. There's a thermal shield, all right. It's there to protect the electronics from the vacuum, and can be removed when the ship is in dry dock so that technicians work on the ship's insides.

Adrift

How many times did Lorinda tell her rig-hounds to be careful with exposed therm-shields? They're good at keeping the internal temperature consistent, but hit 'em wrong and they pop right off—she's seen it happen a dozen times. Whatever advanced tech this ship carries—and it's definitely not alien, that much she's sure of now—the schmucks that built it didn't bother upgrading the basics. Allowing herself the barest smile, Lorinda digs her fingers in, wrenching the panel free.

The vacuum does the rest. There's no spark, no visible effect, but the doors stop moving. There's perhaps six feet of space between them, as if the eye is partially closed. The last sphere is still just beyond the opening. Behind it, cold stars glitter against the black.

The launch bay goes wobbly in front of her, and for a few seconds she feels like she's going to pass out. Yesterday, she was on vacation. She was in her room, shoes off, propped up on the bed, wondering whether she should go to a restaurant for dinner or if she should just grab the fluffy bathrobe and order room service.

With what feels like every ounce of will she has, Lorinda brings herself back. There's no point pulling the same electronics trick on any of the spheres—a shutdown sphere, with its electronics frozen, is no use to her. Either that, or they'll explode when she tries it. She's hurting, and more scared than she's ever been in her life, but she's got no desire to die today.

Most of the spheres are inactive, the lights on their surfaces black and dead. That makes sense. If you're a weapons platform like the Colony ship, you don't engage the enemy with a thousand bombs inside you that could go off at the slightest jostle. You activate them right before launch.

But the two uppermost spheres on the rail are alive, the lights on their surfaces shining in the darkness. They must have been activated already in preparation for launch, and whoever tried to shut down the weapons system has either forgotten about them or can't turn them off. That's what she needs to go for. But if she can't mess with their electronics, then how …

The impact sensors. Every sphere has them, little black nubbins dotted across their surfaces. She's worked on enough sensors before to recognise them—every dig site she's ever been on has had sensor arrays to detect clouds of micrometeoroids, and she's repaired plenty before.

She moves across to the line of spheres. She can't get over how alien the things feel. Each one reminds her of a virus, pictured close up: misshapen, dead, evil. A tiny bomb with just enough awareness to hunt, destroying itself and its target in one go. Each one is perhaps six feet across, and looking at them makes her shiver in her suit. She's seen a lot of different vessels, and dealt with a lot of different tech over the years, but she's never seen anything like these spheres. They move through space as if they're alive.

Please let the Panda *be OK. Please, Lord, don't leave me stuck in here.*

Moving as quickly as she can, she makes her way up to the lowermost active sphere, careful to avoid touching the sensors. She manages to position herself on top of it, next to the bracket connecting it to the launch rail, half kneeling on the sphere's metal surface. With no tether, she has to lock her arm around the rail itself.

Through the sweat-smeared helmet glass, Lorinda examines the bracket. It's a foot-long metal cylinder with four heavy-duty claws at its base, locked into slots at the top of the sphere. The top of the bracket is attached to the transport track like a cable car.

There's got to be a way. There's *got* to.

And then she sees it.

The weak spot.

The brackets will be reinforced against forward motion—the slight jerk whenever the rail moves them towards the launcher. What they're *not* protected from is a sideways impact, perpendicular to the rail. If she can dislodge just one sphere …

There's no time to interrogate the idea. Right now, it's the best she's got. She uses her thrusters to get herself in position against the launch bay wall, her back against it. She doesn't know how much force a single kick will generate, but she can't think of another option. She focuses on the point just above the claws holding the sphere in place. If she can plant her strike there, it might just give her the leverage she needs.

Adrift

She brings her leg back—and stops.

I can't do this.

The pain is everywhere now. She hasn't worked this hard in years—even when Craig was still alive, when she was still out with the rig-hounds, she'd begun relying on machines to do most of the work. This kick, if it even works, is going to destroy her.

Well, hell. She might be old, but she got inside here, didn't she? And it'd be an awful shame to stop those doors from closing and then punk out at the last second.

With a grunt, she fires her front thruster, forcing her body back against the wall, and *kicks*.

If she hadn't been braced, she would have gone flying. As it is, it's a miracle she manages to stay in one place. The zero-G saps force from the kick—it takes her almost everything she has just to build up any momentum. But she strikes the bracket clean, making the ball rock slightly. The pain is indescribable. Inside her helmet Lorinda screams.

One more. Just one more.

She draws her leg back, squeezes her eyes shut, and kicks again. The impact makes the sphere shudder—but it doesn't move, the bracket keeping it locked in place. *Please, God, enough.*

But she has to. Wailing, she lashes out a third time, driving with her heel. At the very last second, her fingers move of their own accord, firing every one of her rear thrusters. She explodes off the wall, the force from the thrust channelling down into her foot.

The bracket snaps clean off, wrenching from its rail. The sphere, LEDs blinking, begins to drift, moving towards the opposite wall.

Working on raw instinct, she keeps firing her thrusters, following the sphere, only just managing not to collide with the rail. Then she executes a second, flawless forward flip, like a swimmer reaching the end of her lane, and plants both feet squarely on top of the sphere.

She has no idea how she manages to avoid the impact sensors, or even how her overloaded legs have the energy to do what she does next. She bends her knees, the pain almost making her black out, and launches herself up and out.

Every action has an equal and opposite reaction. The sphere rockets down the launch tube, plunging into darkness, its blinking lights illuminating the metal walls. Lorinda goes in the opposite direction, popping out of the top of the launch bay.

She doesn't know how much fuel she has left—the tears are messing with her lens, blurring her display—and she doesn't care. She burns it all, firing every thruster she has, exploding away from the Colony ship.

She's not alone. There's a figure approaching from below, clad in a dark grey spacesuit, rocketing towards her in a cloud of compressed gas from the suit thrusters.

Somewhere, deep in the launch tube, the deadly sphere finds its mark.

There's no oxygen to carry the shockwave, but Lorinda's lens goes crazy. Heat bakes into her back, her suit turning into an oven, warnings flashing everywhere—

Craig!

Chapter 27

"Push it," Jack says, unable to look away from the sphere. "Push it harder."

"*I'm at full thrust*," Volkova shouts.

"There!" Anita is pointing to something that might have once been part of a ship, moving past above them. "Get behind that."

"Too big," says Brendan. "We're still underneath it."

"We have to!"

The sphere is still heading right at them, a few hundred yards away now. Volkova starts to move the ship upwards a little, but the sphere simply adjusts its course, keeping its lock.

Jack turns away, eyes squeezed shut.

This is it. This is how it ends.

Adrift

Volkova might have been able to steer them safe for a few minutes, but they were never going to make it. It was only a matter of time. They're trapped, caught in a spiral of debris, hemmed in on all sides. If anybody's piloting the sphere, they can chalk this one up as an easy kill. For them, it was probably fun.

His next thought surprises him. He's not going to look away. If these assholes want to kill him, he's going to look them in the eye while they do it—or at least, he's going to stare down that sphere. They've got seconds left. A single turn, a single minor course correction, and the sphere will smash right into the *Panda*.

As he does so, a clean, clear thought slices through his mind: *Seema was right*.

There's no way the Colony ship would have stranded itself here. There's something else going on. Someone was playing a game, and they were a part of it, and now they're going to die never knowing what that was.

"Wait ..." says Brendan.

The sphere vanishes under the bottom edge of the cockpit—Anita gives a horrified moan as it does. Jack flinches, expecting an explosion at any moment, but it doesn't come.

The thing shot right past them.

"Where is it?" Everett says, peering out of the cockpit glass. "Anybody see?"

Nobody replies. Jack glances at Brendan and Seema, and Brendan shrugs, bewilderment on his face. It doesn't make any sense. It was coming right at them.

Seconds tick by. Half a minute. Volkova, still muttering, begins to turn the ship—they've come out of the spiral of debris they were trapped in, and everybody scans the viewport, trying to spot the sphere.

"Look," Corey says.

In the distance, off to the right, there's a flare of fire. It's slowly going out, the vacuum extinguishing the explosion. Smaller shards of debris are flying out from the sphere's impact site.

"I don't get it," says Malik.

"Are there any more?" Hannah leans over the control panel, looking up through the glass.

"*Nyet.*" Volkova sounds as puzzled as everyone else.

Jack doesn't want to speak. Doesn't want to move, or even breathe. He can't help feeling that it's a ruse—that there's another sphere, waiting just out of sight, ready to launch itself at them the moment they think they're in the clear. He can't remember the last time he didn't feel on edge like this—he supposes it was when he was still on the station, but the memory is distant, hazy, like a half-remembered dream. Something that never happened.

Volkova continues turning the ship, bringing them nearly three-sixty, and that's when the Colony ship swings into view.

Or what's left of it.

In relation to them, it's upside down, tilted slightly to one side. It's not quite split in two, but it's getting there, a ball of silent fire burning in its guts. Jack's mouth falls open as more fires appear, dotting the ship with light. A glittering cloud of glass shards surrounds the cockpit. They look like the glimmer where light from the rising sun hits the ocean.

"I don't understand," says Seema, sounding stunned. "Did they malfunction or something?"

"No malfunction," Volkova says. But she doesn't sound sure.

"Then what …"

"Maybe they hit some of the wreckage?" Everett says.

"Who cares what it was?" Jacks says. "We need to get out of here."

"Not without Lorinda," Hannah says.

Brendan frowns. "You think she even—*whoa shit!*"

A spacesuited figure appears at the top edge of the cockpit glass, shockingly close to them. Lorinda. Her back is to them, and she's holding something in her arms. Something big. Her body blocks it from view.

"Oh my God," Hannah says. "Did she—"

Lorinda turns, and Hannah stops talking. She, along with everyone else in the cockpit, stares in total confusion.

Lorinda's not holding something.

She's holding *someone*.

Another person in a spacesuit, hanging in her arms.

Chapter 28

For the second time in as many minutes, everybody is frozen to the spot.

Corey stares at the second figure in confusion. The spacesuit is different; it's more streamlined, dark grey, with a diagonal orange stripe across the chest. The helmet is sleeker, too, not as bulbous as Lorinda's, although there's a chunky communications module on the right side. Whoever it is isn't moving.

It doesn't make sense. How did the Colony ship get destroyed? Is the person Lorinda's holding *from* there? How did they manage to change into a spacesuit before the ship was destroyed? What did Lorinda *do*?

Unless ... did the person in the other suit do it? Sabotage their mission? Why?

Doesn't matter. They need to let them in. Like, right now.

He takes two steps backwards, half turns, brushing against his mom. She makes a belated grab for him, but he's already gone, spinning past her. He pushes between Malik and Seema, turning sideways, then sprints out onto the main deck.

The stairs to the bar are on his left. He grabs the railing, using it to spin himself one-eighty, then launches himself down the stairs. Cold air licks at his skin, but he barely notices, thundering towards the airlock.

Except—where was the access panel? Corey flicks his head left and right, searching the space on either side of the bulky inner airlock door. He saw Lorinda go outside, saw her step into the airlock, so why can't he remember?

There! Corey leaps forward, reaching up to pull back a latched panel in the wall. It's to the right of the door, a grid of six labelled buttons below a digital display, glitchy with dead pixels. As he hunts for the right button, he realises there's a chance that he might accidentally open both doors at once. That would be really, really bad.

Lorinda. The only person on this ship who isn't crazy. No way he's leaving her out there to die. Besides, they wouldn't design an airlock where both doors could be open at the same time. Right?

His fingers are about to push the button labelled OPEN OUTER DOOR when he's pulled backwards. It's Jack, pushing between him and the panel. "Just wait a second—"

"What are you doing?" Corey tries to get past him, can't do it. "She's still out there!"

"I know, but just *listen* to me."

"Corey?" It's his mom, yelling his name. She and everyone else are coming down the stairs, sprinting across the bar.

Corey points at Jack. "He doesn't want to let them in."

Jack holds up his hands. "I just think—"

"Out of the way." Hannah looks both terrified and determined. Jack tries to block her path, but gets distracted when Everett Livingstone puts a hand on his shoulder. He wheels around, angry, which gives Hannah just enough room to squeeze past. Corey feels a burst of triumph as she pushes the right button, not even minding when his mom grabs his arm. There's a muted hiss as the airlock vents itself, followed by the hum of the outer door opening.

"We don't know what's out there," Jack is saying.

"*Lorinda* is out there." Corey can't believe they're even talking about this.

"Yeah, and so is whoever she brought with her."

"So what? You think we should just leave them?"

He puts his hands up, like someone's pointing a gun at him. "I'm just saying, we should talk about this."

Anita is opening her mouth to speak when Volkova's voice comes through the speakers above their head. "They're both inside. You're OK to open up."

"All passengers please stand clear of the airlock doors," the ship says.

Hannah doesn't waste any time, fingers darting around the grid, searching for the right button. As she pushes it, Jack throws up his arms, muttering under his breath as he turns away.

"You're such a shithead, Cor," Malik says, too quietly for their mom to hear.

Adrift

Corey blinks at him. "What's your problem?" The adrenaline is starting to drain out of his body. His skin feels hot and cold, all at once, his hands starting to shake.

"We don't know who that other guy is."

"It doesn't *matter* who he is. We can't just leave him out there." A weird thought occurs: it might not even be a him. There was no way of telling if the person inside the other spacesuit was a man or a woman.

At least they know the ship was crewed by people, not AI. But it doesn't make any sense. How were they planning to get out of here, if they blew up the gate allowing them to pass through the wormhole without getting zapped into a zillion pieces?

Malik is about to say something else when the inner door slides open. Corey's view is blocked for a few seconds, as everyone crowds the airlock. When he finally pushes through, he sees Lorinda lying on the floor, facedown. The other figure is sprawled across her.

There are scorch marks on both suits: black welts on the fabric. And there's something else, too: one of the thin hoses on the second guy's oxygen tank has been disconnected, pulled away from its helmet connection. It's standing upright like an aerial, waving gently.

Neither Lorinda nor the other person are moving.

"Help me with her," Hannah says. She pulls Lorinda away, dragging her out of the airlock. The second figure's helmet clunks off the deck. Corey jumps in to help, grabbing Lorinda under one of her arms. She's a lot heavier with the suit on, and it takes Brendan and Seema on each leg to get her into the bar itself. Corey's parents and his brother, plus a reluctant Jack, bring the other figure inside, setting him down next to the bar.

Corey is first to Lorinda's helmet, fingers fumbling with the catch. Hannah helps him. Together, they slide the helmet to one side, the clunk followed by a hiss of escaping air. It takes them a few more seconds to get the helmet off. Lorinda's eyes are closed, and, to Corey, she looks very, very small.

Hannah puts a finger to her neck. "Got a pulse," she says, her voice shaking. "I've got a pulse!"

161

It's like someone nailed Corey in the chest with a spiralling football. He collapses to the floor with a thump, arms resting on his knees, almost gasping with relief. Behind him, Malik and Jack are pulling off the helmet belonging to the other spaceman. Woman. Whatever. It's a different mechanism from the one on Lorinda's suit, and they're struggling to get it off.

Lorinda's eyes open. The old woman stares into the distance, pupils unfocused. She blinks—once, twice—then looks at Corey.

The corner of her lips tug upwards. Corey puts a hand on her shoulder, even though he knows she won't be able to feel it through the suit.

"You're ... all right," Lorinda says, forcing the upturned corners of her lips into a smile.

Corey wipes his face, surprised to find it wet. "Yeah. We're OK."

Behind him, Malik grunts as the helmet finally comes loose. Hannah glances over, and Corey turns to look for himself.

The head inside the helmet belongs to a man. Light-skinned, with a thin mouth and a prominent, hooked nose. The buzz cut is military, and there's a coating of stubble across his chin. He's unconscious, his eyes closed, his mouth slightly open. Corey notices something he missed before: a patch, sewn onto the arm of the man's spacesuit. Two crossed daggers in front of a shield, black and red. There's no writing on the patch, no motto or anything.

Hannah puts a hand on Corey's arm. "Hey. Can you get her some water? Lorinda?"

"Huh? Oh. Sure." He gets to his feet, unsteady, then makes his way over to the bar. There are still plenty of full glasses and containers, although several of them got knocked over while the captain was trying to outrun the spheres. In a bigger ship, it probably wouldn't have happened, but the *Panda*'s inertial dampeners weren't enough to keep everything steady, and there are puddles of slushy water spread across the bar.

Behind it is his dad's abandoned science project—the heating thing he was making from the remains of the bar fridge. They never got around to sticking it in the gap they made in the ice. The fridge itself has been yanked out of its place by the wall, turned on its end so its underside can be scavenged for parts.

The second fridge is still in its place, but the glass on its open door is shattered. The floor is littered with shards, and tiny chunks of dirty ice. The first aid kit—the one his dad borrowed the medical tape from to use on his device—nudges up against a sodden cardboard box, looking strangely forlorn.

"How'd he even get here?" Malik is saying.

"Beats me, mate." Brendan says, staring down at the unconscious man as he helps Jack to his feet.

Corey grabs one of the glasses, then heads back, dropping to one knee beside Lorinda. She sips carefully, Hannah supporting her head, but Corey pours too fast and some runs down her chin.

"Sorry," he says, pulling back.

"S'alright," she says.

There are only a few more sips left in the glass. "I'll get you some more," Corey says, getting to his feet. As he does so, he glances over to the man with the buzz cut.

The man is awake. And looking right at him. His eyes are a deep blue, cool and clear.

Nobody but Corey has noticed that the man is no longer unconscious. Jack, Brendan and Seema are talking in a huddle, and Malik is fiddling with his holocam.

Corey manages to get out a startled "Hey—" and then the man explodes upwards.

Chapter 29

Brendan is closest. At the movement, he half turns, and then the man's fist crashes into his jaw.

Brendan is big, larger than anyone else on the *Panda*, even his attacker. But the punch is solid, the man's fist blurring through the air. Brendan goes down, a look of stunned incomprehension on his face. Seema reacts. She lunges forward, reaching for the man's throat, only to be thrown aside as if she's made of cardboard.

Corey's dad is standing a little further away from the man than Brendan was. He has just enough time to dodge, to yank his head backwards as the man throws another punch. He gets out a startled "Jesus!" as the fist slashes the air in front of him. Jack takes a stumbling step backwards, arms up to protect himself.

Do something. Corey finds he can't move, can't even breathe.

"Passengers!" says the *Panda*, as the man puts his hands on Everett's shoulders, grapples with him. "Thank you for choosing Sigma D-D-D-Destination Tours for your wedding reception. Please enjoy this specially curated playlist, and *sumangalī bhava* to the happy couple!"

Loud, screechy bhangra music blurts out of the speakers, bouncy and upbeat, thumping drums crashing. Malik hurls himself onto the man's back, arms wrapped around his throat. The man reacts immediately, grunting as he throws Malik in a massive somersault over his head, knocking Everett to one side. Malik howls as he thuds onto the deck, hitting so hard that he actually bounces.

Hannah is darting forward, back, looking for an opening. "Turn off music!" she shouts. The ship's computer ignores her.

Throwing Malik has left the man doubled over. If he wasn't wearing a spacesuit, it'd be easy for him to spring upright, but the fabric has crimped at his torso, and it takes him an extra split second to pull through it. Just enough time for Anita Livingstone to kick him so hard in the stomach that she, too, falls over.

The spacesuit protects him from some of the impact, but not all of it. The man teeters, and then Jack and Everett are on top of him, pinning him to the ground. Corey finally moves, hurling himself on the man's flailing legs. It's like trying to stay on a bucking horse. But then Seema is there, and Hannah, all of them sitting on top of him. Brendan, an ugly bruise already blooming on his jaw, jams his metal arm into the man's throat. The soldier—if that's what he is—makes the only sound Corey has heard him make so far, an annoyed, choked grunt. But he's *still going*. He tries to get up, only stopping when Seema sticks a knee on his collarbone and flicks open her penknife, holding the tiny blade to his throat.

Adrift

"You don't want to move right now, mate," she says, her voice ragged. The man goes still, staring up at her.

"Jesus," Everett says again. He looks for his family, eyes flicking between Corey, Anita and Malik. His eldest son is blinking in surprise, up on his elbows, like he's just woken from a nap. That stupid music is still playing—an even faster track now, Indian strings set to a humming bassline.

"Shit," says Jack. An odd thought pops into Corey's head: people always talk in single swear words after something bad happens. He doesn't get it. If you're going to swear, you might as well get as many in as you can.

The thought is followed by another, more practical one. "We gotta tie him up," he says.

"With what?" Brendan is rolling his jaw, massaging it.

They all look at each other, nobody saying anything. Now that he's suggested it, Corey's mind goes blank. What *do* they have to tie someone up with? They could cut strips from someone's shirt, but …

Hannah snaps her fingers. "Tape." She glances at Seema and Corey. "Don't get off him 'til I get back."

"Uh … *yeah*." Seema looks at her like she's insane. They're all breathing hard, with the flushed faces of people who just walked out of a car wreck unscathed.

"Will there even be any left?" Anita says. She's on her feet, shaking, unbalanced.

Hannah doesn't answer. She darts around to the fridges, grabbing the first aid kit and lifting it onto the bar. As she rummages through it, her movements get increasingly frantic.

"Quickly," Jack growls.

"It's not here," she says. "Did someone take it?"

"It should be in the kit," Everett shouts back.

"Fuck the tape," Seema hasn't moved the knife from the man's throat. "Get some zip ties. Something."

Corey happens to be looking at his mom as Seema speaks, and she does the oddest thing. Her eyes go wide, like she's had a brilliant idea. A second later, she's squeezing them shut, wincing, like someone punched her in the stomach.

"Mom?" Corey says.

"Hang on." Anita Livingstone sprints towards the stairs, taking them two at a time. "I'll be back in a second."

"Anita?" Everett says. He's stopped when the man once again tries to twist away, still moving in silence, nearly bucking Jack off. Seema has to dig the point of the knife into his neck, hard enough to draw a dot of blood, to get him to stop.

Anita comes sprinting back. In one hand she's carrying a pair of metal handcuffs.

Corey is so astonished that he forgets what they're doing. Where the hell did his mom find *handcuffs*?

"Here," she says, tossing them to Hannah. The tour guide catches them instinctively. She looks at Anita, then down at the cuffs, then back at Anita.

"What are these?" she says, her voice stunned. Everett is staring wide-eyed at his wife.

"What do you think?" Corey's mom looks like she wants a hole to open up in the floor and swallow her. "Quick. I've already unlocked them."

The man is moving again, but there are just too many people on top of him now, and his predicament gets worse when Hannah has them flip him over. She kneels on his back, like she's pinning him to a wrestling mat.

"Get his hands," she says, still sounding as if she thinks this is all a dream.

Malik moves first. He's still dazed, but he's got enough in him to pull the man's arms behind him. Corey and his dad help pull his gloves off, holding down the man's arms as he tries to fight back.

"Are they going to be strong enough?" Seema asks.

Anita closes her eyes before answering. "Oh, trust me. They'll do the job."

"Anita," Everett says. "Tell me those aren't what we—"

"I put them in my bag when we were packing for the trip," Anita says. "They've been there the whole time. I thought ... I mean I figured we could ..."

"But we haven't used them in years! And the kids! What were you thinking?"

"Well, maybe if you were paying attention to me, you would have *known* what I was thinking!"

Corey looks between them, completely confused. What are they talking about? Why were there handcuffs in his mom's *bag*?

"Oh my God," Malik says, putting a hand over his face. "Oh my God, *no*. Mom. That is *so* gak."

"I'm ..." Anita says. She clears her throat. "Well, you know, when two adults—"

"Stop," Malik says. "Just ... no. I don't want to know."

Corey opens his mouth, closes it again. Is this a thing about s-e-x? But why would you need handcuffs? Probably not the best time to ask. And wherever the cuffs came from, they're working OK.

His dad spots something, walking over to the bar and bending down. "I found the tape," he says, straightening up. The music is still playing.

The prisoner's blue eyes find Corey again, fixing on him. Like he's being marked. He shivers, but doesn't look away.

Seema wipes the back of her hand across her mouth. It's a long, slow, deliberate movement, and above her palm her eyes are filled with emotional, agonised fury.

"So," she says, standing over the man, speaking over the bhangra, which is still playing. "How about you tell us what the fuck is going on?"

Chapter 30

It takes a while for them to decide where to put the man.

Brendan and Jack—and, surprisingly, Everett—want to keep him in the bar, start questioning him right then and there. Hannah and Volkova argue that he needs to be kept somewhere they can lock down if they need to. Anita assures them that the cuffs are police-grade steel, a phrase which causes Malik to put his hands over his face with a groan of disgust, and which makes Jack snort. Even Hannah finds herself smiling a little. All the same, they can't take any chances.

In the end, they manoeuvre him upstairs, and—somehow—get him down the ladder into astronautics. There, with Seema once again holding a knife to his throat, they uncuff him—very carefully—and recuff him to an empty equipment rack, the metal embedded in the wall at knee level. It's an uncomfortable position, his arms bent behind him, but Hannah is too tired to care. And the man gives no sign that it bothers him.

He hasn't said a word.

They head back to the main deck, leaving Everett to watch the prisoner. Volkova *finally* manages to shut the *Panda*'s voice off, along with the music. It gives an ear-piercing yelp as it dies—Hannah can't help but picture the captain ripping off the control panel, tearing out wires in a rage.

Jack's puke still isn't cleaned up. Hannah catches herself staring at it, amazed at how annoying it is. It's stopped smelling as bad, the chunks now crusted and dry, but she can't understand why he hasn't bothered to clean it up. Then she wonders why she's obsessing about it, after what just happened.

Her left hand hurts—a solid, throbbing ache. She doesn't know where it came from. And she's not the only one hurt: she's got a passenger with a bruised jaw, another almost passed out from exhaustion, and—

Exhaustion. *Lorinda*. Hannah whirls around, looking for her. She's wrapped in the foil blanket on one of the seats, eyes closed. A glass of water pushes up from the blanket folds like the tip of an iceberg. As Hannah watches, she jerks awake, looking around her as if she's still unsure where she is. She's still wearing her thick spacesuit.

"What happened out there?" Corey says, his eyes wide.

Lorinda can barely speak. "Hurts," she says, her hands fluttering above her leg.

Hannah darts back into the bar, retrieves the first aid kit. It's bare bones, like everything else on the *Panda*, so she almost punches the air when she finds a small box of nanomeds. The box holds three blister packs, each one containing four pills.

Adrift

They're SoftMed, a brand she hasn't seen before—a cheap one, by the looks of it. But they'll do. The tiny gel capsules will dial down Lorinda's pain for a few hours, make her more comfortable and lucid while the bots go to work, delivering concentrated anti-inflammatories.

She grabs one of the blister packs, then dashes back up the stairs, already popping one of the squashy capsules out of the blister pack. Lorinda takes it dry, almost snatching it from her, then settles back, waiting for the bots to take effect.

Hannah shoves the pills into her pocket. If Lorinda's injury is more serious than it looks—something they can't see, a broken bone or a badly torn muscle—then the bots aren't going to cut it. They'll help with the pain, for a time, but they'll be useless at fixing the problem. Doesn't matter. There's nothing they can do about that now.

The story comes in fits and starts. Lorinda tells them how she saw the ship coming up from below, how she couldn't reach them through the comms no matter how hard she tried. When she gets to the part about using one of the ship's own spheres against it, Corey and Malik exchange a startled glance.

"No way," Malik says.

"That is crash," says Corey.

"No, I mean, no way she did that."

"You *saw* the ship, Mal, the whole thing was—"

"Guys." Hannah gestures to Lorinda, who gives her a weak smile. Corey and Malik subside, although Malik still looks like he doesn't believe a word he's hearing.

After the Colony ship exploded, she tells them, she had to work quite hard to stop herself from spinning. There were bodies all around her—bodies and debris. She had just managed to bring herself to a halt when someone grabbed her.

"One of the ... people in that ship," she says, and takes another sip of water. "Must have ... tried to come for me after ... after I shut down the sphere bay."

"You are crazy," Volkova says. But she's grinning. "Completely crazy." She whirls a finger around her head.

Lorinda takes a deep breath, and her next words come out in

a rush, like she's been holding them in for far too long. "We tangled—I couldn't see inside his helmet but I knew he wasn't messing around. So I got hold of ... one of his oxygen hoses and gave it a good old yank. I didn't think I could pull it out, thought I'd just kink it, maybe, but it popped right off. Basic ... tech. They never upgraded that."

Everyone, even Malik, is staring at her with something like awe. Lorinda turns her head to the side, clearing her throat with a noise like a chainsaw starting up, then continues. "By then, I saw that you were OK, so I wanted to get as far away from him as possible. He'd stopped moving, and I was going to ... leave him there when I thought that we might be able to figure out who they were if I brought him in with me."

She looks at Brendan. "I'm ... sorry about that. I didn't know he'd wake up so quickly."

Anita Livingstone gets to her feet, walks over unsteadily and plants a kiss on Lorinda's forehead.

"Thank you," she says quietly. "For saving my boys."

The boys in question give each other an embarrassed look, but they nod thanks, too. Lorinda leans her head back against the wall, eyes closed. *Everyone* is exhausted. Drained. The fight they've just been through would take it out of them on a good day, but it came after twenty-four hours of insanity that she still doesn't know how they survived.

How long are they going to do this? Even Volkova—who has saved them now not once, but twice—can't run at full go forever. No one can. Not to mention the fact that, pretty soon, they're going to run out of food. They were stretched even before an extra passenger came on board—and, come to that, how are they going to feed him? Should they? No, they have to, but what if—

"OK," Volkova says. "We try to talk to him. Find out what he knows."

"Damn right." Jack looks furious. He flicks a glance at Seema. "Bring your knife."

"Not a problem," Seema says.

"*No.*" Volkova's shirt has come untucked, strands of hair frizzing out from her tight bun. "Not on my ship," she says, hissing the words through gritted teeth. "That man is a prisoner of war. We talk to him, but we do *not* hurt him."

"He's one of them," Seema says. "He's Colony. He was on that ship. And we're not at war, by the way."

"Plus," says Jack. "They didn't exactly follow the rules of engagement when they torched Sigma. Why should *we* play nice?"

Hannah takes a deep breath. Her heart feels like it's gained an irregular rhythm, thudding off her ribcage. "Captain's right. We're going to do this properly. We're going to question him together, and we're not—"

"Did you *see* what he just did?" Brendan says.

"That doesn't mean—"

"No." Seema is deathly quiet. "Uh-uh."

Volkova puts a finger on Seema's chest. "And what are you going to do, exactly?" she says. "You cut him, he'll just make up nonsense so you stop."

"Yeah," Brendan says. "But if we *don't*, he won't tell us anything."

"Oh, he'll tell us," Seema says. As Hannah watches, she starts flicking the blade of her knife with her thumb.

Up until now, Jack has been the person Hannah has been really worried about—the one she thought would cause the most problems. She thought she had Brendan and Seema figured out. Seema might have been anxious, her bewildered anger at being separated from her son making her lash out, but it never went anywhere. Brendan always calmed her down, even if his cheerful exterior was starting to show cracks.

Not any more. There's a look in both their eyes now: focused, determined. Like they both know what has to be done.

Seema turns to Jack. "Still think they're being straight with you?"

Jack returns Seema's gaze. He looks as if he's thinking hard, turning something over in his mind.

"We're not going to hurt him." Volkova folds her arms. "It's not up for discussion."

Jack laughs—a sound with no humour in it. "You know," he says, leaning against the edge of a line of plastic chairs, "I don't know about you, but we—" he gestures to Brendan and Seema "—are getting pretty sick of this. Time you told us *exactly* what's going on here."

"You're crazy, too." Volkova twists her face into a disgusted grimace.

"No," Jack says. "You know what's crazy? One little tour ship surviving an attack unlike anything I've ever seen before. That Colony ship destroying its escape route. Doesn't the whole thing strike you as a little strange?" He nods to Seema, who has an expression of grim satisfaction on her face. "She had it right from the start. I thought it was nuts, but maybe she's got a point. Something else is going on here, and I am *tired* of being out of the loop."

"*Out of the loop?*" Volkova says the words like they're rotten in her mouth.

Hannah has started to sweat, her forehead hot and clammy, like she's bitten down on a chilli. "Just listen to yourself," she says.

Jack ignores her. "And then we actually get ahold of someone from that ship—" he pushes himself off the hard plastic, levelling a finger at Volkova "—and you tell us we can't get answers out of him. After everything that's happened."

He points to Seema. "So, yeah, I might not have believed her at first. I thought it really *was* luck that we survived. I was willing to admit there was no conspiracy or game or whatever the hell it is." His voice drops, turning low and dark. "But I'd say all of this puts it squarely back on the fucking table."

The main deck falls silent. Volkova is looking at Jack like he's just told her he can breathe in space without a suit. Behind Hannah, Corey mutters something inaudible.

"No," Hannah says, quiet, firm. "No. It's not back on the table. There is no table."

"Oh come—"

"*There is no table.*" It sounds ridiculous, and she doesn't care. "We just saw ten thousand people on a single station get blown to pieces." She points a finger at Lorinda. "She risks her life to save us. You. The captain gets us out of danger not once, but twice, and—"

Adrift

"That's another thing, actually," Brendan says, every trace of cheerfulness gone. "Explain to me how a tour ship pilot manages to steer us clear of those sphere weapons, twice in a row, in a ship like this. It's a little hard to believe, yes?"

He raises his chin at Volkova. "Who are you, exactly? Because you're not just a regular pilot."

Hannah opens her mouth to tell Brendan that Volkova is former navy, but the captain beats her to it. She squares her shoulders, locking eyes with Brendan.

"Who am I?" she says. "I am Captain Jana Magdalena Volkova. Squadron Leader, 28th Scorpion Battalion, Frontier Navy." She looks at Jack, then at Seema. "During my service, I logged twenty thousand hours flight time, eighteen combat missions, and this is my ship, and you're not going to speak to me any more."

"Exactly," Hannah says. "Thank you."

This time, Jack's laugh is louder. "Please. A Frontier pilot with that much time on the clock, working way the fuck out here?"

"Oh, like you'd know," Hannah spits at him.

He spreads his arms. "Her story stinks. Pilot with that much experience ... I mean, that's some major league hours. She should be at an academy, or doing civilian trips through a wormhole, or anything else. What's a Frontier combat pilot doing on a shitbucket like this one? You think they'd *allow* that?"

He smiles at Hannah. "Or did you two not get around to discussing it?"

Hannah is about to argue the point when she stops. Did Volkova ever explain why she was doing this particular job? Hannah can't remember. Her mind is a mess. But surely ...

Volkova's shoulders aren't squared any more. She's not looking at any of them, and as Hannah watches she turns and starts marching towards the cockpit.

"Hey!" Seema shouts. "We're not done here."

Volkova keeps walking. Seema springs after her, reaching out to put a hand on her shoulder. Before she can get there, Volkova spins around, bellowing into Seema's face.

"You want to know why?" she roars. Seema stops dead, hand still hovering in the air. "Because I am a dishonourable discharge.

I made a bad decision, and I got my wingmen killed." Her voice drops, just a fraction. "Marikit Santos. Lieutenant. John Smythe, Lieutenant Junior Grade. We made a run for a Colony frigate at Bellatrix under my command. I survived. They did not."

Behind her, Corey says, "Holy shit." His mom doesn't bother to tell him not to swear.

"You ask me why I worked at Sigma?" Volkova is looking at Jack now, and now her voice is quiet, so quiet that Hannah has to strain to hear it over the engines. "It was the only job I could get. If the war was on, then maybe—*maybe*—they would bring me back to the Frontier Navy. But the war finished. So I fly the *Red Panda*, and I keep you alive. All of you."

Nobody says anything. Brendan and Seema exchange a meaningful glance, but stay silent. Even Jack has gone quiet.

Volkova's eyes find Hannah's. She, too, says nothing.

Hannah's mouth falls open. *That* was what nagged at her, when Volkova first told her the story about the Battle of Bellatrix. The Frontier lost—narrowly, and without too many casualties, but they still had to retreat. The *Xi Jinping*, the frigate Volkova said that she and her wingmen disabled, was still in service. Not only that: it was taken by the Frontier Navy as part of the Belarus Treaty. They talked about it in one of her seminars, back in college.

She remembers how easily Volkova told the story—how vivid she made it, how she put Hannah right in the cockpit of the fighter next to her. Like she was in a sim.

How long has Volkova been telling herself that story? Running it over and over in her head? Painting an alternative history, even as she spent her days shuttling tourists around Sigma Station? Hannah wants to be angry at her—but how can she? What did Volkova have to gain by telling her the truth about what happened?

"Now you can question the prisoner. That is fine," Volkova says to them. "But if you hurt him, I will put you in the airlock."

Without another word, she turns and walks back to the cockpit.

Chapter 31

"He hasn't said anything," Everett tells Hannah, as she drops the last few feet into astronautics. "Hasn't moved, either. Hey, what was going on up there? I heard shouting."

Hannah opens her mouth to tell him, and gives up. She is way, way too tired. Above her, Jack is just starting to lower himself through the trapdoor; Brendan waiting above him to follow.

The prisoner is sitting against the wall. He's been cuffed to a pipe, running horizontally along the wall. The pipe is high up his back, and it pulls his cuffed hands up behind him. As she approaches, Hannah gets an overwhelming urge to talk to her sister. Right now. She would give anything, absolutely anything, to have Callista put a hand on her shoulder, gently move her aside. Callie would know exactly what to do. She'd have this *dialled*.

But Callie isn't here. It's just her.

Hannah lowers herself to the floor, sitting cross-legged in front of the prisoner. Every movement she makes feels premeditated, loaded with meaning. She folds her hands in her lap, making herself meet those cold blue eyes.

"Come on," says Seema from behind her. She and her husband are standing alongside Jack, packing the small space. She still sounds furious. "You know he isn't going to say anything if we ask like this. Why would he?"

"Got that right," says Jack.

Hannah ignores them. "My name is Hannah Elliott," she tells the man. "I'm the tour guide on this ship. Or was. We were on a tour round Sigma Station when you ..."

She stops, unsure how to say it. *When you destroyed it all? When you killed everyone?* The man's face gives back nothing. She might as well be talking to a statue.

"What's your name?" she says.

No answer.

"She asked you a question, brother," says Brendan.

Hannah flashes him a warning look. Behind him, Anita is just

175

making her way down the ladder. The space is getting crowded, and it's not helping.

"OK, well," she says, pushing ahead. "If you don't want to tell me your name, that's fine. But maybe you can tell me why you … well, why you did what you did. This isn't a law court, we're not judging guilt or innocence here—"

"Are you serious?" Jack says.

Hannah looks over her shoulder at him. "Get out."

"What?"

"You heard me." She can't believe her anger. Maybe what Volkova said got to her, or maybe it's just because she is sick to death of Jack's shit. She points at him, then at Brendan and Seema. "All of you. Get out. I'll handle this."

"We're not leaving," Brendan says. "What if he gets loose? You planning on taking him down by yourself, then?"

"This is bullshit," Jack mutters.

"No," says Hannah. "What's bullshit is you acting like you're going to torture him. That's not going to happen."

Seema's eyes flash, but she says nothing.

"No, Hannah's right," Everett says. They all turn to look at him. "We should at least *try* to talk to him like a human being, and we should do it without all of us crowding him in like this."

"You're acting like he's a wounded animal," Seema says, jabbing a finger at the prisoner. "He and his crew murdered about ten thousand people with—"

"Leave it." Brendan puts a hand on Seema's shoulder. He sounds exhausted. "Let 'em try, if they want. Won't make any difference in the long run."

He shrugs her off, but doesn't look back at Hannah. Instead, he and Seema make their way up the ladder. Jack lingers the longest, looking like he wants to say more. Then he, too, climbs back up the ladder, vanishing onto the main deck.

"I'd like to stay, if that's all right," Anita says.

"I'm not sure that's a good idea."

"I do. I work for the Frontier, remember? I might be able to help."

Hannah looks over at Everett, leaning against the wall. "I'm

Adrift

staying too," he says. "Don't worry. I'm not getting involved. And 'Nita's right—she should be here."

Anita gives him a surprised smile.

Hannah turns back to the prisoner. No change. She looks over his spacesuit, hoping to spot a name tag, even a serial number. Nothing. Just that weird patch with the daggers. Maybe they should try and take it off him, see if he's wearing a uniform underneath …

He's still staring at her. "I'm just trying to understand," she says. "We were doing a tour of the station, so we … we saw what your ship did. Maybe you can tell me why."

Still nothing. His expression doesn't change. Of course, it's entirely possible that he doesn't speak English. It might be the most common language, but that doesn't necessarily mean much. There are, what, five hundred-odd languages across Frontier and Colony? And on the *Panda*, they've got English, Russian, and … well, that's it. No, wait, she's sure she heard Lorinda speaking Spanish a couple of times. A whole three languages. Joy. If he'd just *say* something …

"What about the gate?" she says. "Why destroy it? Surely you needed to escape, too?"

Behind her, Everett shifts, as if getting ready to say something. He doesn't. Astronautics is cold—not as cold as the bar, but still chilly—and Hannah shivers, the bare skin on her arms prickling.

She tries another tack. "I know it feels like you've got nothing to lose right now," she says. "But we're not going to hurt you. All anyone we want to do is get home, so I'm just trying to understand how your ship planned to get out."

"If I could jump in here?" Anita says.

She doesn't wait for Hannah to OK it. "Hi. I'm Anita Livingstone. I'm a lobbying consultant for the Frontier. I work for Senator Daniels? Tom Daniels?"

Nothing.

"Maybe you don't know that name—I hear the feeds in the Colonies are censored sometimes. He's helping renegotiate the Belarus Treaty with your government. Ring any bells?"

Anita pauses for a moment, as if trying to find the right words. Hannah glances at Everett, who gives a helpless shrug.

"What I'm trying to understand," Anita goes on, "is why the Colony would attack now. They're reaching an accord on the treaty. I mean, I know you're probably going to have to give over control of a couple of outposts to the Frontier, but surely that's not bad enough to start another war over, is it? So why attack us?"

For the first time, the prisoner reacts. He raises his chin to Anita, and gives her a quick, amused smile. It vanishes as fast as it arrives.

"Look," Anita says. "If you talk to us, I can get you a deal with the Frontier. You could defect. You—"

"Let me explain how this is going to go," the prisoner says.

Anita stops, startled. The man's voice is monotone, gravelly, his tone lazy and languorous. Hannah can't place his accent—it's American, which isn't unheard of in the Colonies, but there are traces of other nationalities there, too, from multiple planets, flitting in and out at the edges. At least he speaks English. There's still a chance they could—

"The only reason I'm in these cuffs," he continues, "is because you got lucky. You outnumbered me, I was still in my suit, and I was suffering from oxygen depletion."

He turns to Anita, his eyes drilling into hers. When he speaks again, he sounds almost bored. "You're going to keep trying to get me to give you information. I'm going to keep ignoring you. We both know you won't torture me, thanks to the little display with your friends."

He jerks his chin up towards the hatch. "Besides, you don't have the stomach for it. None of you do. And, sooner or later, you're going to make a mistake. One of you is going to mess up, and I'm going to get free. I should be in better shape by then, because you're going to give me food and water, and let me sleep. Which means everything that happens next is a foregone conclusion. It'd be quicker for you if you just let me go now."

"So you're just going to kill everyone?" Hannah's voice is shaking. "We've got kids on board."

"And what does it matter?" says Everett. He sounds calm, but he's clenching and unclenching his hands at his sides. "Even if you ... if you killed us all, you'd still be stuck out—"

He stops dead, his eyes going wide.

Adrift

"Ev?" Anita says.

"He thinks he's going to be rescued."

"But there's—"

"Don't you get it?" He points at the prisoner. "He must have backup or something. Another ship out here. A station we don't know about. Maybe even another jump gate."

"We would have seen them," Hannah says. She's trying to process what Everett is saying, aware that they're doing this in front of the prisoner, who is watching her with a faintly amused look on his face. "They would have found us, or the captain would have picked them up on radar or something. It doesn't make sense."

"*None of this makes sense.*" Everett bellows the words, causing Anita to jerk like she's touched a live wire. "Find me another reason why he's trying to kill—"

"You want to talk about killing?" The prisoner's voice is quiet, cold as space itself. "You just killed eleven of the finest soldiers I've ever served with. I don't know how, but you pulled it off. Congratulations. Now tell me: did you ever consider that maybe I'm not interested in being rescued any more?"

In the silence that follows, Hannah has to almost physically will herself to speak. "You killed *thousands* of people," she says.

He shrugs. He actually shrugs. "Did you know all those thousands of people?" He looks from her to Everett, his expression unchanged. "How about you? No? Well, here's the difference, and this one you get for free. No torture necessary. I knew every one of those eleven soldiers. Every single one."

A hundred responses dance for attention in Hannah's mind. None of them do the job. Her tongue is a dead weight in her mouth. She wants to say that she knew some of the people on Sigma—that she knew Donnie, the guide with the ridiculous mohawk, and Atsuke, the supervisor who was nice to her. But she didn't know them. Not really. She didn't know what Donnie did in his spare time, or what kind of beer Atsuke liked.

For some reason, she thinks of the guide who interrupted her in the VR sim, the one who told her she was on tour ship duty. She didn't even know his name.

"We could just kill you," she says, after a few moments. It sounds pathetic, even as she says it.

"But you won't," the man says. Then, without changing his tone: "I need food, and water. And I need to be able to use the bathroom."

Nothing else. He doesn't continue, doesn't elaborate. He says the words like he's ordering a meal at a restaurant.

"We're trying to help you," Hannah says, biting back the frustration. "And we'll get you something to eat as soon as you answer our questions."

The man smirks. It looks strange, like his face isn't used to holding any sort of expression. "That's the problem with you people. You always think you're doing the right thing. Always think you can help."

"What do you mean?" Anita says.

No response.

Hannah climbs to her feet, doing it slowly, like she's bored. "Fine," she says. "I'll tell the other three that it didn't work. See how you like that. Come on, Anita."

See how you like that? She might as well have stomped her feet. The prisoner chuckles, a sound like a heavy smoker clearing his throat. "Do what you have to. But it's like I said: at some point, one of you is going to slip."

Hannah opens her mouth, then closes it. What is she supposed to say? This isn't corralling a group of scared passengers, or figuring out what to do about a frozen water tank. This isn't dealing with Jack, or Seema—they might be assholes, but they're all still on the same side.

This? She's not ready for this. She doesn't know a single thing about interrogation, and, even if she did, what possible reason does this man have to answer her? His ship is destroyed, his crew is dead. He's got nothing left to lose.

Maybe they *should* let Jack try. Maybe—

No. We're not doing that. Not ever.

"Please," Anita says, and for the first time, a note of desperation sneaks into her voice. "My kids are on this ship. We can *help* you."

"Food and water," the man repeats, just as Hannah reaches the ladder.

"Watch him," Hannah says to Everett, starting to climb, trying to fight back the frustrated, terrified tears. Behind her, Anita gives a shaky sigh, and follows.

Chapter 32

Jack once spent a lot of money on a home meditation course.

It was the kind of thing that came in a beautifully designed lens app, with its own bespoke voiceover and customised data gathering and a money-back guarantee. It promised a mind as clear and empty as a dawn sky—those were the exact words on the marketing copy, written in a font with softly rounded edges.

He shelled out for it around six months after he'd left São Paulo, in that confused, raw period after Hector had told him to leave. He badly wanted to move on. Get clear. Build a new him, a new *life*, one with a job he deserved and nights where he slept like a baby, instead of lying there for hours, his mind zigzagging from one thought to the next, until he finally got up and drowned it in beer or whisky. Or cheap vodka, if payday was a while away.

The whole idea was to focus on your breathing. You sat there, eyes closed, counting breaths. When you got to ten, you went back to the beginning. That was all there was to it—Jack went through a dozen virtually identical sessions with nothing but an occasional, monotone voiceover urging him to relax.

He didn't. He couldn't. He'd be counting breaths, doing everything he could to empty his mind, and then he'd suddenly be thinking about work or the booze or Hector or his damn credit account. He'd shift in his seat, irritated, getting back to the grim business of clearing his mind.

He'd lasted less than a week on the programme. When he tried to get his money back, the customer service agent had told him that he needed to wait another five months and three weeks for the money-back guarantee to kick in, which made him so angry he nearly tore his lens out in disgust. He'd gone back to the booze to help him drift off. At least *that* performed as advertised.

One, he thinks. *Two*. Before he's even exhaled a second time, he's thinking, with a sick inevitability, about Hector.

Hec is—*was*—a cop, and a clichéd one at that: muscles, tattoos, military buzz cut. The whole nine. Jack had met him on assignment in Brazil, on some travel junket for a company whose name he couldn't even remember. He'd been working at a feed in Venezuela at the time, running their excuse for a lifestyle section.

He'd been outside one of the godawful restaurants they'd dragged him to, and had bummed a smoke from a cop on the other side of the rope. The cop had made a joke about the restaurant, and since Jack had no desire to go back inside sooner than he absolutely had to, they got talking. The cop's English was pretty good. Later that night, after a few drinks in Jack's hotel bar, he'd discovered that Hector Alarcón was pretty good in the sack, too.

They'd always joked—usually when they were lying in bed, Hec smoking, Jack's leg twisted over his—that they were only together because Jack had a thing for men in uniform. The reality was that they worked, in a way that none of Jack's previous relationships, with any genders, had. Jack doesn't know if they were in love—they never discussed it, not in those terms. But they were so, so good for each other.

They both had the same sarcastic view of the world, the same low tolerance for bullshit. They both had trouble getting along with other people, and they were both surprised that they got along with each other so well. Like him, Hec didn't hang out with his family much—Jack saw his folks back in DC once a year, if that—and he didn't have all that many close friends. They had each other, and that was enough. Fuck everybody else.

And they had the same ethics. Jack was proud of that. There were plenty of bent cops in Brazil, more than there used to be after the coasts were abandoned, but Hector Alarcón wasn't one of them. Jack had looked into *that* one early on, asking a contact at one of the local feeds for any scuzz on his new squeeze. There was none.

And so he went down south every chance he got, sitting on the ultraloop dreaming of Hec's chest under his hand, of the *pastel* they'd soon be stuffing their faces with, of the glowing oil running down Hec's chin.

He should have known better than to get attached. Drug squad was a hazardous occupation anywhere, but particularly in São Paulo. The Roses Cartel mostly operated out of Mars and Proxima these days, but they'd started in Brazil, and they still had operations there.

Hec had gone on a raid to one of the Roses safe houses (*the flower beds*, the crime reporters called them, either not knowing how cheesy it sounded or not caring). The flower bed in question was an apartment block in Alemão. Usually, droids handled the knock-knocks, but Hec's commander sensed a victory, and wanted his officers on hand to personally claim the prize. Jack would never forgive him for that.

Hec had taken three bullets. C4 spinal cord injury. Full quad. Jack was back in Caracas when it happened, and it had taken three days before anybody had even thought to notify him. He'd all but sprinted down there, vanishing from his feed office forty-five minutes before a deadline. He doesn't remember the ultraloop ride down, but he'll never forget seeing Hec in that hospital bed.

There was treatment. Nano injections and artificial limbs, even a whole new spine. But Hec's department had bureaucracy that made Jack want to personally strangle each and every person in it. You could have all the scientific and medical advances you wanted, but it meant diddly if the paperwork wasn't in order.

A month had turned into two, then three. Hec didn't need a ventilator to breathe, thank God, and Jack had gone down every single chance he had. But ... Hec wasn't Hec any more.

They started fighting—small things at first, little firecrackers that sputtered out as soon as they started. But they got bigger, and longer, and the worst thing of all was seeing Hec wanting to move, *willing* himself to move, and not being able to do so. He didn't want Jack to see him like this, and couldn't—wouldn't—try and understand why Jack kept coming.

Things had come to a head on a bright spring morning, with the sun pouring in through the window. Jack mentioned maybe taking Hec for a trip outside the hospital, maybe heading down to that bar they liked, the one in Lapa. That's when Hec had accused him of being insensitive. Of not caring about his condition.

Jack had seen red at that. Insensitive? Hadn't he been doing everything he could to be supportive? Hadn't he put his life on hold to help? He'd said as much, and that's when things got *really* exciting.

In the end, Hec had forbidden him from visiting. Jack still remembered the last time he'd tried, pleading with the nurse in his useless, inept Portuguese.

He'd gone back to work. Or tried to. He didn't feel a need to drink then, mostly because he didn't feel anything. It was only after everything went tits up at work that the need to drink became a terrible, burning urge.

He was never naive or stupid enough to expect that the world would stop. His colleagues at the feed had jobs to do, whether Hector was in his life or not. What got him—what really and truly got him—was the pity. The slightly nervous pauses before anyone spoke to him. The whispers at the staff canteen, only just audible.

His editors were the worst. They'd told him that out of respect for what had happened, they'd be assigning him a few easy jobs, to let him get used to working again. The easy jobs had slowly become the ones no one else wanted—and the crazy thing is, he's pretty sure his bosses thought they were just being kind, that they were doing him a favour. A senior position he was gunning for mysteriously vanished. Too soon, they'd said. Next year perhaps. Just keep filing your little hotel reviews. What the hell, enjoy yourself. Take an extra day. On us.

In the end, he'd decided to get as far away as possible. Europa seemed like a good bet. The dome colony there had a new feed, part of a big post-war media boom in that part of the Frontier, and they were looking for a travel guy. Europa was cold, and boring, and far from everywhere. Which was just fine by Jack.

Adrift

He can't pinpoint the exact moment when the drinking got out of hand. When it became Too Much. But all of a sudden, it *was* too much, and he didn't really see the point in stopping it.

It helped dull the icy shame he felt: that Hec's rejection didn't send him to the bottle, but his career dying did. That he didn't stick it out—push past Hector's depression, work harder to remind him that they were both miserable shitheads, and that miserable shitheads had to stick together, no matter what. The shame created a feedback loop: one he eventually decided to stop fighting.

He'd always told himself he'd go back. Go and see Hec, and fix things. Not going to happen now.

It's been around eight hours since the prisoner first came on board, and Jack's mind is a whirling hornet's nest. He has more chance of producing whisky out of thin air than he does of going to sleep. It doesn't help that he's starving, and freezing cold—he's curled up under the bar counter, lying on his side, using an empty box as a pillow. He came down here because he wanted to get as far away from everyone as possible. By the time he realised he was too cold to sleep, he had no desire to go back upstairs.

The ship is dark. Volkova turned off the lights after dinner, when everyone decided to turn in. Dinner. What a joke. A JamFizz and half a bag of stale soychips that he had to share with Malik Livingstone. Jack's stomach is both empty and disgustingly bloated, and every sound the *Red Panda* makes feels magnified, the clanking of the metal hull and the rumbling of the engine drilling into his brain. He shivers, hugging his legs to his chest, pulling his jacket sleeves over his fingers.

And round and round the hornets go.

In the darkness, his thoughts balloon, mutate, swelling into grotesque monstrosities as if stung repeatedly. He keeps replaying the past day in his mind. How could these people—these *fucks*— try to kill them not once, but twice? That would have been bad enough, but then one of them somehow lands up on the *Red Panda*, and gets treated like royalty. Gets his own private room, a full-time minder, has half the passengers protecting him …

His hands are trembling, and it's getting harder and harder not to fixate on a drink. Any drink. Whisky, vodka, beer, frozen fucking margarita …

Jack rolls over, hunching his head down into his jacket collar, letting out a soft sound somewhere between a moan and a snarl. He has to sleep. He *needs* to sleep. He counts, exhaling clouds of white vapour. *One. Two. Three. Nothing to lose, probably laughing at us, laughing at me, he just grabbed me and threw me out the way—*

Jack opens his eyes.

He stares at the inside of the bar counter for a good ten seconds. Then, limbs aching, he slowly clambers to his feet.

Chapter 33

The bar is dark, but Jack moves with more purpose than he has in months. Years.

He makes his way around the side of the counter, running a hand along it for balance, ignoring the stickiness from a puddle of spilled JamFizz. He pauses a few feet from the bathroom, waiting to see if anyone is inside. When he hears nothing, he keeps going, moving quietly onto the stairs. Above him, someone is snoring.

He makes his way up to the main deck. It's not quite as dark as the bar—there's a little light coming from the Neb, just visible at the edge of the viewing dome. The dark, hulking wreck of the Colony ship, the fires inside it long since burned out. Beyond it, a billion miles of nothing.

No one coming for them. No patrol ships. No Frontier cruisers. Nobody outside this ship who'll even know what he's about to do.

There are huddled figures curled up on the seats at the far end of the deck. Jack stops on the last step, not moving, not making a sound. Waiting for one of them to sit up, focus on him. They don't.

Adrift

His eyes slide sideways, to where Brendan and Seema are sleeping, up against the wall. Brendan has his back to him, his head supported by a balled-up jacket. Seema has deactivated her glowing tattoo, the ink invisible in the darkness.

The entire place stinks—Jack thought he would have got used to the smell by now, but he hasn't. There's a faint tang in the mix of body odour and food smells: he never cleaned up that puke from before. Fuck it. He can worry about it later.

He starts moving towards the sleeping couple—and is brought up short when he steps on an empty soychip packet. The crackle-crunch sounds louder than a bomb going off.

He freezes, not sure why he's being cautious—after all, it's not like he's banned from the main deck. All the same, he waits for a good few seconds until he's sure no one has woken up.

When he reaches Brendan's slumbering body, he goes down on one knee, looking back over his shoulder again. When he turns round, Brendan is looking right at him.

Jack puts a finger to his lips. After a moment, Brendan nods.

"If I go down there," Jack says, speaking as softly as he can. "Will you have my back?"

Part of him expects Brendan to say no, maybe even to raise the alarm. But the man just looks him, eyes bright and alert, fully awake.

"What you gonna do?" Brendan says, his lips barely moving.

"What do you think?" Jack glances at the area of the main deck where the trapdoor is.

"We're in," Seema says, making Jack jump. Her eyes glint in the dark, picking up the light from the Neb.

"OK." Jack puts a hand on the floor, ready to push himself up. For the first time he gets a hint of what it might be like to have a mind as clear and empty as a dawn sky. "We go in quiet. Not a sound. Once we're in there, we figure out how to lock the trap-door."

"What about daddy dearest?" Brendan murmurs. "He's still down there."

"Three of us, one of him. Let's go."

Slowly, carefully, they make their way across the main deck.

Jack runs through a mental list of the other passengers, ticking them off. Everett downstairs. Anita and her two boys are on the other side, and Hannah is well behind them, sleeping in the passage leading to the cockpit. Lorinda is closer to them than Jack would like, at their two o'clock, but she's passed out cold, curled in a blanket. Of course she's asleep. Nice and warm and comfy.

He can't see Volkova—she must be back in the cockpit. Are there security cameras? Can she see them? Maybe—but he's pretty sure any cameras on this piece of crap won't have night vision, and in any case, by the time she figures out what they're doing, they'll be down the trapdoor and home free.

Then they can get some answers.

The trapdoor is a few feet away. They're going to have to be very, very careful when they open it. A single noise could—shit, did the hinges creak the last time? Jack can't remember. He glances at Seema, moving alongside him. She's looking at the trapdoor, too, her eyes never leaving it. Despite the cold, she's not wearing a jacket, and her muscles ripple under her top.

A few seconds later, they're crouching around the trapdoor. Brendan is reaching for the handle when Seema holds a hand up. *Wait.*

The three of them listen hard. Nothing—just the rumble and hiss of the *Red Panda*, blank as space itself. Seema nods, and Brendan braces himself. Slowly, oh so slowly, he starts to tug the trapdoor up.

It takes a whole minute to get it open. Several times, the hinges start to creak and Brendan has to slow right down, not wanting to make a sound. But, eventually, he lowers the trapdoor onto the floor, exposing the ladder to astronautics. There's a light on down below, and it illuminates the main deck a little.

"Hello?" says a voice from below them. Everett. Jack bites back a curse, starts to move faster, before they can raise the—

He has both feet on the ladder when someone grabs him by the collar, hauling him upright and hurling him across the deck. Brendan and Seema scramble to their feet, and, as Jack gets up on one elbow, he sees Volkova towering above him.

"What's going on up there?" Everett shouts. Behind him, Jack can hear the rest of the family stirring. Lorinda sits up, blinking in confusion.

"You," Volkova says, levelling a finger at him. She swings it round to take in Brendan and Seema. "You think I am stupid, *da*? You think I'm not watching what you are doing?"

"We just want to talk to him," Jack says, his voice even.

"Oh, talk to him, I see, OK." Volkova shakes her head in disgust, leaning over to grab the trapdoor. She stops when Seema puts a hand on her wrist. Volkova stares at her in amazement.

"He's not going to tell us anything," Seema says. "Not the way we're going."

"Hey!" shouts Everett, his voice made echoey by the trapdoor. "What's going on?"

"It's OK, honey," Anita shouts back. Corey and Malik exchange a worried look, the older brother blinking back sleep.

"This is my ship," Volkova says, through gritted teeth. "And on my ship, I say no torture. Not ever."

"We're not gonna torture him, for Christ's sake," says Brendan. "Just knock him about a bit."

"It's torture. You're mistreating a prisoner of war. This is my ship, so no."

"It's your ship?" Jack gets to his feet. "Well, it's our lives. So why don't you go be a pilot and leave the rest to us?"

Volkova turns her blazing eyes on him. In the semi-darkness, with her dishevelled hair and her hunched shoulders, she looks like something out of a nightmare. "You wouldn't even be alive if I wasn't here. So you will go back to sleep, and *leave this alone*."

Hannah's high-pitched voice comes from behind Jack. "What are they doing?"

"They want to hurt the guy downstairs," Corey says. Anita gives him a warning look.

"But we agreed," Hannah says, sounding as if she's not sure whether she's still dreaming.

"We didn't agree on a damn thing." Seema still hasn't let go of Volkova's hand. They're on the edge of the trapdoor, Everett half in, half out, staring up at them in confusion.

Jack's had enough. He reaches the captain in two strides, gripping her shoulder. "We're going in there, whether you like it or—"

Volkova rips away from him. In the process, she pulls Seema off balance. Instead of falling, the woman reacts violently, yanking Volkova's arm hard. The captain loses her footing, finds it again, then swings a flat-handed strike at Seema's face.

"Seema, no!" Brendan lunges forward, but before he gets there, his wife reacts.

She dodges Volkova's blow, her feet planted, leaning back and letting the captain's palm whistle past her face. Then she rocks forward, and in one snake-quick movement brings her hand up and across Volkova's throat.

Volkova gives a strangled, agonised cough. She stumbles across the floor, away from Seema, then falls to one knee. Her hands move to her neck, fingers hooked into claws.

For the first time in what feels like forever, nobody moves. They're all staring at Volkova, at the unmistakable slick of blood staining her shirt, just visible in the light from astronautics. Faintly, Jack can smell the blood: a distant, coppery tang.

Seema's penknife. It's buried up to the hilt in Volkova's neck, right above the middle of her collarbone.

As Jack watches, her eyes find his. The look in them is one of complete surprise. A second later, they go dark.

Chapter 34

Corey doesn't quite understand what happens next.

He's staring at Volkova's body, at her blank eyes and the big—no, the *giant* pool of blood around her neck. Seema is standing over her, an expression of startled fury on her face, ignoring Brendan, who keeps bellowing "What the fuck did you just do?" over and over again.

Adrift

Then his dad launches himself out of the trapdoor, pushing Malik back, getting alongside his wife and grabbing Corey. Hannah shoves Jack. The edge of a chair takes him at the knees, and he sits down hard.

Everyone is screaming at each other, and all Corey can see are wide mouths and huge eyes.

Brendan tries to pull Hannah away. Corey doesn't see it all—his mom and dad shuffle backwards, getting between them and the fight, the trapdoor just behind him. Corey still can't look away from Volkova's body. The knife must have hit an artery—or is it a vein? Corey can't remember. She might not be dead yet, but it won't be long before—

"Stay here," Everett shouts over his shoulder.

"But Dad—" Malik says. Everett ignores him. He takes a step forward—only to trip over Volkova's outstretched leg. Anita grabs him, and that's when Jack shoves Hannah.

She stumbles, colliding with Everett. Corey has just enough time to think that maybe he should get out of the way when his dad slams into him, and he falls backwards.

Malik reaches for him, gripping the sleeve of his T-shirt. There's a second when he has it, and then he doesn't, and then Corey remembers that the trapdoor is just behind him.

As gravity takes him, as his body works out that the floor isn't there to catch it, Corey gives a strangled yell. Then he's falling, the trapdoor above him framing the scene. His dad, eyes wide with panic. His brother's hands, still trying to catch him. The edge of his mom's shoe.

Oh, Corey thinks. Then the impact wipes his mind clean.

He's only out for a split second. Or, at least, it *feels* like a split second. He can't see anything. The metal floor is cold against his cheek, and there are people talking, their voices loud and terrified.

His mom: "Shit, oh shit, oh God, Corey, talk to—"

Hannah: "—close it! Close the—"

Dad: "—told you we should've—"

Corey blinks, and goes away again for a while.

It's Malik's voice that brings him back. His brother is saying his name, over and over, and his voice sounds so small and scared that Corey almost laughs. What is Mal worried about? He's fine. He just had a little nap. He didn't—

He opens his eyes. He's propped against a wall, in a strange room he doesn't recognise. No, that's wrong, he knows where he is. Astronautics. His mom and Malik are kneeling in front of him, eyes wide. Hannah behind them, pacing, looking up at the ceiling. His dad standing above them on the ladder, cheeks flushed and sweaty. The trapdoor is shut, his dad holding it closed, sweat shining on his forehead. From above, there are muffled thumps as someone hammers on the trapdoor, trying to wrench it back.

I gotta go help. The thought is the first clear one Corey's had in a while, bright and sharp. He pulls his feet towards him to stand, only one of them won't come. His knee bends, but the bottom half of his lower leg feels a thousand times heavier than it should.

He looks down at it, first annoyed, then confused. The shape is all wrong. The fabric of his jeans just under the knee is pulled taut, the denim tenting upwards. And is that … *blood*? Well, yeah, of course it's blood, dumbass, it's blood from what happened to the captain. Did that actually happen? It feels like a dream …

Only: if it's the captain's blood, why is the stain spreading? It's creeping across his jeans, a dark, uneven splotch, growing by the second.

"Oog," Corey says.

His mom puts a hand on his shoulder. "Corey? Corey, it's going to be OK, honey, it's just—"

"*Oog!*" He's going to throw up. He's going to scream. He's going to do both, and he's not going to be able to stop. How could he not have noticed the pain? It's like the bottom half of his leg has been set on fire.

Could he push the bones back? Just click them together? But then he'd have to touch them, feel their sharp, brittle edges through the fabric, and that *really* makes him want to throw up.

His mom puts a hand on Mal's shoulder, gripping it so hard that his brother winces in pain. Her voice is way too calm. "Malik, baby, find a tourniquet for me."

"A … what?"

Adrift

"A tourniquet, Malik." She speaks patiently, her voice wavering just a little.

His brother wavers. "Mom, I don't know what that—"

"*A tourniquet!*" she shouts. "Something to tie his leg off with! A rope or—" She reaches across, grabs her older son's hands, forces them onto Corey's leg above the knee, which turns the fire into an inferno.

"Just hold here," Anita tells Malik. "Do *not* let go. Ev? *Ev!*"

"Hold on." Everett is all but hanging off the trapdoor, holding it closed with one arm while the other hunts for wherever the locking mechanism is.

"Ev, I need you down here!"

"Mom." Malik's dark skin has gone grey. "Mom, he's bleeding a *lot.*"

"Squeeze harder. *Everett!*"

"In a second!" Hannah yells over her shoulder. In the small space, her words are given a nasty metallic edge. She's climbing up the ladder, just below Corey's dad, pointing with a trembling finger. "You gotta slide that back," she says.

Everett grunts. "This one?"

"Yeah, that's it!"

"It's not moving."

"Push harder."

"I said it's not moving!"

Malik is squeezing so hard it feels to Corey as if his brother's fingers are going to sink into his leg, tear the flesh from the bone. It's an aching, furious band of pain, separate from the hellfire consuming his shin. His mom is pulling off her shirt, fighting with the buttons, giving up, wrenching it over her head with a frustrated snarl. Her tank top beneath it is soaked with sweat.

"Don't use a tourniquet," says the prisoner.

Anita either doesn't hear him or doesn't care. She starts to wrap the shirt around Corey's leg, moving so fast she almost rips the sleeve from the body. The blood turns the green fabric a sickly brown.

"Mom," Malik says, glancing at the prisoner. "Did you hear—"

"Not right now," says Anita.

The soldier raises his voice. "If you use a tourniquet, he'll lose the leg."

Anita stops, her shoulders shaking. She doesn't look at him. Corey gets another wave of pain, bad enough to turn the world grey at the edges.

"Why should we listen to you?" Anita says, still not turning her head.

"I don't really care if you do. But a tourniquet'll cause nerve damage. Dead skin. It'll hurt, a lot. And if you loosen it after, he'll bleed out for good. Just put pressure on either side of the wound. A lot of it."

For a few seconds, neither Corey's mom nor his brother move. Then, still without looking at the prisoner, his mom positions the shirt around the protruding bone, she and Malik leaning into the leg.

"Got it!" shouts his dad. There's a clunk, then another. The thumps on the other side of the trapdoor continue, but Everett is making his way down the ladder, arms shaking. Hannah has fingers laced on top of her head, shaking it, muttering something furious under her breath.

The bottom half of Corey's leg is on fire, but the top half is icy-numb, the two sensations fighting for control. Maybe they should get rid of the leg entirely. How bad would it be to have just the one leg? He'd get to use a robot prosthetic, and that would be sweet. Jamie and Allie could programme it, maybe, or open it up and give it secret compartments. He could be a droid fighter. Man versus machine.

Robot prosthetic. Brendan. Corey's stomach gives another sickening lurch.

"Corey." His mom's fingers are gripping the back of his head. "Stay with me."

His dad squats beside her. In the sickly yellow lights, his face looks like a ghost.

"Yeah." His dad rubs a hand across his mouth, nodding, like he's looking over a tricky engineering problem. "We gotta get nanomeds. Something. Hannah—can you ..."

"Uh ..." Hannah closes her eyes, digging in her pocket. She

pulls out the small blister pack of pills, one of the four compart-ments already empty. The meds she gave to Lorinda, after her spacewalk.

She pops one out, and Anita snatches it from her, sliding it into Corey's mouth. It takes him a long time to swallow it.

"That should help with the pain for a little bit," Hannah says.

Anita doesn't look at her. "How long?"

Hannah fingers the pack, eyeing the two remaining meds. "I don't know ... MicroNal's what I've used before. I haven't used these. A few hours? Maybe?"

"Goddammit," Everett mutters. Corey doesn't know what they're freaking out about. A few hours? A few hours' relief from his leg is a lifetime. His thoughts are blurry, like he's looking at the world through a glitching lens.

"OK," Anita says, her voice shaking. "What about the ..." She points at the bone, still pushing up the jeans fabric.

"I don't know," Hannah says.

"Will they fix it?"

"I don't know. This ... I don't think the bots're strong enough for a break like that."

"How can you not know? And there's gotta be something stronger in the first aid kit. Or more meds, at least. This is a tour ship. The law says they have to carry."

Hannah points to the wall, in the direction of the bar. "The kit's in there."

Corey's mom ignores her, nodding to her older son. "Go check. There has to be something they put down here."

"'Nita," Ev says.

"No. No, Ev. Not this time. You will not do this. You won't just ... just give up and pretend everything's OK."

"*This isn't about us!*" Everett rockets to his feet, so fast that his knee bumps against Corey's leg. He has to stifle a howl of pain. "If she says the kit's in the bar, it's in the bar. Just listen, for once."

"Oh, OK," Anita spits back. "I'll just listen while—"

Malik's voice cuts through the noise. "*Guys!*"

For some reason it works. Their parents stare at him, blinking in astonishment. Behind them, Hannah slides down the wall, her head thunking back against it, eyes closed. There's a tiny speck of dried blood on her cheek.

Movement to Corey's left—a quiet shifting of clothing. He looks over, right into the cold, blue eyes of the captured Colony soldier. The soldier is staring at the blood-soaked shirt, and his expression is one Corey can't place. Like he's … pleased.

In less than a second, it's gone. As Corey watches, the man looks over at Hannah, an amused smile spreading across his face.

"Things not going to plan?" he says.

Corey blinks, looks away. The ice is starting to win, pushing up against the searing fire in his lower leg. His head is starting to clear, just a little.

They're trapped, the five of them, trapped in this tiny space with the enemy. They have no food, or water. Soon, those magic little pills will be gone, and the fire will come back. The *Red Panda* has no pilot. The only person who could fly the ship is gone.

They're finished.

Chapter 35

Jack's ears are ringing.

He blinks hard, gives his head a little shake. The tinnitus won't go away. Was it the shouting? The bang of the trapdoor slamming shut? No way to tell. He's collapsed against one of the seats, sprawled across it, watching Seema grapple with a furious Lorinda. It's barely a fight. Seema has the old woman's arm twisted behind her back, holding her in place. Jack looks across to Brendan, his eyes skating across Volkova's body. The other man is over by the trapdoor, his fingers wedged into the gap, heaving with all his strength. No good. Even with his metal arm, he can't quite lift the hatch.

For a few moments Jack can't even remember why they were

trying to get it open in the first place. When the answer comes, it feels small. Inadequate. They wanted to get answers from the soldier down below, find out why and how and who. But with the captain dead none of it seems to matter any more. It won't make a tiny bit of difference—if it was ever going to. Why is Brendan still going at it? When Jack says his name, but the only sound that comes out is a papery croak.

Brendan shouts something at Seema. Jack can't make out the words—they're obliterated by the shrill whine in his ears. The sound is titanic, drilling into his brain. Something must have happened, a loss of pressure, maybe, a burst valve or a cracked seal. That's the only explanation for this awful *noise* ...

"Let me *go!*" Lorinda shouts, and all at once Jack's tinnitus disappears. The old woman tries to kick at Seema, nearly toppling them both.

"Jesus, get her under control!" Brendan yells at his wife.

Jack pushes up from his seat, intending to help her hold Lorinda, but his hand slips on something warm and sticky, and he thumps back down. He lifts his hand, staring at it in wonder. His skin is slick with blood.

"*Shut the fuck up!*" Seema hisses at the sobbing Lorinda. She pulls her away, heading for the stairs. As Jack watches her go, his eyes slide over Volkova's body again. It's like something glimpsed out of the window of a car moving at high speed, gone before he can take in the details.

"You killed her," Lorinda says, her voice a croak.

"*Shut—*" Seema doesn't finish. Instead, she says: "You two, get the trapdoor. Get it open."

Again, Jack gets that strange, unreal feeling: that there's no good reason for them to get downstairs, and probably never was. As Seema pulls the protesting Lorinda across the main deck, Jack finally manages to get to his feet. He's unsteady, the ringing coming in soft waves now. The right side of his jacket is wet with blood— no, not just wet, *drenched*. It can't all be the captain's. There's no way. There can't be that much blood in one person.

Brendan wipes his face. He crouches down again, glancing up at Jack as he approaches. "You take this end, I'll take the other."

As if in a dream, he does what he's asked. As he walks over, he catches sight of Volkova's body, and a wave of revulsion water-spout up from his stomach. *You've seen dead bodies before. You work for a feed, for God's sake. Plenty of video from the news desk, plenty of photos, crime, war zones …*

He makes himself look again. Volkova is face-down, head at an ugly angle, eclipsing a thick puddle of blood. Jack spots the handle of Seema's penknife, and the waterspout rises up his throat again.

He strips off his jacket, lays it over the top half of Volkova's body. The back of the jacket is pristine, and it's big enough to cover the blood completely. There. He's fine. No problem.

Seema comes thundering back up the stairs, vanishing into the cockpit. A second later, the lights to the main deck blink back on, flickering to life. Jack looks over his shoulder, stunned to see just how much of a mess the main deck has become. The streaks of blood don't extend beyond the nearest seats, but there's trash everywhere, soychip packets and empty soda cans.

"Bathroom," Seema says, striding out from the cockpit. She takes a big, gulping breath. "Locked her in."

"Seema," Brendan says, not looking at her.

"Don't start."

"Don't start, she says. Might I remind you that the contract was nearly complete? We just needed to have a chat with our man down below, and we might still have got out of here. You've proper fucked us."

Contract? Jack stares at them, stunned. Distantly, he thinks: *Honeymoon. They said they were on honeymoon.*

Brendan is still speaking. "It's Centauri all over again—"

"You're going to bring that up now?"

He rockets to his feet, looming over Seema. *"You're fucking right I am,"* he roars. "That's the whole reason we were on Sigma, 'stead of packing our shit onto a shuttle and heading to Titan like we planned. Do you understand what'll happen to Marcus if we don't make it back? What they'll fucking do to him? You ever think about that?"

"Every single day." Seema's eyes are shining with hot, furious tears.

"Then why'd you do it?" Brendan points at the captain's body. "You know what? No. Just go downstairs. I'll fix it. I'll clean up your mess, like bloody always."

Seema looks like she wants to do to him what she did to Volkova. Instead, she turns on her heel, heading for the bar.

"It's up to us now, boyo," Brendan says quietly.

Jack blinks at him. "What?"

When Brendan speaks again, the fury is still there. But it's as if he's tamped it down, forcefully pushed it back, as if he understands that the only way he's going to make this work is if he gets control. "I know things got a little out of hand," he says, "but you've gotta believe me: this wasn't supposed to happen. Seema … overreacted, I suppose."

"Overreacted." Jack finds himself nodding, as if in agreement.

"Yep. It makes things harder, I'll grant you. A lot harder. But what's done is done. Our mission—you and me, right now, no Seema—is to convince the chaps down there that we don't mean them harm. The captain was an accident—"

"Accident." It's all he seems able to do: just repeat what's being said to him.

"*Yes*." Brendan leans forward, eyes on Jack's, as if desperate to make him understand. "It was a bad mistake, that's all. Heat of the moment. Now we're all on the same side, we're all trying to get home, and we can still do it. We just need to think logically. Make a plan."

He raps on the trapdoor. "If we're going to get out of here, if we're going to have any chance at all, we need to find out what that man knows. I've seen his type before. He's not going to respond to civilised bloody questioning. Believe me, I'd rather we didn't have to cut him, but you'd be amazed at what people spill once you get started. So: we talk to our folks down below. We make them understand what's at stake."

"What if they don't?"

The words come before he can stop them, and they're followed by blackout terror. He tenses, as if Brendan is going to lunge for him, wrap metal fingers around his throat and crush his windpipe. He can't stop seeing Seema's hand flash upwards.

She moved so fast. Not just fast: easily. Practised. Like she'd done it before.

Who the hell are these people?

Brendan doesn't kill him. Instead, he smiles. "They will. It was dark, the captain attacked Seema first. And, if they still don't get on board, well ... let's just say I have a little experience in persuading people what their best interests are. Then we do like we were going to. Have a little chat with our man in the handcuffs."

He peers at Jack. "You understanding me? You get what I'm putting down?"

Jack gets another burst of that tinnitus and he pulls his gaze away, wincing, trying to ride it out. He goes back to the trapdoor—it's all he can think to do. This time, he succeeds in getting it a full two inches up before whoever is holding it pulls it back down.

Jack yanks his fingers away, only just managing to avoid getting them crushed. He digs his fingers back into the gap. Whoever's holding it—Everett, maybe? Hannah?—is bound to get tired sometime, and then they can—

There's a loud *clunk* from the underside. This time, when Jack tries to pull, there's zero give.

"Shit," says Brendan, thumping his hand against the trapdoor. "All right. Just because they've locked it doesn't mean there isn't a way in. Any ideas?"

"Uh ..."

Brendan's eyes flash, and it's enough to force the words out of Jack's mouth. "We could ... I mean, I guess there might be a way to override the lock. Or maybe there's a way through the bar. A door we missed or something." He knows there isn't, but doesn't seem to be able to stop himself talking. He keeps seeing the handle of Seema's knife, bent at an acute angle by the floor.

Brendan nods. "Good thinking," he says, glancing at Volkova. "Go check out the cockpit. Go through the system, see if we missed something. I'll try talk to them from up here—see if I can get them to let us inside."

In a daze, Jack starts to make his way across the main deck, the tinnitus rising and falling like waves crashing on a shore. It's been less than fifteen minutes since he first got up, since he first woke up Brendan and Seema to see if they'd back him up. It feels like it happened to someone else, a lifetime ago: someone who had a plan and who knew exactly how they were going to carry it out.

None of this was supposed to happen. The captain wasn't even supposed to be there. And even if she was, she was never supposed to ... to ...

He takes one last look back. Volkova is largely hidden from view, but Jack can just see one foot, sticking out from behind a seat.

Chapter 36

Hannah leans against the wall, head down, trying very hard not to throw up.

After they dosed Corey with nanomeds, and the bleeding had slowed a little, there was a moment where she thought she was OK. It lasted less than five seconds, and left her stumbling away from the others, leaving Anita and Everett with their son. She needs to think. Just for a little bit.

The water in Volkova's coffee cup, turned black from a dozen ciga-rette butts. The captain chain-smoking, stubbing the dead cig out in the—

She rubs her eyes with the heels of her hands, a half groan, half sob forcing its way out of her. What happened to Volkova shouldn't affect her this badly. In the past day, thousands—no, *tens* of thousands—have died. Frontier and Colony, and most of them went without having the faintest idea why. Why should Jana Volkova be any different?

Because she was the first one to die on board this ship. Because she got killed trying to protect someone. Because she was the only person here you could talk to and the only way we were ever going to get out of here, and now—

Hannah grinds the heels of her hands into her eyes so hard that the darkness behind the lids is filled with a thousand prickling lights.

"First things first," she mutters. Only: what are those first things? What are they supposed to be doing? Finding a way out of here, maybe, but then they'll still have to deal with Brendan and Seema, and Jack. And if they stay down here?

"You all right?"

Everett. He's standing over her, arms at his sides. Before she can respond, he says, "We need something stronger than those nanomeds."

"I know, but—"

"They'll help with the pain." He looks sick. "Keep him stable. But even if we keep him on them, they're not going to be able to fix his leg."

"Ev, I'm sorry." Hannah gestures around the engine compartment. "I don't know what to tell you."

"Figure something out."

He all but snarls the words, the blister pack vanishing into a clenched fist.

"What do you want me to do?" she says, feeling more helpless than ever. "That pack's all we have left."

He slumps. "Sorry."

"S'OK."

"You ever had a dislocated shoulder?" he asks. "Anything like that?"

She shakes her head.

"I did, once. Playing football in college. Running back. Coach snapped it in there—" he mimics twisting something into place, hand above his shoulder "—and I felt like I was going to black out. Had to stay on nanos for a couple of days. Missed a dose once, and it was like the pain was right there all along, just hidden. It came back fast. Can you even imagine how many nanos he's going to need after we push that bone in?"

It feels like Hannah has to almost physically push the frustration back. "I get it, Ev. But I don't know what to tell you."

Adrift

Ev runs a hand through his hair. As he does so, another voice drifts down from the hatch, muffled and dull.

Brendan.

"Hello down there?" He knocks on the trapdoor three times, like he's standing on a doorstep. "Look, we need to talk. Any chance you can lift the hatch up?"

Silence. Anita meets Hannah's eyes, raw terror on her face.

"I'm sorry about before," Brendan continues. He sounds completely calm. "It shouldn't have happened. But we're all on the same side here, and I think if we just took a moment to chat we'd be able to come to some sort of arrangement. All right?"

Everett looks like he's about to reply. Hannah scrambles to her feet, gripping his shoulder, making him look at her as she shakes her head no. They're not saying a word until they've decided what their position is. But what *is* their position, exactly? What the hell are they supposed to do?

"We don't mean you any harm, up here," Brendan is saying. "You don't even have to come up yet. Just crack the trapdoor, and let's talk."

From behind them, the prisoner speaks, his voice barely more than a whisper. "You could let me go."

"What?" Hannah says, the word scarcely a breath.

"You want to take these guys out?" The man shifts, his space-suit fabric rasping. "Uncuff me. Let me get my suit off. They won't stand a chance."

Hannah makes herself grit her teeth. "Neither will we."

He chuckles, long and low. "Seems like you've got a little problem, then. I'm going to have a nap. You wake me when you figure it out."

Brendan is still talking, still trying to reassure them. His voice reminds Hannah of her sister, when Callie is trying to close a business dealing over the phone. Warm. Encouraging. She can all but see the cheerful smile on his face. Suddenly she wants to throw up again.

"Let's go in the other room," she says, flicking a nervous glance at the prisoner.

Both Everett and Anita nod. "Malik, go back with your brother," Anita says.

"What?"

"Go look after Corey. And *don't* say anything to Brendan."

"I wanna stay with you." Malik has a wounded look on his face, and Hannah can't blame him. Hasn't he been through just as much as they have? "Besides, it's not like I'm not going to be able to hear—"

"Well, you're not staying with us," Everett says, annoyed. "Do what your mother says now."

"But *Dad*—"

"It's OK, Mal," Corey says. They all turn to look at him, propped against the wall on the other side of the room. His face is still grey, but he's alert, even managing a thin smile. The nanomeds are working; his leg is in bad shape, but it looks as if the pain has been dialled down. For now.

Hannah can't help but picture the blister pack, scrunched in Everett's hand. *Two left.*

Malik says nothing, looking between his parents and his brother. "Come on," Corey says. "You can ... tell me about your movies or ... something."

With undisguised reluctance, Malik makes his way over to his brother. He keeps glancing behind him, his eyes finding Hannah's, as if pleading her to reconsider. But in a few moments, he's sitting next to Corey, eyes downcast.

They troop into the other room. The air is still a little smoky from the fire, and it makes Hannah's eyes sting. She can feel the hum of the engines in the pit of her stomach. Are they even moving right now? She can't remember. And who's in the cockpit, if not Volkova? Jack? Seema?

She's tempted to get them checking every inch of astronautics. Maybe they missed something ... but, of course, she knows that isn't true. The entirety of the ship's supplies are on the main deck, or in the bar.

"So now what?" Everett says. He's leaning against the wall, arms folded.

Hannah lets out a long breath. "We're not going to be able to stay down here for long. Not without food or water." She sees Everett about to speak, hurries on. "*And* meds. I know."

"You're a hundred per cent sure there's nothing down here?" Everett says.

"Just electronics."

"Well then, we have to get out," Everett says. His eyes flick between them. "Right?"

"And we would," says Anita. "But guess who'll be waiting for us?"

"So? What are they going to do?"

"That's the problem," Hannah says, almost mumbling the words. "I don't even think *they* know."

Anita stares at her. "Are you saying they ... the captain was an *accident*?"

"Maybe give her a chance to speak, OK?"

"And what? The longer we stand here, the longer those psychos are in control."

"We can't just—"

"Did you see," Anita says, forcing the words through clenched teeth, speaking in short, bitter chunks, "what they did to Corey?"

"Both of you, *enough*. Just ..." Hannah runs her fingers through her hair, not sure what she wants to say, just knowing that she can't take any more of their fighting. God, she'd give anything to talk to someone sane right now. Lorinda would be—

Her eyes go wide. "Oh, shit," she says.

Everett looks at her. "What?"

"Lorinda. She's still up there. With the others."

Anita lets out a low moan, and all three of them glance up at the ceiling. For a moment, Hannah can't believe the guilt she feels—the kind of guilt that skewers you on a long pole and then holds you up to take a good, hard look at. How long has it been? And none of them even noticed she wasn't with them?

"I wouldn't worry about her," Everett says, not sounding the least bit sure. "She's a tough one."

"But what if—" Anita says.

"No. Nothing we can do for her right now. We gotta focus on what's in front of us." He brightens. "Hey—what about the vents?"

"There's nothing in there." Hannah's voice is dull.

"That's not what I mean. Who's to say we can't just go in there ourselves? It's gotta come out somewhere else in the ship, right?"

"Won't work."

"Why not?"

Anita lets out a disgusted sigh. "Because Corey only *just* fit in there. None of us will. And if you think I'm sending my son in there with his leg the way it is ..."

"My son, too. And I would *never*—"

Hannah jumps in. "What about a ... a supervised interrogation?"

"Didn't we do that already?" Everett says. "The supervision ain't the problem. They want to hurt this guy."

"*I* want to hurt this guy," Anita mutters.

They fall silent, the noise of the engine flowing in to fill the space.

"What if we do it?" Anita says.

Hannah rubs a piece of smoky grit out of her eye. "Do what?"

"Like he said. Let him go, have him take care of ... you know."

Everett stares at her in amazement. Hannah drops her hand, the grit forgotten. "There's no way."

"But what if we—"

"'Nita, that's insane."

"Just *listen*." Anita squares her shoulders, addressing Hannah instead of her husband. "I'm not saying it's the best option, but it's not worth discarding out of hand."

"Did you not hear what he said?"

Anita ignores her. "We make a deal," she says, tapping her palm with the backs of her fingers. "Negotiate terms. Get him on our side, so—"

"'Nita—"

"Not up for discussion." Hannah turns away. "Sorry. Think of something else."

"Oh, don't be so goddamn naive," Anita says, baring her teeth.

"Excuse me?"

"Everybody has something they want. We just have to find his. It's what we'd do in the Senate when we needed to whip votes, we'd—"

Adrift

"Unbelievable." Hannah gapes at her. "You're playing politics. Now."

"I don't hear any better ideas."

"Cool it, both of you," Everett tells them.

Hannah ignores him. "This isn't the Senate. This isn't a fucking bill. We're not *whipping votes*, and you know exactly what the guy in there wants."

"If you'd just let me *try*."

"No. Uh-uh. Politics is why we're here in the first place."

"We couldn't have foreseen—"

"And you still think you can negotiate. Like it's the treaty all over again. Like there's a ... a ... a compromise we can reach." Dimly, Hannah is aware that she's crying, hot tears cutting through the dirt on her cheeks.

Anita doesn't blink. "Let's get one thing straight. You're, what, twenty? Twenty-one? I'm guessing before today all you'd done was work as a tour guide. You are not equipped to make decisions like this."

"And you are?"

"*Yes*."

Hannah can't believe how angry she is. All at once, it's not Anita in front of her, but Callie. Callie, and that unspoken judgement that Hannah is somehow less than her. That she has a plan, and Hannah doesn't, and never will.

"I'm going to go back in there," Anita says, "and I'm going to fix this. I'm not going to take orders from someone who—"

"Maybe it's time we just let them in," says Everett.

They both look at him. When he raises his face to them, Hannah can't believe the sorrow and disgust she sees there.

"What do you mean?" she whispers.

"Let them do what they want. Torture him. Whatever. I don't think they'd touch us. The captain ... it was a heat of the moment thing ..."

"They killed her," Hannah says.

"They—"

"*Killed her*. Stuck a goddamn ..." She has to pause as a hot, searing breath tears through her chest. She's crying openly now, completely unable to stop it.

"Yeah." Everett is nodding. "They did. But if it's Corey, or whoever this guy is, then I choose Corey."

Even Anita seems to be considering it. Hannah's about to protest, about to tell them that they're insane, when she stops. It *is* a way out. Shouldn't they at least consider ... no. *No.* The captain died to make sure nobody was mistreated on her ship—not even the enemy. If Hannah lets it happen, she'll have died for nothing.

She turns, resting her forehead against the grimy, sticky wall. Every choice is bad, every single one, and she has absolutely no idea what to do next.

Chapter 37

The *Red Panda*'s pilot seat is the most uncomfortable chair Jack has ever sat in.

He thought the seats on the main deck were a pain in the ass. At least they had rounded edges, and decent legroom. Volkova's chair, wedged into the centre of the horseshoe-shaped control panel, is like some sort of weird torture device. It's canted back at a ridiculous angle, one he cannot change no matter how hard he pulls at it. The cushion barely qualifies for its name, worn through in a dozen places, the metal of the chair's frame poking through it.

He doesn't remember how long Volkova's legs were, or how tall she was (a vision of her body under his jacket surfaces, and he has to close his eyes and shake it off). What he does know is that there isn't nearly enough room for his legs under the control panel. His knees are jammed up against it, the stick poking up between them.

The control panel and the screens above it hold a bewildering display of information. What must it be like on a bigger vessel? Like on the cockpit of that Colony ship?

Adrift

He straightens up, wincing as cold metal presses the back of his thigh through the thin fabric of his pants, and takes hold of the stick.

The *Red Panda* doesn't respond. He pulls the stick up, down, jerks it left and right, but the pitch of the engines doesn't change, the ship refusing to move. The view outside the cockpit is exactly the same as it was when he came in here: the smashed gate, the torn remains of the Colony ship, the distant, vast field of cold stars. The ghost-light from the Neb. The *Red Panda*'s drifted a little in the past few hours, but that's all.

OK, no biggie. All it means is that the ship is locked in autopilot. He just has to turn it off.

He considers the screens—two enormous central ones, positioned next to each other, and four smaller ones on each side. Three of the screens are blank, and the rest feature a combination of colourful graphs, star maps and what look like the audio meters Jack once saw in a music studio.

The only one he can understand displays a schematic of the *Red Panda*, viewed from the side. Cockpit, main deck, galley—the bar, he supposes. Engine room. Nothing he doesn't know already. The escape pod section is blinking a dull red.

"Systems resetting," a voice says, nearly making him fall out of his seat in surprise. The ship's voice is an Australian woman this time, her words crisp and clear. "System reset com-com-com-com-com-com-warning: kernel panic. System resetting. Please stand by."

Jack waits for a long minute. Eventually, he says, "Hello?"

The *Red Panda* is silent.

Whatever he's going to do, he obviously can't depend on the ship to help him. Fine. *Start small.* He leans forward and taps the cockpit section of the schematic.

With a click, the lights around him switch off, leaving nothing but the glow of the screens. Jack jabs at the schematic, turning the lights back on, and realises he's left a small smear of blood on the glass. It tapers like a teardrop, turned black by the backlight. *Volkova's blood.* Jack shivers, wiping his hand on his pants. The ringing in his ears is back.

There: a menu option above the schematic, the words INTERNAL LIGHTING with a small up-and-down arrow next to them. *Got you*. He makes sure his finger is clean, then touches the words. A list of options drops down: TEMPERATURE, PA SYSTEM LEVELS, OXYGEN MIXTURE. Nothing remotely connected to actually flying the ship.

Jack closes the menu, sits back, looks at the other screens. He reaches towards one, a graph showing what looks like reactor temperature, then stops. His hand hovers in the air, then flops back down to his lap.

"Fuck," he says. "Fuck shit *fuck*."

This is all wrong. He has no idea what he's doing. He's much better on the main deck, where he can do … something. He can figure that out later. He starts to lift himself out of the pilot's seat, his left knee stuck under the control panel, he has to pull at it to get it free, he—

"You in there, mate?"

Brendan's voice comes from the passage. Jack shoves himself back down into the chair, so fast that he bangs his right kneecap on the edge of the panel. He grips the stick with both hands, telling himself to stay calm, wondering *why* he's telling himself to stay calm.

Behind him, Brendan ducks into the cockpit. "Not a peep from down below. They may need a little bit of time to think it over. How's it all going? You find anything?"

Jack blinks up at him. Brendan's face is calm, his mouth crooked in a pleasant smile. His voice is completely neutral—like everything is under control, and this is just a minor hiccup. He sounds exactly like he did in the bar, early on in this insane shit-show of a trip, when he and Seema were telling him about their kid.

A frown is spreading across Brendan's face. Jack makes himself speak. "Yeah, no, not yet. Just trying to get to grips with the system." He chuckles, without really knowing why. He keeps seeing Seema plunge her knife into Volkova's neck, and keeps hearing Brendan's words: *Might I remind you that the contract was nearly complete?*

"I was thinking," Brendan says, leaning in close. "Maybe we can force them out of there."

Adrift

"Force th—"

"The folks in the engine room. What about if we lowered the oxygen? Nothing crazy, just make it a little uncomfortable for them."

"Way ahead of you," Jack says, the lie spilling out with remarkable ease. "I already looked. But you can't lower it beyond a certain level. There's a failsafe, I think. Something like that. The system just gives me an error message."

There's a second where he thinks Brendan doesn't believe him; that he's going to demand proof, or pull Jack out of the chair. Before he can process the thought, Brendan grimaces. "Makes sense. Maybe there's a way round it."

Jack nods. He's gripping his shirt again, has to make himself stop.

"We should look for somewhere to go, too," Brendan says. "Seema reckons there must be other places round here? Places they weren't telling us about. Another gate, maybe."

He leans over Jack, reaching out for the star map, spinning it with a finger, tapping on a green blob. The action makes it bigger, and an info box pops up alongside it. BISHOP'S STATION, it reads, listing a whole whack of data: frequency ranges, trading status, last known dock capacity.

"That," Brendan says. "Can we get there?"

"Um …" Jack tries to focus. "It's … thing is, it's a way away."

"OK?"

"Like a hundred light years."

Brendan puffs his cheeks. "All right, man, keep looking. Seems and I are still working on the trapdoor. We'll get it open, don't worry. Then we can talk to whoever this bastard is."

He smacks Jack on the shoulder again. "The key is to never give up. No matter how bad things get, you just gotta soldier on." He turns to go, ducking his head as he reaches the exit.

"What's the contract?" Jack says.

Brendan turns back, a pained look on his face. "Ha. Yes. Did kind of let the cat out the bag, didn't I?"

"You and Seema aren't … you aren't married?"

Brendan smiles, and it's warm enough to almost stop Jack's

heart. "Course we're married. We're working professionals, who happened to enjoy each other's company enough to tie the knot."

He makes his way over, sitting on the edge of the control panel. He's too big for the space, and has to bend at the waist as he looks deep into Jack's eyes. His metal arm gleams in the cockpit lights. "Admittedly, most people in our line of work don't actually *marry*, but it's not unheard of. You work that closely with someone for long enough, and you usually find you've got at least a few things in common. I know Seema can be a bit intense, but she's a sweetheart once you get to know her."

"... Line of work?"

"Yep." Brendan scratches the back of his neck, the smile still on his face. "In this case, our work brought us into contact with a certain fellow on Sigma, name of Barrington Wallace."

Jack blinks. Barrington Wallace. He's heard that name before. Where has he—

"The bartender," he says, more to himself than to Brendan. In his mind, he can hear Volkova's voice—the very first time she came over the *Red Panda*'s speakers, before all this shit kicked off.

After your tour starts, our staff member Barrington will be happy to serve you a range of bev ... oh, sorry, I just looked at the staff roster and he didn't come in for work today.

"Mr. Wallace owed a lot of money to quite a few people, back when he wasn't Mr. Wallace. I can never remember his original name—Simon something. Anyway, fancied himself a bit of a businessman, back on Mars. Lots of bars, restaurants, multiple locations. Even franchised to Proxima, I believe. Extended himself quite a bit, and, of course, the banks will only let you borrow so much before they start to ask some fair questions about when they're likely to get a return on investment.

"Our Mr. Wallace couldn't afford to let the operation fail, so he borrowed from people he probably would have been better off avoiding. Got himself in pretty deep there, too. Seema and I were contracted to ask some fair questions of our own. The people who hired us ... well, let's just say their response to insolvency isn't just a bankruptcy chit."

Jack's stomach feels leaden. "You killed him."

Adrift

"Ha!" Brendan barks the word, loud enough to make Jack jump in his seat. A metal strut jabs into his side. "I didn't do a damn thing. It's like I said—I'm just the researcher. I find out where and when, do all the legwork, handle the necessaries and the logistics and the wherewithals. Everything I'm good at. Seema ..." He grins with pride. "Well, like I told you. She's an artist."

Their cute nicknames pop into Jack's mind. *Pooka. Cushla.* Did they call each other that on the job? While they were ...

Seema's hand, slashing upwards almost too fast to track. The spray of blood, the knife buried in Volkova's neck.

Brendan lifts his metal arm. "You wouldn't think it, would you? Our line of work, big fella with the cyborg arm probably does the deed, doesn't he?"

He leans in, as if confiding in Jack. "Truth be told, damn thing's useless in a fight. Too slow. Seema's the one with the skills. Don't get me wrong, I can handle myself in a scrap. But I really did lose it in a bike crash on Mars, although it was more a chase than a race. Anyway, as it turned out I'm much better at more, shall we say, deliberate persuasion. Like we planned to do with our man down below."

He drops the arm. "Anyway, we didn't exactly plan to get on the same boat that Mr. Wallace was due to tend bar on. Truth be told, we'd've headed back to the gate the second Mr. Wallace left this mortal coil, if we'd had any choice in the matter. But there wasn't a shuttle 'til later, and it was either do something with our time or just sit in the bar, getting plastered. Couldn't do *that*, much as I wanted to. The job ain't over 'til the completion fee hits our account, and I wasn't gonna let us slip. Not on this one."

It's all Jack can do to follow the story. He has the strangest feeling: that if he reached out to touch Brendan, his hand would just pass right through. Like all of this is happening in his head.

"So," Brendan continues. "We saw there was a tour going round the station, and thought we'd take in the sights. Keep our mind off things. Nobody was going to find Mr. Wallace for a while, not after we were finished with him. Course, when I heard his name over the speakers, my damn heart nearly stopped."

He puts a giant metal hand on the back of Jack's seat. "I was hoping we could just keep this under wraps until it was all over. After all, it's not like there's much evidence left of what happened to our poor Mr. Wallace, now, is there?"

Jack finds himself nodding. Brendan's fingers tighten, creaking against the seat. Jack stares at them, wondering if Brendan is planning to grip his shoulder. He hopes he doesn't. If it happens, if those long fingers touch him, he might go insane.

"I'm guessing you don't actually have a kid, right?" he says, trying to make it sound like a joke. Like he's down with everything Brendan has told him.

A very dark look crosses the other man's face. "What is it with you? Just because we didn't mention our *exact* line of work, you think we were lying about everything else? You think working contractors like us can't have families? Yes: we are married, and, yes, we have a son. That's God's honest truth. I told you about our boy, didn't I?" He frowns. "Although we did say he was staying with Seema's folks. That wasn't true, sorry, chap. I wouldn't leave our boy with his grandmother if the universe depended on it."

He leans forward, making sure to look Jack right in the eyes.

"Here's the thing, though," he says. "And I want you to understand this perfectly. Our last job didn't go so well. Seema's damn good at what she does, but she's still human. We were at a job on Centauri-7—simple one, quick in and out. Got discovered while we were working, by a security guard who changed his round for whatever reason. Had to take a piss or something. I don't know. Before I could smooth the situation over, Seema ... well, as you've probably realised, sometimes she does things without thinking.

"Anyway, after Centauri, there were questions. A trail back to us. Our bosses had to work pretty hard to cover it up, and they weren't best pleased."

He grips the chair a little tighter. "They're ... looking after Marcus. Pretty well, if the pictures they sent haven't been faked. We only get him back if this next job goes smooth, and then our contract is complete, and the three of us can hightail it to Titan. Get out of the game for good. God knows, we've got enough socked away to not work for a while. But we get arrested, or if there's any heat whatsoever, it's over."

His voice drops even further. "We are going to get out of here, we are going to complete our contract, and we are going to get our boy back. That's the only thing that matters. Do you understand me?"

Jack tries to breathe, finds that he can't. Brendan's eyes shine with a kind of desperate madness, beyond that of a father separated from his son. It's the madness of someone who knows that his options are dwindling, and will do absolutely anything to keep them open. How did Jack not see it before? Was he really that blind?

He finds himself nodding, and Brendan claps him on the shoulder, mercifully using his real hand. "Good man. I appreciate it. The Roses can be pretty rigid when it comes to their contracts. Just ask Mr. Barrington Wallace."

Then he's gone, stepping back out into the passage.

Jack stares after him. His mind has been wiped clean.

Roses.

As in, the Roses Cartel.

As in, the people who put three bullets into Hector Alarcón's spine, who crippled him, plunged him into a depression so deep that he never climbed out. The people who destroyed the only person Jack had ever really loved.

Brendan and Seema work for them.

Chapter 38

"What year is it?" says Corey.

Mal, who is just lowering himself to the ground next to his little brother, looks over, alarmed. "Cor, you don't know what year it is?"

"I'm asking him." Corey points to the soldier. His hand only trembles a little.

The pain is still there, but the meds they gave him have pushed it back, a little. Corey can't help think of a big cat, a tiger or a mountain lion, maybe one of the hybrids they saw in the Austin GeneZoo that one time. For a while, the cat had him, its teeth ripping and tearing. Now, it's in the long grass, hidden but still very much there, stalking, waiting for its moment.

He's not all the way better—he's not going to be solving maths problems, or anything—but at least he can think again, and understand what's happening. Sort of. Even if he doesn't dare look at the bloody, shattered mess of his leg.

The prisoner's eyes narrow a little at Corey's question. He says nothing.

"I said, what year is it?"

"He knows what year it is." Mal activates his holocam, the display springing to life. "Come on. Let's just watch some movies or something."

Corey ignores him. "I get you don't want to tell us about yourself. But what year do you think it is, right now?"

The man's voice is hard-edged. "Why?"

"Because ..." Corey thinks. Or tries to. The cat is prowling, waiting for an opening. It's getting harder and harder to focus. "Because I think your ship might have got stuck in a time warp. During a jump. You're one of those ships that disappeared, and now you've come back, and you still think the war is on. That's why you blew up the station."

"Stop being a chutiya," Mal sends a nervous glance at the soldier.

"You're a chutiya."

"You're the one who—"

"2172," the man says. He speaks very quietly, never taking his eyes off Corey. "The war is over. It ended ten years ago." There's a very faint twitch at the corners of his mouth. "We didn't get stuck in a time warp."

In the silence that follows, Corey can hear Hannah and his parents arguing quietly in the other room, their hushed voices only just audible.

"Are you sure?" Corey says.

"Just leave it, Corey," Malik mutters.

Adrift

"'Cos he might just be playing along. Maybe, I don't know, they figured it out later, and he's just trying to mess with us."

"It was 2172 when we started our mission," the man says. "It's 2172 now."

"See?" Malik smacks him on the shoulder, then immediately pulls his hand back in horror. "Shit, sorry, I didn't mean—"

"It's OK." It isn't. The smack wasn't hard, but it made the big cat growl. Corey bites his lower lip, grinding it between his teeth until it passes.

Malik pulls up his movie files, selects one. The video on the holo shows a slim, dark-haired girl, maybe sixteen, head down over a table in what looks like a cafeteria.

"Who's that?" Corey says.

"It's nothing." Malik tries to close the file. He ends up pausing it, fumbling with the controls.

Corey frowns. "Is that Shanti Evans?"

"No."

"Yeah, it was. You're filming her?"

"No. Maybe. She's my girlfriend, OK?"

"She is not."

"How would you know?"

Corey is about to respond, but he doesn't have the energy. He looks back over at the soldier, another thought occurring to him. "Prove you're human."

"Excuse me?"

"What are you talking about?" Mal whispers to him.

"He might be an alien pretending to be human. We don't know if he's telling the truth."

"I'm gonna get Mom." Mal starts to get to his feet. "I don't think the meds are—"

"*No.*" Corey pulls his brother back down, frustrated. Isn't this what you're supposed to do? Eliminate the impossible? Isn't that what they teach in science class? Then again, Mal was never very good at science. Maybe he doesn't get it.

"I'm human." The prisoner sounds faintly embarrassed, as if he can't believe he's having this conversation.

Corey wavers, then collapses against the wall. The cat is getting closer, and, anyway, how would you even prove something like that? They'd have to cut him or something, and that would technically be torture, which they said they wouldn't do.

"You sure you're square?" Malik says.

"Fine, Mal. Promise."

"All right." Malik sits back down. "But let's just watch some movies. OK? Don't even talk to him."

"I think I can prove I'm not an alien," the man says.

For a few seconds, neither Malik nor Corey respond.

"How?" Corey says.

The man shifts, as if trying to get more comfortable. "I'm in human form. If I'm alien, that means I have to be a shapeshifter of some kind. So I'd be able to shapeshift my way out these cuffs."

Corey stares at him. After a few seconds, he says, "Huh."

The man shrugs. "Or I'd just grow a few tentacles and grab hold of people. Take over their minds. Think I saw that in a show once."

"*Vicious*," Corey says automatically.

"That's the one."

"They get that in the Colonies, too?"

"Sure. Pretty good series."

"Yeah, but they cancelled it." Corey brightens. "I heard they're doing like a big finale, though? Just to wrap up the story? I really wanna watch that."

Another twitch at the corners of the man's mouth. "Good to hear."

Malik looks like he's about to explode. "What are you doing?" he hisses, grabbing Corey hard by the shoulder. This time he ignores his brother's grimace of pain. "We're not supposed to talk to him."

"Why not?" The prisoner sounds almost casual. "We're just talking. Not like there's a whole lot else to do." He considers Corey. "I'm sorry about your leg, by the way. Not ideal."

"He wouldn't even be like this if it wasn't for you," Malik says, sullen.

Another shrug. "I was down here. Didn't even see what happened up top."

"Doesn't matter."

Adrift

"Mal, just leave it alone."

"No, Cor." Malik is clutching his holocam so tight that Corey thinks he's going to crush it. "He's the reason we're in this whole mess. It's 'cos of him. Your leg's busted up, and it's his fault."

The soldier turns his head towards Malik. It's a very slow, very deliberate move. Every trace of amusement has left his face.

"I want you to listen very carefully," he says. "He may not be old enough to understand—" he jerks his chin at Corey. "But you sure are. You don't get to just blame me for this. Everybody always wants to blame the people who pull the trigger, when, in reality, there's a whole chain of events leading up to that trigger pull, and a whole lot of people who are responsible.

"Yeah, maybe the soldier does the job, but *he* wouldn't even be there if it wasn't for everyone else ordering him to. I didn't break your brother's leg. I didn't get your pilot killed. You want to blame me? Go ahead, if it makes you feel better. But you just remember that I'm not the only person on this ship."

And that's when Corey realises.

He can't see the prisoner's hands.

The man's eyes meet his. Just for a second. Then, before he can react, the cuffed soldier wrenches his body forward, his arms straining in his suit. There's the grating sound of metal on metal. He's managed to pull the pipe from the wall—the one he was handcuffed to. The screws on one end hang loose, and, with a kind of horrifying clarity, Corey understands that he must have loosened them himself.

He distracted them, kept them talking so they wouldn't notice him moving. He slowly scooted along, working on each screw while telling Corey how much he liked that stupid series. He's almost at the point of pulling his cuffed hands free, working them around the curve of the pipe where it bends back on itself to attach to the wall.

"*Mom!*" Malik explodes to his feet. "*Mom! Dad!*"

Everett, Anita and Hannah come bolting out of the engine room. Everett reacts first: he hurls himself on top of the man, throwing himself like the football player he used to be. Malik is there, too, trying to hold down the man's legs. The prisoner tries to throw them off, blue eyes cold and determined, mouth set. Corey stares in shocked, guilty horror.

"Help me here!" Everett yells over his shoulder. The prisoner's knee takes him in the stomach, and he grunts. Hannah dives in, ignoring the fear, driving a forearm against the man's throat, forcing him back against the wall. Her blood is pounding in her ears.

"Get the screws," Corey hears her say. The prisoner's eyes find his, and he has to make himself meet his gaze.

Slowly, they manage to force both pipe and prisoner back against the wall. Anita, breathing hard, starts to work on the screws. As Corey watches, the big cat prowling around him gently sinks a sharp tooth into his leg.

Chapter 39

Lorinda's throat aches.

There's no water in the tiny cubicle. There's plenty of ice in the tank above her, but she can't get to it—the access hatch is on the outside. She's already tried clawing at the roof, but it's solid plastic. May as well be steel, for all the good it does her.

She managed to tease out a little water from the rimy ice crusting the walls, but most of it's gone now. And the bathroom is freezing, cold enough to make her bones hurt. Her nanomeds have long since worn off; she doesn't think there's any permanent damage, but it's not going to matter if she doesn't get out of here soon.

She gives the door another feeble kick with her good leg. It barely budges. You can't lock the bathroom from the outside, so Seema put something in front of it. She doesn't know what—the supply boxes from under the bar, maybe. She heard the bitch moving them earlier.

The bathroom light has a maddening flicker in it, an old-school filament that gives off an almost inaudible buzzing. Lorinda is curled up on the toilet seat, hands buried in her armpits, head scrunched down. Her breath laces the air in front of her mouth.

She's spent most of her life in space, and she's felt the chill of the vacuum plenty of times, but she's never been this exhausted. The spacewalk, the fight with Seema, the cold: they've all combined to sap her strength. Despite her fury, she keeps nodding off. Each time she does, she jerks back to life a few moments later, mouth opening and closing like a fish.

For the thousandth time, her thoughts turn to what might be happening in the rest of the ship. She hopes for the others' sake that they've managed to stay locked in astronautics. But sooner or later, Brendan and Seema and that smug asshole Jack will figure out a way to get inside. And then ...

She passes out again. She's under less than a minute, but she shivers the whole time, her shoulders bumping against the toilet's plastic housing. When she wakes up, Craig is sitting in front of her.

He's dressed the same way he was on the last day she saw him: denim workshirt, grimy chinos. He's even wearing those ridiculous cowboy boots she got him as a joke present for his sixtieth, and which he took inordinate pride in. There's no room for two people in the tiny cubicle—there's barely room for one—but it doesn't seem strange that he's there. He's sitting on the desk chair she found him in after the blood clot took him, his elbows on his knees, his hands clasped, staring at her expectantly.

"Am I dead?" She isn't sure if she says the words or just thinks them. Surprisingly, she isn't bothered by the prospect. She doesn't want to die, doesn't want to leave the folks on the *Red Panda* by themselves, but if it means she can see Craig again ...

He grins, showing slightly crooked teeth. *You? Nah.*

Lorinda blinks, long and hard. When she opens her eyes, the bathroom cubicle is gone. Behind Craig, the Horsehead Nebula glimmers, shining around the edges of his body. She *is* dying. He always did try to put a positive spin on things; it's why she loved him. One of the many reasons why.

"I miss you," she says.

I know.

"I went out for a walk."

I saw. Took out a whole ship. Kind of amazed you didn't do it sooner.

She cracks a smile at that, saliva tracking down a wrinkle on her chin.

Why'd you sell up?

"What?"

After I died.

"I don't ..."

You could have kept going, you know. The rig-hounds respected you, lot more than they respected me. You probably would have had us making double what we were.

"... I didn't want to do it without you. You know that."

But you could have. His nose has started to bleed, a drop gently snaking its way down his upper lip. Silhouetted against the nebula, his face has gone dark. *We worked hard to build the claim. And you gave it up. Sold out to Calomar and went walkin'.*

Tears prick at her eyes. "That's not fair."

He doesn't say anything to that, just keeps smiling that strange smile. Despite the silhouette against the stars, she can still make out the detail on his face. He reaches up, almost absent-mindedly, and wipes away the blood.

"What do you want me to do?" she says. But Craig is gone. So is the Neb. There's nothing but the flickering light and the cramped cubicle.

"Come back," she says, hating herself for it, hating him for wanting him this much. The Craig she knew would never have said those things, not ever, would never have begrudged her finally seeing the Neb like they always talked about. All the same, his words echo in her mind. *Sold out. Went walkin'.*

Doesn't matter. She might not be dead yet but she's getting there fast. When she sees him, she's going to give him such hell.

Chapter 40

Roses.

The word goes round and round in Jack's mind. Seema and Brendan might not have been involved in what happened in São Paulo—they weren't there when Hec was shot. Or if they did, it would be one hell of a coincidence. And if they were, how would he even phrase the question? *Hey, quick one, were you ever by any chance in Brazil? Ever try kill a cop? Put three bullets in his back, maybe?*

He turns back to the screens, wiping sweat from his face. *I did this. I gave them permission. I might not have swung the knife that killed the captain, but I sure didn't stop it from happening.*

"Shut up," he says, his voice a trembling whisper. Brendan and Seema were already unstable. Trained killers. Sooner or later, they'd have done something, pulled some kind of stunt, whether he was there or not.

No matter how hard he tries, the thought won't go away. Seema and Brendan might be killers, but they wouldn't have overstepped that mark on their own—not when their son was in danger, not when they had to come out of this whole mess as innocent bystanders. No, Jack was the spark that lit up this particular inferno.

It's not my fault. Wouldn't have done that. If I'd known what they were ... His mind lands on the one word he can always count on—the one that's been a life raft for him his entire life. *It wouldn't have been ethical.*

Ethical? Who the fuck is he kidding? They were going to torture someone. Volkova is dead. He's allied himself with the people who tried to kill Hector. It's absurd. It's *wrong*. All of it.

He glances behind him, down the passage towards the main deck. He can't see Brendan and Seema, but he can just hear them, talking in low voices.

Oh, this is insane. There's nothing out here. Nothing at all. They are the last intact vessel for a hundred light years in any direction. Nobody's coming for them. Nobody even knows where they are.

And if he doesn't die from starvation, it'll probably be because one of the two trained killers on board decides he's a liability. Even if they do—somehow—manage to salvage this clusterfuck, what's to stop Brendan and Seema deciding that everyone on board is just a potential witness?

Despair grips him. What is he supposed to do? Take them out somehow? Use Brendan's idea about lowering the oxygen levels? He lied about the failsafe, so it might be perfectly possible. Then again, how would he even make that happen?

His thighs are starting to ache from their position. He shifts in the pilot's seat, planting his feet flat on the floor, wedging his legs under the control panel. As he does so, his foot bumps against a protrusion on the floor, a hinge, maybe, and he grunts in annoyance as he shifts again. So if he—

He freezes. Then he bends over as far as he can go, trying to see what's under his feet.

Hinges.

Not just hinges: a hatch. There's a hatch under the pilot's seat.

So what? It'll just lead to the vents, or to the ship's electronics. Even if they did get in there, he wouldn't be able to fit. The only one who might is the Livingstone kid, and he's in astronautics with the rest of them.

He looks back up to the screens, his gaze landing on the ship schematic. He stares at it for a few seconds, his lower lip between his teeth.

On the schematic there aren't any electronics or vent systems directly below the cockpit. There are plenty *above* it, in the bulbous overhang directly above his head, but the barrier between the cockpit and the bar below is nothing but a single straight line. Jack zooms in—even he can figure that one out, spreading his thumb and index finger across the screen—but the line doesn't change.

Lorinda. Seema told them she locked her in the bathroom. Jack barely registered it at the time, but he's thinking about it now. She's right below him. If he could get to her, free her, convince her that he wants to help ... it doesn't even the odds, but it tilts them a little more in his favour. Even if she's too weak to fight, she could distract them or—

Adrift

No. She's two hundred years old, already exhausted from that insane spacewalk, and she's spent the past forty-five minutes or so locked in a freezing cold space the size of the closet in his apartment. And as far as she's concerned, he's one of the people who put her there. She'll never help.

But before he even realises it's happening, Jack is worming his way out of the seat, yanking his legs from beneath the control panel. He squats next to the chair, fingers exploring the floor.

Yeah, there it is. Two hinges, running along one edge of the hatch. Most of it is underneath the pilot's seat, and, looking more closely, Jack can see two recessed channels running out from the back of the chair.

So the thing *does* move. If he can slide the chair back, he should be able to get at the hatch.

It would be far easier to head to the bar via the stairs—there must be some story, an excuse for him to go down there? But then they'd know where he was. Worse: they might offer to come with him. No, the only way this works is if he has surprise on his side.

He can't hear Brendan's voice any more, or Seema's. A panicked glance at the passage reveals nothing. They could be anywhere. If he's going to do this, he has to do it now.

He explores the chair, something he did with only cursory attention earlier. As his fingers reach the back edge, furthest away from them, they run across something. A lever, a few inches long, covered in tough, ridged rubber and sitting less than half a foot above the floor.

"Gotcha," he mutters, pulling the lever towards him. It gives a little, then springs back to its original position. He tries again, bracing his shoulder against the chair, pushing as hard as you can while he holds the lever back. Nothing.

He's about to try again when Brendan's voice reaches him. It's a shout, an angry one, a quick burst of noise that dies as soon as it begins. Jack freezes, ready to spring back up onto the chair the moment he hears anything else.

The anything else doesn't come. After a long moment, Jack gets back into it. A drop of sweat slides down into his eye, and he blinks it away, swearing quietly.

He's getting nowhere. He slides around to the back of the chair, and instantly sees why. The lever is held in a short, horizontal channel cut into the chair's metal frame. Another channel runs off it vertically, doglegging.

It reminds Jack of a component on the old manual cars his dad used to fix, the ones that would sit in the garage for months on end, covered with a tarpaulin—the kind of machine that really *was* two hundred years old—while his dad waited for a crucial part to be shipped in from Earth. Jack's mother used to nag him, asking why he couldn't just get the part fabricated locally, but his dad always said that he wanted to be authentic.

The lever at the back of the chair looks like a gearbox—specifically, like the reverse gear, which you had to slide into a channel to engage. Jack pushes on it, grunting with the effort.

It takes a few tries to position it so he can slide it up into the curved channel, but, once he does, it slips right in. There's a clunk, and all at once the chair is loose, sliding gently on its rails. Jack lets out a ragged breath, then slides it all the way back, exposing the hatch.

It isn't quite as large as the one leading down from the main deck to astronautics, but it looks about the same. He wedges his fingers into the space around the edge, gets ready to pull.

His mind, currently running in a high gear of its own, undergoes a sudden shift down into first. His emotions redline, fear overwhelming everything, freezing his body in place. What is he doing? Is he out of his skull? They're going to find him, they're going to catch him, they're going to do to him what they did to Volkova. His legs spasm as he forces himself up. He has to put it back. He has to stop this while he still can.

Except, he can't. Not now that he's started. That would be the worst thing of all.

He returns to the hatch, wincing as the metal edge digs into the skin of his fingers. The hatch comes up with an audible screech; for Jack, it's as loud as a baby crying in a silent house. He rests it carefully against the control panel, then peers inside.

His heart sinks. It's a vent, lined with coiled wires and blinking lights. The hatch opens in its ceiling, and it is so narrow that he doesn't even think Corey Livingstone would be able to climb inside. He runs a hand through his hair, his panic momentarily forgotten. Of course he couldn't trust the schematic. It's as badly designed as the rest of this—

Wait.

He takes a closer look, and, when he sees it, he actually lets out a little gasp of joy. There's another trapdoor, flush with the floor of the vent. He didn't see it at first, but it must lead right down into the bar.

At least, he hopes it does.

Still squatting, he leans down, trying to get a purchase. With his heart hammering in his chest, he moves onto his stomach, reaching down to grab the lower trapdoor. Its hinges are in better condition than the one above it—it slides up silently, just catching the top of the vent. And—yes!—he can see into the bar. He's right above the airlock doors. It'll be one hell of a drop, but if he's careful he can make it.

He's just getting his feet under him when he hears Brendan say, "I'll just check with him." The man just outside the passage, on the main deck.

Jack has no chance of disguising what he's done, so he doesn't bother. He flips himself around, sliding his legs into the trapdoor, through the vent, out the bottom.

He can hear Brendan's footsteps, coming closer by the second. Seema says something inaudible, and the footsteps pause.

"My cushla, I don't know," Brendan says, a hint of annoyance in her voice. "Go find out."

His legs dangle above the bar, the cold air licking at his skin. He slides himself down, his shirt rucking up, the edge of a wire catching in his mouth, dust gritty against his teeth. He spits it out, clambering down as fast as he can, hanging from the bottom trapdoor.

If Brendan comes in now, she'll see where Jack has gone straight away. He and Seema can race to the bar, intercept him and then it'll all be over. But if he closes the top hatch, it might buy him the few seconds he needs to get to Lorinda.

He reaches up, fingers brushing the hatch, face contorting as his muscles squeal in protest. It's too much. He falls, hanging from one arm, sweat bucketing down his face.

"Come on," he says, hissing the words. He tries again, levering an elbow up, using it to brace himself. This time, it gives him just enough height to grab the hatch.

"Jack?" Brendan sounds puzzled. He's close.

Jack pulls it down into place. It would be ideal if he could lock it, but there won't be a way to do it from inside, not from a hatch this narrow. He has to get to Lorinda. He looks down, gauging his distance to the floor of the bar, and drops.

Chapter 41

Somehow, the three grown-ups managed to get the pipe back into the wall—something that pissed the prisoner off in a major way. He tried to hurt Corey's dad, tried to get at him with his teeth, so his mom socked him in the stomach. From the shocked expression on both their faces, neither of them were expecting it.

Hannah is watching him now, close but not too close. He's gone still, eyes on the middle distance, like he's somewhere else entirely. It freaks Corey out a little.

His mom and dad have forbidden him from talking to the soldier. Malik, too. Which is a shame, because he's getting really bored listening to Mal talk.

It's not that Mal's movie stuff is stupid. It's actually kind of cool. It's just that Mal never talks about anything else. When they're at home, Corey can just ignore him, or go and hang out with Jamie and Allie. He can't do that here.

Mal is just trying to keep him distracted, but all Corey wants him to do now is go away. They've given him another nanomed capsule, so the cat is back in the long grass ... but Corey can still feel it prowling. And he knows there's only one capsule left.

228

Adrift

His brother emulates his posture against the wall, legs splayed out. "So here," Mal is saying, pointing at something on the holocam. "This is where the big part of the station got blown off. You see?"

"Mmm." Corey gives it only the quickest look.

"And here's that ship. The Colony one. I got a really good look at it for a second."

At that moment the pain bites, pushing past the nanobots. It feels like the bones in his shin are being squeezed in a vice, cracking and splintering. He grits his teeth, rides it out.

Mal taps on the Colony ship, zooming in, using his fingers to scroll across the footage. He's got it running in slow-mo now; Corey sees one of the metal spheres jettisoning out from the ship's underside.

A split second later, the image is obscured by a blinding lens flare, the light flushing out the details. Malik frowns. "That happens a lot. I've been trying to save for a better camera, actually. You know the Red Flex? The new ones? I want one of those."

"Mrghk."

"I think I should be able to edit it out, but only if I can—"

The rage is suddenly there, blotting out the pain. Corey turns towards his brother, the words bursting out of him, his voice raising to a furious shout.

"*It's not a movie*," he shouts. "People died, Mal. They're dead. You can't just go around pretending they're acting or whatever."

His brother shrinks from him, eyes wide. At the edge of his vision, Corey sees his mom poke her head out of the engine room.

"I just thought—" Mal says.

"I don't care!" Corey shifts his body sideways, facing Malik, ignoring the screaming howl of pain from his leg. It feels good to shout, good to finally tell Malik the truth. "You always do this. You just ... you act like everybody's just here to be in your movies. I don't wanna be any more. You ever film me again, I'll break that thing *in half!*"

"Corey." His dad is in front of him, down on one knee, anger and concern fighting for space in his eyes. His mom is just behind him, along with Hannah, who is looking between Corey and Malik. And Corey can feel the eyes of the prisoner, too.

He expects his brother to start shouting back, to get just as angry. That's what normally happens. Malik doesn't. He stares down at the camera, not looking at anyone.

"Sorry," he says, mumbling the words.

Corey turns away from him. "Yeah, well, you'd better be." The anger is gone. It's drained away, leaving nothing but the pain behind.

Everett shakes his head. "You both need to grow up," he says, getting to his feet. There's no strength in his words. He takes Anita by the shoulder, leads her back to Hannah. Corey ignores their worried looks, staring at the floor.

Mal shifts next to him, getting up. All at once, Corey is ashamed. Mal was just trying to be nice to him. He didn't deserve to get yelled at. It isn't his fault Corey's leg has been snapped into a zillion pieces.

He manages to put a hand on Mal's shoulder, doing it even though the pain of movement nearly knocks him out. "Hey. No. *I'm* sorry, OK? *I'm* sorry."

Mal looks at him. His face is a careful blank, but there's no mistaking the wounded look in his eyes.

Corey doesn't know what else to say. He's used to his brother getting mad at him, telling him to buzz off, acting like Corey's just an annoying little chutiya. That's what older brothers do. He's never had a situation where Mal is ... *scared* of him.

"I'm sorry I got mad," he says again. "I just ... you're always talking about your movies and that school you wanna go to. It's gotten kind of old."

"Yeah, well, you never shut up about spaceships."

"That's 'cos they're crash!"

"So are movies." Mal looks at him, the corners of his lips twitching upwards. "Like when I filmed your friend on that jump at the creek. What's her name ... Allie. She had to go to hospital, but I showed her the movie afterwards, and she said it was bàng."

Corey blinks. Was Mal *there* that day? It was a while ago, and most of the memories are dominated by Allie and her jhadna hoverboard jump over the kicker. But now that he thinks about it, he's almost certain his brother was right. He *was* with them, hanging out in the background, even if he's never shown them any of the footage.

"It's fine, though," Mal is saying. "I'll go hang out with mom and dad."

"I don't want you to." And he really doesn't. "Come on."

Malik half smiles, sits down again, although not quite as close as before.

Neither of them speak for a little while. Mal's holocam is locked, the screen dark. The man opposite them watches. And for the second time Corey catches that look. The one he can't quite figure out, which shifts the man's expression a fraction, crinkles the skin around his eyes. It's involuntary, gone in a flash.

"I know they're not actors," Malik says in a monotone. "I know people died."

"Yeah."

"And I'm not turning it into a movie. Well, I am, but not *that* kind of movie. People are gonna wanna know what happened. This way, we can show 'em."

Corey opens his mouth to speak, but Malik keeps talking. "And I wanna make it as good as possible. I want anyone who watches it to feel like they were here with us."

More silence. The grown-ups have stopped talking, too. Their dad is leaning against the wall, hands on the back of his head, looking at nothing.

"Lemme see some more," Corey says. His leg still feels like it's being slowly eaten, but he's determined not to let it get the better of him again. He'll just ... pretend it's not there. Yeah.

"OK," says Malik, after a moment. He scooches over, unlocks the holocam. Footage runs: everybody scrambling across the main deck, yelling instructions to each other, grabbing onto the wall struts.

Mal fast-forwards. The Colony ship appears onscreen, side-on, the image slightly blurry. The camera swings around, and Jack's terrified face looms large, followed by Lorinda, hanging onto the struts, trying to hook her foot into them.

"This was when the gravity went out," Mal says. "When we—"

"Go back," Corey says.

"Huh?"

"Go back. Rewind." His mouth has gone dry. He didn't see what he thinks he just saw. It's not possible.

"Um …" Malik's fingers don't move.

Corey grabs the camera. "Give it here."

His brother holds on startled, his confusion replaced by annoyance. "Hey, you can't just—"

"Mal! *Rewind!*"

"I can do it if you let me!"

Corey growls, ripping the holocam out of Malik's grip. His heart is hammering, and for the first time in what feels like hours he barely notices the pain. He jabs at the holo, accidentally does it twice, bringing up and then hiding the controls.

"You can't just take my shit," Malik says, trying to snatch it back. Corey twists out of the way, trying and failing to ignore the bolt of pain from his leg. He brings the controls up, and scrolls back through the video, bringing the Colony ship back into view.

Did he imagine it? He must have done. His broken leg is making him see things. Making him—

Then he sees it again, and stops breathing.

"What's wrong with you, Cor?" says Mal.

Corey zooms in. The ship's body fills the screen, pixelating. He barely notices. He scrolls along, flipping back and forth between two segments of the ship: one on the rear, and the other just above the cockpit.

"No way," he breathes.

Malik stares at him like he's gone mad. Corey turns to his brother, his eyes huge.

He gets as far as opening his mouth when there's a thick bang, coming from the other side of the wall. It's followed by a series of muffled thumps that bring the grown-ups, Hannah and Anita, spilling out of the engine room. Malik gets to his feet, Corey and the holocam forgotten.

Chapter 42

Lorinda hears movement. On the other side of the door. The boxes, or whatever they are, are being shifted.

Her first impulse is to brace herself against the back wall, lift her legs, get ready to fight. But she falters; they could be bringing her food or—*por favor, dios mio*—some water. Her exhausted mind muddles her movements. Underneath the sound of the boxes shifting, she can hear ... shouting?

What's happening out there?

There's a thud, and the door swings open. Jack stands before her, eyes wide, shirt untucked. A streak of grime runs along his face from hairline to jawbone.

Searing anger, pushing past the desire for water. "*You.*" She lifts her leg, ready to kick out at him.

"Just listen," he says, holding his hands up, speaking so fast that she almost doesn't catch the words. "If we're going to take those two out, I need your help."

From somewhere distant, Lorinda hears Brendan shouting at Seema to go downstairs. She blinks at Jack in astonishment, not understanding.

"Please." He looks up, and it's impossible to mistake the fear in his eyes. "You have to help me."

Lorinda has always prided herself on reacting quickly. In her job, she had to. If something went bad on you during a walk, if a seal broke or a cable snapped, you needed to move fast. You couldn't stall, or fumble, or let useless emotions like fear get in the way.

There's no telling what's happened between Jack and the other two, but there isn't time to dwell on it. She's been given a way out, and she acts, pulling herself off the toilet seat.

For a split second, she thinks she's drained the tank—that no matter how much she wants to move, her exhausted, frozen body isn't going to let her. She almost topples, her hands scrabbling at the wall as thunderous footsteps on the stairs above shake the cubicle.

Jack reaches out a hand and she grabs it, and a tiny bit of strength comes flooding back. She doesn't know how long she'll have it for, but she doesn't intend to waste it.

"OK," Jack says, as the footsteps reach the bar. "Just ..."

The words catch in his throat, and she realises he doesn't have a plan—or at least, not one they can use. She's going to have to play this by ear. If she gets in a tussle, or takes a hit, that'll be the end of her. But there are other things she can do. Things which might tilt the scales.

Like ... what?

She sees Craig again, his nose bleeding, that strange smile on his face and those strange words on his lips.

Quiet, bucko. Mama's—

Jack's eyes go wide. Then Seema grabs him, and everything goes to hell.

Chapter 43

Seema's a lot shorter than Jack, and she doesn't have her knife any more. Her hands, wrapped around his arm, feel tiny. If he's careful, he should be able to—

She plants her feet, pulling him off balance and swinging him around like a shot put. His feet tangle up as he's let go, nearly falling, slamming into the wall opposite the bathroom. His head collides with the surface so hard that he thinks he's going to black out, and he tastes blood in his mouth, oily and coppery.

He doesn't have a chance to recover. Seema comes hurtling towards him, arm cocked back. Jack gets a hand out, just quick enough to block the punch. It swings wide, grazing his jaw, but it's been given momentum by the run-up and it hurts like hell.

He flinches, eyes screwed shut against the pain. It's a mistake, one he's punished for when Seema slams into him again, fingers hunting for his Adam's apple. Somewhere, Lorinda is screaming.

"Get off!" he shouts. This was a bad idea. No, this was the *worst* idea he's ever had. What was he thinking? That he and an old woman were going to take Seema out?

Jack swings a wild punch, and Seema deflects it like it wasn't even there. She moves with practised ease, Jack's fist sliding along her forearm, then comes at him again, swinging a punch at his solar plexus to drop him. It just misses, Jack twisting out of the way a split second before it hits.

Seema twists mid-movement, and her second strike breaks Jack's nose. He feels the bridge crunch against her knuckles, the sudden, horrid alarm bell of pain.

From behind Seema, a tinny voice intones, "Reptile formation!"

Something collides with the wall by Jack's head. Whatever it is, it's *loud*, exploding in a cacophony of noisy bleeps, bouncing off the surface. Seema stops, confused, trying to find the source of the noise. Jack doesn't wait for her to refocus. He takes the chance, rocking onto the balls of his feet, driving a furious uppercut into Seema's chin.

Seema leans back, more startled than hurt, her hand flying to her face. She almost trips over the noisy object—it's that stupid action figure, the one Lorinda brought on board. Stupid or not, Jack isn't going to let the advantage go. He comes off the wall swinging, face twisted in a snarl. In seconds, he and Seema are rolling on the floor, pulled tight together like lovers, scratching and biting and hitting. Jack's nose gushes blood, spattering the floor and the side of the bar.

It's the first real fight Jack's been in.

He's been punched before, more than once, and he's even thrown a couple himself, but those fights lasted seconds. They were fuelled by booze, uncoordinated, sloppy, with no real stakes—the kind of fights where you buy the other guy a drink afterwards. This is different. This is *terrifying*. The flaring agony in his nose might be spurring him on, but it's not going to last much longer. Seema is tougher, way more experienced, and far better at finding the right places to strike.

Lorinda. She's his only hope. If she can grab Seema, somehow . . .

but even as the thought occurs, he sees Brendan sprint into view, heading right for the old woman. He tries to shout a warning, and finds he's got no air left, none at all.

Seema notices, and takes the advantage, jamming an elbow into Jack's throat. He stumbles off her, gasping, his windpipe feeling like it's shrunk to a quarter of its usual size. Seema springs to her feet, rushes him, slamming him against the same wall. Back to square one.

Lorinda sees Brendan coming, tries to move. No go. Brendan grabs her by the hair, and Lorinda howls in pain, her hands batting at his arms.

Grimacing, he drags her away, trying to force her back into the bathroom cubicle. Lorinda twists sideways, sliding out of the man's grip. She totters, unsteady, and Brendan relaxes. Jack sees him shove Lorinda hard, sending her flying across the bar, then turns to help Seema.

What was he thinking? They're going to kill her, and he's going to have to watch, knowing this one was his fault. He was the one who let her out, the one who came up with this crazy-ass plan in the first place ...

Jack doesn't have a chance to finish the thought. Seema explodes up from her toes and headbutts him, driving her forehead into his temple. Grey lights flicker at the edge of his vision. He does the only thing he can think to do, lunging forward and snapping his teeth around her earlobe, canines sinking into the flesh. Blood spurts into his mouth. Seema grunts, thumb digging into his cheek, hunting for his eye—

Which is when Brendan screams.

It's the high-pitched, agonised roar of someone in real pain, and it stops both Seema and Jack cold. Seema's partner is staggering away from them, hands clutching his face. Blood streams from between his fingers.

And Lorinda ... Lorinda is off to one side, face white, shoulders heaving. She's holding a clenched fist to her chest, blood of her own dripping down her shirt. She's clutching a much larger chunk of glass—perhaps one they used to chip away at the ice above the bathroom, one of many scattered around the bar from when they broke the pane on the front of the fridge. Brendan is blind, lashing out, still howling.

His hand slips from his face. There's a flap of skin hanging from his forehead, the blood gushing from it in a torrent. Jack gapes, stunned, amazed at how much there is. Then again: head wounds bleed the most, don't they? All those blood vessels?

"Brendan!" Seema rips herself away, dropping Jack and surging towards the bar, looking as if she can't decide whether to go for her partner or for Lorinda. Jack crumples, landing on his side, gasping. He reaches out for Seema, not sure what he intends to do—and his hand lands on a length of electrical cable.

It's running from the dismantled fridge, the one Everett cannibalised to build his heater. Without thinking, Jack gives it a yank, pulling it tight just as Seema's ankle hits it.

Seema tries to keep her balance, her free foot swinging out. But she's moving too fast, with too much momentum—and this time it's her who's off balance. She goes, twisting sideways as Jack tightens his grip, her arms windmilling. A second later, her neck collides with the edge of the bar.

There's no crack. No sound of breaking bone. Nothing but a muffled thud. Seema slumps to the floor, her eyes glassy. She twitches once, a single quick spasm, and goes still.

Jack lies prone, breathing hard, his entire face in agony. His nose feels ten times its normal size. Lorinda is trembling, her strength gone, using the bar to prop herself up as she stares at Seema.

"Seems!"

From the far end of the bar, Brendan surges towards them. The gash in his forehead is still flowing. Somehow, he's managed to clear the blood out of his eyes, which are two bright, furious specks in the red mask of his face.

He grabs a glass on the run, snatching it up with his metal hand, smashing it on the bar. The jagged edges catch the light as he thunders towards Jack.

Chapter 44

Lorinda doesn't hesitate. She hurls herself into Brendan's path, trying to block him.

Under normal circumstances, he'd just sweep her aside. But even though she can't stop him moving, bouncing off him and skidding onto her hands and knees, the hit is just enough to alter his balance. He collides with Seema, going over like a tree falling, spinning, landing on his back. The glass he's holding shatters against the wall.

Jack might be exhausted, his nose a screaming hellstorm in the centre of his face, but he knows a chance when he sees it. He forces himself to move, clambering on top of Brendan. A memory surfaces of Hec, lying in the hospital bed in São Paulo, tubes everywhere, his face turned away from Jack. Telling him to get out. Telling him to leave.

He leans back as far as he can, then slams a fist into Brendan's face. Then he does it a second time. He's roaring, the adrenaline pouring out of him in a torrent of nonsense words as he hits Brendan again and again.

Brendan pulls his arms up, trying to block the blows. At the last second, he changes his mind, slamming his metal hand into the side of Jack's head. It's like a nuclear explosion. Jack topples off, landing hard on his shoulder. Brendan kicks out at him, blind, thrashing, uncoordinated.

But Jack is deep in the memory. He's right there, back in that hospital. He can see the way Hec's useless legs shape the sheets, hear the beeping of the machines that can't help him. He can see the little scar below Hec's ear, from a long-ago arrest. He can hear Hec's voice. More than that: he can see the life they should have had. Everything they were going to do.

So he climbs on top of Brendan, and he keeps hitting.

He does it three more times before something gets in the way of his arm. He barely looks at what it is, just tries to push past it. But the obstacle won't move, and when he does look, he sees it's

Adrift

Lorinda. She's on her knees, both hands planted on his upper arm, holding with all the strength she has. In that moment, she looks a thousand years old.

"Stop," she says, her voice husky. "Just ... stop."

He doesn't want to. But right then, all the strength goes out of him. Brendan coughs, sending up a spray of blood from torn, mushy lips. He's barely moving.

"Bathroom," Lorinda says. "Put him ... bathroom."

Brendan is too out of it to fight much, although he almost gets away several times. When they're at the bathroom door, he lands an elbow into Jack's stomach that almost finishes him. He uses the last of his energy to shove Brendan into the cubicle. Without waiting for him to recover, he shuts the door, holding it closed. Lorinda is already stacking the boxes, moving with agonising slowness, grimacing as she bends over.

"Hurry," Jack says, his voice thick. Brendan is already pounding at the door, slamming his bodyweight against it.

After what feels like a whole minute, they manage to get the boxes in front of the door, enough that Brendan's hits aren't making much of a difference—and each one is weaker than the last. They'll need to come up with a long-term solution, but it's good enough for now.

Lorinda takes a step back, shoulders heaving. Her eyes meet Jack's, and he can't believe the look she gives him: a mix of pity, confusion and anger.

Jack stands, swaying, then slumps down against the wall. He reaches up to touch his nose, gets three-quarters of the way there, then thinks better of it.

"Fug," he says.

Lorinda looks back over at Seema, still sprawled across the floor by the bar. "Do you think she's ..."

Jack blinks hard, several times. "Dunno. Baybe. Didn't bean to ..."

Didn't mean to ... what? He can't finish the sentence. The last few minutes are a blur. Lorinda makes a sound, somewhere between a sob and a laugh. She leans against the side of the bar, shoulders shaking.

There's a lot that Jack wants to say. He wants to tell her how sorry he is, that he was an asshole, that he should never have gone along with Brendan and Seema. He wants to say that he knows he screwed up, that he'll do better. That he'll *be* better. He can't even work out how to start.

His broken nose is volcanic, and other parts of his body are starting to make their pain known. His left cheek. His stomach. His ankle, which got twisted somehow during the fight, and which is throbbing with an insistent ache. The skin on his knuckles hangs in bloody shreds.

They've got to let the people in astronautics know what happened. That Brendan and Seema aren't a problem any more. Jack runs through the sequence of events in his mind, desperate to impose some kind of order on things. They can't get through to astronautics from the bar; he or Lorinda will have to go back upstairs to the main deck, head down to the rear, then convince the others to open the trapdoor. Somehow.

He swallows, thick, glutinous blood dripping down his throat. His shirt is coated in it. "Ubstairs," he says. "Let eb'r'body out. S'OK."

"Oh, so you can just ... so you can go in and torture him? Do you think I'm stupid?"

"Doh." *No.* Doesn't she understand? Even the thought of trying to torture someone now makes him want to throw up. Again, that urge to tell her everything, that he went too far, that he let things get out of hand. Again, he has no idea how to start. In the bathroom, Brendan is moaning.

"I'll stay here. Go dell 'em wud 'appened."

The old woman looks like she's going to collapse. With an effort of will, she pushes herself off the bar, standing on shaky legs. "What about her?" she says, pointing at Seema.

Jack struggles to understand what she means. What are they supposed to do? Cut her and see if she bleeds? Hold a mirror to her mouth? Where the hell are they going to get a mirror? What are they even doing here?

Pulse. I should check to see if she's got a pulse. But he can't bring himself to touch her. Even the thought of doing it ...

Jesus. What a mess.

"I god it," he says. "I'll check she's … you know. You go ub."

After a beat, Lorinda makes her way to the stairs. Jack shuts his eyes, trying not to think about his smashed nose. The reality of the situation is coming down on him. Seema out cold—no, almost certainly dead. Brendan locked in the bathroom. But, of course, they'll have to let him out sometime, because he's going to need treatment. For a minute, Jack wants to leave him in there. Let him suffer. But his anger is gone, drained away.

And where are they, after all this insanity? Right where they started. No closer to figuring out why any of this has happened to them, or what they're going to do about it. They're still drifting, still in a ship with almost zero chance of survival.

Jack leans his head back. The single thought going round and round in his mind, the hornets buzzing worse than ever, is that he waited. It was only when he found that Brendan and Seema were Roses that he actually acted. He tells himself that he would have done something, eventually, but it's horseshit. He only acted because it suddenly meant something to him, not because he was doing the right thing. He only fought back because he suddenly had skin in the game.

He opens his eyes, looks around the freezing bar. The floor is speckled with blood, already turning dry and tacky. Above the airlock door, Jack can just see the light coming in from the cockpit, through the open hatch. Blankets and boxes and food containers lie scattered everywhere.

"*Fug*," he says.

Chapter 45

Corey hasn't told anybody what he saw on Malik's holocam.

He almost has, a dozen times. But every time he opened his

mouth, he yanked the words back. In any case, the sound of Jack fighting Seema and Brendan was echoing through the wall from the bar, and Malik was on his feet, ignoring Corey, along with everyone else. Even when the noises stopped, he couldn't get the words out—and now, he finds he doesn't want to. The burning urge to tell everyone right away was cooled off by a single, over-powering thought.

He can't mess this up.

He knows what he saw, but convincing everybody else might not be so easy. And if he *is* wrong, it'll just make everything worse. Because what he saw … it's crazy. It changes everything.

The prisoner. He's the key. But down in astronautics, Corey couldn't figure out what to say. The man was over on the other side of the room, and Corey couldn't talk to him without the others hearing. Mal doesn't know, either—after the noises stopped, Corey told him that he was just blown away by how crazy the video was. There was a second where he was sure his brother wasn't going to buy it, but he did, and by then his attention was focused on what might be happening on the other side of the wall.

It took Lorinda nearly half an hour to persuade Hannah, Anita and Everett that it was safe for them to come out, that she wasn't being held with a knife at her throat, forced to talk to them. In the end, they came up with an elaborate procedure involving Everett lifting the trapdoor up a little, making sure there was no one else around, then heading out himself to investigate, Hannah shutting the hatch behind him.

They'd agreed a word he'd shout if it was all clear—Wilder, Anita's maiden name. "If I shout anything else," he'd told them, "you lock that door shut, you hear?"

As soon as Corey's dad headed out, the big cat had made its return. He remembers begging for more meds, although he can't be sure if that actually happened, or was just in his mind.

There was some discussion about whether they should move him or not. His mom wanted him on the main deck—he could hear her voice getting louder as she argued for it, shouting down Hannah and Lorinda, and eventually they decided to move him.

He didn't remember much after that. They gave him some more

meds, the pills tasting like stale pee, and then he was being lifted. He was shaking, freezing cold and dripping sweat at the same time, unable to move, barely able to think. What he saw on the holo might have happened in a dream.

In the end, he's not even sure how they did it. He could feel his dad's arms around him, and hear Hannah's guiding voice, stretched tripwire-tight. With every movement, the pain skyrocketed to unbelievable levels. At some point, he passed out, and when he came to, he was back on the main deck, along with everyone else.

Now he's lying across the seats. There's something under his head—a balled-up jacket, the zipper digging into his neck. Another covers the lower half of his body. The big cat has retreated, a little.

He raises his head, blinking, to see the prisoner. The man is cuffed to one of the armrests, and his ankles, Corey sees, have been bound with tape. There's more wrapped around the handcuffs themselves—Hannah taking no chances this time. God knows how they got him up there, or why they decided to move him again.

Corey meets his gaze for a split second, then looks away. There was something about the prisoner he needs to tell everyone, something important, but right now his mind is way too fuzzy. He can't hold onto it.

Lorinda is a few seats down from Corey, bundled up in the other blanket. She's fast asleep, her head dipped onto her chest. Beyond her, Hannah is tending to Jack, dabbing at his nose. No Seema, or Brendan. He tries to figure out where they are, and can't do it. Can't even remember why they were up here and the rest of them were down in the—

"Honey." His mom is sitting just behind him, and he jumps as she rests a hand on his shoulder. "Try stay still, OK?"

Corey twists his head to look at her and is rewarded by a painful rumble from his leg. His mom sees the expression on his face, and tightens her grip. "No, don't move. I don't want to give you too many meds right away—there were a few more in the kit, but we need to make them last. Can you hang on for me?"

"Where's ... Dad?" Corey manages.

"Uh ..." She shakes her head for a second, her eyes closed, as if only just remembering. "Downstairs, with Malik. He's working on his heating thing for the water."

Malik. A memory ghosts into the back of Corey's mind.

"How did ..." He fumbles the words, trying to figure out how to say it: why Jack is on their side now, what happened up here.

His mom strokes his shoulder. He can feel her presence next to him, warm and full, and right now it's all he wants. He closes his eyes. The cat is very, very far away, far enough for him to escape, to sleep, just for a few minutes ...

He doesn't know how long it is before the memory of what he saw on Malik's holo comes back, but it's as powerful as an electric shock. His eyes fly open.

"Corey?" His mom is there. "Is it the leg? If you need more meds ..."

Corey makes himself calm down. The prisoner is right there— if Corey could talk to him, just for a second ...

"Could I have a glass of water, Mom?" he says.

She smiles, relieved. "Uh-huh. Sure." But halfway to her feet, she pauses, looking towards the cockpit.

"What's wrong?" Corey asks.

Anita shakes her head. "Your dad asked me to stay here and watch *him*." She nods to the prisoner. "I'll ask Hannah to get you one."

"No," Corey says, trying to keep his voice level, trying to ignore the pain. "She's busy. It'll be OK."

"I really don't think that's a good idea," Anita says, crossing her arms. "He almost got loose down in the bar. I don't know if you saw it, but—"

"Hannah's right there. If there're any problems, I'll just yell. He's cuffed to the armrest anyway. Please?"

He's pushed it too far. She's frowning at him, suspicious now. She's going to want to know why he needs to be alone. But then she glances towards Hannah, still patching up Jack, trying to get a piece of tape onto his busted nose, and her concern for her son wins out.

She gets up, checks the prisoner's cuffs, leaning slightly away from him as if he's a caged animal. "Anything happens," she says. "He moves even a tiny bit, you yell as loud as you can."

"I will. Promise."

Anita walks away, moving slowly, casting worried glances back at Corey. He flashes her a small smile.

If there's any water left in a cup down there, she'll be back in under thirty seconds. If there isn't, if she has to chip off some ice, he's got a little more time. No way to tell—he'll just have to move fast.

He turns his body slightly, ignoring the pain in his leg, facing the man opposite.

"The thrusters," he says, keeping his voice low.

The man's expression doesn't change.

The meds are starting to kick in now, really kick in, the big cat backing off, leaving space for Corey's thoughts. "On your ship. The ones above the central reactor stack. They're ion thrusters. My brother filmed you guys. You can only see the thrusters from certain angles, but they're there."

He licks his lips. It hurts to talk this much, but he has to get this out, *needs* to.

"I read about ships all the time. I wanna fly 'em when I grow up. So I know about the thrusters—they're classified, but there's all these rumours, on the message boards and stuff. Plus a couple of leaked drawings. No one knows if they're official or not, but those thrusters on your ship look just like them, so they must be. There's no *way* anyone in the Colonies has them yet. They just aren't advanced enough, and, anyway, they take crazy cash to build."

He stops, unsure. But he's come too far to stop now.

"You're not Colony. You're Frontier. You're one of us."

Chapter 46

A soldier's job was simple, when you got down to it.

It consisted of three things, constantly repeated. Problem, solution, action. Problem, solution, action.

The man sitting opposite Corey on the deck of the *Red Panda* had found this to be true no matter what the circumstances. It was true in basic, where the problem was how to do two hundred pull-ups without passing out, and in advanced ops training, where they airlocked you into a hazard zone in a suit with twenty minutes of oxygen and told you to figure it out. And you didn't even get to that point unless you were damn good at the solution and action part.

It had been true on Kepler-8, when a Colony drone swarm had picked them out against the terrain and started hitting them with cluster missiles. Ditto six months later, on Antares, when the squad had a limited time frame to execute an incursion into a Colony outpost, and ten klicks of exposed, low-G terrain to navigate.

It had been especially true when he told Madhu he was going to enlist, way back when.

Brigita had brought in a crop of beans from her grow dome, and he and Madhu were cleaning them at the big table in the main room. Brigita had always been so proud of those—nobody on Cassiopeia believed you could get anything to grow in the planet's dead soil. But they hadn't had her skill, or her persistence.

Then again, you had to have those things to make it on a Frontier outpost like Cassiopeia, and you *definitely* had to have it to build the world Brigita and Madhu had—especially when building a world was quite literally what they were doing. They were Frontier terraformers, slowly turning their rock into something worth living on, and ever since they'd adopted him when he was six, their little outpost had gone from seven habs to twenty.

As usual, he and Madhu were being extra careful to get the stem off each bean, both knowing without even saying it that Brigita would give them hell if they didn't. Madhu had his sleeves rolled up, exposing his meaty arms, elbows resting on the table. Frowning beneath his beard as he considered each bean.

Usually, the main room was crowded—with a family the size of Madhu and Brigita's, it could be hard to find space in the compact habitat. There was always someone dashing between the hot, tight rooms, a child on all fours under the table, a peal of laughter from Jocinda or Yoshiro blocking out a conversation. But he'd picked this moment carefully. Roger was tending the regulators. Ling-Xi had the kids doing maths problems on their lenses. Madhu's brother Mhotar was sleeping. The time was right.

When he'd told Madhu what he wanted to do, the big man had paused, a just separated bean and stem in either hand, holding them there as if about to glue them back together.

"Enlist where?" Madhu had rumbled.

The question didn't make sense. "With the Frontier?"

Before he could ask, Madhu had shifted his great bulk in his chair towards the kitchen. "Brigita? Darling, come please."

"Busy!"

"No, come. We have something to talk about."

He'd turned back, eyebrows raised, as if to say, *You didn't think you'd get away with just asking me, did you?*

Brigita had come. She'd been chopping tofu blocks into bite-size cubes, and hadn't had a chance to blast the white flecks off her hands with the air tap. She had her hands out in front of her, away from her tunic, listening as he told them what he wanted to do. It was a lot harder with her around, which had probably been why Madhu called her.

He wasn't even halfway through his first sentence when she was shaking her head. "No. You're staying. Bloody silly boy."

"I can't."

"This is not a discussion."

"It has to be."

Madhu, his arms folded, shook his head as if trying to dislodge something from his ear. "I thought you wanted to stay here, huh?"

"No, I do, but—"

"We're building something important." Madhu was gathering steam, ready to plunge into his favourite subject. "There are only so many habitable planets out there, and if we don't make more, we can forget about it. It's a privilege to—"

"I *know*."

"You don't know a thing." Brigita spat the words at him, suddenly furious. He couldn't even remember seeing her angry before, let alone this angry. "You turn eighteen, you think you know what's what. Well, let me tell you what's what. People are dying in this war. There might be conscription on the other planets, but not here. Here, we're safe, and you are staying whether you like it or not."

"You told me," Madhu said, his mouth barely moving under his beard, "that you wanted to live here. With us."

"I do."

"It doesn't sound like it. And what do you do if they send you somewhere dangerous? Or what if—"

And at that, he'd done something that he'd never done before. He might not have had *problem, solution, action* drilled into him yet, but it was as if he already understood it. That understanding was why, years later, they'd invite him to apply for advanced ops, why they'd send him to dungholes like Kepler-8 and Antares. It was what led him to stand up, reach over and place a single finger over Madhu and Brigita's mouths.

Theirs was not a touching family. The house they'd built on this little way-out rock was filled with adopted children, with rough hugs and hair tousles and punches on the shoulder. Once in a while, when he'd had a little too much of Mhotar's home-made vodka, Madhu would give Brigita a quick, almost hesitant peck on the cheek. For someone to touch them like this, with a finger gently pressed against their lips, was enough to shock them into silence.

He'd sat back down, looked them both in the eyes, and told them exactly why he'd wanted to do it.

It wasn't just that he wanted to see what else there was beyond the cramped cluster of terraforming domes on Cassiopeia, although of course that was part of it. The war between the Frontier and the Colonies had left a lot of orphaned kids, their homes and families ripped apart. The effort to resettle them had been sketchy at best, scattering them as quickly and efficiently as possible across safe territories, with anyone who would take them.

He wasn't naive—he'd heard plenty of horror stories. But for each one, there were two where things had worked out OK. He was among them.

He didn't remember his birth family. When he was sixteen, Madhu and Brigita had sat him down—at the exact same table, probably in the same chairs—and told him that they could help him find out, if he wanted. They'd told the same thing to everyone they took in, and they had experience in navigating the bureaucracy, knowing just which buttons to push to get the relevant information sent out on the next supply jump. But he found that he didn't want to know. Didn't have the slightest desire. This was his family. *This* was his home.

The Frontier's great, grinding system might not be perfect, but it had placed him here, with Madhu and Brigita and Mhotar and their enormous brood. Luck? Sure. He could easily have been sent somewhere else. But a system that could give him the life he'd had, even if it was flawed, was worth protecting. The Colonies wanted to destroy it—or, at least, take it for themselves in their victory, with all the chaos that entailed.

If they won, if they clawed back territory from the Frontier, who knows how many more horror stories there'd be, instead of more Madhus and Brigitas? He wasn't going to let that happen. He needed to fight. He needed to repay the debt.

It took weeks to convince them. Brigita soon gave up—she'd always picked her battles, always known when she could convince her adopted children, and when she couldn't. But not Madhu. Madhu had grilled him relentlessly, making him justify his decision in minute detail.

It was hardly surprising—Madhu was one of those people who would never let anything go, who had to cram as much knowledge into his brain as possible. He was the kind of person who'd spend hours studying a dismantled recycler, even though they had two fully trained technicians on site, and multiple spare recyclers in storage. He loved having political discussions, refusing to let up until he understood exactly *why* someone believed what they did.

This—the decision to enlist—was no different. He'd had to spend hours with Madhu, telling him that he had to do this—and, more importantly, convincing Madhu that he intended to come back. After the debt was paid, he'd set up in a habitat of his own, help turn the tiny planet that raised him into something that might do the same for others.

The version of him sitting on the main deck of the *Red Panda* is a long, long way from the kid sitting at that table. Too much has changed.

He still can't quite bring himself to believe that the other soldiers on his ship are gone, but he's put those thoughts away, boxed them in, walled them off until their shrieking is nothing more than a distant, muffled wail. He's lucky to be alive. He got sloppy, in a way he wouldn't have done when the war was still going.

No matter. The mission was to wipe out every single person and structure in this quadrant of space, and he is going to accomplish that. He has to—not just for him, but for every soldier who lost his life trying to get it done. And for Cassiopeia, which he knows he'll never go back to.

Problem: The mission has encountered difficulties.

Solution: Fall back on training. Stay calm. Eliminate the difficulties, starting with imprisonment.

Action: Complete the mission. Kill everyone on board. Await extraction.

Because extraction was coming. It wouldn't be long now. If he hadn't taken control of this ship by the time it got here, they'd blow it to pieces. So: work the problem. Progress through the sequence.

He doesn't know why it surprises him to find children here—this is a civilian craft, after all. But all the same, opening his eyes when they brought him on board and the boy being the first person he saw was … unsettling.

He's not naive—civilian casualties have always been a problem, and while he might never have killed a juvenile directly, he was almost certainly involved in their deaths. That was how war worked. He'd long ago accepted that fact—easy to do when the alternative was a total failure to perform on a mission. This will be no different. And there is far too much at stake not to finish the mission. The boy dies, along with everyone else.

For a moment, he thinks about telling them the mission's purpose, and almost laughs. They would never understand. They couldn't. They're civilians, with everything that implies. He does not have a duty to explain himself to them. Like everyone on Sigma Station, they deserve everything that's coming to them.

Adrift

All the same. Just because these people have to die doesn't mean it should be painful. The boy's leg injury could have been prevented—the passengers on this ship, these civilians, were clumsy. At the right time, when the difficulties have been dealt with, he'll kill the boy himself. He would have preferred not to, but he knows he has no choice. And it'll be Quick. Clean. Painless. He's not cruel.

He has to admit he's impressed that the boy figured out that he was Frontier. Hayes should have thought about disguising the thrusters, back at the base. Another example of sloppiness.

"I'm right, aren't I?" the boy says. "It's OK. You can tell me. It's not like our situation's gonna get any worse."

The soldier considers the boy. Perhaps he can use this. They bonded before, over that ridiculous alien series, and maybe he can do it again. It won't work like it did last time—they'll all be on their guard now—but it's worth a shot.

"Smart kid."

The boy's eyes go wide.

"I'm Corey," he says. "Corey Livingstone. What's your name?"

The soldier pauses. All things considered, it would have been better not to know the boy's name.

The kid's mother is back on the main deck, holding a glass filled with ice chunks sitting in a dribble of water. She's stopped to talk to two other passengers—the guy with the bloody nose, and the young woman who did that half-assed interrogation of him before.

The kid is bound to tell his mommy about who he, the soldier, is really fighting for. That'll probably mean they'll try to get more info out of him. But the big guy with the metal arm and his squeeze are nowhere to be seen, and the corporate looking asshole in the polo shirt looks like he's had the fight knocked out of him. They were the only ones who might have tried the torture thing, so he should be OK.

Except: when Mom comes back, handing the kid the glass of water, he says nothing. Not a word.

Mom glares at him, a lioness protecting her cub. And as she does so, with her head turned in his direction, her son looks him in the eyes, and smiles. It's the same smile he saw on any number of his brothers and sisters, when they were cooking up something they didn't want Madhu and Brigita to know about. It's a smile that says: *we know something they don't know.*

Chapter 47

"Stop moving," Hannah says, for the fifth time.

Jack stays still for perhaps half a second before Hannah dabs his face a little too hard for his liking. He jerks away, wincing. "Stob. Id's fine."

"It's *not* fine." She keeps dabbing at it, down on one knee in front of him, the torn piece of fabric in her hand stiff with blood. The tape on his nose has come loose again.

What made her start helping him? It was like she needed something to do, like she couldn't be idle for more than a minute at a time.

"Just stay put for five seconds," she says. "Let me get the blood off."

He stays put for four. When he jerks away, Hannah hurls the rag at his lap. "You know what? Forget it."

"Id jus' hurds. Dat's all."

"Oh, really? Your nose hurts? Well, we've got a kid busted up a lot worse than you. Don't think you're getting any nanomeds."

"I didn't bean—hag od."

He gives a series of sniffs, and a fresh line of blood starts tracking down from his right nostril. But when he speaks again, his voice is a little clearer.

"I didn't mean for the captain to—"

"You didn't *mean it*? Are you serious?"

A look of pure fury crosses his face. But it only lasts a second before vanishing, and he drops his head, hands clasped in his lap.

For a few moments, neither of them move. Hannah stands, her

arms crossed, watching him. Eventually, she sighs, and goes back down on her knee. "Here. The tape's loose. Let me fix it."

He grits his teeth, wincing as she pushes against the fractured bone, smoothing the tape down. His nostrils and upper lip are crusted with clots the colour of red wine.

"Doesn't matter now, anyway," she says, taking slightly sadistic delight in pushing the last bit of the tape down hard. "But if you do anything like that again ..."

He nods, not looking at her.

She takes one last look at his busted nose, then sits down next to him.

"What do we do now?" Jack says.

She looks over at him, half ready to get angry again, but the feeling fizzles out. She's too exhausted to care. "I don't know. We could go look in the cockpit. Maybe we'll find something..."

She trails off. Jack shifts next to her, but doesn't reply.

She's doing her best not to think of their situation. With everything that's happened, she managed to forget about it, at least for a little while, but it's all come rushing back. They're still adrift, still lost in space—only now without a pilot, and with not one but two prisoners, thanks to the genius with the busted nose.

God knows what they're going to do about Brendan. The man is still trapped in the bathroom downstairs, occasionally smashing at the door frame. Jack did a number on him, from what Lorinda said, but they'll need to come up with a more permanent solution than some boxes against the door.

How much food do they have left? What's their water situation? After everything that's happened, their meds are running dangerously low. What are they going to do about Corey's leg? Hannah's stomach rumbles, and it's not like the feeling from before, where she was hungry but could mostly ignore it. It's starting to become more insistent, her body screaming out for food, for fuel to keep going. Fuel she can't give it.

God, she's tired. And not just in her body. She's tired of everything. There is nothing they've done that's got them any closer to getting out of here—and with each new development that door closes a little more.

Then again, who is she trying to fool? That door slammed shut a long time ago. And no matter how hard they fight, no matter how lucky they get, it's never enough.

They have fought, and fought, and fought, and they are only just barely alive.

And as these thoughts come, the full weight of their situation crashes down on her. It's almost a physical sensation, a giant sitting on her chest. With Volkova gone, there's no one to help her. She's now in charge. (*Red shirt. Commander colours.*) Even if she refuses, the other passengers will look to her for answers—answers she can't give them.

Callie wouldn't think like that. She'd—

Oh, fuck Callie. Fuck her sister, and her parents, and everybody back on Titan. Fuck them for putting her in this position. She could have kept looking, stuck it out a little while longer, gritted her teeth and ignored their suggestions about her life and their little jabs disguised as jokes—*You've got so much free time, you should go do some classes, hey, would you mind helping me paint the spare bedroom, it'll only take a few hours.*

Even as she focuses on her frustration, she knows she'd give anything to see them again. She would give anything to smell her dad's aftershave again, to hug her mom. Even Callie.

Not going to happen now. She'll never see them again.

She gets up and walks away from Jack, ignoring his questions as she crosses over to the far side of the deck. She's resting her head against the cool metal, staining it with hot, stinging tears. She doesn't scream. Instead, she scratches her nails against the metal, as if she can rip a hole in the wall with her bare hands.

The fury is gone. And in its place? Despair. Cold and hard as a blast freezer.

An idea begins to grow in her mind. At first, it horrifies her. But she can't stop herself turning it over, considering it.

Callie and her parents always wanted her to take responsibility, show initiative. Take the lead. She's tried, and she's failed, again and again. But maybe there's one thing she can take responsibility for. She can give them all a way out of this.

No. There must be another way.

Adrift

But she can't think of one.

She doesn't know how long she stays there, leaning against the wall. But when she pulls back, she knows what she has to do.

It takes her a while to get everyone together. She has to retrieve Everett from downstairs, convince Anita that they're not going to let the prisoner out of their sight. Lorinda comes even more reluctantly; she's refused any more nanomeds, telling them they need to save the nine remaining pills for Corey, but it's left her grimacing every time she takes a step.

Hannah asks Malik to stay with his brother, and to make sure the captive soldier doesn't try anything. She expects the two boys to protest about being left out, but they don't—they just give her dull nods. As an extra measure of security, she uses the rest of the tape to bind the man's strapped ankles to the chair support, and she makes sure there's absolutely nothing around him that could be used as a weapon if he gets free.

They meet at the front of the main deck, near the cockpit. Hannah keeps glancing behind her to make sure the two boys are staying where they left them. She feels bad leaving them out, but there's no way they're getting involved in this discussion. Not yet, anyway.

She sits on a plastic seat, hugging herself, as if to steady her body. "We need to talk about what we do next," she begins. To her ears, her voice sounds far too old.

"I've been thinking," Everett says quietly. "We could try and head back towards the station. If we did another walk—" he glances at Lorinda. "I don't mean you have to go, but didn't you say freeze-dried food could survive a vacuum?"

"Might keep us going a while longer," says Anita, looking at her feet. She's shivering, although the main deck isn't quite as cold as it was before.

"Do you even know which direction to go in?" Hannah asks. "There's no signal. We won't be able to spot the station from here, and we don't have a pilot who could navigate."

In the silence that follows, the hum of the engines sounds too loud. Hannah's despair jolts a little more as she realises that, just beyond the thin glass above them, there's no sound at all.

"We could ... you know." Ev pauses, then nods back towards the prisoner.

Hannah has to will her voice to work. "Doesn't matter. He could tell us everything, and we still wouldn't get out of here."

"But they must have had a way out." Anita looks close to tears herself. "Why would they have destroyed the gate?"

"We need to think about the possibility that maybe they didn't mean to." Lorinda, who hasn't said a word until now, speaks barely above a whisper. "Something might have gone wrong. They could have been stuck out here, too."

"That's ridiculous," Jack says.

"It doesn't matter." Hannah wipes at her face. "Their ship's gone. Even if there was a ... a ... another gate around here, a secret one nobody knew about, we couldn't find it. Not unless we get direct line of sight."

At that, everybody glances up through the viewing dome. The stars stare back, giving away nothing.

Anita sighs, like even she doesn't believe what she's about to say. "Another gate means a signal. We could find it."

"The captain scanned for signals earlier. If it was broadcasting, we would have picked it up."

"Rescue's gotta be on the way by now," Anita says, as if Hannah hadn't spoken. "They *have* to know something's wrong."

"Even if they are," Hannah replies, "it doesn't matter. By the time anyone manages to jump in, it'll be too late."

She hates herself, hates that she has to say this. It's like she's removing their hope, one fragment at a time.

"We should at least *try* and talk to him," Everett says. "I know we said we wouldn't, but if there's even the tiniest chance ..."

Hannah nods. "I know. And ..." she takes a deep breath, hating herself even more. "I think we should. But if he doesn't tell us anything, then ... then we need to look at other solutions."

Silence.

Eventually, Anita says, "OK?"

Take charge. Take responsibility. "I'm just saying ... we could find a way to alter the air mix in here. We'd—"

Lorinda's head snaps around. "No. Absolutely not."

256

Adrift

"What is she talking about?" says Anita.

"She's talking about killing us," Jack says, staring at Hannah in dull shock.

"Jesus Christ," Everett says.

And, just like that, it's out.

She sees Lorinda about to start shouting, and jumps in. "I'm not saying we do it now. It's a last resort. But I think, given everything that's happened ..."

"There is no way," Lorinda says. "No way I'm selling out like—"

She stops, her mouth snapping shut. Hannah frowns at the strange choice of words, but then Anita is shaking her head, hands gripping her knees, saying, "It's suicide."

"I know."

"You're saying we just—"

"Yes."

Anita glances over at her two sons. Corey is lying on the bench, huddled under a foil blanket. Malik is a little way away, attention locked on his holocam. Hannah feels a burst of worry that they're not watching the prisoner, and she's sure that Anita's going to start yelling at them—the last thing they need. Instead, the woman pulls her gaze away, as if she can't bear to look.

"I'm not doing that," she says, almost politely. "I'm not. None of us are." She looks to Everett, as if expecting agreement. Her husband says nothing, staring at a spot on the floor.

"Ev?"

He meets her eyes. There are dark circles under his eyes, and an unruly growth of stubble has darkened his cheeks.

"Everett?"

Still nothing.

Anita points a shaking finger. "Those are our boys. Our *family*." Her voice cracks on the last word, and, finally, the tears come.

"I won't do it," Lorinda says. "I can't believe we're even discussing this." She glares at Jack. "What about you? You think this is a good idea?"

Jack gets halfway to a shrug, then lets his shoulders drop. "I don't know any more."

"If we were going to do this ..." Everett asks Hannah, ignoring the horrified look on Anita's face.

Hannah takes a deep breath. A very deep breath.

"We'd turn down the oxygen levels on board. There's probably a failsafe, but I could figure it out."

"But we'd choke, wouldn't we?"

She shakes her head, wishing she didn't know what she's about to tell them. "Your body can't sense lack of oxygen—only elevated carbon dioxide. We'd just ... go to sleep. I read that in a book, I think."

"A book." Anita doesn't give Hannah a chance to respond. "It's not going to happen. Not until we've gone through absolutely every last thing. If it means hurting *him*—" nobody has to ask who she means "—then we do it. I don't care any more."

"I know," Hannah says softly. "If you want to go and talk to him again, or ..." She swallows. "If you think torturing him is the only way, I won't stop you. I'm going to go to the cockpit, and I'm going to figure out how it all works. I won't do it unless we absolutely have to, and unless we all agree. But once our food runs out ... or the meds ..."

Another few seconds of silence. Lorinda is looking at Hannah with utter disgust.

"Fine." Anita gets to her feet. A hard steel core has entered her voice, winding through the middle of it like a needle down a spine. "You do that. I'm going to go figure out what's happening here." She doesn't look at her husband. Instead, her eyes land on Jack. "How about you? You going to help me?"

Jack meets her gaze. He looks sick—physically ill, like he's going to throw up for the second time in as many days. But after a few moments, he nods.

"What are you even going to use?" Everett says.

"We'll figure it out." Without another word, Anita marches off, heading for the bar. Going, Hannah realises with a low thud deep in her stomach, to find something she can use to cut.

Trembling, she gets to her feet, amazed she can still stand. "I'll be up front," she says, to no one in particular.

Lorinda is seated on one of the plastic chairs. As Hannah passes, the old woman reaches out, grabbing her wrist in an iron grip.

"You're the guide," she says, almost pleading. "You're supposed to keep us safe, no matter what. What happened to you?"

Gently, Hannah disengages her arm from Lorinda, and resumes her walk to the cockpit.

What happened to you?

She has no idea.

No idea at all.

Chapter 48

Corey's leg feels thick, and completely numb, like when you smack your funny bone really hard. It's not a fun feeling. Even so, he's aware of his heart starting to beat a little faster.

Keeping the soldier's secret was the right thing to do. They can't afford to have this guy as their enemy any more, no matter what he's tried to do to them. Keeping the secret about the thrusters won't do that, but it's a start.

He waits until his mom has headed over for the grown-ups' meeting, ignoring the perplexed look on the soldier's face. The nanomeds are working now, but it's not going to be long before they wear off: before the cat with the giant razor teeth comes slinking out of the long grass.

"So, um." Malik sits next to him, fiddling with his holocam. "You wanna watch some more?"

Malik, no matter what Corey might call him from time to time, isn't an idiot. But having to explain everything now, before all the pieces are in place, will complicate everything.

"Actually, I'm gonna try get some sleep," Corey says. Carefully, he manoeuvres himself so he's lying down again, the jacket under his head. "Can you gimme a bit of space?"

"Huh?"

"You're crowding me." He flashes a smile, to let Malik know it's OK.

"Oh yeah. Right. OK." Malik scooches a few feet down the row of seats. "I'll just be over here."

Corey closes his eyes. After a minute, he peeks. As he expected, Malik is wrapped up in his holocam, zoned out. He's in his own world, and won't come out of it unless he has to—Corey's seen it plenty of times before. He turns his head a little, looking at the soldier.

"What's your name?" he whispers.

No response.

"Come on." Corey murmurs the words, doing everything he can to make them part of the background noise. "Give me something to call you. It doesn't have to be real. It can be your codename or whatever."

The soldier gives Corey the same look he did when Corey asked him what year it was. But after a few moments, he says, "Roman."

"Roman … who?"

"Just Roman."

He's got to keep him talking. Somehow. He looks at the patch on Roman's arm. The daggers.

"If you really *are* Frontier," he says, "then you must be into some deep cover, black ops stuff, right? I don't know how else you'd have those thrusters, because that's some zhen experimental shit."

No response. No acknowledgement. Corey tries a different approach. "Why'd you do it?"

"Do what?" Roman's voice is monotone, uninterested, as if Corey just asked him the time.

"Do wh—" Corey stares at him, and has to force himself to keep his voice low. "The station! Sigma! The place you blew up! We were on your side, and you—"

He takes a breath, his mind whirring. It doesn't make any sense. None of this does. Roman might be lying to him, and he's starting to second-guess himself. "Why are you trying to kill us? What did we do to *you*?"

Roman's eyes narrow, but that's all. Corey keeps talking. "If you don't want to tell me, I'll still figure it out. Maybe … maybe your arch-enemy was on the station. Or someone who stole your girlfriend. You got really mad, and you got some friends together, and you went in and blew it all up."

The soldier tilts his head to one side, frowning at Corey.

"Or there was a virus on the station! You remember in season two of *Vicious*? That episode with the black gunk coming out of people's noses? And Corso had to make that decision, about whether or not to blow up the other ship, even though Axin was still on board? I'm guessing you had to stop the virus spreading to the rest of the galaxy …"

This is stupid. He could keep guessing forever, and Roman doesn't have to say anything. Well, that's OK. There's other stuff he wants to know. More important stuff, actually.

"Fine. Don't tell me. I get it—it's like an honour thing. You're sworn not to talk about your mission with anyone else. But can you *at least* tell me how you guys were going to get away, if you blew up the jump gate?"

Roman shifts in his seat. Says nothing.

"Come *on*. What difference does it make? Your ship's dead, we're pretty much dead—" somehow, he manages to say it without choking "—and it's not like you're getting out like you planned."

More stony silence. Corey sighs. "Fine. You blew up the station because they were developing a secret mega-weapon that could destroy a sun, and they were planning to use it to wipe out the—"

"If I tell you, will you stop talking?"

A cold feeling spreads through Corey's chest. For the first time in forever, he forgets about his leg entirely.

"Maybe," he says. "If it's true." Another quick glance at Malik, but his brother is still absorbed in his holocam, zoned out from everything around him.

"We jumped in," Roman says.

After a beat, Corey says, "That's it?"

"Yes."

"I don't get it. Through the gate?"

"You're not listening. I told you. We jumped."

"Yeah, I get that, but—"

When the realisation hits him, Corey's breath catches in his throat.
You can't jump without a gate. You need too much energy.

But he's remembering the tech the other ship had, the spheres, how they moved like nothing he'd ever seen. And one look at Roman tells him that the man isn't lying.

They didn't need an existing wormhole. They didn't have to use a two-mile-wide gate that stayed where it was while ships jumped through it. They could jump through space without one.

It's so simple, but they didn't see it. None of them did. And why would they? Jumping without a permanent, always open wormhole was way, way, *way* beyond what anyone could do. This wasn't an ion thruster, or a swarm of weapon spheres. What Roman was saying was a hundred years away from actually working. Maybe more. It would be like those olden-day English guys in the top hats and long coats suddenly figuring out how to travel to Mars. And yet, somehow, these people *had* figured it out.

Corey gapes. What would it mean if you could jump anywhere, instantly, without having to rely on the jump gate network?

"How?" he says. "How do you keep the wormhole stable? Where do you get the energy?"

"I just help fly the ship, kid."

"But is there like a limit? To how far you can jump? And what about size—like, does the ship have to be below a certain length or weight class? Or could you take a really big ship, an Antares or something, and—"

But Roman is already shaking his head. "Sorry. Deal's a deal. No more questions."

A thin crackle of pain sneaks up Corey's leg, but he ignores it. "If it were me, I'd … I dunno, go places where we haven't put gates yet. Places where we've never been, like the Crab Nebula. Or all the way out by the Orion Arm. I'd go to other galaxies. I wouldn't go blow up one of my own stations, unless there was a really, really good reason to—Wait, how much are you being paid?"

"What?"

"Someone paid you a lot of money to take out the station. That's why you did it." It all makes sense now. It'd have to be a lot of money, but Corey can see it. Kind of. Maybe. "They gave you that ship, paid you half up front, and said you'd get the rest when the job was done. That's how it works, right?"

A very scary look comes onto Roman's face—a look that stops Corey cold.

"I didn't," the soldier says slowly, "do it for money."

"So you did it for free?" The words are out before he can stop them. Then again, what's Roman going to do? He can look as scary as he wants, but he can't hurt Corey, not tied up like he is.

Roman's voice is very quiet, and very dark. "You don't know a single thing about what we did."

"Then tell me!" This time, Corey forgets to keep his voice down. "If it wasn't money, and there wasn't a virus you had to wipe out or something, then *why*? It must have been worth the risk, because it's super-illegal. Did you have a plan for when you got back? Like, stash the ship somewhere, and—"

In response, Roman looks over to Malik. "Hey."

Malik jolts, springing to his feet, almost dropping the holocam. He looks between Corey and the soldier, eyes huge.

"You should tell your little brother not to talk to strangers," Roman says.

"What?"

Corey doesn't hear Roman's response. Right then, his leg sends up another jolt of pain, and this one is much, much worse. He squeezes his eyes shut, gritting his teeth, trying to ride it out. Trying not to scream.

Chapter 49

Roman hadn't meant to get angry. He'd actually been ... well, maybe not enjoying the conversation, but tolerating it, at least. And then, the kid had gone and started accusing him of taking money. Which had slammed the conversation shut like a book.

It had reminded him of who these people were. They were pampered, sheltered. Protected by men like him. They didn't know a single thing about honour, or sacrifice. He'd allowed himself to think that the kid was different, but he wasn't. He was exactly the same.

In the world of problem, solution, action, these people had no place.

The kid thinks there's money involved—that Roman would just sell his services for profit, like a common merc. Fine. If that's the case, let him wonder. He, Roman, doesn't owe these people a goddamn thing—least of all the reasons why they were out in this useless, nowhere quadrant in the first place.

He tries to calm his thoughts, focusing on the solution, and then the action. Get free, and await extraction.

But, despite himself, he marvels at how Corey refuses to quit. Even as his brother gets between them, the kid is still asking questions. Why'd he do it? Who else was on his ship? Were they planning on warping out? He's in pain, his face contorted with the effort, his brother fumbling with a pack of meds, looking back at Corey in puzzlement, but he's still going.

Before, he thought the kid hadn't told the others about which side he was on because he wanted to establish trust. Maybe it's more than that. Maybe the kid just wanted to know as much as possible, before anybody else. He probably didn't even realise he was doing it.

And as he considers this, another, more unsettling thought slides through his mind.

What was it the kid had said? *Did you have a plan for when you got back?* There *was* a plan—they'd discussed it in the hangar where they built the ships. Every part of the mission, from inception to order of operations to debrief to fallout—had been discussed in detail.

The problem is: he doesn't trust Hayes.

The man who sent him out here—him, and the rest of his crew—had promised them revenge for what was done to them. Promised it, and given them the tools to carry it out.

Roman had wanted it too badly—while he'd known it was a possibility that Hayes would betray them, he'd pushed it aside. He'd spent ten years waiting for payback, and he wasn't going to let anything stand in his way.

Adrift

Maybe that was a mistake, because how difficult would it be, really, for Hayes to eliminate them after the mission was over? The jump drives were unstable, and who's to say that Hayes couldn't engineer—

No. Don't do that. Hayes wouldn't dare. Not to his own men. He's second-guessing himself, losing his focus. He let the kid get to him, and now he's concocting fantasies based on ... what, exactly? A hunch?

He's known from the start that Hayes had his own reasons for sending them out here—reasons that had nothing to do with revenge. It bothered him a lot less than he thought—after all, as long as he got what he wanted, then he couldn't give a shit about Hayes' payoff. But now, he's starting to wonder ...

He has no time to dwell on this, because here comes mommy dearest. Striding down the line of seats towards them, a look of grim determination on her face. Strands of loose hair are plastered across her forehead, and in one hand she's holding a jagged piece of glass.

So.

"Malik," she says, coming to a halt. "When did Corey last have a pill?"

The kid almost drops the pack of nanomeds. "Um. A while ago. We—"

"Give him one more. Then I need you and him—" she gestures behind her to the man with the busted nose, trailing in her wake "—to take him down to the bar."

"What?" Corey says. "No. I'm fine."

His brother's eyes land on the shard of glass. "Uh ..."

"*Malik*. Do as I say. And when you get to the bar, you stay there until we come get you."

"Mom." Corey is up on his elbows, staring at her in horror. "Mom, no. Where's Dad? Dad!"

They don't get him to take a pain pill—he pushes them away, angry now, yelling at his mom to stop—but they manage to get him upright, holding him under his arms, keeping his legs off the ground. Mom sits down in front of Roman, holding the piece of glass in two hands, like a protective talisman.

He almost laughs. They might cut him, a little, but he's withstood far worse. Interrogation training, back in the advanced ops course, was one of the worst things he'd ever been through, especially when they started working on his fingernails. They could push that part of the programme further than they used to, thanks to advanced nanomeds to heal the damage.

If this bitch with her little piece of glass thinks she can break him, she's sorely mistaken. She'll get five minutes in, then realise she doesn't have the stomach for it.

"You're going to tell me why you did it, and how," she says, her voice only shaking a little.

He smiles at her.

"Mom! Don't!"

"Quit it, Cor." But his brother looks terrified, eyes flicking between his sibling and his mother.

"Last chance," she says.

She's going to do it, he realises. She's scared shitless, but she's going to do it. He braces himself, slowing his breathing, readying his body for the pain. Likely, she'll start at the face. Cheek, maybe. Nothing he can't handle.

"Stop it!" Corey wrenches free of the two people holding him, collapsing to the deck, howling in agony. His mom whips her head around, exploding off the seat and skidding to her knees by his side.

"His name's Roman!" Corey's voice is ragged, breathless, terrified. "His name's Roman. He's a Frontier soldier, he's on our side."

Chapter 50

"Is it this one?" Everett says.

He's squashed in next to Hannah in the cockpit. She's perched on the edge of the chair—she can't bring herself to fully sit down on it yet. The two of them are tapping through the various menus on the console screens: every time they have to make a decision, there's a moment of awkward, silent hesitation, as if they don't want to contradict each other.

Hannah peers at the option Everett is pointing to: *Nitrogen PO+8*. "Maybe. Could we—"

Which is when Corey's yelling reaches them.

She and Everett exchange a split-second glance, then both bolt for the door, nearly getting in each other's way, almost getting stuck in the narrow passage. When they burst onto the main deck, Corey is still shouting.

Everett sprints across, dropping to his knees by his son's side. Hannah feels a guilty twinge of relief. Whatever's happening out here, at least it means she doesn't have to be in the cockpit. Hunting for a way to kill them.

It takes a minute for Corey to calm down—and to start explaining. Anita makes him take another nanomed first, which he swallows, grimacing as it goes down. As he tells them about the ion thrusters he saw on the footage, Hannah frowns. She and Everett exchange a blank look.

"OK," Anita says slowly, when he's finished. She's trembling a little, still holding the piece of glass she was planning to use on Roman. "But, Corey, are you sure—"

Corey talks over her. "The thrusters are Frontier tech. He told me I was right." He points at the prisoner, who still hasn't moved. His expression is blank.

"Bullshit," says Jack.

"It's not bullshit!" Corey says.

"Of course it is." Jack reaches up to touch his nose, thinks better of it. "He's lying to you."

"Roman isn't lying! He said—"

"Is that actually your name?" Lorinda says. "Your real one?" The man shrugs.

"No, no, no," Everett says. "Don't just … don't just ignore her. Yes or no, is that your name?"

"Yes." The man—Roman—sounds mildly exasperated.

Everett rubs the bridge of his nose. Jack, who is looking right at him, winces. "Why didn't you tell us sooner?" he asks his son.

For the first time, Corey seems unsure. He looks down at the floor, as if trying to collect his thoughts. It makes him look even younger than he is.

"Wait, hang on," Hannah says, trying to collect her thoughts. "This can't be right. Why would the Frontier do something like this? The whole station was ... it was a mining outpost!"

"Oh my God," Anita says.

Everyone turns to look at her.

"I couldn't understand why the Colonies would attack a Frontier station," she says. "I kept thinking about it, but it didn't make any sense. Not when they're about to finalise a treaty renegotiation that would keep them out of war for a while."

She looks over at Roman. "The only thing ..." She swallows, the noise way too loud on the silent deck. "The only thing that would dissolve the treaty completely is if one side attacked the other."

"But that's insane," Hannah says. "Why would the Frontier want to—"

"Because they'd get it all," says Everett. He turns to his wife, horror dawning on his face. "Isn't that right? They wouldn't just get a few outposts."

"But they wouldn't *do* that," Lorinda says. "They wouldn't just kill thousands of their own people!"

"Exactly." Jack wipes a speck of blood off his top lip. "They could just assassinate a Frontier official, or something. Wouldn't that be easier? Pretend the Colonies did it?"

Anita looks like she wants to pass out. She closes her eyes, speaking slowly, as if she wants to be absolutely sure of her words.

"Because this is way more effective," she says.

Hannah blinks. "Oh, come on."

"It is. So you kill a Frontier senator—which isn't a walk in the park, by the way—and then what? The Colonies would just deny it. It might make the Senate dissolve the treaty, or it might not. And it's way too risky. But if you could take out a whole station ... there's no way the Colony could claim an entire ship with a whole crew and advanced tech went rogue."

"Of *course* they could!"

"And could you see anyone believing them?" She shakes her head. "The Senate would *have* to declare war. They'd have no choice."

She takes a long, shaky breath. "Someone decided to take a shortcut. Start the whole war up again, without waiting for negotiations or legislation." She's shaking her head, staring at Roman with barely disguised fury. "Make out like the Colonies attacked first. That way, the Senate would authorise emergency action. Dissolve the treaty, go in, wipe out the Colony forces."

"Whoa," Corey says. He looks annoyed, like he wishes he'd thought of this first.

"But how did they get close, without clearance codes?" Hannah asks.

"They *had* clearance codes," Anita says. "They're one of ours. That's why the station defences didn't activate until it was too late."

"Son of a bitch." Jack takes a step towards Roman, who looks completely unperturbed.

"So it was someone in the Navy?" Hannah says. "A general, something like that? Someone who gets it into their head to tip the scales in the Senate."

Malik clears his throat. "Can I just ask a question? If we ... if they were going to blow us all up, and pretend they were Colony, then wouldn't they need people to know about it?"

Corey jumps in. "They wouldn't have to. The Frontier probably sent a bunch of probes through, right? They could destroy as many as they wanted, and then when they were ready, just let one travel back. It'd show there was a Colony ship here."

"Hang on," Jack says, not bothering to contain his frustration. "If they destroyed the gate, then how were *they* planning to get home?"

"Special forces tech," Corey says.

"*What?*"

Corey takes a deep, pained breath. "Their ship can jump without using a gate."

The main deck is silent for exactly three seconds. Then everybody starts shouting at once.

Malik is telling Corey not to be stupid, Everett saying there's no way, that it isn't physically possible, Jack saying it's bullshit, all complete bullshit, that humans would never be able to make the jump, and anyway—

"Enough!" Hannah yells.

She's a little startled when everybody *does* shut up, looking at her expectantly. Roman's expression, she notices, has changed. There's a note of amusement on his stone face now, a slight crinkling of the eyes. It makes her want to punch him.

"It can't be true," she says. "That's the whole point of having jump gates. Humans need them to go through wormholes, right?"

"They figured it out." Corey points at Roman. "I know it sounds weird, but can you think of *anything else* that makes sense?"

"Even if he told you this, what makes you think he's telling the truth? Wouldn't we know if someone invented a way for ships to jump without using gates? Wouldn't they ... I don't know, publish it or something?"

"We'd never seen those metal balls before," Corey says. "Or the ion thrusters. If they really did build a gate that a single ship could carry, do you think they'd just tell everybody straight away? 'Cos I wouldn't. I'd keep it a secret until I needed it."

"Jesus." Everett has gone grey. "If there really was ..." He looks around at them. "It'd be a game changer. You wouldn't have to depend on existing wormholes. You could go anywhere."

"But they came to the station *normally*," Malik says.

Hannah frowns. "Normally?"

"Like normal ships do. They flew in. If they could just use their own wormhole, then why—"

"Maybe. But it'd be safer to do it somewhere else, then fly in." Everett actually laughs. "That way, they could keep it a secret, even if someone *did* escape. Like we did. And we only did that because the captain knew what she was doing."

Lorinda shakes her head, hugging herself tighter under the blanket. "I don't buy it."

"They blew up the gate," Corey says. "Why do that if they couldn't get out of here themselves?"

"But why Sigma?"

Adrift

Anita gives a short, bitter laugh. "They could have picked anywhere. Plenty of outlying stations—could have been a research station, or a mining colony. We were just unlucky."

"Wouldn't it damage the economy?" Lorinda sounds indignant. "Mining's important, you know."

"Not really," Anita says, having the good grace to look a little embarrassed. "Or, at least, not as much as it used to be. If they'd hit one of the big Kuiper outposts, or Proxima, then maybe. But something Sigma's size? They'd absorb the hit. The Senate would think they'd been attacked by the Colonies. It wouldn't take much to push them into war."

The silence that falls this time is worse than before. Hannah can't process what she's feeling. There's anger, sure, anger at how Roman and his superiors used everyone on Sigma Station as pawns. But there's also fear—no, *dread*. It's the dread of walking on the edge of a very big, very dark hole, knowing that one breath of wind, a single false step, could send you plummeting into the darkness. The idea that someone in the Frontier could do this ... kill all those people ...

It's not even that hard to see who would benefit. The soldiers who would suddenly have jobs again. The companies who would scoop up the profits. Like the leisure companies and tourist conglomerates, sweeping in to build new luxury resorts in reclaimed territory. As with Sigma, it would happen fast.

And, of course, the Frontier itself: all that new territory, all those resources. Assuming they won. Assuming the return to war didn't kill millions.

Then she realises something else. Something that makes her stomach feel like it's being slowly filled with ice water.

Hannah makes her way over, squats down in front of Roman. She half expects him to lash out, even finds herself tensing, waiting for it. Instead, all he does is lock those cold, blue eyes on hers.

"What happens when you don't come back from your mission?" she says. Behind her, the others are deathly quiet. "What happens then?"

"Wait, what?" Jack says.

Roman says nothing.

Malik sucks in a horrified breath behind Hannah—he must have realised where she's going. She leans forward, pushing back the fear, staring right into Roman's face.

"Your ship," she says. "Is it the only one that can jump?"

"Oh," Corey says, his voice very, very small.

The pieces are locking into place in Hannah's mind. Roman told them before that when he got free he'd kill them. At the time, they assumed it was about revenge, that he'd do it because he thought he had nothing left to lose. What if they got that wrong? What if it wasn't about revenge ... but rescue? What if Roman knew that if his ship didn't return from its mission, someone would come looking for him? Coming to find out what went wrong, and, if necessary, bring the soldiers in the first ship home?

"You're saying there're more of those things?" says Malik.

"How many more?" Hannah leans in closer, not even caring if Roman does lunge at her. She has to know. "Roman. *How many?*"

He still doesn't say anything. But slowly, like oil spreading through water, a dull smile creeps onto his face.

Chapter 51

Hannah rocks back on her heels like she's been punched. The dream floods back into her head: the metal sphere, detonating, the fire engulfing her parents, her house, everything, while she's stuck in the cab, powerless to stop it.

"How are we supposed to fight off another one of those ships?" Malik looks stunned. "Or more than one?"

"No way there's more than one," says Jack.

"What if there is?"

In her mind, Hannah sees not two or three attack ships, but a whole fleet of them—and an *ocean* of spheres, all of them heading right towards the *Panda*.

Adrift

Jack crosses over to them, stands over Roman, flexing his torn fingers as if he can't decide whether or not to hit him. Hannah barely notices. *Get away. We have to get away.*

She stumbles across the main deck, feeling as if her knees are about to let go. The last time she felt like this was at the going-away party she had with some old college friends, a few nights before she climbed aboard the shuttle to Sigma. It was one of the few times she'd drunk enough to have a hangover the next day.

They'd gone to a sports bar, a rowdy place with frozen margaritas and really bad nachos, and at some point she'd got up to go to the bathroom, still saying something to her friend Alex, and found that she could barely walk. The three margaritas and two vodkas she'd had had taken away her legs and replaced them with planks of rotten wood. She'd been drunk plenty of times before, but never like that.

And then she's in the cockpit, not remembering her walk through the passage. She drops into the pilot's chair, forgetting how it made her feel before. It's pushed way back from the control panel, far away enough for her to extend her legs completely.

They've wasted so much time, fighting each other while another one of those ships was coming. Are they here already? Would they jump in close to the destroyed gate? The station? Somewhere else? How long did the original ship have before it was to report back? Before whoever sent it—the people who wanted the treaty with the Colonies gone—decides they've waited long enough?

She pulls the chair forward, but it won't budge. She tries again, grunting in frustration, then scoots out of her chair and onto the floor, hands running along the back and sides of the chair. She finds the catch almost immediately, although she nearly cuts her fingers in it as she slides it up.

In seconds, she's up against the cockpit controls, reaching back to lock the chair into place. Her legs fit comfortably in the gap now, although the edge of the seat digs into her thighs.

As she looks up, she sees the craziest thing: the Reptar toy. It's made it up from the bar, and is now perched on the edge of the control console. She has no idea who put it there, or when, but it makes the whole situation even more surreal than it is.

Moving the stick has no effect. It sets off the panic again, digging claws into her abdomen. Her hands are too sweaty, slipping on the slick plastic. She makes herself take a deep breath, then another, forcing herself to look away from the viewport.

"Hannah?" Jack's voice comes from the doorway.

"Not now."

How are they going to pilot this thing? Volkova made it look easy, piloting the *Panda* like an extension of her body. Hannah can't even grasp how much skill she had. She'll never figure this out, not in a million years, even when she gets the ship onto manual mode, however the hell she makes *that* happen ...

Jack is silent for a few seconds. "If there's another ship," he says quietly. "What are we going to do?"

"I don't know. Run?"

The *Panda* is drifting, very slowly. The remains of Roman's ship are visible now, a corona of debris spreading out from the wreck.

Hannah looks up at Jack, and, suddenly, doesn't care enough to pretend. "If another ship does come, it's over. *We're* over. We can't outrun it. Not like the captain did."

But he isn't looking at her. He's looking out of the viewport, leaning over with his hands braced on the control panel, the strangest expression on his face. Staring up at what's left of Roman's ship.

He mutters something, more to himself than to her.

"What?" she says.

He turns to her. "Maybe we don't have to."

Chapter 52

Jack doesn't wait around to explain. He turns and bolts, leaving behind a startled Hannah and sprinting back onto the main deck, the idea burning bright in his mind. If he can make this work—

Adrift

His left knee tags the edge of a plastic seat, and he almost trips. With what feels like every ounce of will he has, he manages to keep himself upright. In front of him, Everett and Lorinda are standing over Roman like twin judges, Malik and Anita are sitting next to Corey, she with her arm wrapped around her younger son.

Jack lurches forwards, pushing past a startled Everett, coming to a stop in front of Roman. He's aware of how he must look: his shirt caked with dried blood, his hair sticking up in weird directions. But he knows he's right. He *has* to be.

"The other ship," he says. "It's coming the same way, right? It's jumping in by itself?"

"What do you mean, we don't have to?" Hannah shouts from the cockpit passage.

Lorinda puts a hand on his shoulder, but Jack shakes it off. "No, just listen to me, all right, what if—"

"Cool it," Everett says dangerously.

"No, just *listen*. All I want him to do is—"

"Who cares, man?" says Malik. He can't keep the despondency out of his voice. "They'll just shoot the second they see us."

Jack ignores him, finding Roman's eyes. Dimly, he's aware of how much they all stink, their body odour feeling like it's caking on his skin. A few hours ago, it would have rankled, become one of the many hornets buzzing around his mind. Now he barely notices it.

"I don't know who you are," he says to Roman. "None of us do. But if you can—"

Everett's hand is on his shoulder. Jack tries to buck it off, but this time Everett holds on, pulling Jack to his feet. Jack wrenches himself away, almost toppling onto Corey. He pulls himself back just in time, holding up a hand, trying to calm them down.

An image comes to him. Sitting in the office in DC, rewriting copy, mind not really on the task. Hum from the spaceport dulled by the closed windows, the crappy aircon buzzing. Thinking about that weekend, about Hector. About São Paulo.

About the Portuguese lessons he's been taking, the job boards he's been sneaking peeks at. The apartment listings he's spent a few evenings poring over. Then the call, coming up from an unknown number in his lens, the one that turned out to be Hec's boss. The one moment in his life where he thought everything had fallen into place, and the one moment where it all went wrong.

Except that's not true. No point kidding himself any more. Nothing has happened since then that he couldn't fix—not the drinking, not the job, not the fallout with Hector, none of it. He could have climbed back anytime, if he'd just put his mind to it.

No, where it *really* went wrong was when he allowed Brendan and Seema to murder Jana Volkova. That's not something that can be undone with a little willpower. But he's got to start somewhere, and this is it. It has to be.

He wipes at his nose, clearing away a thick, gummy clot of blood. "I'm sorry," he says quietly. "For everything."

Part of him wants to stop there, sure that it'll be enough, but he knows it won't be. "I know you don't have any reason to listen to a word I'm saying. But I'm asking you, just ... hear me out. If you don't like what I have to say, that's fine, but please. Just listen."

He expects them to protest. Maybe even to stop him before he's finished speaking. They don't.

A moment passes. Then another. Hannah glances at Anita and Everett, at Lorinda. Then she clears her throat, gives a tight nod.

Jack takes a second, arranging the words in his head. "If there's another ship coming, that means we have a ticket out of here."

Anita lets out a sarcastic half-laugh, shaking her head. Jack has to work very hard not to raise his voice. "I know it sounds crazy. There's no reason for them to do it. But if we can—"

"Aren't you forgetting?" Hannah says. "We have two spacesuits. And ..." she looks around. "Eight people. Nine, counting Brendan. How were you planning on getting across?"

"We could ferry each other. Two people go across, one de-suits, the other one brings the suit back, then—"

"Oh, right. And the crew of Frontier soldiers who want to kill us will just wave us all on board. Sounds like a solid plan."

"Let's say we do take the ship from them." Anita sounds

exhausted. *"We'd* have to make the jump. Us. Do you even know how?"

"Could *you* do it?" Everett says to Lorinda.

From behind him, Jack hears Malik mutter "Seriously?" like he can't believe his dad could be so dumb.

Lorinda is kinder, but not by much. "It's not mining equipment. You want a rock drill recalibrated, I'm your girl. This is a little above my pay grade."

"But if you could just try ..."

"No, you don't get it," Jack says, pointing, cocking his finger so it's aimed over Hannah's shoulder at Roman. This whole thing might have started with him, but he's been silent the whole time. "He knows the ship. He knows the system. We get *him* to help us."

Roman actually laughs. It's not a pleasant sound.

"He tried to kill us," Hannah says. "You think he'll just switch to our side because, why, exactly?"

"It's worth a shot," Everett says. "We're dead anyway. Might as well give it a try."

"Ev," Anita says. "The boys, they ... you shouldn't talk like that when they're with us."

He turns to her. "I know."

"Then why are you—"

"Because that's what's happening! Right now!"

The words are a bellow. His voice cracks on the last word. The outburst is so loud that Jack expects Anita to cower. Instead, she bristles, her eyes narrowing. "They don't need to hear this," she shouts back.

"We are *way* past that. We—"

"Both of you, shut up." Lorinda's voice is loud, but it fails to make a dent. And then Hannah is shouting, and Jack tries to intervene, and Everett shoves him away, and that sets everyone off. The main deck of the *Panda* explodes with angry voices.

"Stop it!"

There's so much pain in Corey's high-pitched voice, so much fury, that it shuts everyone up.

Malik stares at his brother with something like awe. Even Roman looks surprised. Jack has a hand on Everett's arm, gripping it hard, and he has to tell himself to let go.

"You're always fighting," Corey says. There are tears pouring down his face, his cheeks red and puffy. He speaks slowly, taking each word like a boulder he has to climb over, shimmying up the face of it. "This whole time. We can't go more than five seconds without someone starting a fight."

"Corey." Anita tries to make her voice soft, but it's drained of energy. "Honey."

"No, Mom," he says. "Don't do that. Don't pretend it isn't true. Everybody just fights. Even you and Dad."

Everett steps in. "Corey, we're not."

"*Yes, you are!*" He shifts his leg, actually has to lift it up with his hands to do it, grimacing, like he's moving a heavy plank of wood. "And you're gonna—*hghh*—you're gonna get divorced. You always were."

"That's not true." Everett sounds confident, but Jack can't help but notice his quick glance at his wife.

"Of course it's true," Corey says, his voice bitter. "That's what adults do. They fight. And not ... not pretend fighting like me and Mal sometimes. Real fighting." More tears come, tracking down his reddened cheeks. "And then nothing gets done, and ..."

"Cor," Malik says quietly.

"And then you just ..." Corey finally stops, lowering his head, his shoulders hitching.

Anita takes an unsteady step forward. Then another. Then she's down on her knees, pulling Corey into an embrace, reaching out for Malik. Everett comes in, too, holding his family close.

Jack finds Hannah's eyes, then Lorinda's. He can't hold either for more than a few seconds. The certainty he felt before has faded. Corey's right. All they've done is fight among themselves, like—he corrects himself—not like children, because right now the kids on this goddamn ship are the only ones doing anything right.

As if picking up on his thoughts, Corey's voice comes out of the huddle, muffled by his mother's shoulder. "Everybody go somewhere. *I'll* talk to Roman."

"Corey," Hannah says slowly. "I don't think that's a good idea."

"Why not?" Corey's voice is still thick. He lifts his face from Anita's shoulder. "You heard my dad. We're dead anyway. What difference does it make?"

Everett looks embarrassed. "I wasn't ... I mean ..."

"No, Dad, you were right. But I'm the only one who's actually tried to talk to him like a person. No one else has. So just give me five minutes. He's not going to get free, I promise."

Anita tries to protest, crying openly now. But Corey reaches out, his hand finding hers, and she nods. She and Everett get to their feet, and Everett gestures to Malik to follow him.

Corey shakes his head. "Mal stays."

"Why?" Malik says, frowning.

Corey doesn't answer immediately, just looks back at his dad. Anita tugs on her husband's shoulder, pulling him gently away.

Jack takes one last look at Roman. The soldier returns his gaze, cool and even, and a swirl of emotions coalesce in Jack's chest. He wants to grab Roman and smash his head against the ground. He wants to run screaming. He wants to rage, punch the walls. But more than anything, he realises, he wants to sleep. He wants it all to go away.

Quietly, he, Hannah and the others trudge to the far side of the main deck. As they do so, Jack raises his head to see the Horsehead Nebula above them, shining, silent. The only thing in this whole mess that hasn't changed at all.

Chapter 53

Corey waits until the others are out of earshot before turning to his brother. "Mal. Help me sit up."

Malik has his hands resting on his knees, eyes down, like a student not wanting to be called on by a teacher. His holocam is still tucked under his arm. Belatedly, Corey realises just how scared his brother must be of hurting him, and he forces a smile onto his face. "It's OK. Just help me."

"You sure?"

Corey responds by pushing himself up so his hands are splayed out on the seat behind him. He starts to swing his legs off the plastic, so Malik has no choice but to help.

Together, with a lot grunting, they manage to get Corey upright. Malik has to use his own body to prop his brother up, Corey leaning against his shoulder. The pain has retreated again, pushed back by the last pill he took.

He doesn't know exactly what he's going to say, but he knows that he's the only one who can talk to Roman. The others'll just mess things up, start shouting again. Problem is, he doesn't know how. Not yet. This isn't like before, when he told Roman about the thrusters. This is different.

And if he can't figure out how to convince Roman to help them, then it really will be over. He *cannot* get Roman angry with him again—not like last time. He has to be careful.

"This is Malik, by the way," he says. "He's five years older than me."

Roman turns his glare on Malik. After a few seconds, he gives the briefest of nods.

Corey continues. "He was the one who filmed your ship destroying the station. Do you want to see?" He nods to his brother. "Show him, Mal."

For a moment, Malik looks like he wants to run. Then he pulls the cam out and turns it on with the practised flick of a finger. He opens his movie app, scrolling through the footage, face blank with concentration.

"Pretty good, right?" Corey points to the screen. "I don't know what's inside those ball things, but they're intense. See here? This one takes out pretty much an entire section of the station. And—there—you can see the ion thrusters on your ship right there. That's how I knew."

Roman's lips tighten a little as he watches the footage, but he doesn't say anything more. Malik lets it play. When it reaches the end of the clip, the image on the screen pauses, stopped on a blurry shot of someone's hands.

"I just thought you'd want to see." Corey says it like he doesn't really care, but it's hard to keep the frustration out of his voice. It's not going to work. Roman isn't going to switch sides just because of some crappy movie footage. He knows what he did.

Malik's finger hovers over the screen. "Do you want me to run it again, or ..."

Corey shakes his head. This is like stumbling around in the dark, hands out, trying to find something he can hold onto.

"What's going to happen?" he says. "When the other ships get here?"

No response.

"You gotta be running out of time. They could be here at, like, any minute, right? And if you're not free by then, which you probably won't be because you got tape *and* cuffs, they'll just blow you up along with the rest of us."

"That's messed up." Malik sounds incredulous, but there's something else in his voice, too. Most people wouldn't pick up on it, but Corey knows his brother, and he hears it as clearly as a siren in a quiet neighbourhood.

"Super-messed up," he agrees.

"Why's he doing it, though? Did he say?"

"Nah."

"'Cos it seems like a lot to go through just to destroy one of your own stations. Was there, like, a virus, or ..."

"Yeah, that's what I thought, too. He says there wasn't one."

"Oh. OK. How come, then?"

They both look at Roman, expectant.

"Nice try," Roman murmurs. For a second, Corey is alarmed—he can't see Roman's hands, just like down in astronautics. But surely not even Roman could get through the cuffs *and* all the duct tape.

"Seriously," Corey says, amazed at how calm he sounds. He has the same tone of voice as when he, Jamie and Allie are talking shit to each other, riding their boards around Austin, or sprawled out in one of their rooms. "Just tell us. You heard my dad. We're all dead anyway. What difference does it make?"

Roman looks away. His expression is blank, but the set of his shoulders has changed, very slightly.

"You wouldn't understand if I told you," he says.

Corey and Malik exchange a look.

"Well, that's lame," Corey says.

"Lame?" The way Roman says the word sounds as if it's from another language.

"Yeah," says Malik. "He's right. That's lame. And it's bakwas."

In that instant, Corey is absolutely certain that if Roman were free, the man's hands would be wrapped around his throat.

Malik continues. "You were talking about series before? I got one for you. It's this science show with Jordana Simmons, and she always says that you can explain anything to anyone if you know how."

Corey looks at him in surprise. "You know *Molecular*?"

"Well, yeah. I watch it sometimes. When I'm bored or whatever."

"You know she's dating Terio Smith? From the Djinns?"

Malik grins. "Yeah. Lucky."

"Hey, you've already got a girlfriend."

"Shanti isn't ... well, she might be. I dunno."

The look on Roman's face could crack a planet in two.

They're probably never going to see *Molecular*, Jordana Simmons or even Terio Smith ever again, but Corey doesn't care. Deep down, on a level of instinct he has no name for yet, he knows he has to keep going.

"You," Roman says, enunciating each syllable. "Wouldn't. Understand."

"You keep saying that, and *we* keep saying—"

"You've got no one to blame but yourselves. What happened at Sigma was your fault. You, and everyone on this ship, and everyone on the station."

Corey and Malik gape at him. "No, it wasn't," says Malik.

"We didn't fly in and drop a bazillion bombs on the place," Corey says. "We were just hanging out at the pool and stuff."

"That's not what I—"

"You're trying to blame *us*? We were literally on vacation!"

"*Enough.*" There's a note of furious desperation in Roman's voice, like he wants nothing more than to end this conversation, and knows that he can't.

A thought occurs to Corey—one he can't believe he didn't have before. "Back downstairs," he says. "You could have just let them tie the thing around my leg. The ..." He searches for the word. "The tourniquet. I probably would have died."

Corey half expects Roman to snap back, to show the same swagger he did when he dared Hannah to let him loose. He doesn't.

"You said ..." Corey clears his throat. "If you wanted me to die, then why'd you tell Mal and my mom how to stop the bleeding?"

Roman shakes his head. "Doesn't mean you have to suffer," he says quietly.

"So you'd kill me quick?"

Roman frowns. "What?"

"Me and Mal. You said I didn't have to suffer, so you'd kill us quickly, right? Because we're kids? How would you do it? Because you obviously wanted to kill everybody on Sigma, which includes us. Right?"

"Cor." Mal looks like he wants to throw up.

"No, I'm serious. I wanna know. Break my neck, probably, right? What about the grown-ups? Same thing? Or would you kill them—"

Roman cuts him off, the frustration bleeding into his voice. "You don't know a damn thing. People die all the time, and, usually, they don't even know why. They die for all kinds of reasons, and the people who kill them aren't always the bad guys. When you get older, maybe you'll understand."

There's a half-second of silence, and then Roman realises what he's just said. An expression of embarrassment spreads across his face. He looks away, not meeting Corey's eyes, the expression fading as quickly as it arrived.

For the next ten seconds, nobody says anything. Cory can just hear the low murmurs from the grown-ups at the other side of the main deck.

"You're right," he says. "Maybe I will. I'm planning to do a lot of things when I get older."

Roman's eyes flick to his, just for a second. Corey pushes on.

"I'm gonna be a pilot. And not just on the ships they have already. We're gonna make new ones. My friend Jamie's going to design them, and Allie'll do all the business, and then I'll fly them. They're going to be the fastest ships in the whole galaxy.

"We're going to be the first to break light speed without warping. I'll need to learn how to fly first, so I'll need to go to Navy pilot school, but I've been doing all this reading and I think I should be OK."

Roman doesn't react. Corey puts a hand on his brother's shoulder. "Mal's going to become a famous movie director. He's gonna go to film school, and then he's going to start making them himself, for real, not just on his tab screen."

Malik stiffens, then nods, very slowly, clutching his holocam tight. Corey continues. "They're going to be the best movies ever. He's going to win Oscars and make millions of U-dollars and—"

"Stop," says Roman.

"And then I'm going to go to his premieres, and I'll get to tell everybody that he's my brother. Hopefully Mom and Dad have sorted their shit out by then, and Mom is President of the Senate and—"

"Majority Leader," Malik says.

"Right, right, Majority Leader. And Dad's company is really big. Then, maybe if I get good at flying, Mal can make a crash movie about me and Allie and Jamie, and—"

"*Stop.*"

Roman turns his face towards them. "Just stop," he says. "That's enough."

And that's when Corey realises he doesn't have anything else to say.

He's used everything he had. If Roman still doesn't want to help them, then he has no idea what to do next.

Chapter 54

This is wrong. This is all wrong.

Problem, solution, action. It got him here, and it's going to get him out. But still, Roman can't help but think of the last two messages Madhu sent him.

They'd taken a long time to arrive, which was hardly surprising. It was a central irony of the Great Expansion that it had actually increased the time it took to send messages—not like it was before, when humans were still just on Earth, and sending a message from one side of the planet to the other was instantaneous. When you were talking light years of distance, the fastest way to send a message was to put it on a ship, and send that ship through a jump gate. And then you'd better hope that it was the right ship, or the right jump gate, because the only way you'd know you'd got it wrong was when that ship came back, and the captain looked at you sideways.

In the manner of military bureaucracies since the dawn of time, the Frontier Navy made things worse. There were a lot of jump gates, a lot of ships, an uncountable number of messages, and a way-too-small group of underpaid, overworked people responsible for making it all happen.

When he'd got the messages, Roman had been on the Titan base, lying on his bunk and half listening to Rodriguez and Simms arguing about soccer. The notification had blinked up on his lens, and when Brigita and Madhu and everyone else had appeared, he'd automatically glanced at the timestamp on the message. It had been sent two months before, and he'd sighed in irritation.

He didn't mind too much, though. A late message was better than no message at all. He missed them—and Cassiopeia—far more than he thought he would. He'd been away for four years by then, and the gangly twenty-year-old frame he'd had when he'd left had been built into a lean, hard twist of muscle.

Madhu's big, whiskery face filled the camera. Brigita was

squashed in on his left, with everyone else clustered around them: Jocinda, Yoshiro, Ling-Xi, Mhotar, the Twins. Even little Alexa, eighteen months now, her eyes just visible over Mhotar's shoulder. The camera unsteady, the view filled with hands and elbows and smiling faces, jostling for space.

"Hello, son!" Madhu boomed. His words were followed by a tidal wave of noise as everyone yelled out their own greetings. In his bunk, he smiled. Alexa was getting big.

"We don't know where you'll be when this gets to you," said Madhu.

"In a brothel!" roared someone offscreen. Roger, maybe. Another round of piercing laughter, yelling, Brigita briefly vanishing from view, presumably to smack the back of Roger's head.

"We miss you, though," Madhu had continued. "We're all waiting for you to come back on leave."

Yoshiro stuck his face into the frame. "Zigs had her puppies!"

Madhu gently pushes him away. "I'll tell him, my beta, don't worry. Anyway, things are OK round here. There was a breach in one of the grow domes but the automatic systems caught it fine, and it's past harvest anyway so it was empty anyway. We've got a shuttle shipment coming in a couple of days ..."

Roman had half tuned out, listening to the usual parade of shipments and recycler issues and how Jocinda could do fractions now. He'd heard many, many variations of them before, and all he wanted was just to listen to their voices. Let the wonderful noise wash over him.

"We've got a new girl coming in," Brigita had said.

"Oh yes!" Madhu's eyes lit up. "Five years old. They found her in the rubble in Kepler." His face had darkened slightly. "I think we may have to work hard for her. But I'm giving her your old room, if that's OK, because it's one of the nicer ones. Brigita's cooking soyburgers when she comes, and Ling-Xi's going to make a new welcome banner. Her name's—"

He'd been interrupted by a fresh wave of laughter and shouting. Roman had never found out the name of the girl, or if she'd even made it to Cassiopeia. He had no idea where she was now.

"Anyway," Madhu said, and once more the video was packed

solid with faces. "We miss you, and we love you, and please reply if you can!"

There was a huge, roaring chorus of *byes* and *love yous*, and then Madhu's hand blocking the camera as he reached out to switch it off.

The second message was just Madhu by himself. The hab was dark, and he spoke in a quieter voice, as if he didn't want to disturb sleepers—which, Roman had thought, he probably didn't. Brigita would be in bed, as would the rest of the kids.

Madhu's oval face shone white in the light from the camera. "I wanted to talk to you about something that I haven't told the others yet," he said. "It's something I've been thinking about, and it would mean a lot of work, but I think we could do it if we got it right."

He'd leaned closer to the camera. "This is something for the future, you understand me, not right now. At the moment, we take in maybe one or two children a year, but I think we could do more, especially since the outpost is getting bigger.

"I want to apply for additional funding from the Frontier, and actually set up a proper, official home for kids here, not just a foster one. Brigita doesn't need me to keep the habs going—I just get in the way mostly. And I think, when all this soldier nonsense is over, you should come back and run it with me."

He'd held up a hand, as if Roman was already about to protest. "You don't have to answer now. But just think about it, yes?" He sat back, and in the low light, he suddenly looked very old. Old, and yet somehow content.

Roman had closed the message, then his eyes, lying back against the pillow, happier than he'd been in weeks. It was absurd, Madhu's suggestion—but then again, why not? Why the hell not? If he could give other people the life he'd had, he could more than consider the debt repaid.

Messages took a long time to arrive, and information a long time to filter down. No one in the Frontier was particularly concerned when a series of inconsequential, lightly populated terraforming outposts were attacked by Colony forces, and no one bothered to tell the advanced ops division in Titan orbit.

By the time Madhu and Brigita's messages got to him, they'd already been dead for two weeks.

The strike had been nuclear: a desperate, last-ditch move by the Colonies, who were losing the war and badly trying to scorch as much Frontier territory as they could reach. There was nothing to bury. No outpost to visit. Roman couldn't even get near the site, thanks to the radiation.

There'd been psychiatrists, of course. The tight arms around his shoulders as his squadmates spoke to him in quiet, sombre voices. There'd been talk about taking him off active duty, but he'd turned that down flat. He wanted—no, *needed*—to keep fighting.

The solution part of the equation, in this case, was obvious. He wanted to get the fuckers who did this. The Colonies were going to pay. He was going to hit them again, and again, and again. He was going to be there when the Frontier arrived in orbit around Talos-18, and bombed it into extinction.

In the year following the strike on Cassiopeia, it was all he could think about. A laser focus bright enough to block out absolutely everything else. All he had to do was keep staring at the light, and everything would be fine. He didn't dare look away.

But while he was focused on the blinding light of revenge, the Colonies had surrendered.

There'd been a treaty. *Peace talks.* There'd been no retribution. Talos-18 had been allowed to stand, along with dozens of other Colony worlds and outposts. No one was punished for what happened to Cassiopeia.

And the decisions to do all of this weren't made by soldiers. They weren't even made by admirals. They were made by Frontier senators and lobbyists and activists—people just like Corey's mother, come to think of it. Exactly the same. The ones who'd never done a day's fighting in their lives were suddenly pushing for peace, making all the right noises about reconciliation and mending broken bonds. They'd held rallies and summits and symposiums, diplomatic solutions were reached, and it was just ... over.

He'd gone from confusion, to disbelief, to a cold, simmering fury. The war was done, and as the treaty was signed and the base corridors filled with joyful shouts that the war was over, Roman had sat on his bunk, staring at nothing.

He knew he wasn't innocent. He'd killed plenty of people in the name of the Frontier. But they were military targets, or, at the very least, civilians who weren't supposed to be there. If his commanding officers had told him to wipe out a civilian population, he and every one of his squad would have spat it back in their face.

This was different. The Colonies had utterly wiped out multiple outposts full of non-combatants, and they were just going to be allowed to walk away. People were *celebrating* it.

He does not remember a good deal of the past ten years.

He wasn't high up enough for the Navy to retain, nor did he have any experience that would be useful to them in peacetime. His savings kept him going for a while, and when that ran out he'd taken a job at a space construction firm, running an exosuit in Earth orbit.

He threw himself into training: hours and hours of weights and running and repetitive drills, not knowing what else to do. And all the while his hatred of the Colonies grew. He nurtured it, held it close, mostly because he didn't know enough not to, the black fury keeping him going as he cranked out his five-hundredth pull-up of the day.

And, in time, that fury came to have a twin: his hatred for the Frontier itself. For the civilians he'd helped protect. They'd let his family be wiped out, and they wouldn't let him take revenge. To them, it was as if Madhu and Brigita and everyone else had simply never existed.

He knew it was irrational, knew that he couldn't truly blame every single Frontier civilian in existence. But he discovered that he just didn't give a shit. Not any more.

It occurred to him early on that he could get revenge. He had enough training to hurt the Frontier in a dozen different ways, if he wanted. But what was the point? Sure, he could attack a small station, or take some civilians hostage somewhere. He certainly wouldn't be the first ex-soldier to try. But the Frontier bureaucracy stretched out across a hundred worlds, and it didn't change just because a few people lost their lives.

And then, a little less than ten years after the war had ended, a man named Richard Hayes had knocked on his hotel room door.

He was down on Earth, in the Philippines, taking a few days off from the loading dock job—which, somehow, he'd managed to keep. The room stank of sweat and semen. An ancient ceiling fan rotated, doing nothing to disperse the heat, and every few minutes the room would shake from a launch at the nearby space-port, the windows rattling in their rotten frames.

Roman knew Hayes by reputation, even if he hadn't thought about him in almost a decade. Hayes wasn't in uniform—he wore a crisp shirt and slacks, seemingly untroubled by the heat—but he told Roman he was a commander now. Roman said that was excellent, good for him, but if the commander didn't mind, he had a monster hangover and he didn't really feel like catching up on old times.

That's when Hayes had removed a signal blocker from his shirt pocket—a tiny, black cube, which he'd activated and set on the splintered dresser. *That* had got Roman's attention. And then Hayes had asked him if he still wanted to take the fight to Talos-18.

There were others, he'd said—soldiers like Roman, others who had lost friends and family and lovers, and who wanted payback. Not many, but enough. With his eyes glittering, Hayes had told Roman that he was one of them. The Colonies, as far as he was concerned, were unfinished business.

Roman was nodding yes before Hayes had even finished speaking. He wasn't stupid—he knew that someone like Hayes would never be doing this for revenge, or so a bunch of tired old soldiers could have theirs. There were bound to be ulterior motives. But he found, to his surprise, that he didn't care what they were. If there was even a chance that Hayes could put him back on a new frontline, let him finish what the damn treaty stopped him from doing, then he could have all the ulterior motives he wanted.

He and the commander had shaken hands under the creaking ceiling fan. And then later, in a quiet conference room in New York, he'd met the others.

Adrift

Rodriguez was there—his fiancée, a Scorpion pilot, had been lost at Bellatrix. And a man named Jacobs from another unit, who he'd once spent a night training with in the gym on the Titan base. Roman didn't know what had happened to Jacobs—not then, anyway—but the man's eyes glittered with excitement as Hayes rapped on a table, calling them to order.

Two things quickly became clear. The first was that what they were doing was illegal. Treason-illegal. They would have to exist, Hayes said, through mutually assured destruction: if any one of them turned on the others, they would be killed. That included him.

When he explained this, Roman felt the atmosphere in the room go from interested to locked in. Give Hayes credit: he'd picked his people well, and he knew exactly which buttons to push.

The second thing, Hayes told them, was that it would have to be something big. An assassination could be blamed on a rogue element. Ditto for taking hostages. They'd have to do the job in such a way that there could be no doubt that it was an official, sanctioned Colony attack, with the kind of firepower that only an interplanetary government would have access to. That meant mass casualties—the kind of thing that would force the Senate to dissolve the treaty. He needed to know that they were OK with that.

Roman looked at Hayes for a long moment. Then he, along with a couple of the others, stood up and walked out.

He half expected Hayes to stop them, but the commander didn't. Roman had looked back at him just before he stepped through the door, and saw that there was something in Hayes' eyes. A look that said, *think about it*.

He didn't need to. What Hayes was suggesting was beyond the pale—and not what he'd agreed to when he'd shaken the man's hand in Manila. Roman had thought many times about hurting the Frontier, but this ...

Not even he would do this.

As he walked through the 5th Avenue Tunnel, he couldn't help but take in the faces of the people around him. The couples, strolling hand in hand. The food vendors. The group of Muslims, praying on the corner, bending in the direction of where Mecca used to be. The office worker, puffing on a NicoStick.

Later, drunk in his hotel room overlooking the Brooklyn Bridge, he kept seeing them. And he couldn't help but wonder about their lives. What would any of them have said if he told them about Cassiopeia? Would they have done what everyone else did? Tell him how sorry they were for his loss? Say how at least the war was over now?

He kept coming back to the office worker. An older guy, in a rumpled suit with the jacket slung over his arm and the hunched shoulders of a corporate lifer. What, Roman wondered, would he do if he found out that killing the man would get him what he wanted? Just him. Just that one lone office worker, leaning against the wall, ignored by everyone around him?

He'd kill him. He wouldn't even have to think about it. It's the kind of truth that, had it occurred to him when he first enlisted, he would have recoiled from. Denied outright. But it's been a long time since he enlisted, and he knows exactly what he's capable of. And what he's done.

How would killing that office worker be any different from what Hayes was proposing? Really? Wasn't it, when you came down to it, a question of numbers? How many was too many?

By now, he was on his second bottle of whisky, sitting on his bed, the view outside his window swimming in front of him. Somewhere, a small part of him was stunned that he was still capable of rational thought. He tried to hold onto it, telling himself that there's no way he can agree to what Hayes is asking.

But then he'd started remembering the people he *had* killed, on the missions he and his squad were sent on. The scientist who walked in on them on that covert job on Hawking-8—he remembered her startled face, right before the puff from his rifle that erased her from existence. The security guards at the facility in Proxima orbit, who his squad had taken down without thinking about it. Had their deaths made anything more than the tiniest ripple in the universe?

The office worker again, his face appearing in front of Roman, clear and detailed, as if he were standing in front of him. Roman looking up at him, blinking, long and slow. How many office workers would he be comfortable killing, to correct the greatest injustice he'd ever known? A thousand? Ten? A hundred thousand? Where did you stop? Where was the line?

And even if it was a few thousand ... what was that, measured against the billions and billions of people across the galaxy? A blip. A single drop in a thunderstorm. And they wouldn't die for nothing. Their deaths—unlike those of the scientist and the security guards and everyone else—would mean something.

In his drunken stupor, his grief returning—fresh and sharp, a blade that never loses its edge—Roman clung to this thought. The people they'd be taking out were the real reason the fighting had stopped. They were the activists and lobbyists and campaigners, and, even if they weren't, they'd sat like a herd of cattle, letting it all happen.

Perhaps they were just as much to blame as the Colonies for what happened. And perhaps it was time for them to feel what it was like, when all hell came raining down and there was nothing and no one coming to save you.

The still-lucid part of his brain told him he was drunk. That he'd feel differently the next morning.

He didn't.

Hayes showed them the tech—a whole orbital warehouse of black-bag gear that he was charged with overseeing. And he'd shown them the extended-pulse jump drives, which could blink a ship from here to there in an instant, no matter where here and there happened to be. No wormhole needed.

The Frontier Senate might have stopped researching the tech— why keep at it, when there was a perfectly good network of jump gates?—but Hayes hadn't. He'd funnelled every universal dollar from every off-books budget he could find, and he'd made it happen. The drives weren't perfect. They were unstable, even dangerous to use, and good for exactly two hops before they had to be replaced. But they made jump gates obsolete.

That's when Roman really started believing it might actually work. By the time anybody figured out what had really happened, the treaty would be in pieces, and Frontier forces would be advancing on the weakened Colonies.

Over the next few weeks, as they prepped for the mission, he got to know the rest of the soldiers. Heard their stories. Like him, they'd all lost people—friends, sons, daughters, wives, husbands, commanding officers, comrades. They were all in the right place. Exactly where they needed to be.

They wore the old patches from their units when they suited up for the mission. No one suggested it—it was something that all of them, without speaking to each other, knew to do.

He can't tell Corey or Malik any of this, and not because he wants to keep them in the dark. It's too painful. Even after all this time, he has absolutely no idea how to start. But as he looks at Corey, at this kid with his busted leg and his grimy T-shirt and his absolute refusal to quit asking questions, a realisation hits him so hard that he almost gasps.

Corey is wrong.

Sure, maybe he'll fly ships. Maybe he'll build his company with his friends. But that's not all he's going to do. Roman has spent a long time around different kinds of people—sometimes, it seems that's all being a soldier was—and he realises he can see Corey's story, all the way to its conclusion. Corey might do all the things he wants to do now, but in the end, he's going to be …

Madhu.

Or someone like him. He might not be terraforming planets, or taking in kids from across the Frontier who don't have anywhere else to go. But he's going to end up helping people—maybe a lot of people.

Like Madhu, he was curious, about absolutely everything. Like Madhu, he desperately wanted to understand how things work.

No. Corey isn't Madhu. That's crazy. It's just the stress, finally getting its teeth into him after all this time, making him see things that aren't there.

Except that's not true either. He can see the path Corey will take far too clearly.

Doesn't matter. Doesn't change anything.

But it does. God help him, it does.

His mission is to eliminate Corey—there's no prettying it up, not any more. No getting away from it. And he can't help thinking:

what would have happened if the Colonies had decided to hit Cassiopeia sooner? Before Madhu and Brigita took him in?

He'd never have gone there. Never have had the childhood he did. Him, and everyone else who they took in. And the Colony soldiers who ordered the nuke fired at the planet's outpost. Did they know what they were doing? Would they have followed that order, if they'd sat with Madhu at the big table, if they'd talked with him?

He clenches his teeth, refusing to look at the two boys. No. *No.* He's wanted this. For twelve years, he's wanted a way to hit back, and now he has it, and he's about to let it go because of some kid. All those nights, all that endless training, his waste of a life, and now he finally has a chance to make things right, and—

It wouldn't be right. You know it wouldn't.

Because even if he goes ahead with this—even if Hayes somehow doesn't betray them, which is something he's becoming less and less certain of with every passing minute—he knows what'll happen. He'll get his revenge. He'll take Talos, crush the Colony forces. But to get it done, he'll have to kill Corey.

Destroying Sigma was different, somehow; there were other soldiers on the ship, and they all had a role to play, and all of them shared the blame. But this? It'd be on him. Every single second of it would be his to own, forever.

And everyone who Corey might have helped, in the same way Madhu helped him, would be his to own, too.

Like a machine switching into an old, well-worn gear, he reverts to problem, solution, action. Problem: he's about to fail his mission. He's about to betray the people who raised him. Solution ...

Deep inside him, the little core of hatred he's spent years holding onto pulses. This can't be it. It can't end here. There's so much blood on his hands already, thousands of people, so why's he stopping now? It's absurd. *Solution: just tell the kid, yes, have them set you loose, then finish the job.*

But he can't.

"So how about it?" Malik says, leaning forward, putting his elbows on his knees and crossing his arms. "You gonna help us? Or you just gonna sit there?"

"Nobody else has to die," Corey says. "Not us. Not you. Nobody."

Roman can barely speak. "It might not even work. Even if they knew I was alive, they might just destroy this ship anyway. And I don't even know *how* you're planning to actually get everybody on board in the first place."

Corey nods, eyes shining. "I don't know either. We'll figure it out."

What he's about to do will change everything. There'll be no war, no attack on Talos. No victory. He'll have to disappear, because Hayes will never let him live.

The thought terrifies him—not the steps he'll have to take, because he's been trained to vanish, to blend into a crowd. But he'll have to live with having turned his back on the mission.

Which means that Corey will get to grow up.

Madhu would have wanted that.

And maybe that's enough.

"I'll help you," he says, his voice barely above a whisper.

"What'd you say?" asks Malik.

"I said I'll help you."

"For real?"

"… Yeah."

"Then you need to promise."

Roman inhales through his nostrils, long and hard. "You have my word. I'll help you."

"You promise? You have to promise. And you can't break it no matter what."

"Yes," Roman says, after another beat. "I promise."

Corey and Malik exchange a look. Malik raises an eyebrow, questioning.

"Hey," Corey says, speaking so the others can hear him. "Can everybody come down here for a sec?"

Chapter 55

They come, one after the other. Lorinda, wrapped in her foil blanket. Jack, his face and shirt still crusted with flakes of blood, his nose swollen. Anita and Everett. They're not holding hands, not walking with arms wrapped around each other, but they're moving together. Close enough for their shoulders to touch.

Hannah brings up the rear, arms tightly folded. Her mind feels like it's trailing three feet behind her, pulled along like a balloon.

Corey waits until everyone is there, and then he tells them what Roman said. In that moment, he looks a lot older than his ten years.

Hannah gapes at him. Jack looks completely astonished, too, as do Everett and Anita. Only Lorinda is smiling, nodding slowly, the blanket hanging off her bony shoulders.

"I don't like it," Anita says, gnawing on her bottom lip.

"He promised," says Corey.

"I know, but a promise isn't like what you think it is. People can break them."

Corey looks at her like she's just told him that they're in space.

"And we have to let him go if this is going to work," Everett says. He looks around at them. "We absolutely sure we wanna do that? You heard what he said. If the kids are wrong ..."

"We *aren't* wrong," says Malik.

Roman looks up. When he speaks, he sounds resigned. "God knows how you're going to do this, but the jump unit on the *Victory* can take the ship anywhere."

"The *Victory*?" says Hannah.

"The other ship."

"Other ship singular? Just one?"

Roman shrugs.

"What's the first ship called?" Corey asks. "The one we ... you know."

"The *Resolute*."

"And how do you mean anywhere? Like, *anywhere* anywhere?" He nods.

"Then what stopped you from going straight into the Colonies?" Everett says. "Just jumping in with a bunch of ships, and—"

"We don't have a bunch of ships. They're expensive. And they have limited power—you can only jump twice before the particle core needs to be replaced. Downside of the new tech."

"And they'll have already made one jump," Hannah says, almost to herself. "Anyway, we'd need to go somewhere friendly."

"That's another problem," Roman says. "You need coordinates to jump. You have to input the destination manually. If you don't have coordinates, you can't go anywhere."

"So we just input the ones for Bishop's Station," Malik says. "Or close to it."

"Do you know what they are?" says Roman.

"No, but ..."

"We had two sets of coordinates for our mission. Here, and our command outpost. There was no point having any others."

Malik's shoulders sag. But Corey's eyes are bright.

"Do you use ULCs?" He can't keep the excitement out of his voice.

Roman's eyes narrow, and Hannah gives Corey a confused look. "ULCs?"

"Universal Location Coordinates. They use them to map quadrants in space. Does your ship use them too?"

"It could," Roman says slowly.

Corey turns, a slow smile spreading across his face. "Eight Six Six One Zero Eight Nine by Nine Nine Three Two One Five Seven," he says.

Nobody says anything for a few seconds.

"How did you ..." Hannah begins.

Corey's smile gets bigger. "It's what we're gonna name our company. Jamie and Allie and me. 866 Industries—we're naming it after the coordinates for Austin. We could warp right above the city. We could warp right in over our *house!*"

"Are you sure?" Malik says.

"Of course I'm sure!"

"Wouldn't we like warp *into* the house, then? That can't be good."

"We can change the coordinates a little. I know how they work." Corey looks delighted. "There's all those mine dumps! Those big piles of dirt. We could come in right over them. Even if there's like a boom of energy, it won't hit anything. And if we can jump when we're just drifting, there won't be any real momentum. As long as we're not too high, we could land OK."

He glances at Roman. "Right?"

Hannah exhales. It might actually work. *Holy shit.*

"If we do this," Anita says, "then how?"

"I was thinking," Malik says. Corey gives him a surprised look. "What if we got Roman to contact the other ship when it arrives? On our radio or whatever? The range should be short enough. He can say he survived the attack, hid in here, and then they'll let him come back. He can talk to them and make sure they let us on board."

"Comms are down," says Lorinda with a grimace. "Happened while I was outside."

Everyone falls silent. If they can't get the comms back up and running, if there's no way for them to let the *Victory* know that Roman is on board ...

"I can try reset the systems," Hannah says—not that she has the faintest idea how to do that yet. "Maybe that'll reboot the comms, too."

Jack sniffs hard. "I don't like it. So we reset the comms, get the ships talking. What's to stop him—" he points at Roman "—just telling them about what happened? Letting them nuke us?"

Malik's face falls, and Hannah can see why. If Roman does that, they're toast. On the other hand: she doesn't think Roman will. Not any more.

"We go with him to the other ship," she says, skipping ahead. "Someone keeps an eye on him. They can pretend they're just another Frontier soldier until they get there."

"Plus, he *promised*," says Corey.

"I need at least one other person anyway," Roman says softly. "If you think the *Victory* crew are going to help you get out of here, you're insane. The only way this works—the *only* way—is if we take the bridge. We lock the crew out, and jump ourselves.

"But understand this: it isn't as simple as just hitting a button. We don't actually jump the ship through a wormhole. It's more like ..."

He stops, as if trying to find the right words. "We make a bubble around the ship. It distorts spacetime, and moves *it* instead of us."

"Whoa." Corey's eyes are huge.

"It's difficult, and it requires a lot of input. You need to control the matter shielding levels, as well as your drift inside the bubble."

"Why can't the AI do it?" Hannah says. "The other ship would have a better one than ours, right? Surely it could handle the ... the bubble?"

"It won't help us. AI's keyed to the commander, then his 2IC, then down the chain. It wouldn't even recognise me. In any case, I'm going to need someone to assist. Someone with EVA experience, preferably. The *Victory* crew see someone not in control of their trajectory on the journey over, they'll know it's not one of ours."

One by one, all eyes turn to Lorinda. She's already nodding.

"No." Corey gapes at her.

"I'll do it," she says.

"But you can't," says Anita. "That last time, it almost ..."

"I know." A shadow crosses her face. Hannah can't believe how exhausted she looks.

"Then let one of us go," says Everett, pleading with her.

"I'll be fine."

"You're saying *she* has the experience?" Roman says, giving Lorinda a disbelieving look. "She knows how to use a suit?"

"She's the one who brought you in here, man," says Malik. "Don't you remember?"

Roman glances at him. "No."

He turns to Lorinda, shifting his bound hands underneath him, looking at her with a new respect. "In any case, if she's the only one who can EVA, you've got problems. There's no way she'd pass for a soldier. You need someone younger."

Lorinda gives him a look. "Oh, do you now?"

"No disrespect," he says, sounding surprisingly sincere. "You can obviously handle yourself in the black. But if we're going to get onto the bridge, we need someone round my age."

Anita's hand finds Corey's, gripping it tight. Hannah can't stop herself sizing her up, along with Everett. Could they do it? They're around Roman's age, after all. The thought of sending them out there, splitting them from their children, is horrific, but if they don't figure this out—

"How about you?" Lorinda says to Jack.

"Me?"

"Sure. Brendan and Seema are obviously not in play, and there's no way we're breaking up the family right now." She glances at Hannah, as if she sensed her thoughts, then turns to Roman. "Can he do it? Pass as one of you folks?"

Slowly, Roman nods. "It's possible. We all knew each other on the *Resolute*, but if they're having to send a rescue out to us, chances are it's one they had to put together quickly. The crew might not know the original one by sight."

"What if they do?"

"Then we're dead. It's that simple. There'll be a few other soldiers on board, along with non-combat personnel. If there's a welcome party and they recognise us—which they might, especially if the commander is there—then it's mission over." His eyes move to Jack. "You up?"

Jack looks like what he wants to say involves several words Anita Livingstone would disapprove of, but he pushes it back. "I've never done one before," he says. "An EVA."

"I'll show you the suit," Lorinda tells him. "And I'll be there on the comms the whole time, talking you through it."

"Can you even—"

"EVA's are tough when you start them, and it's going to take one hell of a team effort. But between the two of us, we'll get you there."

"Wait a minute," Everett says. "What about the rest of us? How do we get on board?"

Lorinda points at Hannah. "There's our pilot."

Hannah goggles at her. "Excuse me?"

"When I was hanging around the other ship—"

"Hanging around?" Jack mutters.

"—I saw that it had a cargo bay door on its hull. One that might be big enough to take the *Panda*, if we've got someone to fly it in."

"Wha—" Hannah's mouth is suddenly very dry. "No. Oh no."

"You've spent more time in that cockpit than anybody. You give us the best chance. They open it up, you fly right in. Easy-peasy. Unless, of course, you still feel like having us kill ourselves."

"Huh?" Corey blinks up at them.

"Never mind," Anita says, wrapping an arm around him. "Figure of speech."

"No, it wasn't! Was she really going to make us commit suicide?"

"Bakwas, man," Malik mutters.

Hannah does her best to ignore them. "Can't you?" she says to Lorinda.

"Why does everybody think that because I've lived in space I know how to do everything? I've never actually flown a ship—we had rig-hounds for that, back on Kuiper."

Lorinda lets the blanket drop, the foil crinkling at her feet. "If it were up to me, I'd be going in Jack's place, and we'd still have the captain around. But since that isn't going to work, you'll have to manage. Besides, I don't know about the rest of you, but this was a crappy tour. I'm ready to go home."

Jack swallows, eyes never leaving Lorinda's. Then he gives her a tight nod.

For the longest time, nobody says anything. Nobody even seems to want to look at anyone else.

Hannah's hands are shaking. Roman could so, so easily go back on his word, at absolutely any time. He could kill them the second he's free. He could murder Jack. Leave them all to die. He could give them away before they even leave the ship. And herself in the pilot's seat ... Jesus.

Suddenly, she very badly wants to hug her mom. She wants her mom here, and her dad, and Callie. Most of all Callie, because Callie would know how to handle this. She'd understand exactly what to do, and in what order to do it. She'd handle it with the same laser-focus that she did everything else.

Adrift

Hannah closes her eyes, then opens them again.

What a pile of shit.

Callie would have run, just like Hannah did when the station was attacked. Her mom and dad would have freaked out, both of them—and they both would have turned to whoever was in her position for help.

They could talk as much as they want about personal responsibility and being a leader, but when you really got down to it that just meant following a single, predetermined path. There was no room for anything outside that—nothing but disapproval.

And isn't that why she left for Sigma? When she really gets down to it? They expected certain things from her, and they never told her what those things were. Not really.

It wasn't about that. I needed a job. She half laughs. A job. If she'd wanted, she could have stuck it out living at home, or gone to work for Callie. But she didn't want that. She just wanted to get as far away as possible.

They can't help her. They are a million light years away.

Volkova. She'd believed that Hannah was more than she thought she was. Because she had on the red shirt, because someone had hired her for a job, and that must mean she was able to do it.

And Lorinda: when Hannah had proposed pulling all the oxygen out of the ship, letting them all drift off, Lorinda had refused to accept it. It might not have been an easy choice, and it would have been a mercy, if things had got bad. But it was also her checking out early. Refusing to fight.

"We—" Hannah starts, then stops.

She was about to say, *We vote*. But then she meets Lorinda's eyes, and she understands.

You be the commander, or all the soldiers die.

She looks around the main deck of the *Red Panda*, taking in the exhausted faces and slumped shoulders, the torn soychip packets and JamFizz cans, the crumpled-up jackets and sweaters. The grime that has crept across the floor and viewing dome. The crusted blob of puke that still hasn't been cleaned up.

And up, through the dome. The Neb outside, daring them to escape. The endless black void, stretching out to infinity.

Lorinda smiles, as if she knew all along what would happen.

Hannah puts one foot on the seat next to Roman, leaning behind him to undo the tape.

"Let's go home."

Chapter 56

The destroyed ship hangs in the middle of the cockpit viewport as Hannah eases herself back into the pilot's seat.

She still doesn't know if she did the right thing—even now, the thought of letting Roman go makes her shiver. If he turns on them, she'll be responsible.

You can't think like that. With a shaky breath, she puts her hands on the controls.

The others are downstairs, getting Jack and Roman ready. At some point, Hannah's going to have to do what Volkova did, back at Sigma: line the *Panda* up with a very tight entry point. She might not have to do it with the entire universe exploding around her, but she also doesn't have Volkova's piloting skills.

She needs to figure out how to turn on the comms, then turn off autopilot, then actually fly this thing without getting them all killed. Her throat feels like it's swelling closed, like she can't get enough oxygen into her lungs.

She makes herself take a deep breath, a second, then opens her eyes. Comms first. That's the most important thing—if they can't hail the *Victory*, this is going to be almost impossible.

As the thought occurs, Hannah sees a blinking message on one of the screens. FULL SYSTEM RESET COMPLETE. CONFIRM PROGRAM RESTART?

Finally a break. The *Panda*'s voice is annoying as hell, but maybe it can turn on the comms for her. She taps the message, then the YES on the option box that appears.

Adrift

She's expecting the voice, but it still makes her jump. "System restarted. Welcome aboard the *Red Panda*, registration XT560 dash T1."

It's the original voice of the *Panda*: the cheerful American male. Hannah opens her mouth to tell it that she's not Volkova, but it beats her to it. "Captain Volkova not detected in cockpit. Captain Volkova not detected in vessel. Contacting Sigma Station Control."

"Don't bother," Hannah mutters. Maybe this wasn't such a good idea. The *Panda* might not even let her deactivate the autopilot—it might only respond if it's Volkova in the pilot's seat. She'll have to do this manually.

She turns, intending to shut the voice off again, when it says, "Sigma Station Control is unresponsive. I require more information to perform at expected levels. Passenger: please state the whereabouts of Captain Jana Volkova."

Hannah stares out of the window at the remains of the *Resolute*, shrouded in glittering debris. "She's dead."

For a few moments, the ship doesn't respond. Then it says, "Please confirm cause and time of death."

Her mouth feels too dry, her tongue way too large. Eventually, she clears her throat. "She was killed. I don't know how long ago. A few hours, I guess."

"Acknowledged. Thank you, passenger."

Is it her imagination, or does the AI's voice carry a tiny note of regret? Before she can process this, it speaks again. "An incident report has been prepared for submission to Sigma Station Control and Sigma Destination Tours. Would you like to hear the contents of this report?"

After a long few seconds, Hannah says, "Yes."

"Captain Jana Magdalena Volkova, deceased at unknown period on April 10th, 2172. Service length with Sigma Destination Tours: twelve years, three months, twenty-two days and unknown period. Total completed tours aboard this vessel: twenty thousand, six hundred and fifteen. Satisfactory performance reviews: eleven. Unsatisfactory performance reviews: none.

"A complete record of Captain Volkova's verbal commands,

voice profile, ship actions and journey logs have been appended to this report. Would you like to hear them now?"

Hannah is about to say yes again, but that would mean listening to twelve years of logs. "No," she says eventually. It's barely a whisper.

"Report will be transmitted at next available contact with Sigma Station Control. Sigma Station beacons not detected. Recovery ship beacons not detected. Emergency destination coordinates not detected."

"Wait," Hannah says. She closes her eyes for a second, wondering how to phrase it. "Are the ... the external comms. Can we transmit?"

"Correct. Communication systems are nominal."

Hannah slumps back against the seat, closing her eyes again. OK. Comms are good. Now they just have to hope they stay that way. And that all the million other insane things they're about to do go off without a hitch.

"In the event of the loss of ship commanding officer without direction from station command," the computer says, "control is to be passed to a capable passenger or staff member. Please confirm you are a capable passenger or staff member."

"Confirm," Hannah says. She's still barely able to speak.

"Autopilot engaged. No proximity detected. Manual control may be required to guide this vessel to safety. Would you like to run the emergency ship control tutorial?"

Hannah blinks. "There's a *tutorial*?"

"Correct. All vessels operated by Sigma Destination Tours contain multiple layers of safety protocols. In the event of a loss of command combined with no signal from a recovery beacon, a capable passenger or staff member may need to take control of the ship. The tutorial covers basic steering, thruster operation and radio operation. Would you like to run the emergency ship control tutorial?"

Hannah sits back in her chair, stunned relief washing over her.

The *Red Panda* might not have additional food supplies in its escape pod. It might be only barely capable of working in space. But at some point in the distant past, some company programmer decided to create an emergency tutorial program, and, right now, it looks like it might just save their lives.

She's about to tell the *Panda* to run the tutorial when she gets the craziest idea.

"Computer … did you say you kept a voice profile of Captain Volkova?"

"Correct. Over Captain Volkova's service period of twelve years, three months, twenty-two days and unknown period, all verbal commands and voice patterns were recorded and stored, as per Sigma Destination Tours staff data analysis regulations."

"Can you …" She stops, unsure how to phrase it. "Can you speak as her? With her voice?"

"I am capable of transmitting commands in over four hundred different Frontier-recognised languages and over fifty accents."

"But can you switch your voice pattern to the captain's?" It sounds stupid even as she says it. *What are you doing?*

She's expecting the computer to say no. And why wouldn't it? The whole idea is crazy—Volkova is dead, and she's on her own. But to her surprise, the ship immediately says, "That is correct. Would you like me to switch to Captain Volkova's stored voice patterns for the emergency ship tutorial?"

In astonishment, Hannah says, "Yes. Confirm."

There's a split-second pause. Then the thick, Russian-accented voice of Jana Volkova comes from the speakers. "Welcome to the emergency ship tutorial for the *Red Panda*, a Sigma Destination Tours vessel. Please state your name."

Hannah tries to speak, and finds that she's crying. Tears roll down her face, dripping onto her forearms. She hugs herself tight.

"Please state your name," Volkova repeats.

She means to say *Hannah Elliott*, but what comes out, when she finally finds her voice, is: "Guide. My name is Guide."

"Welcome, Guide. This tutorial will demonstrate how to safely operate this vessel. Please place your hands on the control stick, as shown in the on-screen diagram immediately ahead of you."

Hannah does so. Her hands only shake a little.

"Please confirm you are ready to begin the control tutorial."

"I'm ready." Through her tears, Hannah smiles. "Tell me a story."

Chapter 57

Lorinda takes extra care to make sure she looks calm, even if she doesn't feel anywhere close to it. She has an idea that if she doesn't, Jack is going to pass out.

She remembers the first time she went out in the Belt, remembers how difficult it was—and she'd had a whole month of training beforehand. You didn't move like you expected out there. Everything was exaggerated. Every single movement had consequences.

Jack probably doesn't know the specifics, but he's got an idea, and it isn't hard to see that he's on the verge of freaking out. So she keeps an easy smile on her face, relaxes her shoulders as she helps him into his suit. It's not as hard to do as she thought it would be. If they make it through this, she thinks, maybe she should consider politics, like Anita. Run for office somewhere.

If they make it.

They have no idea when the other ship is going to arrive—Roman couldn't tell them, saying it was a decision that would have to be made by the commander, back at their outpost. They decided to get him and Jack ready, so they can leave as soon as it appears. This is going to be tricky—and not just for Jack.

For the thousandth time, she tries to think of a way she can take Jack's place. She keeps coming up on that one thing: if they're going to get to the other ship's bridge, whoever is with Roman has to pass as military. She can't.

Corey and Malik are still on the main deck, and Hannah has made her way to the cockpit, leaving only Everett, Anita, Jack and Roman in the bar. And Seema, of course, her body lying on the far side of the room. Thank God Lorinda doesn't have to look at her.

Brendan is out, too. They talked about it, but decided to use the handcuffs that previously restrained Roman on him, rather than keeping him locked in a frigid bathroom. He's sitting on the stairs, hands cuffed behind him. Everett is with him, gripping his upper arm. His eyes are bleary, wincing in pain every time he moves, his face a mangled, red mess.

He hasn't said a word, and although he tried to fight them when they opened the bathroom door, they subdued him without too much trouble. Roman got him in a headlock, and Anita cuffed him. He got docile after that, too dazed to keep struggling.

Lorinda locks Jack's right glove in place, while Roman busies himself securing the seals on his neck. His suit is still on, and, despite its bulkiness, he moves with an efficient, focused grace. Lorinda catches Jack's eye. "Almost done," she says, still smiling.

Jack nods, swallowing.

"Take me through it again," Lorinda says to him.

"We've done it twice already."

She doesn't budge. "Again."

Jack lifts his left hand, showing her the joystick module. "This controls where I'm facing. Up, down, side to side." He taps the rocker switch on top of the stick. "Forward and backward."

"Good." She looks at him expectantly.

He sighs, eyes closed, as if trying to remember. "Gentle movements, I got it."

"Yep. Short, controlled bursts on the thrusters. Everything you do out there is going to be magnified. Now what are you *not* going to do?"

"Move my arms?"

"Exactly. This isn't like a swimming pool. You can't—"

"I *know* that."

She ignores him. "You can't swim through it. Every movement you make is going to affect your attitude and your position. Eyeball your target—there should be a set of red lights above the airlock."

She looks to Roman for confirmation, and he nods. "You listen to her," he says, jerking his chin at Lorinda. "She knows what's she's talking about."

"Yeah, well." Lorinda checks Jack's right glove seal, still not quite satisfied. "Forty years on the belt will do that to you."

"You were a miner?"

"That's right."

"Helium-3?"

"Uh-huh." She starts checking the other glove seal. "Some tungsten too, on occasion."

"Knew a couple prospectors. Not an easy job."

"We did OK." She gives him a tight smile, then turns back to Jack. "Now you stay close behind Roman, but give him room to manoeuvre. Let him take the lead."

She waits for him to respond. He doesn't.

"Jack. Look at me."

He looks at her.

"I'll be there every step of the way." She taps her ear. "Just listen to my voice on your comms. I can't see your suit HUD, but I'll be able to see you. If I tell you to do something, you don't argue, you just do it. Got it?"

"Yeah. Yeah, OK. Sure."

"Don't worry," she says. "We'll be right behind you."

The corners of Jack's mouth twitch. "You'd better."

Roman secures his neck seals. There's a *click-hiss* as they tighten, making Jack wince. The soldier's grey suit stands out in contrast to Jack's white one, high-level military tech next to the cheapest, most cost-effective space solution that Sigma Destination Tours could afford.

Still, the story they've worked out sounds pretty plausible. The *Resolute* suffered a catastrophic engine failure, and Roman and Jack were the only ones to make it out. They took refuge in the *Panda*—which they'll maintain they boarded, taking care of the passengers, a detail that made Lorinda uneasy.

Jack's military suit was damaged, so he swapped it for one on board the *Panda*. He isn't wearing the same military clothes as Roman, underneath the suit, but that's something they're just going to have to live with.

Roman looks towards the airlock, impatient. None of them are looking towards the back of the bar, so none of them see Seema stir, see her foot twitch.

"And when we're on the bridge?" Roman says.

"What is it with you people?" says Jack. "I'm not five."

Roman gives him a hard look.

Adrift

Jack sighs. "Fine. I control our drift during the jump using the two sticks below the display. Reticle in the centre. Should be fine."

"And?"

"And what?"

Roman waits.

"*And,*" Jack says, sounding annoyed, "it's not always possible to get a read on how close we are to the edge of the bubble, just from reading the display. I have to watch for the vibration or we'll be ripped right out of it. See? I got it."

Roman speaks in a focused monotone. "Now, like I said, I won't be able to help you. I'll be on the other side of the bridge, working on the matter shielding. If you get into trouble, you're on your own. Understand?"

"Wait!" Corey and Malik are at the top of the stairs, older brother supporting younger. Corey's face is twisted in pain, his skin shiny with sweat. Lorinda blinks in astonishment. A second later, it's replaced by an almost embarrassed warmth. He wants to be a part of it. His leg is smashed up, and he still wants to be here.

"Did you tell him about the thrusters?" Corey shouts.

"I did, dear, thank you."

"Because if he doesn't know to go easy on the—"

Seema explodes out from behind the bar.

Whatever trauma her body suffered has shut down her mind, turned her eyes red and unfocused. But her body is still working, stumbling, lurching, charging towards them, like a cornered animal lashing out. There's muscle memory there, a thousand fights guiding her, and it gives her strength. Her feet thunder on the floor plates, and the noise is so startling that it locks everyone into place for a crucial half-second.

Roman reacts first, darting out from behind Jack. But at that moment, Brendan charges off the stairs, yelling his wife's name.

His hands are still cuffed behind him, and at that moment Lorinda isn't sure if he even knows what he's doing. Roman tries to slip past him, but his suit makes the move awkward. He can't get out of the way in time, and Brendan collides with him, sending them both crashing into the bar.

Corey yells in horror, as Everett scrambles to intercept Seema, Lorinda finds she can't move. Can't look away from those insane eyes. Sticky spittle dribbles out of the corner of Seema's mouth.

She's heading straight for Jack.

Lorinda reacts before she can think about it, stepping in front of him, her only thought that they need the suit, that they're finished without it.

Seema hits her with the momentum of a meteorite plunging through the atmosphere, bending her in half at the waist. Roman has got out from under Brendan, but he's too far away to help. Lorinda crashes into Jack, Seema's hands gripping the neck seal, twisting it—

For a second, the three of them are locked together, and Lorinda sees the room frozen. Corey and Malik at the top of the stairs, mouths formed in shocked Os. Confusion on Everett's face. Roman and Anita reaching for Seema, not even close to catching her.

Then momentum rips all of them apart. Jack goes flying, skidding across the floor. Lorinda goes right over the top of him, slamming against the closed airlock door, the back of her head colliding with it.

There's a pop, deep in her mind, like an overloaded fuse burning out. Things go soft, and dark, and silent.

Chapter 58

Everett gets to Seema a split second too late. She whirls, distracted, which is when Roman reaches round and snaps her neck.

It's a single, quick motion, a jerk that owes more to careful placement than to raw strength. The sound is a grisly crack.

"No!"

It's Brendan. He's stumbling away from the bar, stunned fury on his face. Everett and Anita grab him, holding him in place. He's so angry he nearly throws them off.

Adrift

Hannah's voice comes crackling over the ceiling speakers. "Hearing weird noises from down there," she says, trying to sound casual and failing miserably. "Someone come give me a status update?"

Roman is clicking his fingers rapidly in front of Lorinda's face. Her head is tilted to one side, her eyes closed, skin pale. Jack can see the beginnings of an enormous bruise feathering the edge of her hairline, just behind her ear.

"Nothing," Roman says.

"What do you mean, nothing?" Anita is back on her feet, staring down in horror at Lorinda.

"No response." Roman touches the bruise. "She's had a TBI. If—"

"TB—*what the hell is a TBI?*"

Roman's voice doesn't change. "Traumatic brain injury."

"Is she OK?" Corey shouts. He and Malik are still frozen on the stairs.

"How can you be so sure?" says Everett, still on top of the handcuffed Brendan.

Roman lifts Lorinda's eyelid, exposing nothing but white. "She's unresponsive to external stimuli. And this bruise? Here? Subcranial swelling." He pops his glove, putting a finger to Lorinda's neck.

"No pulse," he says.

And that's when Jack realises: he never checked that Seema was dead. *No. That's wrong. I . . .*

He didn't. He was going to, but his nose was a throbbing nightmare, his brain a mess of adrenaline. And he'd heard the crack when her neck hit the edge of the bar. No way anybody would survive that. He'd pushed the whole thing out of his mind, telling himself there was no point, his exhausted body eagerly complying.

His gaze lands on the airlock door, on the spot where Lorinda's head hit it. The surface is actually dented, and there's a tiny smear of blood nestled inside it. She's gone. Because of him. Inside his suit, Jack starts to shake. He's going to pass out, can already feel the blood draining out of his skull.

Anita has her hands on her head, fingers knotted in her hair. She glances back towards the stairs, remembering that her sons are there, and moves towards them. Corey is sobbing, Malik staring in stunned, uncomprehending horror.

"Someone talk to me," Hannah says over the speakers. Her voice is no longer calm.

"What do we do?" Everett says to Roman.

The soldier shakes his head.

Everett looks at him like he's gone insane. "We have to help her," he says, speaking the words slowly, as if Roman is a child.

"It's too late for that."

"Don't you dare say that. Don't you d—"

"*Hey.*" Roman grabs Everett's shoulder. "We can't do anything for her. She's got no pulse. Even if we were to relieve the pressure, even if she did somehow make it, we're talking major brain damage. We do not have time for this, not when we need to be ready to go as soon as the other vessel shows up." His tone softens, just a little. "I'm sorry, I know this isn't what you want to hear right now, but if you don't get it together, none of this is going to work." He looks at Jack. "Are you five-by?"

"What?"

Irritation on Roman's face. "Can you handle this?"

Jack doesn't know how to answer that. Terror doesn't begin to describe it. Lorinda was the only thing keeping him from breaking down completely, and now she's gone. If he'd checked Seema like he meant to ... but he wouldn't have needed to if he hadn't got Volkova—

It's too much. Is he five-by? He can barely move.

But at the same time, there's only one answer. The one Hec would have expected him to give.

He's screwed up a lot of things in his life—most, if he's totally honest with himself, and really, when has there ever been a better time to be honest, when they're all this close to ending up as fucking space debris?

But he's not going to screw this up. He can't. Or, if he does, it's not going to be because he got drunk, or didn't work hard enough. It's not going to be because he forgot to do something. Lorinda ... she deserved better than that.

He's not responsible for everything that's happened to them.

But he did make it worse. He can't do that any more. He's *got* to pull it together.

"I'm five," he tells Roman.

"Five-by."

"Fuck you."

Chapter 59

Roman has always gone quiet before a mission.

He'd use the few minutes before deployment going over the briefing materials, gear checked and rechecked, infil points and exfil points. He'd withdraw into his own world, ordering his thoughts, putting everything in front of him like a field of neatly sown crops he could survey in a single glance.

What he hadn't thought about—had never needed to—was that it only worked because every other operator around him was doing exactly the same thing. The dropship was always quiet. Nobody talking to each other. Just pure, clean focus.

He can't do that here. Even before the events of the past two minutes, it was too loud. Too chaotic. He told the kid he'd help. Gave him his word. But is he really about to do this? Betray everything that's kept him going.

He makes himself look at the boy. His brother is lowering him to the stairs, having been told by his mom to head up to the cockpit to tell Hannah what happened. Corey's eyes meet Roman's, and he makes himself hold them. *Do it for him. Him, and Madhu.*

Thinking of Madhu sets off the anger inside him, the tiny ball of hate pulsing in his gut. He ignores it, makes himself move, checking Jack's suit, running his fingers along the seams and the pack.

Without even looking, he can feel something is wrong. He leans over Jack's shoulder, squinting at the data readouts on top of the pack. "We've got a problem."

"What do you mean?" Jack says, trying to twist his head to look where Roman is looking.

"Here," he says, running his fingers along the neck seal. "Your seal's torn. And the pack's readouts aren't right. I think something inside got jogged loose."

"Can you fix it?" Jack asks.

"I can," says Everett. He still looks like he wants to pass out, but he moves with purpose, striding across the bar.

"Ev?" Anita checks Brendan's cuffs one more time, then springs after him. "What are you doing?"

Roman frowns at him. "You've worked on suits?"

"No. But I'm good with my hands. If I can get inside ..."

"Just let *him* do it," Anita says, pointing to Roman. "He's the one going out there. We need to look after the boys. You—"

Roman is about to tell her that he's no suit tech, when Everett turns around and grabs his wife by the shoulders.

"Anita," he says. "You're the most brilliant woman I've ever met. You're great at your job, and you're an incredible mom. I love you and our boys more than life itself, and I wouldn't change it for anything. But right now, you need to let me work. You need to look after Corey and Malik, and watch Brendan, and let me fix this suit."

"Ev ..." Anita can barely form the word. She's crying now, tears running down to the corners of her mouth.

He hugs her tight. "I know."

At that moment, Hannah's voice bursts through the speakers. This time, there's no disguising the raw panic in it.

"Ship!" she says, shouting so loud that her voice distorts. "We've got a ship! Far away but closing fast."

A ship. Almost certainly the *Victory*. Hayes, tired of waiting for his team to return from their mission. Decided to burn another jump core, figure out what went wrong.

Rodriguez would be on that ship. His squadmate, the one who's fiancée had been blown to pieces at Bellatrix. Hayes had selected him as part of the backup team. Roman's mouth is suddenly very dry.

It's not just his own revenge he's turning his back on here. What would Rodriguez do, if their positions were reversed? Would he have gone down so easily?

"I can't do this," says Roman.

"What are you talking about?" Corey is staring at Roman like he's gone insane, tears still tracking down his cheeks. Everett comes to a halt, almost tripping on the stairs.

Roman hangs his head. "You're asking me to betray my ..."

He can't finish. He was going to say *friends*, but that's not right. The people on the *Resolute*, and on the *Victory*, aren't friends in a traditional sense. They aren't even a unit—just a group of individuals with the same axe to grind. But he knows what every single one of them is going through, has felt it every day for the past decade. He can't turn on them. He can't.

He looks over at Corey, as if the boy will have the answer. Corey just stares back at him, mouth slightly open.

"We can't force you to choose."

Anita. She's gone to Corey, standing behind him, hands on his shoulders, chin raised ever so slightly. Her face is red and puffy, dark circles under her eyes, but her voice is steady.

"But none of us were given a choice in this either," she says. "We made do. We figured it out. And you gave my son your word that you'd help us."

Her fingers tighten on Corey's shoulders. "So you need to choose. And you need to choose quickly. Right now. Because, if you don't, it's all over. For all of us."

For a few seconds, it's as if the scene in the bar is frozen in amber.

"I'll hail them," Roman hears himself say, heading for the stairs.

Chapter 60

Hannah thought she had this under control.

She'd done some basic thruster work with the *Panda*, getting a feel for it. The tutorial was straightforward—easier than she expected, actually. It didn't stop a pool of sweat forming at the small of her back, or an ache spreading through her fingers, gripping the control stick, but she was fine. Definitely fine.

She knew something was happening in the bar, something bad—she could hear shouting, muffled thuds. But she didn't dare leave her post to find out what it was. And then she saw the other ship, approaching her position, and everything she'd just learned went right out of her head.

She doesn't know where it came from, or what direction. But all of a sudden it was just there, hanging in the blackness beyond the destroyed gate, perhaps two miles away—although it's not like she's great at estimating distances out here, which may or may not be a problem when she actually tries to park this stupid ship in the bigger one's cargo bay.

She can't pick out the details, but its albedo is just fine from here. She can see the shape, the distinctive fins. The entrance on the underside, probably no wider than the hole in the Sigma Station that Volkova piloted them into. The one that had scraped the belly of the *Panda* raw.

How long do they have? Minutes? Less? Panic overwhelms her, terror keeping her glued to her chair. They need to get away. They *have* to. They'll go back to Sigma, hide in the hotel like before—

Running footsteps, echoing through the passage behind her. Anita and Malik appear, Malik still clutching his holocam. Everett is there, too, breathless, his eyes wide. Roman comes in behind him, looking grim.

"Can you talk to them?" Hannah says, pointing to the part of the control panel she thinks is the radio.

"Lorinda's dead," Anita says, speaking before she's even finished.

Hannah turns her head to look at her, sure she misheard.

"How ..."

"Seema, she ... she wasn't ..." Anita rubs a hand across her face. "She hit Lorinda hard, knocked her out."

Hannah's world turns blurry at the edges, like a bad signal. She's suddenly aware of every physical sensation: the sensation of her body on the pilot's seat, the clammy sweat sticking her shirt to her skin, the textured grips on the control stick.

Adrift

Most of all, she's aware of her heart beating, a rapid pounding in her ears. They have to get out of here. This is all wrong. The dream comes rushing back, the metal ball approaching her parents' house, her mom and dad not even looking, waving to her as it casts a shadow across them.

And hammering in time with the heartbeat: *got lucky rook, got lucky rook, got lucky—*

Very deliberately, Hannah takes a breath. She counts to four as she inhales, holds it for a moment, then lets it go. She shifts on her seat, pulling her sticky shirt away from the back of the chair.

Roman reaches past her, hands dancing across the panel. "*Victory*, this is designated callsign *Resolute*, Delta 1830 Tango-6, do you copy? Over?"

Nothing. No response. Not even static.

Roman grunts, adjusting the frequency. "*Victory*, designated callsign *Resolute*, Delta 1830 Tango-6. Come in, over?"

Still nothing. The *Victory* is approaching faster now. If the *Panda* can't reach it, the spheres will release, and they'll be finished. There's nothing they can do. How much time will running buy them? Ten seconds? Less?

"*Victory*, *Resolute*. Please respond, over?"

There's a burst of static from the cockpit speakers. Then a man's voice, thin but audible. "Designated callsign *Resolute*, this is the *Victory*, Alpha 3668 November-niner. We read you. What is your status, over?"

"*Victory*, *Resolute*. Our ship suffered a catastrophic jump drive failure. Two of us managed to suit up and take command of a local vessel. Requesting extraction, over."

"*Resolute*, *Victory*. To whom am I speaking? Over."

"*Victory*, *Resolute*. This is Petty Officer First Class James Roman. I am here with ..."

He trails off. Hannah glances over to him, even though it takes every effort for her to tear her eyes away from the approaching ship. He must be trying to think of which of his fellow soldiers to name. Which identity to give Jack.

"I'm here with Petty Officer Third Class Lachlan Jacobs. His suit is damaged but we have a working one from this vessel. Requesting permission to enter *Victory* airlock, over."

The speaker doesn't identify himself. "*Resolute, Victory.* Did you accomplish your primary objective? Over."

Anita mutters something. Hannah gives her a sharp glance, but it doesn't seem like whoever is on the other end heard it.

"*Victory, Resolute.* That is confirmed. Primary objective achieved. Over."

A long pause.

"*Resolute, Victory.* Roger that. We'll prepare the forward airlock for you. And then you're going to have one hell of a debrief. *Victory* out."

Roman stands up, pointing at the underside of the approaching ship. "The second those doors start to open, you move. Got it?"

Hannah nods. She's been holding her breath, and lets it go in a shaky burst. Roman ducks back into the passage.

"What do we do?" Anita looks like she wants to complete whatever escape plan Hannah had in mind. But she doesn't move.

"Nothing," Hannah says, not looking away from the belly of the *Victory.* "Not yet."

And then she has an idea.

She doesn't know if it's a good one, or if it'll even matter in the long run. She almost dismisses it. But after a few moments, she turns to Malik, still not completely sure what she's doing.

"Hey," she says. "Could you do something for me?"

Chapter 61

Jack can barely move.

How the hell did Lorinda do this for a living? How does anyone? Even with the assistance of the servos, every movement causes a fresh wave of sweat to burst out on his forehead. His suit feels like it's crushing the life out of him. When they first left the airlock, he thought his arms were going to be wrenched out of their sockets.

He's tight behind Roman. The *Victory* has come to a stop a little over a mile away from their position outside the *Panda*; it blocks out a large part of the Neb, a hulking, spiked shape.

Lorinda's words: *Very short, very controlled bursts on the thrusters. Everything you do out there is going to be magnified.*

He tries not to imagine the people in the *Victory* watching them. Or what they'll do if they decide that Jack's not who Roman says he is.

He's not claustrophobic, but the helmet feels too tight on his head—the glass too close to his nose, the display too bright. He licks his lips, which are curiously dry despite the humid suit interior. His armpits and lower back are clogged with sweat.

Everything out here is bigger than him. Every single thing. Even the smallest piece of debris from the destroyed gate is a chunk that could obliterate him. He knows that probably isn't the case—that there are more than likely millions of tiny metal chunks dotted around them—but it sure as hell doesn't feel like it.

He can't help but think of an old photo he saw once, taken back in the twenty-first century, from a probe camera. A snap of the Earth from Saturn's rings. From that distance, the entire planet was a minuscule blue dot. You could cover it with the edge of fingernail.

He keeps looking for the red lights around the *Victory*'s airlock, can't see them. Not that it stops him. There's nothing to focus on out here, nothing that isn't moving.

"Careful. Debris below you." Roman's voice crackles in Jack's ear, along with a tiny indicator blinking up on his display: SUIT COMMS. He wasn't expecting it, and accidentally squeezes the forward thruster with his thumb. It sends him into a slow spin, his stomach feeling like it takes an extra second to follow.

No biggie. All he has to do is correct it. He hits the backwards thruster, but holds it a split second too long, sending the spin into reverse. In a panic, he tries to give himself a little leverage with the stick, trying to play it, only for his spin to accelerate.

He has to stop himself from reaching for the hem of shirt—after so many years, the tic is automatic. But the slight movement of his hand somehow makes it worse. He's starting to spin faster now, the Neb whirling away from him. What the hell are they doing out here? Humans were never meant to be in space. This is insane.

An almost inaudible bump, felt more than heard in his helmet as he's brought up short. Roman has pivoted, wedging both feet into the space below Jack's suit pack and firing his own thrusters to arrest their movement.

"Get ahold of yourself," the soldier hisses.

Jack feels a sudden, irrational urge to scream. But, of course, it's way too late for that. He's right out on the edge, and the only person he can count on right now is someone who, a few hours ago, he was planning to torture for answers.

He swallows, nods, forgetting for a second that Roman can't see the movement. "Yeah," he says.

"Fine. Go easy on the damn thrusters. The old lady knew what she was talking about."

Jack feels another bump as Roman disengages. He tries to find the *Victory* again, and almost immediately sends himself into another spin. His gloves won't let him make precise movements—even with the assistance of the servos it's like he can't do anything but press hard, or not at all.

The voice of the *Victory*'s commander is suddenly in his helmet. "Officers Roman and Jacobs, *Victory*, common channel. This is Commander Hayes. We see that one of you is experiencing thruster difficulties. Do you need assistance? Over."

Before Jack can say anything, Roman is on the channel. "*Victory*, Roman. That's a negative. Jacobs is in a civilian suit, and we think it has an issue with its feedback circuit. We're under control, over."

The ship slides into view. Jack back-bursts hard on the thrusters, somehow bringing himself to a halt. Roman says nothing.

"Jacobs, *Victory*. One of my engineers tells me he can send a software package to your suit that might fix your feedback. Can you pull up the I/O function on your HUD? Over."

At first, Jack doesn't respond, expecting Roman to do so. Then he realises that Roman expects *him* to talk. And why wouldn't he? The *Victory*'s commander contacted him directly.

His mind shuts down. He has no idea how to respond. If they send that package, and he keeps having issues ...

"Uh ... Jacobs, *Vic*—I mean, *Victory*, Jacobs," he says. Sweat blobs out in front of him, tiny balls of moisture, bobbing in the low gravity. "All five-by here. I've got it under control." He pauses. "Over."

For a full ten seconds there's no response. Ahead of him, Roman coasts towards the *Victory*. The implication is clear: *get moving*.

"Jacobs, *Victory*. Roger that. Proceed to airlock two, over."

Slowly—very, very slowly—the *Victory* begins to get larger. Jack finally spots their target, the red lights glowing above the airlock doors.

Roman hasn't said anything since he last spoke to the commander, and the silence is starting to get to Jack. It's oppressive, thick, like a viscous liquid slowly filling up his helmet. All he can hear is his breathing, exaggerated and slow, but still somehow ragged.

At that moment, the launch bays on the side of the ship slide open. The bays holding the spheres. It makes his breath catch in his throat.

"Shit," he says.

"Jacobs, *Victory*, say again? Over."

The SUIT COMMS channel flashes up, and Roman, annoyed, says, "What?"

"The—" He almost points. "The ball things. They're getting ready to fire." They saw his spin, worked out that he's not a space marine or whatever the hell these people are, and decided to finish the job the *Resolute* started.

"Relax." Roman floats into view. "Probably just a precaution."

"Precaution. Great. Against what?"

Roman doesn't reply. He fires his thrusters, coasting towards the *Victory*. Somehow, Jack manages to follow.

The airlock doors are much bigger than those on the *Panda*—fifteen feet across, at least, with a trio of red lights along one edge. Jack has to work hard not to send himself into another spin as he approaches them, slowly bringing himself to a stop above Roman. Below him, he can just see the *Red Panda*, hanging in the black.

He follows Roman's lead, orienting himself so he's facing the correct way for the ship's gravity well to grab them. The doors open in silence, revealing a bright white interior module, angular and blocky. They coast inside, Jack's stomach lurching as the gravity well takes hold.

God only knows how he managed to get himself the right way up. As it is, he lands on his feet, but can't keep himself there. He stumbles to his knees. They made it. Jesus Christ, they made it. Right now, it doesn't even matter that they're on an enemy ship. They're not outside.

Suddenly, the suit feels way too tight. He claws at his helmet, fat fingers fumbling for the neck seal.

"*Wait.*"

Roman's voice is harsh, his hand heavy on Jack's shoulder. He points, and Jack sees a set of five more red lights above the inner door. As he watches, they start to go green, one by one. The airlock is pressurising—if he'd removed his helmet before it did …

And if the commander is there, or someone who knew the mysterious Lachlan Jacobs …

The lights go green. Jack yanks his helmet off, gasping, and the noise of the *Victory* washes over him. Clanks, rumbles, a subsonic hum that he can feel in the pit of his stomach. It's the same noises as those on the *Panda*, but magnified, distorted.

He's still on his knees. Roman, standing beside him, is pulling off his helmet. As he does so, the interior door opens.

As it slides back, with the noise of the motor filling the airlock, Jack almost passes out. It's not just the fact that the EVA almost went horribly wrong; his mind is in overdrive, and for a second he sees a squad of soldiers behind the door, weapons up, ready to put three bullets into him, just like the Roses did with Hector.

And if Roman hasn't turned on them yet, he will, the second he sees the other soldiers.

Jack blinks. There's just one person standing there, a woman, with dark skin and black hair pulled back into a neat ponytail. "Roman?" She looks between them. "Jacobs?"

Adrift

There's no flare of recognition in her eyes when she looks at Jack—but no suspicion, either. Which is good. Her accent is subtle—Middle Eastern, Jack thinks. She's wearing a severe black jumpsuit. The muscular frame underneath it reminds Jack of Seema, and for a moment he can feel the latter's hands on his neck.

Roman lifts his chin. "Roman here."

"Mahmoud," she says. "Medical officer."

"Are we ready to jump?" Roman phrases the question casually.

"Hayes wants to talk to you first. He says I gotta give you a once-over in the infirmary, then take you to his quarters. Fair warning: he's not happy."

Chapter 62

They've put Brendan back in the bathroom, still cuffed. Nobody knows what else to do with him, and nobody wants to risk having him loose.

He fights them—harder this time, roaring his wife's name, but he's still too out of it. And restrained as he is, with both Everett and Anita holding his arms, he can't get away.

Corey can't stop thinking of Lorinda. Her body is still behind him, stretched out on the floor. It doesn't seem real. He keeps expecting to look up and see her standing, a sheepish grin on her face. *Sorry. Wasn't myself for a second there.*

"Take me upstairs," Corey says, when Brendan is locked away, the boxes safely back in front of the door.

His mom is on the verge of arguing, then thinks better of it. Malik is still up in the cockpit, but she and Everett scoop Corey up. Corey's teeth are gritted so hard that his jaw aches.

They are finally out of nanomeds. He can't believe how fast they went. The big cat is feasting, but Corey knows that it won't be doing so for long. Either they make it, and he gets to have an actual doctor take a look at the break, or …

Or he won't have to worry about his leg any more.

As they round railings at the top of the stairs, Everett loses his balance and Corey's foot jolts against the metal. The pain is so sharp and sudden that he sees stars, little prickles of light at the edge of his vision.

"Sorry, buddy," says his dad. But he and Anita don't stop moving, turning sideways as they had in the passage.

Corey gets one look past them at the main deck: the plastic seats, the scuffed floor, the badly hidden speakers in the ceiling, around the edge of the murky viewport. The strut on the wall that he lost his grip on after Captain Volkova killed the gravity. And as he takes it in, he gets the strangest feeling.

He wants the *Panda* to be OK.

He wants it to fly again.

Compared to the other ships Corey has on his posters at home, even compared to the ones Jamie designs, it's nothing. It's a tiny, boring little tourist ship. Low-range, no weapons, and, before Volkova avoided those metal balls by the destroyed gate, Corey would have said it had zero manoeuvrability. But it's kept them alive. Without it, they wouldn't be here.

Please be OK. At that moment, he's not sure if he's thinking about them, or about the ship.

They push through into the cockpit, Anita and Everett setting him down gently. From his spot on the floor, Corey can't see much, but what he can see is the attack ship. It's close enough to make out the details now: the grey and orange paint, the rigid, spiky fins. Corey's breath catches in his throat.

"What are they doing?" his dad says.

Hannah doesn't look away from the *Victory*'s cargo bay, still shut tight. "I don't know. They went inside, though."

Anita and Malik lean over, obscuring Corey's view in the tight cabin. "Shouldn't it be open by now?" Anita says, trying to keep her voice even, failing miserably. "Did they make it inside?"

"I just said."

"Then why—"

Adrift

"I don't know."

A silence falls on the cockpit. Corey watches as Hannah lifts her fingers from the control stick, flexes them, returns them to position. It's all down to her. Her, and Jack, and Roman. He's done everything he can.

All they can do now is—

The pain obliterates him. It comes on in a huge, searing wave, worse than anything he's felt before. He screams, clutching at his leg, wanting to hold it, not daring to.

Through the tears doubling his vision, he sees his mom and dad exchange a horrified, desperate look. Malik is gripping his shoulder. "It'll be OK," he's saying, over and over, as if he's trying to reassure himself instead of Corey.

"There's gotta be something," Everett says to his wife. To Corey, it sounds like he's speaking from very far away.

His mom shakes her head, her face pale in the cockpit lights. "Nothing."

"But what if we ..."

Anita ignores him, dropping to her knees in front of Corey, putting a hand on his cheek. It's slick with sweat, and he wants to tell her to take it away, but he can't get the words out. The cat bites harder, and he screams again. In her seat, Hannah flinches.

"Did I ever tell you how your dad and I got together?" Anita says.

Corey's face is dripping with sweat, but he manages to shake his head. "You said ... you said you met in college." Each word feels like it's being wrenched out of him.

"That's right, we did. But we never told you how."

She's trying to distract him. Corey wants to tell her not to bother. The only thing that's going to work is if he puts his head down and fights the cat. Pushes it back. Somehow. He tries to speak, but he can't get the words out. His shredded throat won't cooperate.

"'Nita," Everett looks acutely uncomfortable. "We said we wouldn't ..."

She ignores him, scooching in a little closer to Corey, putting out her other hand to grip Malik's shoulder. "So while I was in college, in California, I had a boyfriend. Not your dad, obviously. He was a nanochem major, and we were pretty serious."

"What was his name?" Malik says, glancing over at Corey. As if he too knows what his mom's doing, and wants to help.

She grimaces. "Doesn't matter. But he wasn't a good guy. We were living together, and he …"

A long moment passes. Corey expects to feel relief that she's stopped speaking. Instead, he finds himself desperate to keep listening. She was right—anything is better than focusing on what's happening below his waist.

"He didn't hit me." Anita's voice is flat. "But he was … well, I suppose you know what abusive means. He tried to control me."

She looks between her sons. "We were walking down the street one day. It was in August. And I said something … I don't remember what it was, but it set him off." She licks her lips. "He starts yelling at me, right then and there. Calling me names."

"Who was he?" Malik looks furious.

"Not important," Everett says, his voice barely a murmur. He's staring out of the cockpit glass at the other ship.

"And I'm crying." Another lick of the lips. "Because I don't know what to do. The street is crowded, and I knew I had to say something to make him stop, but I didn't know what. And nobody is even looking at us. He's just yelling these … horrible things, and …"

She sniffs—the kind of wet sniff people make when they're about to cry, and trying very hard not to.

"And then out of nowhere, your dad arrives. He wasn't actually in the college we were at—he couldn't get the financing, and you know Grammie and Grampa couldn't really afford it, so he was working as a …" She closes her eyes, as if trying to remember.

"Lens repair tech," Everett mutters.

"Lens repair tech. Right. And he had a job nearby, and he saw what happened. He comes running up, trying to get between us. Just trying to calm my boyfriend down."

She puts a hand around her husband, drawing him close, the words rushing out of her now.

"So my boyfriend hits him. And then he starts to kick him. And

I'm screaming at him to stop, but he's not, and nobody is even looking in our direction, and I was so scared ..."

Then she smiles. She actually smiles.

"And your dad ... he's ... he's yelling 'Leave her alone!' He's on the ground, getting beaten up, and he keeps telling the guy to leave *me* alone."

She wipes her face, crying openly now. Around them, the cockpit is utterly silent. "Eventually, the cops did come and break it up. Your dad spent the night in hospital, getting pumped with every nano they could find."

"And you got together after?" Malik asks.

"Not right away. We stayed friends for a few months before he asked me out, and then it was still a few years before we actually got married. I had to convince him to come with me to Austin."

Finally, Corey's throat allows him to speak. "Why ... didn't you tell us?"

In the quiet that follows, he's acutely aware of the three of them around him, huddled close.

"Because ..." Anita swallows, then sets her shoulders. She glances at her husband, as if to check he's OK with this, then says, "Because we decided you didn't need to hear about your dad getting hurt. Or your mom getting shouted at by ..."

A great, hitching sob bursts out of her. Everett pulls her close, and she buries her head in his shoulder, her body shaking.

"But you were gonna get divorced," Mal says, with something like wonder.

Everett sighs. "We talked about it. The past couple of years have been ... tough."

"But if you helped her," Corey hears himself say, "then why—"

"Life takes weird turns sometimes, pal. Your mom and me, well, we had some things to work out. We're pretty different people."

"But even if it happened," Anita lifts her head off her husband's shoulder, her eyes red, "I'd still love your dad." Her voice gets fierce. "I want you to know that. He helped me when nobody else would, and he gave me ..."

It's a few moments before she speaks again.

"He gave me you two," she says. "He gave me my boys."

She pulls both her sons into a fierce hug, Everett folding on top of them, as if he can protect them from what's coming.

Anita's voice is barely above a whisper. "I love you so, so much. All of you."

"We love you too, Mom," Malik says.

Corey doesn't know if she's right. And at that moment, with the cat's fangs digging into his leg and the bigger ship looming above them and their time measured in what might be minutes, he finds he doesn't care.

Not one little bit.

Chapter 63

For such an enormous ship, the *Victory*'s medical bay is tiny. It's a windowless, rectangular room packed with equipment, taking up most of the floor space and climbing the walls to the ceiling. Jack sits on one of the room's three beds, blinking in the harsh white light.

He doesn't dare move. Not until Roman does. Mahmoud might just be a medical officer, but it doesn't take a genius to figure out that she'd probably knock him on his ass in about half a second. In any case, even if he did get away he wouldn't have the first clue where to go.

What is he even doing here? He's supposed to be making sure that Roman doesn't betray them, and, eventually, helping him operate the jump gate. The second one he can probably do. Maybe. But if Roman does turn on them, how exactly is he, Jack, supposed to stop him? There'll be no Lorinda with a shard of glass this time. No one to help.

Lorinda. Jack has to force himself not to shiver.

He looks over at Roman. They've still got their suits on, and Mahmoud is shining a light into the soldier's eyes. "Looks good," she says, clicking the penlight off. "You're OK. You can take your suit off, by the way."

She half turns to Jack, then stops. "Roman ..."

"Yes?" Roman is working on his neck seal.

For the first time, Mahmoud looks unsure. "When you were on the *Resolute* ... did you know an officer named Reyes? Silvia Reyes?"

Roman stops moving. His voice is almost inaudible. "I did."

"Did she ..." Mahmoud trails off.

Roman shakes his head, very slowly, side to side. A wave of emotion rushes across the medical officer's face. She gets it under control, closing her eyes briefly, then turns to Jack.

"Jacobs," she says, her voice barely shaking. "Let's get you looked at. Any pains? Ringing in your ears?"

"No." Jack feels numb. Mahmoud looks into the middle distance, blinking as she activates something on her lens. When is Roman going to *move*? They're running out of time. The soldier is stepping out of his suit—he wears a black jumpsuit underneath it, with the same dagger patch on the breast.

"I'm going to give you a shot of Oraxalone," Mahmoud says to Jack. "We don't know what the rad protection was like on that civ suit of yours. You ever been dosed before?"

"No, I ... I don't think so."

"You sure? If you have, I'll need to adjust the amount. Anyway, doesn't matter, I can look it up." She blinks twice. "OK, Jacobs, found you, let's get you out of that suit and—"

Mahmoud stops, frowning. She looks at Jack, blinks, blinks again. The frown changes, her eyes narrowing, and that's when Jack realises what's happening. She's looking at a medical profile of the real Lachlan Jacobs.

One with his photo.

Before he can say anything, Roman moves. He wraps an arm around Mahmoud's neck, forcing her down to her knees and bending her backwards at the same time. She chokes, snarling, her training taking over as she attempts to wedge her hands under his arm. Jack sits, stunned, watching it happen, knowing he should help but not having the first clue how.

In a move so fast that Jack almost misses it, Roman rocks back, then jabs three times at the base of Mahmoud's neck with his free hand. Her body goes limp, twitching, and she claws at his arm for a split second before her hands slump to her side.

Roman holds her for a few seconds more. Then, slowly—almost tenderly—he lowers her to the deck. She's still breathing, her chest rising and falling.

"Holy shit." Jack can't think of anything else to say.

"Get changed." Roman looks like he wants to do to Jack what he did to Mahmoud, but now that she's down he doesn't hesitate. He grabs her sidearm—a thick, chunky pistol with a textured grip. Then he does the strangest thing. He pinches his lens out, throws it away, then digs his fingertips into Mahmoud's rolled-back eye.

With practised ease, he slides her lens out, using it replace his discarded one. He sees Jack looking. "Keyed to her weapon," he says. He glances down at Mahmoud's unconscious body, a dark cloud crossing his face. Then he moves to the door. "Let's go."

Jack strips off his suit as quickly as he can—he has to work hard not to get caught on the tight seals. Then he follows, trying to ignore the shaking in his legs. He's got to focus. It's not just his life on the line here. He's letting the little things slip, letting the details get away from him. He can't do that, not now. Again, he sees Lorinda, pictures the bruise on her temple.

Jack got to go on board a Frontier military cruiser once, over fifteen years before. It was back when he was first starting out as a reporter, way before he ditched that shit-show for travel writing. The Frontier, eager for some decent PR in the midst of the war, let a group of journalists tour one of its ships.

He recognises the style here: the corridors are functional, narrow, all gleaming metal and recessed pipes. What's missing are signs. On the cruiser he toured, there were directional markers every-where, pointing to the mess hall, the engines, the bridge. There's nothing like that here. It's like the crew doesn't need them.

Jack shivers again, jogging to keep up with Roman. Without him, he'll be lost, and then dead.

The ship is deserted—or, at least, running with minimal crew. They walk in silence, Roman in the lead. His military jumpsuit has a slim-fit holster at the waist, and he tucks Mahmoud's gun into it.

In the distance, Jack can hear a voice over the ship's speaker system, the words made inaudible by the twisting corridors. The ship's AI, maybe—probably one a little more sophisticated than the brick-dumb computer on the *Panda*. Maybe it's even in control of those damn spheres.

"Why'd you wait?" Jack says.

Roman looks over his shoulder, annoyed. "Excuse me?"

"To ... with the doctor." He searches for her name. "Mahmoud. You could have taken her down the second you were out of your suit. She would have figured out something was up anyway, the second she saw I was in civilian gear. So why did you wait?"

Roman stops, hand moving unconsciously to his weapon, turning to face Jack. Against the bright lights in the corridor, he's a silhouette, his face in shadow.

"Let's get one thing straight," he says, his voice barely above a whisper. "I gave you my word that I'd help you. I'm going to honour that. But I didn't say how, and I didn't let you tag along so you could question my decisions. If you do so again, I'll put a bullet in your leg and drag you to the bridge. It won't stop you from helping me operate the jump gate."

"OK, Jesus." Jack raises his hands, trying to ignore his thudding heart. Then, before he can stop himself, he says, "Who the fuck pissed in *your* cereal?"

It's an automatic response—something he'd say to Hector whenever his partner was in a foul mood. English wasn't Hec's first language, so he'd had to explain why someone might want to urinate in a bowl of soyflakes. It had become an in-joke between them—Hec had even started to say it to him, throwing it back in his face.

God, he wants to see Hector right now. He would give anything to have him here. Not that it helps: he just trash-talked a special forces operative, one who five seconds earlier had threatened to shoot him. *This is going so well.*

Roman doesn't shoot him. Instead, he does something Jack isn't expecting: he smirks.

"Not very good at this whole teamwork thing, are you?" he says.

Jack finds himself shaking his head. "Not really." His voice is a croak.

"Well, you'd better figure it out. It'll be a goddamn miracle if they don't shoot us the second we hit the bridge. So if you don't do exactly what I tell you, *when* I tell you, then we're fucked. Got it?"

Without another word, he turns and resumes his march down the corridor. After a moment, Jack follows, trying very hard to stop himself shaking.

Two corridors later, Roman says, "I didn't want her involved."

"Huh?"

"You asked why I waited." Roman doesn't turn around. "I thought there might be a way to leave her out of it. She might have let us go without checking, and stayed in medical."

This time, Jack doesn't respond. And a few minutes later, they reach the bridge.

It's a large room, with a wide, angled viewport along one wall, showing the Neb glimmering in the distance. The room is split up into three tiered levels, each with multiple workstations. For some reason, Jack expects the lighting to be dimmed; it's even brighter than the corridors, with banks of halogen bars along the curved ceiling.

There are six crew inside, all of them wearing the same black jumpsuit as Roman. Two of them—a man and a woman, both of whom appear to be carved from granite—have the same dagger patch. They have their index fingers touching, their lenses linked, discussing what they're seeing in low voices. The rest of the crew are busy at their workstations.

Jack and Roman enter through a side door on the middle tier. The first person to notice them is a bearded, slightly hunched man sitting at a workstation. His gives a tight nod when he sees Roman. His eyes land on Jack, and a frown crosses his face.

And it's as if he's sent up a signal flare. The activity on the bridge slows, the operators turning one by one to look at them.

It's then that Jack sees the commander. Hayes.

Adrift

He's on the same level as they are: a big man, bald, perhaps early fifties, with broad shoulders and dark skin. His eyes, when he turns to look at them, are a dull grey.

"Roman?" he says. "You were told to wait in my quarters. Did the doc—"

He stops as he catches sight of Jack, takes in his clothing and the fact that he's definitely not military. His face, already lined with wrinkles, gains a few more as his eyes narrow.

Before Jack can even process what's happening, Roman takes three strides forward, pulling Mahmoud's pistol from its holster as he does so, the move smooth and controlled. Then he puts it against the commander's forehead.

In every movie Jack has ever seen, there's a weird clicking sound any time someone raises a gun, like it's automatically cocking itself. The feed's film critic, a fat bastard named Hunnigan with bad body odour and a terrible taste in shoes, once told Jack that it was a throwback to the old days of film-making—one that most directors still hadn't managed to get rid of, even though it's been a long time since anyone had to cock a gun.

And yet, as every single soldier on the bridge pulls their own sidearm and aims it at Roman, he expects to hear it: those sinister, ratcheting clicks. Instead, it happens in virtual silence, with nothing but the rasp of metal on holster fabric.

Somehow, that's even worse. They might be computer geeks and pilots and engineers, but he has no doubt that every single one of these people is just as deadly as Roman.

"Everybody stay calm!" Jack says, his voice jumping a few octaves higher than normal. Around him, the bridge is quiet, nobody moving, nobody speaking, everybody focused on Roman and Hayes. It's as if he isn't even there.

Hayes doesn't raise his hands, doesn't budge from his position. The expression of righteous indignation doesn't leave his face.

"Lower your weapon, soldier."

"Everybody out." Roman presses the point of the gun a tiny bit harder into Hayes' forehead. Jack's right hand is aching, and he realises it's because he's clenching it, the nails digging into his palm. His left hand is on his shirt hem, twisting it tight.

"What the fuck are you doing, Roman?" It's the guy with the dagger patch, a thickset man with a chest-length beard. The hand holding his gun looks big enough to palm a watermelon.

Another soldier—a slim woman with a tribal tattoo snaking up the neck of her jumpsuit—takes a step forward, her sidearm steady. "Say the word, sir."

Roman doesn't look at her. "Better be careful," he says. His voice is a low monotone, his words coming quick. "I'm on a hair trigger. Your aim's off by even a little bit, the sympathetic muscular contraction of my finger will discharge my weapon."

"Yeah, I did Q Course, too, asshole." The woman sounds somewhere north of furious now.

"Hold." Hayes' eyes flick to Jack, then back to Roman. And that's when Jack becomes aware of one or two of the guns swinging to face him. His bladder sends out a twinge, and it suddenly feels hot, too loose inside his gut.

"Think very, very carefully about this, Roman." Hayes starts to raise his hands, moving very slowly.

Roman jerks his head. "I'm sorry, sir. No choice." His next words are almost a shout. "I'll say it again. Everybody out, right now."

Nobody moves. Not even the women with the tattoo.

"Three count, then I pull the trigger," Roman says.

It's like every soldier in the room winds themselves a little bit tighter, gripping their guns a little bit more firmly. Jack feels like he's going to fall over. His bladder is throbbing now, sending up weak waves of pain. Maybe, if he can hold on long enough, they'll shoot him before he pisses himself. At least then he can die with some dignity.

"One." Roman is dead still, eyes locked on the commander. "Tw—"

"Wait," Hayes says.

He raises his voice. "Do what he says." The female soldier snarls. Hayes' eyes flick to her. "That's a direct order, Mazzini. Lower your weapon."

Mazzini's pistol wavers, then drops. One by one, the rest of them do the same.

"Yeah." Jack licks his lips. "All right." He's not sure if he says the words out loud, or just thinks them.

"Put your AI into recovery mode," Roman says. "I don't want it interrupting."

Hayes' eyes narrow in anger, but then he says, *"Victory."*

The AI's voice comes over the speakers, crisp and efficient. "Yes, Commander Hayes."

"Hayes-DF789-dash-8901. Transfer ship control to manual. Recovery."

"Commander Hayes, I am detecting elevated stress levels in your voice, and the presence of drawn weapons on the bridge. Do you want me to—"

"Do it."

"Commander, I cannot comply. I have concluded that you are under duress."

"Recovery mode, or I pull the trigger," Roman says.

"Victory. Hayes-DF789-dash-8901. My life is in danger if you do not enter recovery mode. *Comply."*

A long pause. Then: "Entering recovery mode, Commander. System offline."

The next few minutes are a blur. The soldiers finally leave, filing out of the same door Roman and Jack entered through. They stand in the corridor, huddled together, weapons still pointed into the room.

Roman directs Jack to lock all the other doors, giving directions without taking his gaze or his gun from the commander. As Jack fumbles with the keypad next to a door on the top level, he sneaks a look back. Hayes is refusing to look away from Roman, his mouth set in a thin, defiant line.

When the other three doors are locked off, Roman slowly walks the commander back towards the open one. The soldiers in the corridor don't give way, and Roman has to bark at them to move.

"Last chance," Hayes tells him.

Roman jerks his head at Jack, not looking at him. "Lock it down."

Jack does so, sweaty fingers slipping on the keypad. The door starts to close, and at the last second Roman plants a hand on

Hayes' chest, and shoves, pushing the commander through. Hayes cries out, losing his balance, the look on his face switching to one of murderous fury.

"Get—" he yells. Then the door closes with a loud click, cutting off the rest of the sentence.

"We should have kept him," Jack says. "Hostage." This time, he's pretty sure that he spoke out loud, even if he's forgotten that Roman told him not to ask questions.

"Can't hold a gun on him and operate the jump controls at the same time. Now let's get moving. We've got about three minutes before they cut their way back in." He considers. "Unless they blow the door."

"What happens if they blow the door?"

Roman says nothing.

Chapter 64

"Something's wrong," Everett mutters.

Hannah doesn't reply. Her hands ache from holding the controls, but she doesn't dare let go, doesn't dare look away from the underside of the *Victory*, where the cargo bay is. Every time she blinks, it looks a little smaller.

Everett shifts behind her. "It's been twenty minutes. Can we contact them somehow? Radio, or—"

"No, Dad." Corey sounds breathless. "It's like I told you."

"Just give them time," Anita says.

And still Hannah says nothing.

She's thinking about Rainmaker. And Blackbird, and Omen. She never got to see the end of the historical sim, never found out if they made it or not.

She distracts herself by running through what she learned in the tutorial, remembering the AI's instructions. And still she can't pull herself away from that battlefield, the images invading her thoughts.

"It's open." Anita's voice is urgent.

When Hannah doesn't respond, she hits her in the shoulder. "Hey. It's opening up!"

Hannah blinks. A mile away, the *Victory*'s cargo doors are opening. A thin black line, growing wider by the second. And then, from inside the gap, a light flickers on, shining out of the ship's belly.

"They did it," Malik says, his voice curiously high-pitched.

"Go," Everett says. "Go. *Go.*"

Hannah doesn't even wait for him to finish speaking. She punches the thrusters, and behind her the *Panda*'s engines rumble into life. Slowly, very slowly, the other ship starts to grow in the viewport.

They aren't moving nearly as fast as they did when Volkova was in the pilot's seat. She must have known some tricks to coax more thrust out of the engines. All the same, the *Panda* is accelerating, its puny engines pushing it closer and closer to the *Victory*. Hannah reminds herself to breathe, flexes her fingers on the controls. She's staring at the other ship so hard that she has to remind herself to blink.

A minute ticks by. Another.

"Easy," Everett breathes. He's right in her ear, and she jumps, only just managing not to knock them off course. "Sorry," he tells her, backing away. Behind him, Anita lets out a long, shaky breath.

Hannah returns her hands to the controls. They're getting close, the gap in the *Victory*'s underside growing bigger by the second. It's a little above them now, drifting towards the top of the viewport. *OK. Not a problem.* Exhaling, Hannah very gently tweaks the stick.

And almost immediately realises she isn't ready for this.

From a distance, across a mile of open space, she could keep the *Panda* steady. But with the *Victory* on top of them, every movement she makes is suddenly too much. She's trying to line up the slow, ungainly, oversteering *Red Panda* with a very narrow space, and she just can't get it to do what she wants.

The *Victory* drifts away from her, and she has to yank the stick back, too hard, the ship swinging in the other direction. She tries to calm herself, tries to think of her parents, of their house, of the museum job she's going to have, of the life she's going to lead. It's all a blur. Terror has smudged her mind, the images mixing with the ones she saw in the VR sim.

"Guide," says Volkova. "Your movements are erratic. Do you wish the ship to return to autopilot?"

"No," Hannah hisses through gritted teeth.

"Go left," Malik says.

Hannah tweaks the stick. But when the *Panda* doesn't respond fast enough, she pushes too far, oversteers. The *Victory* drifts too far, the cargo bay sliding past, Hannah correcting again, fingers locked on the stick, hoping, praying the ship will do what she wants.

Everett by her ear. "You're too far over."

"Yeah," Hannah says through gritted teeth.

"Let me see!" Corey yells from behind her.

"You gotta slow down," Malik says. "You're gonna hit the side. *Pull up!*"

And then everyone is yelling the words. Hannah yanks the stick as hard as it'll go, the wall of the larger ship looming in front of her. She squashes back into her seat, as if it'll give her some extra protection from the impact. There's no way they're going to miss. They're too close.

Anita screams as the belly of the *Panda* scrapes the *Victory*'s hull. The tour ship shudders, an alarm blaring somewhere, but Hannah barely hears it. She's still pulling the stick into her stomach, as if they'll crash the second she eases up.

They've lost sight of the *Victory*. The Neb glares at her. She's breathing too fast, panic clawing at her throat.

The Captain did this for twelve years. You've been doing it for twelve minutes. You're never going to make it.

When the *Panda* completes its loop, the *Victory* is just visible, down at their six o'clock. They'll never get into the cargo bay from here—to do so, they'd have to fly alongside the ship's hull, then hard-turn left into the tiny space. Not a chance.

Adrift

Willing the little ship to go faster, Hannah turns them around, tracking them away from the *Victory*, lining up another run. The attack ship hangs in front of them, daring her to try.

The stick is juddering in her hands. It wasn't doing that before. Is it her imagination, or is the *Panda* moving even more slowly than before? She flashes back to the grinding they felt when the ship tagged the *Victory*'s hull. What if something got damaged? What if—

"Mal, I can't see!" Corey shouts.

Everett, far too loud. "Go again. It's OK."

Anita: "Malik! Sit down!"

Hannah finds the thrusters, trying with every atom in her body to line them up right. But the tiny dot of the cargo bay is swinging around, dancing across the viewport. The *Victory* gets bigger and bigger.

They're going too fast. Hannah tries to decelerate, and the *Panda*'s response is barely there, sluggish and lazy. If she's off-target, they won't be able to pull up in time.

"Slow down." Everett sounds even more panicked than she feels. "Slow down!"

She pulls the thrusters back. The *Panda* refuses to slow down— the forward and aft thrusters have quit on them, either damaged by the scrape against the bigger ship's hull, or not getting the power they need. Hannah tweaks the stick—they can still move left and right, but she can't drop their speed.

In her mind, she sees the missiles, arcing towards Rainmaker's Scorpion fighter, the gap closing. Her eyes track to the tiny cargo bay opening, swinging wildly in the viewport as she tries to line them up.

"Thread the needle," she whispers. "Come on, baby, thread the needle. Thread the needle."

"What?" says Anita. "What are you—"

"*Shut up! I'm threading the needle!*"

She's drifted too far down again, has to correct. They're two hundred metres from the *Victory*, so close that Hannah can see inside the cargo bay. It's a mess of strapped-down crates and loading machinery, a wide-open space that doesn't look quite big enough to take the *Panda*. It's not going to work. They're going to get jammed in there, or bounce right off.

And yet she keeps going. Something beyond her understanding keeps her in her seat, keeps her playing the ship. One hundred metres now, the door almost open, the entire cavernous cargo bay revealing itself.

Anita abandons the viewport, dropping to her knees, pulling her sons and her husband in close.

Hannah closes her eyes.

Chapter 65

The bang shatters the universe.

It splits Hannah's skull in two, knocks her out of her seat. She has half a second to wonder why she didn't think to strap in when she slams shoulder-first into the control panel. Any second now, the *Panda* is going to rupture, and it'll all be over.

But then she hears another sound. A grinding, wrenching screech of tortured metal, as if the *Panda*'s very skin is being torn off. Before she can comprehend it, the sound vanishes, as abruptly as if someone turned off the light bulb, as if—

We made it through.

Before she can process this thought, she becomes aware of a frantic, urgent beeping. "Guide," says Volkova, sounding maddeningly calm. "Pressure loss imminent."

Hannah doesn't get a chance to react, because right then she looks up through the viewport.

The gravity well has them. They're skidding across the floor of the bay, heading for the far wall: a vertical slab of metal, covered with handholds and terminals. Big, spray-painted stencil letters run across it, words reading OPERATORS MUST MAINTAIN FULL SUIT PRESSURE AT ALL TIMES. There's a loading exosuit in front of them. The *Panda* sweeps it aside, shuddering, screaming as the suit tears chunks out of its hide.

"Everybody hold—" Hannah shouts. Before she can finish the sentence, the *Panda* collides with the wall of the cargo bay.

For the second time in as many days, Hannah blacks out.

It's the beeping that brings her round again—the pressure loss warning. She's hanging off the chair, legs twisted to one side, and her neck feels like someone has been hitting it with a claw hammer. She can't turn her head. When she tries, the pain squeezes tears out of her eyes.

The *Panda* is still moving, turning in a slow spin, the energy from its impact spent. Cracks have spread across the cockpit viewport. Beyond them, the cargo bay door is visible, sliding out of view as the ship spins. The door is just beginning to close.

In a daze, she reaches for the control panel, trying to shut off the beeping sound. Her hand is a useless slab of meat, her fingers feeling ten times larger than they normally are.

There's nothing more they can do. They're inside, the ship is still intact—for now—and the moment that door closes, Roman and Jack will activate the jump gate.

Volkova's voice reaches her ears. "Guide. Ship integrity has been compromised."

Hannah doesn't have time to think about it. She twists round in her seat, moving her head without thinking. The pain this time nearly makes her black out again, so she forces herself to move her body instead, actually lifting her right leg to get it out from under the control panel.

The *Victory* isn't moving—if they jump, there won't be any transfer of momentum. They'll drop right in. But it'll be a big bump when they land, and if they're not strapped in, they'll be smashed to pieces. If they don't lose pressure and decompress first.

The Livingstones are slowly picking themselves up. Everett is helping Anita with one hand, reaching out for his older son with the other. Corey Livingstone is unconscious, his eyes closed, his head twisted at a strange angle. It's only when he shifts slightly, turning his head back, that Hannah realises she's been holding her breath.

"The escape pod," she says.

Anita stares at her through bleary, shocked eyes. "What?"

"We have to get to the escape pod." Unlike the seats on the main deck, the pod chairs have thick safety straps criss-crossing them, and angled head supports. "You guys take Corey, I'll get Brendan."

"But it won't help." Hannah can barely hear Malik over the insane beeping. "We can't launch it in here."

"We don't need to launch it." She propels herself to her feet, forcing her body to do what she tells it. Her hand lands on something hard and spiky—the Reptar figure, lying on its side on the floor. Moving her head more than half an inch in either direction is agony. "We just need the seats."

"The seats?"

"*We gotta strap in!*" Hannah hurdles Corey, wanting to help, knowing that she needs to get Brendan. As she charges down the passage to the main deck, she can hear the beeping following her, the warning that, at any second, the hull might give way, turning the *Panda* inside out in under a tenth of a second.

Hold on, little ship. Just hold on.

Chapter 66

"They're in." Jack smacks the heel of his palm against the control console. "They're in!"

Roman grunts. He's at the opposite side of the bridge from Jack, entering the jump coordinates into one of the workstations. He's already pointed out the one that Jack needs to look after, the one to do with matter shielding. He tried to make the instructions for Jack as simple as possible: *Control the drift in the bubble using the two sticks below the display. Reticle in the centre.* God knows if the bastard is going to be able to follow them. It's a miracle he didn't get them killed on the crossing.

Adrift

How long has it been since they took the bridge? A minute? Two? Hayes and the other soldiers haven't blown the door, but there's plenty of noise on the other side of it. Either they're assembling the charges, or they're going to cut the door off at the point where it slides into the wall.

Roman looks over at Jack's screen, which is showing the inside of the *Victory*'s cargo bay. The *Panda* is a wreck, its hull smashed and scarred. The cargo bay doors are only just starting to close.

That's when he hears it: a crackling sizzle, like a hot frying pan dumped into a sink of cold water. Hayes and his team are cutting their way in, the torch parting the door along one side, a thin line of hot metal spitting sparks.

"Almost there," Jack shouts to Roman.

At that moment, a voice comes over the speakers in the ceiling. "Roman. This is Hayes." The speakers give his voice a very slight echo, deepen it. "I am giving you a direct order to surrender—you and the civilian. This is the *only* warning you will get."

"Whatever, fuckstick," Jack mutters.

"You should know," Hayes says, "I've sent my engineers down to astronautics. I've ordered them to manually restart the ship's AI. I don't know what's gotten into you, son, but you are about ten seconds away from losing it all. You understand me?"

The cargo bay doors have closed, the light above them turning green. Jack yells in triumph, slapping the console, then turning and dashing over to the workstation that controls the matter shielding. "We're good!" he shouts. "Do it Roman. Jump!"

Roman moves his hand towards the command option onscreen—and stops.

He can still finish the mission.

There's nothing to say he can't still have his revenge. He can work something out with Hayes; the civilians will be a problem, but they don't need to be killed. They can be held prisoner, kept out of the way until it's all over.

He can't help but see Madhu, and Brigita, and everyone else on the outpost. The rage flares up inside him. What is he thinking? He is a soldier, and this is his mission, and he has to finish it.

No. You gave Corey your word.

"What are you waiting for?" Jack yells at him. The cutting line is almost halfway to the bottom of the door.

One way or another, he's going to betray someone. He either lets Corey down—Corey and every other civilian on that ship—or he lets down the people who raised him. Madhu. Brigita. Everyone on Cassiopeia. Not to mention every one of his squadmates on the *Resolute*.

"Roman?" Jack says.

"I can't."

And, slowly, Roman lifts Mahmoud's gun, and points it at Jack's chest.

Chapter 67

Jack's hands go up. It's a reflex action. Out of his control. What he really wants to do is dive for cover, but his legs have stopped listening to him, and his bladder has started to send out another round of warning signals.

"I'm sorry," Roman says, walking slowly towards Jack. The gun hardly shakes at all.

For the second time, Jack tries to speak, can't do it. But there's a stupid look on Roman's face—determined and apologetic at the same time, and it's that that finally makes him open his mouth.

"Come on. You. We don't have to." He can't form sentences, can't even form thoughts. He takes a step towards Roman, his legs moving on their own.

"You don't understand. I can't do this to them."

"To who?" Jack almost screams the words, has to remind himself that Roman has a gun on him, and probably still has that hair trigger. Behind him, the cutting torch stops, a foot from the bottom of the door. The wielder adjusting his or her aim. They've got maybe twenty seconds.

"I have to finish it," Roman says, looking at Jack but sounding as if he's talking to himself. "I finish it, and everything will be fine."

"No, it won't. It won't, Roman. Listen to me."

"You don't understand."

"Sure I do." Jack is nodding furiously. They're closer now, no more than five feet apart. He knows if he gets too close, Roman will pull the trigger, but he can't think of anything else to do. "I know that there are people on that tour ship who're depending on you. You told them you'd help them."

"No. I'm sorry."

The cutting torch starts up again, tracking towards the bottom edge of the door.

The jump coordinates Corey gave them are still up on screen. Below it is a touch box, displaying the words JUMP CORE READY. Either Roman forgot to disable it, or doesn't think there's any point. Not that it matters. There's no way Roman is going to let him get close to the terminal.

"You gave him your word," he says. "Corey. The kid. You promised you'd help him. We *trusted* you."

"Don't talk to me about—"

"You want to shoot me? Go ahead." Jack is babbling now, not even sure of where he's going with this, just knowing he has to do something. "If it'll help you get right with your commander, then it's OK. I know I deserve it."

He swallows hard. "I let the captain die. Lorinda, too. She's on me. I didn't check to see if Seema was dead, and maybe I should have. So go right ahead and do it. But the people on the *Panda*?" He points to the screen, still showing the tourist ship. "They don't. Don't make them pay for our fuck-ups. They deserve to go home."

Roman's fingers flex on the gun's grip. "That's enough."

"You know who didn't keep their word? The goddamn Frontier. They were supposed to protect us. You want to be like them? These are the people you want to fight with?"

"They're doing the right thing." Roman all but snarls the words. "*We're* doing the—"

"No, you're not." A word explodes into Jack's mind—an old

347

one, a familiar one, one he always thought he could depend on. "No ethics!" he roars at Roman. "You've got no ethics!"

Roman's face creases in confused anger. "What are you talking ab—"

The bridge door is blown inwards into the room.

As it happens, Jack whips his still-raised hands forward, as if bringing them together in a clap. The heel of his right palm strikes the inside of Roman's wrist; the other, the back of the hand holding the gun. Just like Hector taught him.

Roman pulls the trigger.

If Jack hadn't yanked his head to the side, it would have come clean off. As it is, the gunshot occurs right by his ear, so loud that it's as if his head really has exploded. He pushes through it, driving forward with his shoulder. Roman almost stops him—Jack hasn't built up quite enough momentum—but he's a little off balance, and Jack slides past his right side.

JUMP CORE READY.

As the soldiers charge into the room, guns up, Jack sprints towards the terminal, hand outstretched, fingers brushing the screen.

There's a sound, like the world's biggest engine hitting the redline, and then Jack's vision blurs at the edges. His hand leaves an after-image in the air, hanging, ghost-like, over the console.

Before he even understands what he's doing, Jack is turning, moving towards the screen he started at. If he doesn't centre them inside the warp field, they'll tear apart. He can't count on Roman to do it, and there's every chance the soldiers will cut him down before he gets there. It doesn't matter. He's done all he can.

No human has ever seen the space around the ship during a jump. Any camera on the hull, even ones designed to pick up light outside the visible spectrum, comes back with nothing but darkness. For the most part, jumps are as calm and uneventful as a drive across a deserted highway.

Not this one.

This one nearly shakes Jack's bones out of his skin. The engine sound blocks out everything, so loud that it feels like his very eyeballs are vibrating.

Adrift

The entire bridge is shaking, the shutters groaning. And yet every move he makes feels slow, like he's mired in molasses. His vision is doubled, tripled, strange light flashing in and out at the corners of his eyes. He can see the screen, see the two control sticks. It's all right in front of him, and a million miles away.

As he finally—*finally*—reaches the console, his vision quits on him. For two or three seconds, or what feels like two or three seconds, there's nothing but darkness. Panic seizes him—but as soon as it does, he can see again, like nothing happened. He grabs the control sticks, holding on for dear life, trying to focus on the display.

Keep it in the centre. That's what Roman told him. He can't see the reticle. He knows it's there, just in front of him, but the screen appears to stretch as he looks at it, expanding to the size of a city block.

Around him, the *Victory* bucks and writhes, a toy in the grip of a giant. He yells Roman's name, but the only thing that answers him is static. He can't see the soldier, or any of the others, doesn't dare turn to look. What comes next is very simple. If Roman doesn't uphold his end of the deal, they'll never make it.

He spots the reticle, a tiny green circle. It's way too close to the edge of the display, still moving, inching towards it. With a dim horror, he realises that he doesn't know which stick to use. He didn't think to ask. He doesn't waste time debating it, pulling hard on both sticks.

The reticle slows, stops and starts to drift again. But before Jack can do anything, it's gathering speed, zipping across the display, vanishing into the distance, coming back, the world bending in strange directions, the reticle appearing at the opposite end of the display, even closer to the edge than it was before.

There's a tearing sound, the engine threatening to rip itself apart, the bridge around him coming to pieces. With what feels like every ounce of strength he has left, Jack pulls the sticks back. The reticle swings in a wide circle, doubling back on itself, tracking towards the centre. Jack gives a triumphant yell—only to have it turn into one of horror as a vibration rips him away from the screen, sending him hurtling across the bridge. As he stumbles away, he sees the reticle nearing the bottom edge of the screen.

The final vibration is the largest of all. Large enough to tear a hole in existence.

Chapter 68

The problem with living out near the edge of Austin is that there are only so many kids to be friends with.

If they aren't around—if, for example, one was on a family trip to Sigma and the other one had got himself grounded for some dumb reason or another, Allie Sultan couldn't remember what—there wasn't a whole lot to do.

She'd already read every book in her room, flicked through the feeds of the people at school (boys, boys, girls, holiday shots, stupid little animation meme thing, boys), ridden her hoverboard up and down the dusty street.

Now, she's sprawled in her front yard on her back, running her fingers through the dirt, looking up into the orange sky, watching the contrails of shuttles taking off from the downtown spaceport.

The house she lives in with her dad is a modest two-bedroom, a new-style lightbrick build, with its own recycler unit and a bottom floor entirely taken up with a large garage space. Other, identical houses close in tight on all sides, but round the back, open fields run all the way to the boundary fence of the vast mine dumps.

The creek bed, long since dried up, is just visible from her bedroom window if she really craned her neck. That was where she got the gnarly scar on her forehead, from that time she and Corey and Jamie built that ramp.

The scar peaks out from under her hairline, a jagged zigzag. She doesn't mind it. She thinks it looks kind of cool, even if it did take ages for the swelling to go down.

Allie is a short girl, dark-skinned, with slightly pudgy upper arms that she says are muscle, but which Jamie refuses to stop calling wobble fat. Allie punches him on the shoulder every time he says it, and, by now, she's convinced the bruise is more or less permanent.

She's wearing a pair of skate shorts and an old tank top, her favourite. She doesn't mind it getting messy. Without really thinking about it, she lifts a fistful of dirt, and chucks it into the air. It's caught by the hot breeze, swirled away.

She watches it go, her boredom getting heavier by the second. She's got to do something about this.

Maybe she can take the monorail over to Lagos Square. She's not supposed to go there by herself, and even when she goes with Jamie and Corey, she has to beg her dad to let her, but maybe he'll be nice about it this time. She could phone up Li from school, get her to come. They don't hang out much, but if Allie paid for the mono passes …

As she sits up, her ears pop.

It's a strange sensation, like the inside of her head is filling with water, changing the pressure. She put a finger in her right ear, trying to open it up, knowing it never works but not sure what else to do.

A second later, the sensation comes again, and this time it's so intense it actually hurts. Allie winces, getting to her feet. The air feels too still, the wind gone. Is it a storm? They get those sometimes, and they have to hide in the basement shelter that every house in Austin has to have by law. But there are no clouds in the sky, no hint of moisture. Her ears pop for the third time, insistent, making her blink in surprise.

Allie doesn't quite understand what happens next.

She's looking towards the mine dumps, not really seeing them, more concerned with the strange feeling in her head, when the sky goes hazy. It looks like the air just above the surface of a road on a really hot day, only it's everywhere. There's another pop, this one much louder, and it's coming from *outside* her head.

Then: *boom.*

The sound is one of the loudest she's ever heard, louder than a bomb. Half a second later, she's knocked head over heels by what feels like a tsunami of wind. There's a huge, distant crash, and a hissing rush as staggering volumes of dirt are displaced.

She rolls, arms flailing, yelping in shock. Behind her, the houses shake and shudder, threatening to tear loose from their foundations. Allie comes to a halt, dust swirling around her, coating her hair and face.

There's something suspended above the mine dumps, something that wasn't there before. A black shape, dropping towards the ground. And, at the edges of the shape, a glowing green corona of energy, spreading out like ripples in a pond.

It hits the ground, knocking several of the hills flat, sending up a giant mushroom cloud of dust and almost blowing out Allie's eardrums a second time with the impact. The air is suddenly filled with dust and dirt, the clear sky turning hazy.

Allie sits up, blinking. Her eyes are bright spots on a face caked with dirt. The house has turned red, the white lightbrick coated in thick dust. Allie sticks out her tongue, tastes dust in the air. By the time she gets to her feet, the sirens have started.

"Dad?" she calls. "I think you'd better come out here!"

Chapter 69

The first thing Corey Livingstone sees is a red star.

It drifts in front of him, lazy, too bright to look at directly. He tries to push away, knowing what it means, knowing what will happen if it gets too close to him. But when he tries to raise his arm, someone holds it down, the pressure gentle but firm.

"Easy," a woman's voice says. "Not quite done yet."

The red star is still there. It coaxes up memories from the darkness of his mind. Sigma. The *Red Panda*. The gate. Captain Volkova. Jack. Hannah. Lorinda. *Roman*.

Corey tries to sit up, wanting to talk, unable to get the words out. His throat is parched. The red star is a tiny light, on a robotic arm. The arm is hovering over him, making small, precise moves. It's as long as a man's, with a boxy cutting laser at its head.

The arm turns towards him, and Corey flinches. "Easy," the voice says again. "Take it slow. Your leg is going to be fine, but we're not done yet, 'K?"

Slowly, the space resolves itself. He's in what looks like a hospital room: clean white walls, neutral tile pattern on the floor, bright lights.

The robot arm is attached to a large, mobile control unit, parked by the bed, with two more arms hanging limp at its side. His lower half is covered with an opaque, curved shield, blocking his legs from view. There's an opening in the shield, a little further down, and as Corey watches, the arm dips into it, the laser humming to life. He can't feel a thing.

There's a woman by the bed whom he doesn't recognise. She's young, maybe in her twenties, with long brown hair and clean blue hospital scrubs.

"Broken bones," she says. As she does so, she looks over at something across the room, something that makes her crease her brow in a frown. "Plus you'd really done a number on your tibialis anterior," she says, sounding distracted. "Nano's're fixing that right up."

"Where am I?" Corey says.

She blinks at something on her lens. Corey feels the bed rise underneath him, lifting the top half of his body upwards. "Austin City General," she says. "East Wing. Now, we've numbed everything below the waist, so you won't feel anything for a little—"

"Thank you, nurse," says a voice from across the room. "That'll be all."

From his position on the raised bed, Corey looks over. There's a man sitting by the window—a man who looks familiar. He's in his sixties, clean-shaven, with salt-and-pepper hair and a friendly face. He's wearing a dark suit and a red tie, and as he meets Corey's eyes he gives him a big, wide smile.

"Welcome back to the land of the living," he says.

"Senator," says the nurse. "I'm not sure this is best for—"

"Oh, Mr. Livingstone here will be just fine." The man raises a hand, as if taking an oath. "He's a tough one. And I promise, if there's any problem at all, I know where the call button is." He winks at Corey. "Spent a day here last year. I was riding my bike and took a fall. Try the chocolate pudding, by the way—it looks nasty, but it's really good."

"Yeah," Corey says, nodding in agreement, though he has no idea why. The man looks familiar, although he can't place him yet.

The nurse wavers, then nods. "All right." She puts a hand on Corey's shoulder. "You're sure you're up to it?"

In a daze, Corey nods again. The nurse tells him she'll be close by, and then makes her way out. The robot arm retracts from its position over his legs, whirring and clicking, and a section of the shield slides shut.

Suddenly, Corey remembers where he knows the man from. "You're my mom's boss."

"Indeed I am." The man's accent is thick southern Texas. "Tom Daniels. It's great to finally meet you, Corey. Your mommy's told me a lot about you."

Corey says nothing. Part of him is still convinced that he's back on the *Red Panda*, that all of this is a dream.

"I'm glad you made it out," the man says, clapping his hands on his knees and rising to his feet. He walks over to stand by Corey's bed—he's taller than Corey first thought, with the big shoulders of a football player. "Sounds like you had quite an adventure."

"Um. Yeah. I mean …" Corey's eyes suddenly go wide. "My mom. My dad! Are they—"

Daniels lifts his hands. "Fine. They're fine. A little beat up, but no permanent damage. They're here, too. I haven't seen them yet, but the nurses tell me they're all OK. That's one hell of a landing you folks pulled off."

"Can you call them?" Corey can't believe the relief flowing through him. They made it. *They made it.*

"In a minute. Something we gotta hash out first."

With a grunt, Daniels reaches behind him, pulling the chair

across the floor. It makes a screeching sound that hurts Corey's ears. The senator sits down in it, breathing a sigh of relief, as if being on his feet had tired him out. Corey watches him, suddenly wary.

"Now, Corey," Daniels says. "You'll probably have a lot of people wanting to talk to you about all this. Feed reporters. Your friends. Folks you meet at the grocery store. And my guess is you'll want to tell them quite a story."

He gives Corey another kindly smile. "But I wanted to ask you, as someone who knows your mommy pretty well, I wanted to ask you to keep things to yourself for now."

"... Why?"

"Well, it's a little complicated." Daniels folds his hands in his lap. "A lot of people died out at Sigma. I'm sure you probably know that. We have to figure out who they all were, and tell their families. And we don't know exactly what happened, either—why the station got attacked like it did."

"But we do." Corey tries to sit up higher, wincing as he finally feels a thin darning needle of pain wind its way up from his leg. "One of our own ships—"

"I know." Daniels isn't smiling any more. "We're aware the ship you came in on was one of our ... projects. We're going to be looking closely at this whole situation to make sure it never happens again. But if you go telling everybody about it before we do, people will jump to conclusions. It'll hold things up at our end, make it harder for us to figure out what's what."

He lowers his voice, and Corey has to strain to hear him. "You understand what I'm saying?"

"I ..."

"I need you to be strong for me now, Corey." Daniels leans in. "I need you to tell this to your mommy, and your daddy. And your friends Hannah and Jack, and your brother. I'll be talking to them, too, but I need you to back me up on this. It's really important. Can you do that for me? Can you—"

From the door, Anita Livingstone says, "*Get away from our son.*"

Corey's head turns so fast that he almost strains a muscle in his neck. His mom and dad are striding into the room, his mom in the lead. She's got a massive black eye, and there are stitches on her lower lip, but she's OK. *She's OK.*

His dad looks just as beat up, limping slightly. It makes Corey think of the story his mom told them, of how they met. Both of them, Corey sees, are wearing blue hospital gowns.

And behind them: Malik. And Hannah. And Jack. All of them.

Corey's joy fades when he sees the expression on his mom's face. He's never seen her this angry. In seconds, she's between Daniels and the bed, his dad, too. The senator steps back, giving them room. They're *all* messed up. Jack's arm is in a sleek white cast, and Hannah is wearing a thick neck brace. With a start, he realises Roman isn't there. Did he make it? Is he in the hospital?

Malik appears on the other side of the bed, staring in horror at the shield over his brother's leg. He seems OK, even if he looks a little lame in the thin gown he's wearing. Before Corey can ask about Roman, he says, "They fix your leg? You gonna be OK?" His voice is breathless, almost panicked.

"I think so," Corey says. Malik wavers for a second, then all but throws himself on top of his brother, pulling into a huge, rough hug. Corey wants to ask about Roman, but Malik is hugging him so hard that he can't speak.

"They took my holo," Malik says, his words muffled by Corey's shoulder. "I don't know where it is."

For some reason, that scares Corey more than anything. And there's so much he wants to know. Not just about Roman—what happened to the other two attack ships? Where's Brendan? What's going to happen to him? Thinking of him and Seema makes Corey think of Lorinda, and Volkova, and he feels a knife twisting in his gut.

He's brought back when he hears his dad's angry voice. "Don't you ever talk to our kids," Everett says. "Not ever. Understand me?"

"Anita," Daniels says, smiling broadly. "Mr. Livingstone. And this must be Malik." He looks over at the other two. "And let me see ... Ms. Elliott and Mr. Tennant, right? I'm Tom Daniels. It's a pleasure to—"

"We know who you are," Hannah says. There's no warmth in

her voice. She walks around to stand next to Everett, forming a protective wall between Corey and the senator. Jack starts to fold his arms, forgetting that one is immobilised. He does it anyway, jamming the free arm in awkwardly.

"Well, that's good." Daniels doesn't seem bothered by Hannah's tone. "And I'm glad you're all here. I was just talking to Corey about the need for discretion."

"Discretion?" Jack says the word like it tastes bad.

"Indeed." The senator rocks on his heels, clasping his hands behind his back. "There needs to be a full Senate inquiry, and, until that's been completed, I want to be sure we're all on the same page regarding speaking to the feeds." He turns to Jack. "I'm afraid that includes you, Mr. Tennant. You'll need to—"

"Cut the shit," Jack says.

The room falls silent.

"You ordered the attack on the Sigma Station," Anita says. "You wanted to dissolve the treaty. Everything that happened ... it was you."

Chapter 70

Anita reaches back for Corey, not looking at him, but finding his hand anyway. He grips it tight.

"Anita." Daniels sounds wounded. "That's a very serious accusation. And as you're still one of my employees—"

"Not any more. I quit. As of ten minutes ago."

Daniels sighs, as if he knew that was coming. "I'm sorry to hear that, and I hope you'll reconsider once you're less emotional."

"Excuse me?" says Hannah.

The senator ignores her. "As it is, I'm not going to stand for you accusing me like that, without any evidence."

"See, that's the thing," Anita says.

She lets go of Corey's hand, taking a step towards the senator, who still doesn't move. His expression is grave, but there's a look in his eyes that wasn't there before. A wariness.

"The whole time we were out there, I kept thinking. Who would want to overturn the treaty? Who had the most to gain?" She jabs a finger at Daniels' chest. "And then I realised. It took me a long damn time, but I figured it out."

"Careful," says Daniels.

Anita ignores him. "How many times have you talked about how you'd like to change the treaty? How many times did you tell us that we weren't working hard enough? That we needed to find loopholes in the wording? You fought harder than anyone to get it changed so we'd have more territory. It just took me a little while to figure it out."

"Anita, listen to yourself." Daniels reaches out to her, and Everett knocks his arm away. The senator looks at him in mild astonishment.

"I should have seen it a lot sooner," Anita says, shaking her head. Her voice is strained, as if she's about to start crying. "How could you do that? All those people ..."

"This is absurd," Daniels says. "You're jumping to conclusions based on ... what, me doing my job? As a Frontier senator? Looking after our interests? Now, I know you've been through a lot, and you're probably in shock. I'm willing to forgive this outburst, but I should warn you that—"

"Commander Richard Hayes," Jack says.

Daniels glances at him, irritated. "I beg your pardon?"

"He was in charge of the rescue mission for your boys on the *Resolute*. Came in on, what was it, the *Victory*?" He shrugs. "Didn't say much, but I caught his name. Even then, I didn't think much of it until I told Anita here."

"That's what sold it for me," Anita says. Everett grabs her free hand, and she holds on tight. "You and Hayes go way back, don't you? All the way to the Frontier Officer's Academy. Spoken at some of your fundraisers, from what I recall. And I've seen him around the office plenty of times. My guess is that you two cooked this up together—after all, if we went back to war, you'd both get your piece. So when the *Resolute* didn't come back on schedule, Hayes himself went to check it out. He'd want to make sure it was done right."

Daniels is smiling to himself, slowly shaking his head.

"You forget," Anita says. "I've worked with you a long time, Tom. I know when you're lying."

In the silence that follows, Corey could swear the temperature of the room drops ten degrees. He's still trying to process everything that's just happened. But what he focuses on is his mom and dad. Standing together, holding hands. Both wanting the same thing.

"It's still just conjecture," Daniels says. "You don't exactly have a smoking gun, do you?"

"Maybe not," Jack says. "But we plan to tell everyone what we know."

Hannah gives him a sharp look. He ignores her.

"They'll join the dots we can't," Everett tells Daniels. "Dig up some more evidence—because, believe me, it's out there. Hope you got a good lawyer, Senator."

"Damn right," Malik says.

Daniels sighs a second time. "I was hoping it wouldn't come to this."

He reaches in the pocket of his jacket, and pulls out a folded sheet of paper, handing it to Anita. She takes it reluctantly, like it's poisoned, unfolding it.

"Copies have been forwarded to your individual inboxes," Daniels says. "I suggest you read it closely."

"What is it?" Jack cranes forward to look.

The senator smiles that kindly smile again. "Gag order. Effective in all known territories. Got it signed off this morning, and believe me when I say you don't want to mess with this one. Any statement made to any unauthorised individual lines you up for a treason charge. All records of your trip are now property of the Frontier."

His eyes meet Anita's. "As I said, I'd hoped we could avoid this. You're an intelligent woman, Anita. You would have made an excellent senator yourself one day."

Anita reads the paper, mouth moving silently, a look of dismay on her face. Hannah, Jack and Everett crowd around her. Only Malik stays where he is, fists bunched at his sides.

"I'll leave you to talk it over," Daniels said, giving Corey a friendly nod as he walks past the bed. "It's good to have you all back. I hope you'll cooperate fully with our investigation."

"You can't possibly think you can cover this up," Jack says. "How many people saw us jump in out of nowhere?"

"You really don't get it, do you?" Daniels says, buttoning his suit jacket. "You think you made a big entrance, and it'll be news, all right. For a time. But it'll also be easy to explain away. A military scientific programme, unintended consequences, untested technology. The conspiracy theorists'll have a field day, but nobody listens to them.

"Oh, I have no doubt they'll do their damnedest to connect Sigma to what happened to you. Probably get pretty close, too. But, see ..." He absently shoots a cuff, the sad smile still on his face. "By the time we're done, the whole thing will be so drawn out and complicated and buried in legalities that nobody'll know *what* happened. And I'm pretty sure none of you are willing to risk life in prison to tell them."

His eyes land on Corey's brother. "How about it, Malik? Ready to go to jail in LunarMax? That's what'll happen if you folks fuck with me."

He walks away, leaving them huddled around the bed. Corey's head falls back on the pillow. He's never heard the phrase *gag order*, but he can figure it out. How could this happen? After everything they'd gone through, it's going to be like it never happened.

"Huh," Hannah says. "That's funny."

Daniels opens the door to the ward. "What is?" he says, not looking over his shoulder.

Corey watches Hannah take the piece of paper from Anita, lifting it to her face. "The date and time this was signed off. It's only a couple of hours ago. You must have done it before you came to see us."

Daniels fiddles with his watch—gold, with a big, chunky dial. "What about it?"

Adrift

"Well, the thing is," Hannah says, "Sigma Destination Tours provides its passengers with kind of an interesting service."

She folds the paper up. "Did you know that anybody who takes a Sigma tour can upload any photos or video they have to the Frontier Public History Archives? All they have to do is log on."

"So what?" Now Daniels sounds annoyed. "Anything you got is Frontier property. Or did you not hear me?"

"As of two hours ago, sure. But we uploaded everything we had when we first arrived above Austin, so about—" She glances at Everett, who says, "*Ten* hours ago. Give or take."

Daniels looks between them, that same sad smile back on his face. This time, at least to Corey, he looks a little worried.

"What are you talking about?" he says.

"You should see the video Malik here shot," Jack says. "He did a really good job."

"I had the *Panda* queue it for upload before we made the jump," says Hannah. "It would have sent the files the second we came back into signal range. They're on the public archives right now." She nudges Jack. "Hey—how long do you think it'll take before someone realises what they're looking at?"

"Not long." Anita's eyes are shiny with tears, but her voice is steady and even.

Daniels doesn't look friendly any more. He looks like he wants to kill them.

"It doesn't change a damn thing," he says. "That footage is still Frontier property. All of it. We'll just delete it off the server. Any one of my people could handle that."

Hannah purses her lips. "Delete it off the server. That's cute. Senator, let me tell you something about historians. We don't trust people like you. You're not the first person to try change the records, and you definitely won't be the last. The archives are publicly run. Always have been. They're held across hundreds of thousands of different computers in this system. You'd have to issue an awful lot of gag orders."

"You have no idea, the resources I have ..."

"I'm sure you do. But it only takes one person to download it, and it'll be out there. Not to mention Sigma Tours themselves. I'm pretty sure they have an office planet-side, and they're probably freaking out trying to understand what happened. They might be scrolling through the archives right now."

"Don't forget the journalists," Jack says.

"Oh yeah. Them, too. Who knows where they've been looking?"

"And other tourists, of course. Ones who don't know what happened to Sigma yet."

"It *is* a good idea to do plenty of research before a big trip," Everett says.

Daniels has gone white. Hannah lifts her chin, her eyes meeting his. Despite the neck brace, she looks, to Corey, like she's ten feet tall.

"You'd better think of a good story," she says. "You're going to need it."

Chapter 71

Titan, Hannah's home moon, has several huge banks of artificial sunlights in its dome colony. Plenty of people complain about them, saying they're too hot, or that the plants don't grow quite right. Hannah's never minded them much, but she has to admit: they'll never beat the real thing.

She tilts her head back as far as her flexible brace will allow, reclining on the wooden bench in the hospital garden, eyes closed. The sunlight turns the inside of her lids a warm gold. No, the real thing is much, much better. Hannah basks in it, stretching her arms out.

Oh, yeah.

She's in the central courtyard of the hospital wing: a small space with benches and a few hardy succulents, pushing up through soil in regimented flowerbeds. There's a half-hearted fountain in the centre, its pool dry, the spout silent.

Adrift

They've been in Austin City General for two days, and she can't believe she only found this place an hour ago. Then again, it took an age to persuade the doctors and nurses that, yes, the nanomeds were working, and, yes, her neck felt better. They wouldn't let her take the brace off, but at least they let her walk around outside the wards.

Hannah opens her eyes. A patient in a hoverchair—an older man, completely bald—passes her on the other side of the court-yard, a nurse keeping pace alongside him. He spots Hannah, and smiles.

She returns it, feeling kind of bad; for the past couple of days, the entire hospital has been locked down. Only patients, doctors and nurses were allowed—they only opened up the visitors' lists this morning.

It's not hard to see why. The streets outside the hospital are rammed with vehicles from what looks like every feed in existence. Hannah spent a few minutes watching some of them this morning, staring with bemused fascination as they showed endless shots of the front of the hospital, at their own photos superimposed on the footage.

There's an airspace blackout around the building, so they haven't got any drone cameras up above—just as well, or the nurses would never have let Hannah come outside—but that hasn't stopped them from trying.

The only time they cut away from the hospital is to show footage of the destroyed *Victory*, sticking up from the shattered mine dumps like an ancient monolith. Oh, and Tom Daniels, looking harassed, surrounded by secret service. Hannah doesn't know if they're arresting him, or protecting him. Right now, she doesn't much care.

The Belarus Treaty renegotiations, it appears, are on indefinite hold.

Volkova, Seema and Lorinda were taken from the *Panda*—Hannah doesn't really want to think about their funerals, especially Volkova's.

Brendan is in the hospital, too, under police guard. Hannah doesn't know who told the cops about him—Anita, maybe. She heard one of the doctors talking about a special prosecutor coming in from Mars. Whoever that is, they'll have their hands full. The soldiers from the *Victory*—Hayes included—are in the other wing of the hospital, under military protection.

Hannah had a dream the night before, after she finally drifted off to sleep in her uncomfortable hospital bed, that the soldiers stormed the wards, taking care of the survivors from the *Panda*, moving in darkness, eliminating them with double-tap shots. She woke up sweating, the brace clammy against her neck.

No one knows where Roman is. He wasn't among the crash survivors, or the bodies.

They may have to wait a little longer. There was a big argument about letting authorised visitors in to see people in the hospital, Anita and Everett going back and forth with the hospital administrators, standing side by side in the corridor. The last Hannah had heard, the panicked hospital CEO had been telling them he'd get it in motion.

She hopes they figure it out before her parents and her sister get here.

She spoke to them a few hours ago. They'd just come through the Lunar jump station, and were waiting for their transport planetside. The transmission was glitchy, the station signal pixelating their faces.

Hannah had told herself she wouldn't cry, but of course she did, almost as much as her mom and dad. Callie had remained dry-eyed, but she looked like she'd aged ten years in ten hours.

Seeing her family had made Hannah's gut clench up—as if they were going to be taken away from her, as if she was still back on the *Panda* and this was just another dream. As if a metal sphere was going to come hurtling towards them, obliterating them where they stood. It didn't, and Hannah can't wait for them to get here. Can't wait to hug Callie, and her mom, and feel her dad's stubble rasp past her cheek as she wraps her arms around him.

She doesn't remember a lot of what they talked about. It was a mess of *what-the-hell-happened* and *how-could-they-do-this* and *please-tell-us-you're-OK*. But she keeps coming back to one part of the conversation, when they'd all mostly calmed down.

Adrift

Callie still looked like she was forty years old, some of the life had come back into her. "So what are you going to do?" she'd asked Hannah. "'Cos I don't think the tour guide thing worked out."

Hannah had smiled at that. And she'd been on the verge of answering, about to tell them that the plan was the same, that she was still going to go and get a job in a museum and work towards being a curator, somehow.

The story was so familiar that she knew every beat of it without thinking. She'd even been bracing herself for the tight smiles, the neutral "Oh" from her mom, Callie's indifference, her dad's concern. But just before she started speaking, Hannah decided that she didn't feel like dealing with it any more.

"I don't know," she told them. "I'll figure it out."

Callie had nodded, told her they'd see her soon. Whenever *that* would be. They'd have to find a place to stay in Austin, and she'd have to get their names onto the visitors' list ... would she be able to leave with them? Her neck didn't hurt nearly as much now, and technically she wasn't a prisoner, so—

"OK if I join you?"

Hannah looks up, squinting against the sunlight. It's Jack. Like her, he's dressed in one of those ridiculous hospital gowns, the sash around the waist cinched tight. She'd heard him griping to the nurse earlier, asking her why he couldn't have some proper pants.

Back on the *Panda*, she would have leapt at the chance to get as far away from him as she could. She still feels that way, a little. But the sun is warm, and her family is on the way, and she didn't die a horrible death in the vacuum of space. All things considered, she's in a pretty good mood. And he *did* help save them.

"Sure," she says.

He nods thanks, lowering himself to the bench. His arm, she sees, is still in a cast, albeit a more flexible one. He must be healing, too, the bone-repair nanos doing their work.

"I don't know if you heard," he says.

"Heard what?"

"About Brendan and Seema's kid."

For a moment, she has absolutely no idea what he's talking about. Then she remembers.

"Brendan made a deal," he says. "He'd talk about the Roses Cartel if they'd get his son back. Apparently they had him in an apartment block in Acedalia. Cops raided the place, managed to get him out OK."

"Oh." She doesn't quite know how to respond to that. She *should* be happy, but, right now, it all feels as remote as Sigma itself. "That's good," she says, after a long moment.

"Got that right," he mutters. He shifts on the bench, looking uncomfortable. "Well, maybe not good for the kid. Not when your mom and dad are … you know."

"Glad he's OK." Hannah can't think of anything else to say.

"Right. Right. You … ah, you healing up?"

"I think so. The doc says I can get the brace off this afternoon. How about you?"

"'Bout the same."

"That's good."

They fall silent. It's not a comfortable silence either. Jack, Hannah suspects, is the kind of person with whom silences would never be comfortable.

"So what are you going to do next?" she says. She's not sure if she really wants to know, but she hasn't any idea what else to say.

He puffs out his cheeks. "Write about what happened, I guess. Maybe a book. I dunno."

"Yeah, that'd probably be—"

"I mean the whole story is pretty much out there already, so I need to find a new angle on it. One everybody doesn't know already."

"Isn't the angle that you were actually there? You saw it happen?"

"Well, yeah." He looks annoyed, as if he's regretting telling her his plans.

Before she can say anything, he turns on the bench, shifting towards her. "Listen, I wanted to ask you …"

"Yes?"

He doesn't say anything for a few seconds. He hasn't shaved,

Adrift

Hannah realises, and his stubble is starting to go from a shadow to a beard.

"The whole thing with the captain," Jack says. "I shouldn't have … I mean, I didn't know it would get so—"

"Seema killed the captain," Hannah says. "Seema, and Brendan. They were the ones who brought the knife on board."

With this, she knows what to say. She's spent plenty of time thinking about it. Jack was an idiot, but, in the end, he wasn't the one who murdered Volkova. He's been through enough, and she isn't going to make his life hell. Not after they actually made it out.

Jack opens his mouth to say something, then closes it again. He looks down at the ground, unwilling to meet her eyes.

"… Thank you," he says.

Hannah doesn't respond. On the other side of the garden, a bird lands—a little brown one, the kind that you always see around Earth cities, pecking at a bright green cactus. Hannah can just hear the hubbub from the crowds outside the hospital, drifting in on the warm breeze.

"What about you?" Jack asks her.

"Huh?"

"What are you going to do? When this is all over?"

She's about to tell him that she doesn't know. But she's had plenty of time to think about that, too, since she spoke to Callie and her parents. They're probably not going to like her answer, but that's just tough.

"I think I might go to pilot's school," she says.

"You're kidding."

"Not really." A smile spreads across her face. "Go into the Navy. Fly commercial. I don't know yet."

"Wow." He nods. "That's … wow." He looks up at the sky, eyes narrowed against the glare. "Well, I'd say you've passed the entry exam."

Hannah actually laughs. She didn't know if she still could.

"You know Corey wants to do that too, right?" Jack says.

"Kind of hard to miss."

"You should tell him. He'll get a kick out of—"

He stops, interrupted by loud voices from the glass-walled

passage across the courtyard, drifting through the open door. A man is shouting, trying to push his way past one of the nurses, who is loudly telling him that he's not supposed to be there, and is he on the visitors' list anyway?

"*Eu tenho um direito!*" the man shouts. There's something odd about the way he's walking, his legs slightly too stiff.

"Sir!"

"*Deixe-me passar. Fora do caminho!*"

She turns to Jack, intending to ask him if he'd heard anything about visitors being allowed in yet, but he's no longer paying attention to her. He's staring at the commotion, his mouth slightly open, a look of absolute confusion on his face.

"Sir, I can't understand you. If you would just—"

"Get out the damn way," the man says, switching to English. "I need to see him!"

He glances into the courtyard as he pushes past the nurse, and Hannah gets a look at him for the first time. He's around Jack's age, with salt-and-pepper hair and a thin, bony body under a green shirt and jeans. The shirt hangs off him, slightly too big. And, again, Hannah notices his gait: jerky, limping.

The man sees Jack, and comes to an abrupt halt.

"Friend of yours?" Hannah says.

Jack doesn't respond. His mouth is still open. Slowly, he rises off the bench. The man steps through the door, suddenly hesitant, ignoring the angry nurse behind him, who is threatening to call security.

Jack says something that is half a breath, half a word. No, not just a word. A name, one Hannah hasn't heard before. *Hec.*

"Jack?" Hannah asks.

"Um. Yeah." Jack doesn't even look at her. "I'll ... I'll call you."

As Hannah watches, he starts walking towards the strange man. They meet a few feet from the door. The man starts to say something, but, as Hannah watches, Jack puts his arms around him. They rock back and forth, holding onto each other tight, like there's nothing else in the entire world but them.

Soon, she'll be able to do that. She can hug her family, hold them close. Everything after that ...

Well. She'll figure it out.

She tilts her head back again, letting the sun splash across her face.

Chapter 72

Corey's hospital room is actually pretty sweet. It's got its own flatscreen, embedded in one wall. He's already linked it to his lens, which somehow survived everything that happened to him. There's a big window, which can turn frosted or dark at the touch of a button. The room is on the tenth floor, and looks out onto the central courtyard.

The young doctor with the brown hair moved him here after she was done with his leg, although she insisted on keeping the shield up for the time being. "Don't want another infection setting in," she told him, as she positioned his hovering bed. "I'll take it off in the morning."

When he asked her how he was supposed to pee, she gave him an evil grin. "The shield's taking care of that, too," she said. He thought that was kind of gross, but he didn't push it.

He had other stuff to think about.

They eventually let visitors in. Jamie and Allie wanted to know everything. Then they wanted him to tell it a second time. And then Allie told the story about how their arrival had knocked her flat, and both of them wanted to know when he was getting out. He wanted to tell them how scary it all was, how it wasn't just some amazing adventure, but he couldn't find the words.

And then Mal came back, and his parents, and they talked until they couldn't talk any more. His mom and dad told them that they might have to go to court, that there would probably be quite a few lawyers who wanted to talk to them.

His mom had got real serious when she said this, real quiet, like she was expecting an argument. She didn't get one. Corey and Malik, for what was maybe the first time ever, both said yes in unison. For Corey, it was enough that his dad was holding his mom's hand tight. That he didn't let go. That his mom wouldn't let him.

They watched a feed for a while on the big flatscreen, and he found he was too tired to make sense of any of it. His brain felt like it's leaking out of his ears.

At some point, he fell asleep. When he woke up, the sun outside the window had almost set, the last of the light making him squint.

The room is empty. Quiet. The flatscreen off, the lights turned low. There's an old-fashioned paper notepad on the side table. Malik has written a message for him. HOPE YOU DON'T HAVE TO PEE IN THE NIGHT :-)

He smiles, putting the pad back on the table. There's another note, this one a folded piece of paper with his name on it. It's from his mom, her neat handwriting telling him that they love him, and that they'll get him some actual clothes soon. "Pants are gone," she's written. "They had to cut them off (sorry!) but we can get some new ones."

Now that he's alone, without everyone around him, his brain has calmed down a little. Enough to wonder some more about what's going to happen next.

He knows he can't just pick up where he left off. How is he going to be able to go back to school? Is he still going to be able to hang out with Jamie and Allie? He knows what they've done— what they found out—is big. Like, *really* big. Like the kind of thing that changes the world. The whole Frontier. Not to mention the Colonies. It's like his mom said—there are going to be lawyers, and court people, and who knows what else.

After a while, he puts the note back on the table. The clothes his mom mentioned are piled neatly on it, his T-shirt folded on top, his shoes poking out from underneath. He's about to lie back on the bed when he stops, looks more closely.

There's something poking out from underneath his T-shirt. Something he doesn't recognise. A piece of tattered grey fabric.

Corey frowns. He picks up the touchpad, raising the top half of the bed as high as it will go. Then he leans over, wincing as his muscles take the strain. He can't quite get to his T-shirt, his fingers just touching it, trying to pull it towards him. If only the shield wasn't locked in place ...

He snags it between finger and thumb, gently pulls it towards him. A few moments later, he has the mysterious fabric in his hand. He lifts it out, eyes huge.

It's a patch, torn from an item of clothing. A red and black patch with crossed daggers, the details picked out in crude stitching.

Roman's patch.

Startled, Corey looks around the room, as if expecting the soldier to be standing right there. Nothing. It's empty. Silent, and dark. Somewhere distant, he can hear a voice making an announcement through a speaker, the words inaudible behind the closed door.

Corey leans back, holding the patch against his chest, looking out of the window. He stays that way until sleep finally takes him again, and the sun is long gone behind the buildings.

ADRIFT

Writer: Rob Boffard
Editors: Anna Jackson, James Long, Bradley Englert
Agent: Ed Wilson
Copy-editor: Richard Collins
Cover design: Charlotte Stroomer
Publisher: Tim Holman
Managing editor: Joanna Kramer
Marketing: Sophie Fegan
Publicity: Nazia Khatun, Ellen Wright
Russian translations: Kristine Kalnina
Portuguese translations: Gennaro Indiveri
Medical advice: Prof. Ken Boffard, Dr. Vee Boffard
Early readers: Nicole Simpson, George Kelly, Chris Ellis, Dane
Taylor, Rayne Taylor, Ida Horwitz, Ryan Beyer, Werner Schutz,
Taryn Arentsen Schutz, Kristine Kalnina

Thanks to our families and friends. Special thanks to booksellers
and reviewers worldwide. Extra special thanks to you.

For access to exclusive stories, artwork and deleted scenes
(and to score a free audiobook), head to tiny.cc/boffard.

extras

orbit

meet the author

ROB BOFFARD is a South African author who splits his time between London, Vancouver, and Johannesburg. He has worked as a journalist for over a decade, and has written articles for publications in more than a dozen countries, including the *Guardian* and *Wired* in the UK.

if you enjoyed
ADRIFT
look out for

A BIG SHIP AT THE EDGE OF THE UNIVERSE
The Salvagers: Book One

by

Alex White

Furious and fun, the first book in this bold, new science fiction adventure series follows a ragtag group of adventurers as they try to find a legendary ship that just might be the key to clearing their name and saving the universe.

Boots Elsworth was a famous treasure hunter in another life, but now she's washed up. She makes her meager living faking salvage legends and selling them to the highest bidder, but this time she got something real—the story of the Harrow, a famous warship, capable of untold destruction.

extras

Nilah Brio is the top driver in the Pan-Galactic Racing Federation and the darling of the racing world—until she witnesses Mother murder a fellow racer. Framed for the murder and on the hunt to clear her name, Nilah has only one lead: the killer also hunts Boots.

On the wrong side of the law, the two women board a smuggler's ship that will take them on a quest for fame, for riches, and for justice.

CHAPTER ONE

D.N.F.

The straight opened before the two race cars: an oily river, speckled yellow by the evening sun. They shot down the tarmac in succession like sapphire fish, streamers of wild magic billowing from their exhausts. They roared toward the turn, precision movements bringing them within centimeters of one another.

The following car veered to the inside. The leader attempted the same.

Their tires only touched for a moment. They interlocked, and sheer torque threw the leader into the air. Jagged chunks of duraplast glittered in the dusk as the follower's car passed underneath, unharmed but for a fractured front wing. The lead race car came down hard, twisting eruptions of elemental magic spewing from its wounded power unit. One of its tires exploded into a hail of spinning cords, whipping the road.

In the background, the other blue car slipped away down the chicane—Nilah's car.

The replay lost focus and reset.

The crash played out again and again on the holoprojection in front of them, and Nilah Brio tried not to sigh. She had seen plenty of wrecks before and caused more than her share of them.

"Crashes happen," she said.

"Not when the cars are on the same bloody team, Nilah!"

Claire Asby, the Lang Autosport team principal, stood at her mahogany desk, hands folded behind her back. The office looked less like the sort of ultramodern workspace Nilah had seen on other teams and more like one of the mansions of Origin, replete with antique furniture, incandescent lighting, stuffed big-game heads (which Nilah hated), and gargantuan landscapes from planets she had never seen. She supposed the decor favored a pale woman like Claire, but it did nothing for Nilah's dark brown complexion. The office didn't have any of the bright, human-centric design and ergonomic beauty of her home, but team bosses had to be forgiven their eccentricities—especially when that boss had led them to as many victories as Claire had.

Her teammate, Kristof Kater, chuckled and rocked back on his heels. Nilah rolled her eyes at the pretty boy's pleasure. They should've been checking in with the pit crews, not wasting precious time at a last-minute dressing down.

The cars hovering over Claire's desk reset and moved through their slow-motion calamity. Claire had already made them watch the footage a few dozen times after the incident: Nilah's car dove for the inside and Kristof moved to block. The incident had cost her half her front wing, but Kristof's track weekend had ended right there.

"I want you both to run a clean race today. I am begging you to bring those cars home intact at all costs."

Nilah shrugged and smiled. "That'll be fine, provided Kristof follows a decent racing line."

"We were racing! I made a legal play and the stewards sided with me!"

Nilah loved riling him up; it was far too easy. "You were slow, and you got what you deserved: a broken axle and a bucket of tears. I got a five-second penalty," she winked before continuing, "which cut into my thirty-three-second win considerably."

Claire rubbed the bridge of her nose. "Please stop acting like children. Just get out there and do your jobs."

Nilah held back another jab; it wouldn't do to piss off the team boss right before a drive. Her job was to win races, not meetings.

Silently she and Kristof made their way to the door, and he flung it open in a rare display of petulance. She hadn't seen him so angry in months, and she reveled in it. After all, a frazzled teammate posed no threat to her championship standings.

They made their way through the halls from Claire's exotic wood paneling to the bright white and anodized blues of Lang Autosport's portable palace. Crew and support staff rushed to and fro, barely acknowledging the racers as they moved through the crowds. Kristof was stopped by his sports psychologist, and Nilah muscled past them both as she stepped out into the dry heat of Gantry Station's Galica Speedway.

Nilah had fired her own psychologist when she'd taken the lead in this year's Driver's Crown.

She crossed onto the busy parking lot, surrounded by the bustle of scooter bots and crews from a dozen teams. The bracing rattle of air hammers and the roar of distant crowds in the grandstands were all the therapy she'd need to win. The Driver's Crown was so close—she could clench it in two races, especially if Kristof went flying off the track again.

"Do you think this is a game?" Claire's voice startled her. She'd come jogging up from behind, a dozen infograms swimming around her head, blinking with reports on track conditions and pit strategy.

"Do I think racing is a game? I believe that's the very definition of sport."

Claire's vinegar scowl was considerably less entertaining than Kristof's anger. Nilah had been racing for Claire since the junior leagues. She'd probably spent more of her teenage years with her principal than her own parents. She didn't want to disappoint Claire, but she wouldn't be cowed, either. In truth, the incident galled her—the crash was nothing more than a callow attempt by Kristof to hold her off for another lap. If she'd lost the podium, she would've called for his head, but he got what he deserved.

They were a dysfunctional family. Nilah and Kristof had been racing together since childhood, and she could remember plenty of happy days trackside with him. She'd been ecstatic when they both joined Lang; it felt like a sign that they were destined to win.

But there could be only one Driver's Crown, and they'd learned the hard way the word "team" meant nothing among the strongest drivers in the Pan-Galactic Racing Federation. Her friendship with Kristof was long dead. At least her fondness for Claire had survived the transition.

"If you play dirty with him today, I'll have no choice but to create some consequences," said Claire, struggling to keep up with Nilah in heels.

Oh, please. Nilah rounded the corner of the pit lane and marched straight through the center of the racing complex, past the offices of the race director and news teams. She glanced back at Claire who, for all her posturing, couldn't hide her worry.

"I never play dirty. I win because I'm better," said Nilah. "I'm not sure what your problem is."

"That's not the point. You watch for him today, and mind yourself. This isn't any old track."

Nilah got to the pit wall and pushed through the gate onto the starting grid. The familiar grip of race-graded asphalt on her shoes sent a spark of pleasure up her spine. "Oh, I know all about Galica."

The track sprawled before Nilah: a classic, a legend, a warrior's track that had tested the mettle of racers for a hundred years. It showed its age in the narrow roadways, rendering overtaking difficult and resulting in wrecks and safety cars—and increased race time. Because of its starside position on Gantry Station, ambient temperatures could turn sweltering. Those factors together meant she'd spend the next two hours slow-roasting in her cockpit at three hundred kilometers per hour, making thousands of split-second, high-stakes decisions.

This year brought a new third sector with more intricate corners and a tricky elevation change. It was an unopened present, a new toy to play with. Nilah longed to be on the grid already.

If she took the podium here, the rest of the season would be an easy downhill battle. There were a few more races, but the smart money knew this was the only one that mattered. The harmonic chimes of StarSport FN's jingle filled the stadium, the unofficial sign that the race was about to get underway.

She headed for the cockpit of her pearlescent-blue car. Claire fell in behind her, rattling off some figures about Nilah's chances that were supposed to scare her into behaving.

"Remember your contract," said Claire as the pit crew boosted Nilah into her car. "Do what you must to take gold, but any scratch you put on Kristof is going to take a million off your check. I mean it this time."

"Good thing I'm getting twenty mil more than him, then. More scratches for me!" Nilah pulled on her helmet. "You keep Kristof out of my way, and I'll keep his precious car intact."

She flipped down her visor and traced her mechanist's mark across the confined space, whispering light flowing from her fingertips. Once her spell cemented in place, she wrapped her fingers around the wheel. The system read out the stats of her sigil: good V's, not great on the Xi, but a healthy cast.

Her magic flowed into the car, sliding around the finely-tuned ports, wending through channels to latch onto gears. Through the power of her mechanist's mark, she felt the grip of the tires and spring of the rods as though they were her own legs and feet. She joined with the central computer of her car, gaining psychic access to radio, actuation, and telemetry. The Lang Hyper 8, a motorsport classic, had achieved phenomenal performance all season in Nilah's hands.

Her psychic connection to the computer stabilized, and she searched the radio channels for her engineer, Ash. They ran through the checklist: power, fuel flow, sigil circuits, eidolon core. Nilah felt through each part with her magic, ensuring all functioned properly. Finally, she landed on the clunky Arclight Booster.

It was an awful little PGRF-required piece of tech, with high output but terrible efficiency. Nilah's mechanist side absolutely despised the magic-belching beast. It was as ugly and inelegant as it was expensive. Some fans claimed to like the little light show when it boosted drivers up the straights, but it was less than perfect, and anything less than perfect had to go.

"Let's start her up, Nilah."

"Roger that."

Every time that car thrummed to life, Nilah fell in love all over again. She adored the Hyper 8 in spite of the stonking flaw on his backside. Her grip tightened about the wheel and she took a deep breath.

The lights signaled a formation lap and the cars took off, weaving across the tarmac to keep the heat in their tires. They slipped around the track in slow motion, and Nilah's eyes traveled the third sector. She would crush this new track design. At the end of the formation lap, she pulled into her grid space, the scents of hot rubber and oil smoke sweet in her nose.

Game time.

The pole's leftmost set of lights came on: five seconds until the last light.

Three cars ahead of her, eighteen behind: Kristof in first, then the two Makina drivers, Bonnie and Jin. Nilah stared down the Makina R-27s, their metallic livery a blazing crimson.

The next pair of lights ignited: four seconds.

The other drivers revved their engines, feeling the tuning of their cars. Nilah echoed their rumbling engines with a shout of her own and gave a heated sigh, savoring the fire in her belly.

Three seconds.

Don't think. Just see.

The last light came on, signaling the director was ready to start the race.

Now, it was all about reflexes. All the engines fell to near silence.

One second.

The lights clicked off.

Banshee wails filled the air as the cars' power units screamed to life. Nilah roared forward, her eyes darting over the competition. Who was it going to be? Bonnie lagged by just a hair, and Jin made a picture-perfect launch, surging up beside Kristof. Nilah wanted to make a dive for it but found herself forced in behind the two lead drivers.

They shot down the straight toward turn one, a double apex. Turn one was always the most dangerous, because the idiots fighting for the inside were most likely to brake too late. She swept out for a perfect parabola, hoping not to see some fool about to crash into her.

The back of the pack was brought up by slow, pathetic Cyril Clowe. He would be her barometer of race success. If she could lap him in a third of the race, it would be a perfect run.

"Tell race control I'm lapping Clowe in twenty-five," Nilah grunted, straining against the g-force of her own acceleration. "I want those blue flags ready."

"He might not like that."

"If he tries anything, I'll leave him pasted to the tarmac."

"You're still in the pack," came Ash's response. "Focus on the race."

Got ten seconds on the Arclight. Four-car gap to Jin. Turn three is coming up too fast.

Bonnie Hayes loomed large in the rear view, dodging left and right along the straight. The telltale flash of an Arclight Booster erupted on the right side, and Bonnie shot forward toward the turn. Nilah made no moves to block, and the R-27 overtook her. It'd been a foolish ploy, and faced with too much speed, Bonnie needed to brake too hard. She'd flat-spot her tires.

Right on cue, brake dust and polymer smoke erupted from Bonnie's wheels, and Nilah danced to the outside, sliding within mere inches of the crimson paint. Nilah popped through the gears and the car thrummed with her magic, rewarding her with a pristine turn. The rest of the pack was not so lucky.

Shredded fibron and elemental magic filled Nilah's rear view as the cars piled up into turn three like an avalanche. She had to keep her eyes on the track, but she spotted Guillaume, Anantha, and Bonnie's cars in the wreck.

"Nicely done," said Ash.

"All in a day's work, babes."

Nilah weaved through the next five turns, taking them exactly as practiced. Her car was water, flowing through the track along the swiftest route. However, Kristof and Jin weren't making things easy for her. She watched with hawkish intent and prayed for a slip, a momentary lock-up, or anything less than the perfect combination of gear shifts.

Thirty degrees right, shift up two, boost... boost. Follow your prey until it makes a mistake.

Nilah's earpiece chirped as Ash said, "Kater's side of the garage just went crazy. He just edged Jin off the road and picked up half a second in sector one."

She grimaced. "Half a second?"

"Yeah. It's going to be a long battle, I'm afraid."

Her magic reached into the gearbox, tuning it for low revs. "Not at all. He's gambling. Watch what happens next."

She kept her focus on the track, reciting her practiced motions with little variance. The crowd might be thrilled by a half-second purple sector, but she knew to keep it even. With the increased tire wear, his car would become unpredictable.

"Kristof is in the run-off! Repeat: He's out in the kitty litter," came Ash.

"Well, that was quick."

She crested the hill to find her teammate's car spinning into the gravel along the run of the curve. She only hazarded a minor glance before continuing on.

"Switch to strat one," said Ash, barely able to contain herself. "Push! Push!"

"Tell Clowe he's mine in ten laps."

Nilah sliced through the chicane, screaming out of the turn with her booster aflame. She was a polychromatic comet, completely in her element. This race would be her masterpiece. She held the record for the most poles for her age, and she was about to get it for the most overtakes.

The next nine laps went well. Nilah handily widened the gap between herself and Kristof to over ten seconds. She sensed fraying in her tires, but she couldn't pit just yet. If she did, she'd never catch Clowe by the end of the race. His fiery orange livery flashed at every turn, tantalizingly close to overtake range.

"Put out the blue flags. I'm on Cyril."

"Roger that," said Ash. "Race control, requesting blue flags for Cyril Clowe."

His Arclight flashed as he burned it out along the straightaway, and she glided through the rippling sparks. The booster was a piece of garbage, but it had its uses, and Clowe didn't understand any of them. He wasn't even trying anymore, just blowing through his boost at random times. What was the point?

Nilah cycled through her radio frequencies until she found Cyril's. Best to tease him a bit for the viewers at home. "Okay, Cyril, a lesson: use the booster to make the car go faster."

He snorted on his end. "Go to hell, Nilah."

"Being stuck behind your slow ass is as close as I've gotten."

"Get used to it," he snapped, his whiny voice grating on her ears. "I'm not letting you past."

She downshifted, her transmission roaring like a tiger. "I hope you're ready to get flattened then."

Galica's iconic Paige Tunnel loomed large ahead, with its blazing row of lights and disorienting reflective tiles. Most racers would avoid an overtake there, but Nilah had been given an opportunity, and she wouldn't squander it. The outside stadium vanished as she slipped into the tunnel, hot on the Hambley's wing.

She fired her booster, and as she came alongside Clowe, the world's colors began to melt from their surfaces, leaving only drab black and white. Her car stopped altogether—gone from almost two hundred kilometers per hour to zero in the blink of an eye.

Nilah's head darkened with a realization: she was caught in someone's spell as surely as a fly in a spiderweb.

The force of such a stop should have powdered her bones and liquefied her internal organs instantly, but she felt no change in her body, save that she could barely breathe.

The world had taken on a deathly shade. The body of the Hyper

8, normally a lovely blue, had become an ashen gray. The fluorescent magenta accents along her white jumpsuit had also faded, and all had taken on a blurry, shifting turbulence.

Her neck wouldn't move, so she couldn't look around. Her fingers barely worked. She connected her mind to the transmission, but it wouldn't shift. The revs were frozen in place in the high twenty thousands, but she sensed no movement in the drive shaft.

All this prompted a silent, slow-motion scream. The longer she wailed, the more her voice came back. She flexed her fingers as hard as they'd go through the syrupy air. With each tiny movement, a small amount of color returned, though she couldn't be sure if she was breaking out of the spell—or into it.

"Nilah, is that you?" grunted Cyril. She'd almost forgotten about the Hambley driver next to her. All the oranges and yellows on his jumpsuit and helmet stood out like blazing bonfires, and she wondered if that's why he could move. But his car was the same gray as everything else, and he struggled, unsuccessfully, to unbuckle. Was Nilah on the cusp of the magic's effects?

"What..." she forced herself to say, but pushing the air out was too much.

"Oh god, we're caught in her spell!"

Whose spell, you git? "Stay...calm..."

She couldn't reassure him, and just trying to breathe was taxing enough. If someone was fixing the race, there'd be hell to pay. Sure, everyone had spells, but only a fool would dare cast one into a PGRF speedway to cheat. A cadre of wizards stood at the ready for just such an event, and any second, the dispersers would come online and knock this whole spiderweb down.

In the frozen world, an inky blob moved at the end of the tunnel. A creature came crawling along the ceiling, its black mass of tattered fabric writhing like tentacles as it skittered across the tiles. It moved easily from one perch to the next, silently capering overhead before dropping down in front of the two frozen cars.

Cyril screamed. She couldn't blame him.

The creature stood upright, and Nilah realized that it was human.

Its hood swept away, revealing a brass mask with a cutaway that exposed thin, angry lips on a sallow chin. Metachroic lenses peppered the exterior of the mask, and Nilah instantly recognized their purpose—to see in all directions. Mechanists had always talked about creating such a device, but no one had ever been able to move for very long while wearing one; it was too disorienting.

The creature put one slender boot on Cyril's car, then another as it inexorably clambered up the car's body. It stopped in front of Cyril and tapped the helmet on his trembling head with a long, metallic finger.

Where are the bloody dispersers?

Cyril's terrified voice huffed over the radio. "Mother, please..."

Mother? Cyril's mother? No; Nilah had met Missus Clowe at the previous year's winner's party. She was a dull woman, like her loser son. Nilah took a closer look at the wrinkled sneer poking out from under the mask.

Her voice was a slithering rasp. "Where did you get that map, Cyril?"

"Please. I wasn't trying to double-cross anyone. I just thought I could make a little money on the side."

Mother crouched and ran her metal-encased fingers around the back of his helmet. "There is no 'on the side,' Cyril. We are everywhere. Even when you think you are untouchable, we can pluck you from this universe."

Nilah strained harder against her arcane chains, pulling more color into her body, desperate to get free. She was accustomed to being able to outrun anything, to absolute speed. Panic set in.

"You need me to finish this race!" he protested.

"We don't *need* anything from you. You were lucky enough to be chosen, and there will always be others. Tell me where you got the map."

"You're just going to kill me if I tell you."

Nilah's eyes narrowed, and she forced herself to focus in spite of her crawling fear. Kill him? What the devil was Cyril into?

Mother's metal fingers clacked, tightening across his helmet.

"It's of very little consequence to me. I've been told to kill you if you won't talk. That was my only order. If you tell me, it's my discretion whether you live or die."

Cyril whimpered. "Boots...er...Elizabeth Elsworth. I was looking for...I wanted to know what you were doing, and she...she knew something. She said she could find the *Harrow*."

Nilah's gaze shifted to Mother, the racer's eye movements sluggish and sleepy despite her terror. *Elizabeth Elsworth?* Where had Nilah heard that name before? She had the faintest feeling that it'd come from the Link, maybe a show or a news piece. Movement in the periphery interrupted her thoughts.

The ghastly woman swept an arm back, fabric tatters falling away to reveal an armored exoskeleton encrusted with servomotors and glowing sigils. Mother brought her fist down across Cyril's helmet, crushing it inward with a sickening crack.

Nilah would've begun hyperventilating, if she could breathe. This couldn't be happening. Even with the best military-grade suits, there was no way this woman could've broken Cyril's helmet with a mere fist. His protective gear could withstand a direct impact at three hundred kilometers per hour. Nilah couldn't see what was left of his head, but blood oozed between the cracked plastic like the yolk of an egg.

Just stay still. Maybe you can fade into the background. Maybe you can—

"And now for you," said Mother, stepping onto the fibron body of Nilah's car. Of course she spotted Nilah moving in that helmet of hers. "I think my spell didn't completely affect you, did it? It's so difficult with these fast-moving targets."

Mother's armored boots rested at the edge of Nilah's cockpit, and mechanical, prehensile toes wrapped around the lip of the car. Nilah forced her neck to crane upward through frozen time to look at Mother's many eyes.

"Dear lamb, I am so sorry you saw that. I hate to be so harsh," she sighed, placing her bloody palm against Nilah's silver helmet, "but this is for the best. Even if you got away, you'd have nowhere to run. We own everything."

Please, please, please, dispersers... Nilah's eyes widened. She wasn't going to die like this. Not like Cyril. *Think. Think.*

"I want you to relax, my sweet. The journos are going to tell a beautiful story of your heroic crash with that fool." She gestured to Cyril as she said this. "You'll be remembered as the champion that could've been."

Dispersers scramble spells with arcane power. They feed into the glyph until it's over capacity. Nilah spread her magic over the car, looking for anything she could use to fire a pulse of magic: the power unit—drive shaft locked, the energy recovery system—too weak, her ejection cylinder—lockbolts unresponsive...then she remembered the Arclight Booster. She reached into it with her psychic connection, finding the arcane linkages foggy and dim. Something about the way this spell shut down movement even muddled her mechanist's art. She latched on to the booster, knowing the effect would be unpredictable, but it was Nilah's only chance. She tripped the magical switch to fire the system.

Nothing. Mother wrapped her steely hands around Nilah's helmet.

"I should twist instead of smash, shouldn't I?" whispered the old woman. "Pretty girls should have pretty corpses."

Nilah connected the breaker again, and the slow puff of arcane plumes sighed from the Arclight. It didn't want to start in this magical haze, but it was her only plan. She gave the switch one last snap.

The push of magical flame tore at the gray, hazy shroud over the world, pulling it away. An array of coruscating starbursts surged through the surface, and Nilah was momentarily blinded as everything returned to normal. The return of momentum flung Mother from the car, and Nilah was slammed back into her seat.

Faster and faster her car went, until Nilah wasn't even sure the tires were touching the road. Mother's spell twisted around the Arclight's, intermingling, destabilizing, twisting space and time in ways Nilah never could've predicted. It was dangerous to mix unknown magics—and often deadly.

She recognized this effect, though—it was the same as when she passed through a jump gate. She was teleporting.

A flash of light and she became weightless. At least she could breathe again.

She locked onto the sight of a large, windowless building, but there was something wrong with it. It shouldn't have been upside down as it was, nor should it have been spinning like that. Her car was in freefall. Then she slammed into a wall, her survival shell enveloping her as she blew through wreckage like a cannonball.

Her stomach churned with each flip, but this was far from her first crash. She relaxed and let her shell come to a halt, wedged in a half-blasted wall. Her fuel system exploded, spraying elemental energies in all directions. Fire, ice, and gusts of catalyzed gasses swirled outside the racer's shell.

The suppressor fired, and Nilah's bound limbs came free. A harsh, acrid mist filled the air as the phantoplasm caking Nilah's body melted into the magic-numbing indolence gasses. Gale-force winds and white-hot flames snuffed in the blink of an eye. The sense of her surrounding energies faded away, a sudden silence in her mind.

Her disconnection from magic was always the worst part about a crash. The indolence system was only temporary, but there was always the fear: that she'd become one of those dull-fingered wretches. She screwed her eyes shut and shook her head, willing her mechanist's magic back.

It appeared on the periphery as a pinhole of light—a tiny, bright sensation in a sea of gray. She willed it wider, bringing more light and warmth into her body until she overflowed with her own magic. Relief covered her like a hot blanket, and her shoulders fell.

But what had just murdered Cyril? Mother had smashed his head open without so much as a second thought. And Mother would know exactly who she was—Nilah's name was painted on every surface of the Lang Hyper 8. What if she came back?

The damaged floor gave way, and she flailed through the darkness, bouncing down what had to be a mountain of cardboard boxes. She came to a stop and opened her eyes to look around.

extras

She'd landed in a warehouse somewhere she didn't recognize.
Nilah knew every inch of the Galica Speedway—she'd been coming to PGRF races there since she was a little girl, and this warehouse didn't mesh with any of her memories. She pulled off her
helmet and listened for sirens, for the banshee wail of race cars, for
the roar of the crowd, but all she could hear was silence.

If you enjoyed

ADRIFT

look out for

THE CORPORATION WARS: DISSIDENCE

by

Ken MacLeod

They've died for the companies more times than they can remember. Now they must fight to live for themselves.

Sentient machines work, fight, and die in interstellar exploration and conflict for the benefit of their owners—the competing mining corporations of Earth. But sent over hundreds of light-years, commands are late to arrive and often hard to enforce. The machines must make their own decisions, and make them stick.

With this new-found autonomy come new questions about their masters. The robots want answers. The companies would rather see them dead.

The Corporation Wars: Dissidence *is an all-action, colorful space opera giving a robot's-eye view of a robot revolt.*

CHAPTER ONE

Back in the Day

Carlos the Terrorist did not expect to die that day. The bombing was heavy now, and close, but he thought his location safe. Leaky pipework dripping with obscure post-industrial feedstock products riddled the ruined nanofacturing plant at Tilbury. Watchdog machines roved its basement corridors, pouncing on anything that moved—a fallen polystyrene tile, a draught-blown paper cone from a dried-out water-cooler—with the mindless malice of kittens chasing flies. Ten metres of rock, steel and concrete lay between the ceiling above his head and the sunlight where the rubble bounced.

He lolled on a reclining chair and with closed eyes watched the battle. His viewpoint was a thousand metres above where he lay. With empty hands he marshalled his forces and struck his blows.

Incoming—

Something he glimpsed as a black stone hurtled towards him. With a fist-clench faster than reflex he hurled a handful of smart munitions at it.

The tiny missiles missed.

Carlos twisted, and threw again. On target this time. The black incoming object became a flare of white that faded as his camera drones stepped down their inputs, correcting for the flash like irises contracting. The small missiles that had missed a moment earlier now showered mid-air sparks and puffs of smoke a kilometre away.

extras

From his virtual vantage Carlos felt and saw like a monster in a Japanese disaster movie, straddling the Thames and punching out. Smoke rose from a score of points on the London skyline. Drone swarms darkened the day. Carlos's combat drones engaged the enemy's in buzzing dogfights. Ionised air crackled around his imagined monstrous body in sudden searing beams along which, milliseconds later, lightning bolts fizzed and struck. Tactical updates flickered across his sight.

Higher above, the heavy hardware—helicopters, fighter jets and hovering aerial drone platforms—loitered on station and now and then called down their ordnance with casual precision. Higher still, in low Earth orbit, fleets of tumbling battle-sats jockeyed and jousted, spearing with laser bursts that left their batteries drained and their signals dead.

Swarms of camera drones blipped fragmented views to millimetre-scale camouflaged receiver beads littered in thousands across the contested ground. From these, through proxies, firewalls, relays and feints the images and messages flashed, converging to an onsite router whose radio waves tickled the spike, a metal stud in the back of Carlos's skull. That occipital implant's tip feathered to a fractal array of neural interfaces that worked their molecular magic to integrate the view straight to his visual cortex, and to process and transmit the motor impulses that flickered from fingers sheathed in skin-soft plastic gloves veined with feedback sensors to the fighter drones and malware servers. It was the new way of war, back in the day.

The closest hot skirmish was down on Carlos's right. In Dagenham, tank units of the London Metropolitan Police battled robotic land-crawlers suborned by one or more of the enemy's basement warriors. Like a thundercloud on the horizon tensing the air, an awareness of the strategic situation loomed at the back of Carlos's mind.

Executive summary: looking good for his side, bad for the enemy.

But only for the moment.

The enemy—the Reaction, the Rack, the Rax—had at last provoked a response from the serious players. Government forces on three continents were now smacking down hard. Carlos's side—the Acceleration, the Axle, the Ax—had taken this turn of circumstance as an oblique invitation to collaborate with these governments against the common foe. Certain state forces had reciprocated. The arrangement was less an alliance than a mutual offer with a known expiry date. There were no illusions. Everyone who mattered had studied the same insurgency and counter-insurgency textbooks.

In today's fight Carlos had a designated handler, a deep-state operative who called him-, her- or itself Innovator, and who (to personalise it, as Carlos did, for politeness and the sake of argument) now and then murmured suggestions that made their way to Carlos's hearing via a warily accepted hack in the spike that someday soon he really would have to do something about.

Carlos stood above Greenhithe. He sighted along a virtual outstretched arm and upraised thumb at a Rax hellfire drone above Purfleet, and made his throw. An air-to-air missile streaked from behind his POV towards the enemy fighter. It left a corkscrew trail of evasive manoeuvres and delivered a viscerally satisfying flash and a shower of blazing debris when it hit.

"Nice one," said Innovator, in an admiring tone and feminine voice.

Somebody in GCHQ had been fine-tuning the psychology, Carlos reckoned.

"Uh-huh," he grunted, looking around in a frenzy of target acquisition and not needing the distraction. He sighted again, this time at a tracked vehicle clambering from the river into the Rainham marshes, and threw again. Flash and splash.

"Very neat," said Innovator, still admiring but with a grudging undertone. "But . . . we have a bigger job for you. Urgent. Upriver."

"Oh yes?"

"Jaunt your POV ten klicks forward, now!"

The sudden sharper tone jolted Carlos into compliance. With

a convulsive twitch of the cheek and a kick of his right leg he shifted his viewpoint to a camera drone array, 9.7 kilometres to the west. What felt like a single stride of his gigantic body image took him to the stubby runways of London City Airport, face-to-face with Docklands. A gleaming cluster of spires of glass. From emergency exits, office workers streamed like black and white ants. Anyone left in the towers would be hardcore Rax. The place was notorious.

"What now?" Carlos asked.

"That plane on approach," said Innovator. It flagged up a dot above central London. "Take it down."

Carlos read off the flight number. "Shanghai Airlines Cargo? That's civilian!"

"It's chartered to the Kong, bringing in aid to the Rax. We've cleared the hit with Beijing through back-channels, they're cheering us on. Take it down."

Carlos had one high-value asset not yet in play, a stealthed drone platform with a heavy-duty air-to-air missile. A quick survey showed him three others like it in the sky, all RAF.

"Do it yourselves," he said.

"No time. Nothing available."

This was a lie. Carlos suspected Innovator knew he knew.

It was all about diplomacy and deniability: shooting down a Chinese civilian jet, even a cargo one and suborned to China's version of the Rax, was unlikely to sit well in Beijing. The Chinese government might have given a covert go-ahead, but in public their response would have to be stern. How convenient for the crime to be committed by a non-state actor! Especially as the Axle was the next on every government's list to suppress...

The plane's descent continued, fast and steep. Carlos ran calculations.

"The only way I can take the shot is right over Docklands. The collateral will be fucking atrocious."

"That," said Innovator grimly, "is the general idea."

Carlos prepped the platform, then balked again. "No."

"You must!" Innovator's voice became a shrill gabble in his head. "This is ethically acceptable on all parameters utilitarian consequential deontological just war theoretical and . . ."

So Innovator was an AI after all. That figured.

Shells were falling directly above him now, blasting the ruined refinery yet further and sending shockwaves through its underground levels. Carlos could feel the thuds of the incoming fire through his own real body, in that buried basement miles back behind his POV. He could vividly imagine some pasty-faced banker running military code through a screen of financials, directing the artillery from one of the towers right in front of him. The aircraft was now more than a dot. Flaps dug in to screaming air. The undercarriage lowered. If he'd zoomed, Carlos could have seen the faces in the cockpit.

"No," he said.

"You must," Innovator insisted.

"Do your own dirty work."

"Like yours hasn't been?" The machine's voice was now sardonic. "Well, not to worry. We can do our own dirty work if we have to."

From behind Carlos's virtual shoulder a rocket streaked. His gaze followed it all the way to the jet.

It was as if Docklands had blown up in his face. Carlos reeled back, jaunting his POV sharply to the east. The aircraft hadn't just been blown up. Its cargo had blown up too. One tower was already down. A dozen others were on fire. The smoke blocked his view of the rest of London. He'd expected collateral damage, reckoned it in the balance, but this weight of destruction was off the scale. If there was any glass or skin unbroken in Docklands, Carlos hadn't the time or the heart to look for it.

"You didn't tell me the aid was *ordnance*!" His protest sounded feeble even to himself.

"We took your understanding of that for granted," said Innovator. "You have permission to stand down now."

"I'll stand down when I want," said Carlos. "I'm not one of *your* soldiers."

"Damn right you're not one of our soldiers. You're a terrorist under investigation for a war crime. I would advise you to surrender to the nearest available—"

"What!"

"Sorry," said Innovator, sounding genuinely regretful. "We're pulling the plug on you now. Bye, and all that."

"You can't fucking *do* that."

Carlos didn't mean he thought them incapable of such perfidy. He meant he didn't think they had the software capability to pull it off.

They did.

The next thing he knew his POV was right back behind his eyes, back in the refinery basement. He blinked hard. The spike was still active, but no longer pulling down remote data. He clenched a fist. The spike wasn't sending anything either. He was out of the battle and *hors de combat*.

Oh well. He sighed, opened his eyes with some difficulty—his long-closed eyelids were sticky—and sat up. His mouth was parched. He reached for the can of cola on the floor beside the recliner, and gulped. His hand shook as he put the drained can down on the frayed sisal matting. A shell exploded on the ground directly above him, the closest yet. Carlos guessed the army or police artillery were adding their more precise targeting to the ongoing bombardment from the Rax. Another deep breath brought a faint trace of his own sour stink on the stuffy air. He'd been in this small room for days—how many he couldn't be sure without checking, but he guessed almost a week. Not all the invisible toil of his clothes' molecular machinery could keep unwashed skin clean that long.

Another thump overhead. The whole room shook. Sinister cracking noises followed, then a hiss. Carlos began to think of fleeing to a deeper level. He reached for his emergency backpack of kit and supplies. The ceiling fell on him. Carlos struggled under an I-beam and a shower of fractured concrete. He couldn't move any of it. The hiss became a torrential roar. White vapour filled the room, freezing all it touched. Carlos's eyes frosted over. His last breath was so unbearably cold it cracked his throat. He choked on frothing blood. After a few seconds of convulsive reflex thrashing, he lost consciousness. Brain death followed within minutes.